M000170173

THE SERPENT
PAPERS

THE SERPENT PAPERS

Jeff Schnader

THE PERMANENT PRESS
Sag Harbor, NY 11963

Cover photos by *The Columbia Daily Spectator*/John Taylor Lewis and Andrew Farber.

For information, address:
The Permanent Press
4170 Noyac Road
Sag Harbor, NY 11963
www.thepermanentpress.com

Library of Congress Cataloging-in-Publication Data

Schnader, Jeff, author.
The Serpent papers / Jeff Schnader.
Sag Harbor, NY: The Permanent Press, [2022].
ISBN: 9781579626488 (cloth)
ISBN: 9781579626549 (trade paperback)
ISBN: 9781579626501 (ebook)
1. College students—Fiction. 2. Columbia University—Fiction.
3. Nineteen seventies—Fiction. 4. Vietnam War, 1961–1975—
Protest movements—Fiction. 5. Campus fiction. 6. Historical
fiction. 7. Novels.

PS3619.C446543 S47 2022 (print)   2021045310
PS3619.C446543 (ebook)   2021045311
813'.6—dc23

Printed in the United States of America

*To Tristan, Jonathan, Beth, those who fought the Vietnam War,
and those who fought against it*

FOREWORD

So what is conscience? How can we live with it, be true to it, examine it every moment of every day? It's the voice of God inside our heads, it's the awareness of good and evil, the culmination of our sense of morality and ethics that has evolved within us since we were children. *The Serpent Papers* addresses these questions. Every page in this book is right in the intellectual wheelhouse. The war in Vietnam confronted all of us in our generation to define our allegiance to the flag with crystal clarity. The pressure to do so was real and constantly present, the moral lines were being drawn, and we could see it on the news every night. We had to be true to our consciences, and that's what this book is about. This war was like no other that our country had ever been involved with before. Many of us were suspicious that the notion of the domino theory (that the spread of Communism would grow like a cancer throughout Southeast Asia) was really a heavily veiled ruse by The Military Industrial Complex to test our weapons of war and the men who used them, as well as, of course, to make money. We had to decide: will we fight and kill or be killed to fulfill our patriotic duty? Or will we resist and object to the horror, protest the bombs, the napalm, the B-52 raids? Or will we drop out, get stoned, run away to Canada, or join the Weathermen? There it was; we had to make up our minds. Each of us had to define our conscience, take a stand. The vivid and real characters in this brilliant, masterful book bring us right back to those days and remind us of how our decisions—whether to follow our consciences, to ignore them or to justify them—might make us Congressional Medal recipients or murderers. I loved this book. An important book, it is the best I've read in the past ten years.

Michael D. Smar, MD, Bronze Star Recipient
Combat Medic, US Army, 1st Infantry, Vietnam, 1968–1969

TABLE OF CONTENTS

1

Headed to Babylon

There are things I've never told anyone, secrets hidden away in a vault with the doors clanged shut, forty years ago or maybe fifty, in the deepest recesses of my head. Secrets not previously told because they might have jeopardized my future by branding me a pot fiend, a beer hound, a left-wing radical or a white pointy-headed bigot. But I'm older now with a dwindling future, and the story is ready to be told.

In the lifetime of my generation, it was the Vietnam War, a battlefield twelve thousand miles away, which had the greatest stakes. The war created a polemic at the very heart of the age in which we lived, reinforced everywhere in the media and echoed in our minds, hearts and fears. It pitted the forceful convictions of two groups of Americans, one group for and the other against the war, tearing the nation apart so that each half stood across a great rift of enmity from the other. One group called the second group "un-American," while the second called the first "lackeys of imperialism" and worse. It was a miasma of rhetoric, a Babel that made two sides out of the same exploited generation of men.

As Margo explained it, this was the domestic underbelly of the war, the stateside conflict between the forces of two sworn enemies living side by side in America. And it was because of Margo's logic and encouragement that I found myself at the center of a historical confrontation between these two forces, an uprising that all participants knew might transform into massacre. As I stood on the Van Am Quad on the Columbia campus in that spring of 1972, my heart thumped from the adrenaline in my veins, but I was still unsure which side I supported.

I scanned the Quad for Margo, my guide in this new world—she had sworn she would come, but she didn't. I was alone in a sea of hundreds of students, arms pumping in protest against the war's escalation. As we stood on the grass in sunshine, encircled by brick buildings on three sides, it was impossible not to see the lines of New York Tactical Police barring our exit on the fourth side. They were shoulder to shoulder, with clubs and jackboots, and hundreds more poured in: phalanxes in battle regalia, platoons on motorcycles, and horse cavalry.

For a moment the swirl of activity paused, and I could reflect. How was it that I, a warrior by nature and son of a US naval officer, found myself in such an improbable place, on the brink of inevitable bloodshed in a protest which defied the shedding of blood? Did I believe in this fight? And whether I did or did not, was the warrior within me even capable of deserting such combat? Violence had been tattooed on my soul from birth, so I wondered: had I changed so much in my short life that I could now stand with an anti-war rabble against my ingrained identity? Had I changed so much that I had become unrecognizable, even to myself, as I gazed at my reflection through the veil of the cosmos?

Everything starts with the seed, and then come the roots. I was born into an America proud of its pugnacious power, having never lost a war in its history. Flag waving and pride were an integral part of what it meant to be an American in the 1950s and '60s, and the children of this era were brought up on these principles like mother's milk. My father was an officer in the US Navy, and I grew up proud to be his son. I remember when I was a tot, sitting on his lap, facing his uniformed chest, touching the colored ribbons and other baubles of military accomplishment strung there as decoration. He was a broad-shouldered powerful man, and next to him I sat protected by a formidable warrior under the umbrella of the might of the United States armed forces. At home, he bounded around the house and was everywhere at once, painting walls, repairing the deck, building outdoor furniture in the garage. If he spied me while he was planting in the garden, he would suddenly bolt to catch me, grabbing me as I shrieked with excitement, snagging me by the waist in the crook of his arm and then wrapping me up in the garden hose. He would say, "You want me to tie you in knots?" and I would say "No!" though I really meant "Yes!" When I started going to church, I felt I was walking with the most important man there, a paragon of society. I observed the admiration that other congregants lavished upon him. In my mother's face and demeanor, I saw that she idolized my father as well. I bathed in our happiness as a family so that when my brother Jerry came along, he became one of us, and he was mine to protect and nurture as my parents had nurtured me.

Yet nothing so perfect endures. As a boy I wanted to please my father by mirroring his views and his mighty charisma, but as I grew up, either through random misfortune or through a concatenation of irreversible events, I became an angry boy. Eventually in a disorganized emotional state I found myself on the threshold of manhood, and I was confronted by the usual choices young men must make. In the case of choosing where to go to college, I made an impetuous if not unexpected choice, but only after my father sat down next to me one evening and turned the TV off.

"We should talk," he said.

I felt my lips tighten against my teeth. I felt my muscles contract.

"About what."

"Your marks are good—"

"What about it?"

"We should talk about your future."

We looked at each other. Our relationship had changed; I was now beyond his reach. I would choose where to go to college without any pressure to please *him*. I wanted to go where *I* wanted to go, and I wasn't going to discuss it.

"You have choices," he said.

I stared back.

He shifted in his chair.

He was an accomplished man, my father. As an officer, he was either telling others what to do or being told what to do by superiors, and now I watched him struggle through a conversation with a person outside his professional hierarchy—me, his son, over whom he had diminishing control. So much had happened in the prior few years that both he and I had changed individually, and now I felt a pointed dislike toward him. For one thing, he began to drink occasionally in the evenings, and although I knew he could be mean when he drank, I had never really experienced the brunt of it firsthand.

Then one afternoon, my antagonism crystallized. I was sitting in my room, tormented by unyielding acne, brooding a teenage sulk, listening to the Airplane's *Bless Its Pointed Little Head*, *Fresh Cream's* "N.S.U.," and "The Star-Spangled Banner" by Hendrix. I was gazing into the pockmarked angular faces of the Rolling Stones silhouetted in shadow on the cover of their album *Out of Our Heads*. The music was dangerous and foreboding, and I wrapped myself in its darkness. It was a spooky time, a time when the fears of growing up mixed with all manner of other fears from asking a girl on a date to being shipped to Vietnam.

As I sat tapping the floor, singing without a thought in my head, my brain conjured up images of Lola Quinn, a girl in my class whose slacks fit snugly to the meat of her thighs and whose breasts stuck pertly against her pink leotard top. In this state of rapture with fantasies and hormones running rampant, I made an unplanned decision to call her, thinking to use an excuse about homework. Forgetting to turn down the music, I picked up the phone and dialed, listening to the rings with ratcheting tension. As Lola answered the phone, I said "Hello," but my father began banging on the door, which oscillated with his weight as he alternately pushed and released. I heard my mother's voice behind him yelling, "David—you'll break the hinges!" to which he shouted, "Unlock the goddamn door!"

I knew right away they were drunk, and I panicked, shouting, "Just a sec!"

I ran to the door and opened it, and my father barreled in shoulder first trying to keep his balance with his arm outstretched, yelling "Goddamnit!" As he stumbled, he straight-armed me in the chest and grabbed my shirt, ripping it as I fell over backward. He snatched the phone from my hand and slammed it down in its cradle, howling, "No one can think with this racket!" He went to my stereo and whacked it with his arm, scraping the needle across the record, ripping the vinyl with a sound that screeched through the speakers. Horrified by his ferocity, I stood up and watched as the disc skittered off its platter and across the floor.

"I've had enough of this!" His face was red; he reeked of alcohol.

I got to my feet. "Dad—what're you doing?"

"We're trying to have a quiet night downstairs! But you!"

He lifted his hand and slapped me hard on the face with his palm. This surprised me; he'd never slapped me before. I was stung and humiliated, worse than from the whips of the Sisters, and it angered me beyond belief.

I shouted, "Goddamn abusive son of a bitch!"

He replied with a roundhouse and a closed fist, barging forward as he swung. Instinctively I ducked, lifting my arm to deflect the blow, but my elbow caught him on the chin as he lunged, and the impact hit him hard.

He was enraged. He grabbed me with both hands by the throat and squeezed.

I couldn't breathe. I would have fallen over, but he held me up. I felt lightheaded; I saw rainbows. I opened my mouth to tell him to stop, but my throat could only rasp. I vaguely heard my mother's voice, and she was saying, "David! Stop!"

He turned his head, loosening his grip. He threw me on the floor and pointed, saying, "You're not the only one in this house!"

He staggered out the door, banging his shoulder on the jamb and cursing.

I coughed and couldn't stop. My throat hurt. I reached up and touched my head which throbbed everywhere, especially where it had struck the floor. I was dizzy. My mother leaned over me then, and the smell of liquor was so strong, I retched.

"You okay?" she said, bleary-eyed with sagging lids.

"He's a fucking animal!" I croaked.

"He had a bad moment," she said. "We all do."

"He's a brute!" I began to cough and couldn't stop.

She opened her eyes heavily, licked her lips and said, "He didn't mean it. Why'd you get him all wound up? What'd you do that for? I don't understand any of this." She turned and went downstairs, and I heard them talking loudly until my father started to blubber. By the time he came back to speak to me, all teary-eyed and apologetic, I had physically recovered, but the space I once had in my heart for him had vanished.

—⁂—

"Go on," I said as we sat together so calmly that an onlooker would have thought our relationship perfectly normal. "Tell me about my college choices."

I liked to see him uncomfortable; I glared at him. I wanted to intimidate him even though it seemed impossible. I felt possessed— there was a demon in my chest, controlling me from inside, stoking my conviction that my father was somewhere at the root of the violence I had inflicted on others and the damage I had suffered as a result.

I wouldn't let him off easy.

"You have a future to consider," he said. "You have great potential. Given all your options, we think you should go to college at Annapolis which is a fabulous place. Or perhaps Notre Dame. Or the University of Virginia, which has a strong ROTC program."

"Maybe I'll volunteer for Nam instead," I said, enjoying my insolence. I looked him in the eye and flashed a wide fake smile.

"You *could* volunteer," he said stone-faced and austere, preferring to ignore my impertinence. He responded objectively, "We want the best for you—we always have. But the military needs intelligent men like you. Why not go as an officer? Get training and education and then you'll get a commission. Start on the steps to the top—why be a grunt in the mud? There will always be another war; America will always have a fight *some*where. There will be medals for you as you achieve the milestones of a military career; the glory will be greater . . ."

He hesitated, seeming to want to say something more but checking himself. He adjusted himself in his seat, pinched his nose and cleared his throat before adding, "And you'll be somewhat safer as an officer."

I thought of a gathering at my parents' house when they had invited their officer friends and wives. The men came in uniform that day, bedecked in their bars and medals, gleaming with the honor that their ornaments symbolized. My father told me afterward that the medals stood for the great achievements in service to country that he and his friends had garnered through glory. He said that a military career was a story told in sequence, and the ornaments they wore, each medal a tribute to the wearer, were stepping-stones to a place at the table with the military elite. "They are the sum total of a military life," chirped my mother, basking in his radiance.

—◊—

"You know I have connections," said my father. "They can open doors for you. We can get you into the Naval Academy."

"I won't go to Annapolis."

He was surprised. "Why not?"

"I don't want to be a warrior."

"Want or not, you *are* one. I know who you are, and you're a fighter from a long line of fighters."

"How in *Hell* would you know if I'm a fighter?"

"You've been a fighter ever since you could walk. I used to watch you trade punches with that oaf Gilly when you were five and he was six. He would knock you down, and you would get right back up and hit *him*! By gosh, you were half his size!"

I remembered Gilly at that age—he was such a big kid that his older brother had called him "Genghis Fat Boy." I also recalled my anger and humiliation for having been decked by such a stupid lout, which is what I thought of him at the time.

"I also heard about your defiance toward your teachers in grade school."

"You *knew* the Sisters were beating me at Saint Eustace," I said, "and you did nothing? Why'd you let them do it!"

"You *know* what I think about Saint Eustace: those teachers built your character. They've hardened you for the conflicts that lie ahead."

"And *that's* what you think—the beatings were *good* for me."

"You know that's what I think: the beatings aren't good in themselves, but the overall effect is positive."

"Saint Eustace—they're evil. Father Croghan, the Sisters, I see what they are. After what they did to me, I'm not a Catholic anymore. I don't know what I am, but I see what *you* are because *you* sent me there! I used to worship you, but now I see you're no different from *them!*"

"Is that why you don't wear the cross we gave you? Is that why you aren't taking communion anymore?"

"That's right!"

It was a lie, but I wasn't going to tell my father that I had committed what Catholics call a mortal sin—an act of terrible violence that took me to the limit of my self-control in the darkest moment of my life. No, I would never tell him that my impurity in the eyes of God, worn on my soul like disfiguring paint, was the real reason I couldn't take the sacrament.

"By God," he said getting up from his chair, the blood of his face deep red, "I should take my belt and whip you!"

"Do it!" I said, jumping to my feet. "Do it! That's something your goddamned school taught me! They've taught me to take a beating—just like you wanted!"

We stood face to face a few feet apart. Though he was an inch or two taller, I was nearly full-grown. Our gazes met, and his eyes flashed a lack of restraint, but then he smiled unexpectedly.

"It's like I said—you've confirmed it. You're a warrior."

He sat back down and chuckled.

"Sit," he said, sweeping his arm magnanimously. "Stop trying to provoke me all the time and tell your daddy what you want to do with your life."

Maybe I was being perverse, tired of being bossed around, rebelling against the endless control and the weightily expectant yoke of being next in a rigid line of military men. I wasn't a good Catholic boy anymore, and I found myself trapped in the hypocrisy of pretending to be good. I wasn't going to a Catholic college or anywhere close to home—no Notre Dame or University of Virginia for me. I would go into exile, a place with no connection to the military or to my family, somewhere secular where the forces of good and evil could array themselves around me and vie for my soul as I faced the mirror of the greater universe.

Questions hanging over my future stoked the fires of my agitation until finally, in the end, I decided to head to modern day Babylon, Fun City, Gotham, Pleasure Island, where I would study civilization at the jaded but greatest repository of knowledge in the Western world. It was 1971, and I was going to "Hell on earth," as the Sisters of Saint Eustace would say, Columbia University—hotbed of radicalism, den of iniquity, home of left-wing bomb-throwing Jew-boys, stomping ground of Black Panthers and commie-pinko organizers. I would walk the ivied quads at the hub of the Weather Underground, but whether to strike the stone of the liberal hippie world with the conservative hammer of my fathers or to shatter my soul and shake my genealogical tree by joining the forces of as yet unknown, long-haired brothers was unclear to me. A battle was brewing inside me. I was an angry boy, a lost boy, and I would seek redemption or fall into a fissure and tumble into Tartarus, like the dead in a painting by Hieronymus Bosch, rising from the earth on Judgment Day, to be flagellated by demons and roasted in hellfire for the whole remainder of God's eternity.

And for the rest of my waking life.

2

Jerry

It was pain and anger that drove me from my home, out of Virginia and away from the Catholic Church. Such feelings have always triggered memories of my father and the beatings I received at the hands of the nuns. Yet there has been nothing so pure as the pain I've suffered when mulling over the life of my brother, Jerry.

There was something wrong with my brother when he was born. I had heard that the birth was difficult, and Jerry seemed unresponsive in some ways though responsive in others. It was an ordeal that went on for nearly two years. Some of the doctors said he was autistic while others, with a confident doctorly air, said that he had a birth defect with brain damage. Others wanted to know if my mother drank a lot of alcohol during the pregnancy which, I later found out, she had. The voicing of all these possibilities was devastating to my parents who were confused by such disparate opinions and lived in a state of constant torment as they wondered which horrible reality would be the final and true outcome for their son.

I was only seven when he was born, and I was frantic as the months went by because I sensed that Jerry, due to his vulnerability, might be in some kind of danger. My worrying was compounded by the fact that I didn't really understand everything that was happening, only that something was wrong, an intuition heightened by the continuous yelling of my parents at one another. The whole episode brought me a sense of responsibility for another human being that I had never felt before, making me love my brother unconditionally.

As Jerry got older, he seemed to become more normal in some ways. He was supposed to be damaged, but he progressed well. He walked early; he had great balance; he was coordinated. He responded to play with smiles and giggles. Then one day, one of the doctors stumbled on an answer: Jerry was just short of stone deaf, but he would be able to understand language with hearing aids, one in each ear. The doctor warned, however, that his speech might be permanently impaired because of his inability, even while wearing the hearing aids, of discerning the clarity of words spoken *to* him. Further, he said that in order for Jerry to learn, he would have to concentrate much harder than other children, especially on the specific enunciation of his teachers.

I rejoiced at the news, jumping and punching the air. I now knew he had a chance, and I swore I would always be there to bring him safely through the world. I made this pledge at the age of eight, swearing a Catholic oath of protection and acknowledging that I would die to keep that oath, determined in the way of children who see the world in black and white. Every night thereafter, I sang him to sleep with nursery rhymes. As he got a little older, I played blocks with him and read him bedtime stories. When he approached school age, I became obsessed with a fear that he would be sent to Saint Eustace and be vulnerable to abuse and beatings by the nuns. I didn't think he had the fortitude that I had, and his deafness would make him both a target and unable to follow the sternness of his teachers' commands. I knew how rigid a place it was.

He ended up in public school. There were no nuns, but other children supplied the abuse. Groups of boys chased him after school and knocked him down which was why, most days, he came home humiliated or terrified. I knew the bullies. I talked to them and threatened them. I even tried to reason with them, but nothing changed.

On Jerry's eighth birthday, my parents gave him a banana bike. We taught him to ride, but he didn't need help; he was a natural. My father had been a big athlete in high school, and I played soccer at Catholic High, but my brother could ride a bike faster and with more tricks than any kid I'd ever seen. It was during those days that I saw, for the first and last time, my father get a twinkle in his eye for Jerry, his handicapped son. He rode his bike all over the neighborhood and beyond; it was freedom to him, his Promised Land, a release from the torments of his life. The bullies couldn't catch him, and this made him confident and gave him a taste of power.

One day in June, one of those long days when the sun lingers into the evening, my mother called me inside and told me to find Jerry for dinner. I thought I knew where he'd be, down at Bolduc's soda fountain, sitting on the floor next to the comics rack, reading *Casper* and *Richie Rich*. He wasn't supposed to be there because it was on a busy road, only the width of the sidewalk and a line of parked cars between the store and the heavy traffic, ripping down Guinea Woods Pike. It was hot and hazy, and as Bolduc's came into sight, I heard a commotion. Two bigger kids were chasing Jerry, and he was screaming, "No! No! No!" I saw him on his bike pedaling to escape them as fast as he could, catapulting himself between two parked cars, off the curb and into the air.

It all happened fast. I saw him turn his head over his shoulder to see his tormentors, one beefy boy and a taller girl, their faces contorted with bullying rage, shouting obscenities at a child who had done nothing wrong except wear hearing aids. I watched it all as boy and bike launched onto Guinea Woods Pike, followed by a terrible noise, a fatal hideous clank as Jerry crumpled against the metallic wall of cars, headlamps all in the same direction, relentless traffic moving with idiot purpose through time and space.

A delivery truck hit him, snapping his head back and splashing red as he and his bike flipped upward. A second car hit him as he fell, crushing both him and the bike. I saw the tires bounce and the car jolt as it went over his body, extinguishing all remainder of breath. I ran over and stood, powerless, watching his body contract with convulsions and then stop. His chest was flattened; the left side of his face was stove in. His left eye was gone; his head was gashed, and blood pooled onto the road. A woman was out of her car and screaming, but all sound became muffled, all vision became gray as a shroud of numbness enfolded me. I was alone with my pain, kneeling next to his body, begging to God that he spare Jerry's innocence and have me flogged to death by the Sisters instead. And then I had horror and emptiness, and everything disappeared from the face of the earth except anguish and the poor inert body of my brother, lying small on the asphalt, thin, broken and now forever alone.

—ᴍ—

Before the police came, I knelt by Jerry's body as it lay on the pavement, a small crowd of onlookers gathering round. The two bullies who had run Jerry into traffic had evaporated into the night. But I had seen their faces, and I found out who they were. They were in ninth grade, my age, but in the public high school. They hung out at the Bolduc's strip mall every day and would be easy to find.

The police investigated at the scene but found no bullies and no one at fault. "Some deaf kid barreled into traffic on a two-wheeler. Flattened by one of those delivery trucks. Stone dead in a minute." At the funeral, my parents couldn't look at me. My father stood with his mouth all crooked like an open gash across his face, and my mother cried continuously. I hated them for not safeguarding my brother enough. Intellectually, I blamed my father—he had had the power to alter events that I hadn't; I *knew* it was his fault. Yet in my heart I felt unbearable guilt, a desperate and inescapable horror for my own inaction. Recalling my physical proximity to Jerry at his death, I played the scene over and over in my head, reliving my pain. I forced myself to remember that I had done nothing at that moment to intervene to prevent his death. Gilly said that I hadn't had time to do anything, that it happened too quickly, but my heart didn't let me escape. Me, it had been my fault—I had done nothing to protect my little brother when he had come face to face with mortality, his ultimate need for shielding, his irreversible demise.

The coffin was small. It went in the ground, into a hole with dirt piled around it. The priest said a few words about Jesus's love, but what did Jesus have to do with it?

My heart was beating, but it was stony cold. I was going to kill those two kids, and I told Gilly, "They killed Jerry so I'm going to kill *them*. Simple."

"What do you mean?" asked Gilly. "You can't!"

"I *can't*? Watch me!"

"No, listen!" He grabbed my shoulders. "I'll go with you, but you can't *kill* them—it's a mortal sin! Don't throw your life away for those losers!"

I stood looking at Gilly, the big-shot athlete with the handsome face and rippling muscles that captured girls' hearts. But his face wasn't pretty now—the brow was furrowed, and the eyes were dewy. It was a tense, urgent, begging face. Begging me not to do anything rash. He knew me, and he knew what I might do. His expression had more caring than anyone had shown since Jerry's death, and this made me pause.

"Listen!"

"Okay," I said, "but I'm going to hunt them down, and when I find them, I'm going to punish them!"

"Thank the Lord God of Ireland and the Catholic Church of My Fathers!" His words were comical, but he wasn't being funny.

"To hell with the Church—what've they got to do with it?"

"Yeah," he said. "To hell with the Church! And to hell with the Sisters!"

Gilly meant what he said, but I was uncertain about taking him with me, and I brooded over it. If he came, he would endanger himself as an accessory to violence. He would also be a witness against me, however unwittingly. He was my friend, and I wanted him to come, but somehow it wasn't enough. No, this was my problem, and I'd do it on my own.

So I spied on the bullies. After avoiding Bolduc's for a while, they started going back regularly. I watched where they went until I had their routine down pat. They would stay until dusk, and then they walked home through a series of weeded lots, sprinkled with junk, rusted cans, broken cardboard boxes and scrubby trees and vines. Somewhere in the middle of this expansive, unpeopled place was an abandoned trailer that someone had set fire to years ago, standing alone and blackened, its windows shot out with BB guns, its door torn away like a gaping mouth. They always walked past that trailer and then through a small clump of trees on a worn-down path through waist-high weeds.

This was a place for an ambush.

I hardly knew what I was doing, but I spent hours wandering that lot and examining the terrain, both physically and in my head. I thought about it during breakfast as my mother jabbered away at me, in class as the math teacher droned on, and after school, lying on my bed, looking at the ceiling. I was going to do this, and I would do it right or not at all. I had a twelve-inch, serrated Gerber Mark II Combat Knife and a nine-inch BC41 World War II British Commando Knife, but I didn't want to do the kind of damage these knives could effect, nor did I want to risk killing them unintentionally if things got out of control. I wondered whether I might take the knives and brandish them to create fear, but I concluded that a threat of deadly force might create an unpredictable situation. In the end, I decided to take my broom-handle stickball bat wrapped in black tape at one end. I would spring out and catch them by surprise, and they would get a beating they would never forget. Beatings could be fatal, so I would have to be circumspect, not lose my head. However, if the nuns had taught me anything, they had taught me the meaning of violence and abuse, and they had also taught me its technique. I was sure that these softer, public school types would feel the judiciously executed brunt of my learning.

I would have to take the boy first, make sure he was down and couldn't run, and then I would move to the girl. The idea of hitting a girl was bad, but I would have to overcome my feelings because she was as guilty as the boy, and she was just as accountable. She was bigger and taller than me, and she killed my brother, so why would I shrink from making *her* suffer?

But it wouldn't be easy. I would hit her because she deserved it and because she would have to know that I meant it. I would have to threaten them both, and they would both have to believe me. They would have to know that if they talked after, I would come back and kill them. Even if I didn't quite believe it myself. They would have to fear me to make the whole thing work—they would have to believe that if they ratted on me so that I ended up in prison, I would return after my release to hunt them down and make them pay with their last drop of waking life.

I sat in front of the mirror in Jerry's bedroom, planning my attack. I imagined how it would be, meeting them in that lightless, empty lot. It would be dusk, and I would wear charcoal on my face and the camo shirt my father had bought me. I would be invisible. I would spook the bastards.

When the day came, I sat with my back against the blackened trailer, amongst the scrub and broken bottles, and I waited for the sun to go down. They would be coming from the south, and I had placed myself so that they would have to walk past the open door of the trailer and then past me, crouching in silence, hidden in the high weeds. I had the broomstick bat, about four feet long, the taped end in my hands for a good grip, and I listened for voices.

For a long time there was nothing, but then I heard a rustling through high grass, not from the direction I had expected. I stood up fast, without moving my feet, so that I made no noise. I held the bat up, ready to swing it, and I listened. Sweat formed on my forehead in beads that tickled my skin, but I stood still.

The sound moving toward me got closer. It was high-pitched, but it was low to the ground, swishing, and I realized it was an animal, maybe a possum or a snake. It suddenly changed direction and moved away, and I relaxed my grip and eased my breath out. I wiped my brow, careful not to mop the charcoal off the lower part of my face. I put the bat down and took one hand off and leaned, once again, against the trailer wall, feeling the wall give slightly, a soft sponginess of rotten wood, dampening my shirt which wicked up the moisture.

The trailer could be perfect to dump dead bodies, away from the eyes of the world, deep in this empty lot. The aromas of decomposition would be hidden by the musty smell of a thick layer of mold in the rain-sodden structure, far from the humanity of Bolduc's and the noses of shoppers, minding their business, bustling two hundred yards away. My father had told me a story about smell, about rotting bodies and men, whom he knew, who had hidden in a pile of dead soldiers in Saint-Lô to avoid capture. There were maggots and rats, and when they tugged at an arm or a leg in an effort to cover themselves, the limbs of the dead fell apart, and the bellies spilled open, the stench making them retch in waves.

Suddenly I heard voices—their voices—coming up the dirt-packed path from the south. The boy was panting as he dragged along.

"Christ, Laureen."

"Stop worrying about it. They don't even know who we are."

"He was just a little kid."

"Grow up, Stankewicz. You say the same thing every day. There are kids dying all over the world. He was this little *deaf* kid—that's all—and we didn't do anything wrong."

"It wasn't right."

I saw the girl pass first, pirouetting along the path, amongst the vegetation, chattering away, and I hated her. My stomach clenched, and my bowels threatened to flush themselves empty. The anger I had stowed away, a gift from the Sisters, percolated into consciousness, and I trembled with fury.

The boy, Stankewicz, thick necked, broad shouldered and squat, lumbered past me with his head down.

I leapt out, bat over my head, and screamed at the top of my lungs. Stankewicz screamed in terror and put both arms over his head to protect himself as my bat came down with a savage blow.

He screamed again, and I hit him again over his shoulder as he ducked and fell. Then I hit him on his back and on his legs, and he tumbled into the weeds, whimpering. I flogged him, lifting the bat over my head and bringing it down hard, battering him over and over again until I saw blood wetting the back of his shirt where I had pounded the skin off his bones. I realized that I might flog him to death so I stopped, finding a trace of control, panting and sweating.

"Stay there," I said, pointing the bat at him, "or I'll kill you."

Then I turned to the girl who stood transfixed and in terror, her hands over her mouth. She was muscular in the arms and shoulders for a girl her age, and I was a bit intimidated. I faced her and held my bat horizontally and back to my right, ready to do damage but unsure that I would.

"You wouldn't hit a girl, would you?" she whispered, but with scorn, showing her teeth.

"You killed my brother, and you're gonna pay." But I still wasn't sure.

She licked her lips as if thinking. Then she reached for something in her belt and came up with a stiletto. She pressed the button, and the blade snapped out.

"I'll cut you, you little faggot. I'll cut your nose off and your eyeballs out. You better get out of here while you can. I can kill you, and it'll be self-defense."

This wasn't in the script, but it made her a lethal opponent, and an irrational tide rushed through me, a surging unstoppable madness. I swung my bat and hit her hard below the knee. Her legs upended as she spilled to the ground, her stiletto flying up and away into the dark sea of grasses.

She shrieked.

"You'll cut me?" I yelled. "You'll kill me? So do it!"

As she was getting onto her hands and knees, wailing, trying to stand up, I lifted the bat over my head and swung it flush against her back, knocking her flat-faced onto the ground. When she tried to get up a second time, I hit the side of her chest with a hard thud, so hard that I felt her bones give, more than I expected. She grunted and went down again, breathing hard and coughing. I hit her once more, and she coughed again, this time expectorating bloody foam which hung off her lip.

"Oh, God," she said hoarsely, coughing more. "Oh, God."

I wanted to hit her again. I wanted to smash her skull to bits. The adrenaline pumping through my veins was calling me to violence, screaming in my ears, "Crush her! Hammer her!"

But it was enough, and I knew it. I must have broken her ribs, and the bloody foam scared me. And then, like a beacon shining through the jumbled mists of my emotions, I felt Gilly somewhere near me, maybe at my shoulder, so invisibly tiny I couldn't see him, speaking in my ear, whispering, "No, J-Bee—don't do it! Don't!"

I stood up straight and let the bat slip into one hand. I slouched and wiped the sweat off my face.

"Listen up, both of you. You hear me?"

There was no answer, which scared me. But I did hear them breathing.

I raised my voice. "Answer me, or I'll fuckin' hit you again! Do you hear?"

"Yes," said the girl in a tiny, whiny voice. "I hear."

The boy was crying and said nothing.

"I should kill you. You deserve to be killed. I *want* to kill you. But I'm letting you go. It can end here. If they ask you, you can make up a story—I don't care one way or the other. But if you ever tell anyone how this happened, or anything about it, I swear I'll hunt you down and find you. And you better pray that I don't find you because, even if it's twenty years from now, I'll never give up until I end you. And if it comes to that, I'll make sure you *really* understand pain."

"Stop!" said Stankewicz. "Stop." He was sobbing now. "I'm sorry. I'm really sorry. I can't believe what happened—it happened so fast. And he was just a little boy." He looked up at me, and his face was white and bloodless. "I'm glad it's over. I'll never tell. I swear."

I saw his face, and then I saw Jerry's face. I saw his child's smile, saw the hearing aids.

It was dark now. I felt my tears gush, and I turned and ran away. In a small clearing, in a trash-strewn lot, I cried for my brother, knowing it was over and that whatever I did, it couldn't matter because I would never see him again.

3

Fortress Columbia

In May of 1971, a year after Kent State students were shot and killed by the National Guard, I was accepted at Columbia. Later that same summer, as the war in Southeast Asia seemed unstoppable and demonstrators were being arrested by the thousands in Washington, DC, I stepped off a bus from Norfolk, Virginia, into the grime of subterranean New York. I was fresh with hope as I entered the dim underground maze of Times Square, mounting the platform and hopping the subway. An overnight bag slung across my shoulder, I was pressed with countless straphangers, swaying in sync with the rocking of the train while I tingled with the premonition that adventure lurked a mere flicker in time ahead. We hurtled through lightless tunnels, cocooned in a redolence of burnt axle oil and underarm sweat as buzzing bulbs flashed like dull strobes, intermittently highlighting expressionless faces while alternately plunging us all into blackness.

I exited the subway at Broadway and 116th, ready to cross the threshold of Columbia, academic cloister and fortress. As I ascended into sunshine, taxis blared horns, and buses belched soot. Crowds rushed and jammed the sidewalks, and buildings towered above. I was enchanted by the energy and hooked by the strangeness: Fun City curling its finger and whispering, "Come get it," promising pleasure while threatening the Great Pox.

Entering the medieval black gates with their spearhead points at the top, I plunged into the cauldron of the university where the forces of intellect, power, and the history of all learned things churned together in the minds of students and faculty, an infinite stew of creativity and possibility. On either end of the campus stood the great colossi of Butler and Low Libraries, and in the center between them was the famous Sundial, sparkplug of campus revolution and fulcrum of radical assemblies. It was a magical place, lusty, sinful and alluring. Incense was in the air, and Derek and the Dominos blared on speakers, welcoming students back to school. Everywhere swarmed with neckties and long hairs, blazers and djellabas, and now here was I, fresh off the trains, hair cut short, a virgin to drugs and sex and a troglodyte, emerging bleary-eyed from the deep mystical labyrinths of the Catholic Church and the warm soupy swamps of the South.

I breathed it all in. Jostled by crowds moving with purpose, I was accosted by aromas of roasting reefer and by visions of gleaming white buildings. My father had said, "If you end up at Columbia, retrieve its former glory. Take it back from the left-wing boys." But I wasn't so sure. Columbia had been a lightning rod in student revolutionary history, and now I was here. The campus breathed lustily into my nostrils as I traipsed forward, eyes closed, arms outstretched before me in a trance, aware of my submission to forces marshaled both for and against me in my future. I had been given a one-way ticket to the hippie capital of the world, and now I was there, trucking toward a future without definition, plunging headlong into my unpredictable life.

—⁓—

I had shipped my trunk ahead a month before, and once I had dug it out of the pile in the dormitory lobby, I dragged it to stand with a group of the grubbiest and hairiest men in America, unshaven whiskers with layers of oil daubed on their faces and staining their shirts in the armpits, the result of traveling through late summer heat. Their appearance was somehow concordant with something inside me, something I hadn't previously recognized.

"Bell, Joseph," said the monitor, giving me my key and pointing his thumb over his shoulder. "1206B, up the elevator."

The room was Spartan with two desks and two beds. A heavy, opaque, plastic curtain covered the wall-length window, making it dark, and the single bulb in the ceiling cast a dim light on the grayish floors and cinder-block walls. It felt like the inside of a ship's metal hull or even a prison, and I hadn't even started. I was a cog, and this was a factory. If I could finish, I would drop off the college conveyer belt, Columbia's stamp on my back.

I pulled back the curtain and light poured in, revealing a sun-drenched campus: sparkling green quads, meandering redbrick walkways, gleaming white stone buildings and fluttering blue banners. Turning back to the room with new optimism, I noticed the walls were thirteen cinder blocks high, so I left and bought paint to color my half of the room with alternating red and white stripes like the flag. I painted a navy-blue square in the corner with fifty white stars, each star made the same with a hand cut stencil.

My roommate, a short-haired Nebraskan whose Adam's apple stuck out a mile, came in and saw what I had done.

"I'm inspired," he said, picking up the paintbrush and stepping back to admire my work. "Can I use your paint?"

"Absolutely."

"Your flag is Fort McHenry. Me, I'm thinking abstract expressionism, Jasper Johns. I guess you're more the patriot."

I was the antithesis of a patriot, but I wasn't going to confess. As the Vietnam War raged twelve thousand miles away, I recalled a conversation with my closest boyhood friend.

"I enlisted," Gilly had said. "I volunteered. I'm going to be a soldier; they're sending me to Nam. I'm scared, but for once in my life, I'm going somewhere. I'm doing something important."

I felt regret bordering on envy for not having enlisted alongside him. I had deliberately decided to go to college, but my emotions hounded me that I had missed something important—I worried that Gilly was going to war without me to protect him.

"You might end up on the eleven o'clock news, for the love of God!" I said.

He looked at me.

"What the hell did you enlist for?" I went on. "You could get killed."

"What d'you mean, on the news? I'm going to be a GI. I'm going to fight; free Vietnam from the Communists. I'm going to kill Viet Cong for my country. I won't be the one on the news."

"Let's hope not."

More realistically, he was going to dig ditches, be a front man on patrols through the jungle, get foot rot and maybe malaria or encephalitis. After that, he might get shot or kill someone. If he died, they would say he died for his country, and he might get on the news in one of those body bags CBS was showing on the nightly reports, lying on the tarmac at some landing strip with palm trees all around.

"I thought you were going to community college. I thought you got into Tidewater."

Gilly shuffled his feet and stared at the floor.

"My marks. Not so hot."

I was horrified. Grades were not his forté, confirmed by the fact that he had been left back in grade school and was a year older than me.

"Will you write me, J-Bee? I know we haven't hung out together as much as we could've, but you've always been my best friend— more like a brother."

"Of course I'll write."

"Yeah?" He looked up at my face, searching to see if I meant it.

—✕—

My roommate said, "You *do* know who Jasper Johns is, right?"

"Yeah," I said. "So what makes you think I imagine myself a patriot?"

"I dunno."

"Are you saying you think I'm a square?"

"I didn't mean it in a bad way. Our generation is burning flags all over the place against the war, but here we have a flag that can't burn."

I liked his insight, and I said so.

"My name's Nelson Oates by the way," and he stuck out his hand.

"Joseph Bell, but if you want me to *like* you, call me J-Bee."

"That works."

"And if you secretly think that I *do* look square, think twice about *your* name."

"Yeah I know. Some people call me Nellie. I hate it—sounds like an old nag."

"How about Nebraska?"

"Nebraska?" He cupped his hand on his chin. "Well heck, why not?" He smiled. "I like it!"

4

Freshman Smoker

Just as Nebraska was finishing painting his wall, I returned with two armloads of pulp from Salter's Secondhand Books. While I was gone, he had mirrored my work in his half the room, right down to the stencil for stars. We stood together a moment, gazing at something we had created, turning our heads in an arc to take it all in. It was a serious flag, big, and I would live inside it like a cocoon.

A scruffy-looking guy popped his head in and shouted, "Get your asses out! Milo's throwing a party!"

"Who the hell's Milo?" asked Nebraska, wiping paint from his hands.

"No idea," I said, but in seconds, we were off to the source of the noise, Milo's room, fifty feet down the hall. The air in the hall hung with hash smoke, incense, and the lusty smell of male and female sweat soaking tee shirts after a long day of hauling trunks and fighting sidewalk mobs. Drugs were exploding on the scene that year. Some rock stars had made them part of their lives, while others like Joplin, Hendrix and Morrison had given their lives to them. The boys in Nam had discovered them, and so had Timothy Leary who was surfing the astral plane to "tune in, turn on, and drop out." Columbia was in the vanguard, a rat's nest of drugs, and as The Devil lived and breathed in Gotham, He was sure to inoculate me as one of his own. I wasn't looking to get high on dope, and I wasn't yet a user, but I knew the smell of grass, and I knew there was a ton in Milo's room. It scared me to be a willing virgin, but it was only a matter of time.

Outside Milo's room, the hall was packed with bodies. Twenty men and women, student types, clustered in haphazard groups. Some were standing, drinking Bud out of cans and cups, and about ten were sitting against walls, smoking, drinking and chatting. Several bodies sprawled on the floor, and about five or six women were clustered around the door itself, smoking and talking, unsure of whether they wanted to go in or just perch themselves where they could see action on both sides. One guy was sitting and plucking a guitar. Nebraska stopped to chat with the women, but next time I looked, he was gone.

Inside, the room was identical to mine with another twenty kids packed in. Hendrix played "Red House," and the two beds—minus mattresses—were heaped with luggage and clothes. Ceramic pots sat on the one long windowsill, and in those pots were shoots with sprigs in various stages of growth, all the leaves with seven points. Posters of Joplin and the Allman Brothers hung on the walls. Most people were stopping to meet and greet while another six or seven were standing in corners or sitting, laughing, smoking and drinking.

A short, broad-shouldered guy with hair down his back and a tee shirt which said, "Make Love Not War," materialized in front of me.

"Can you fuckin' believe Nixon wants to take away our student deferments? I mean, can you dig this guy?"

"Deferments?" I said.

"Corrupt son of a bitch. Yeah—don't you have a draft card yet? He's going to end our student deferments and assign numbers to everyone's birthday. You know, a draft lottery."

A tall guy in a crew cut moved toward us, stumbling to get to the door, holding a joint. "Care for a toke?" he said.

"Sure."

I took it in my fingers and brought it to my lips, sucking at it, a new sensation. I tried to hold in the smoke but couldn't, expectorating a thick white cloud.

"Good stuff, huh?" Then he poked me in the chest and said, "But it looks like you need practice."

I must have looked ticked off, so he put out his hand. I shook it.

"Name's Steinson. Call me Buck."

"J-Bee."

"Cool. Gotta bolt. You should meet Milo—tall guy with bleached-white hair." He pointed, "That's him with the stupid preppy tie. Great guy though. Later."

Steinson blew out of the room and down the hall, leaving me with the joint in my fingers, facing a wall of churning bodies, the short guy with the "Make Love Not War" tee shirt standing at my side.

"That guy Steinson you were talking to," he said.

"Yeah. What about him?"

"His father's a three-star general. Mind if I have a hit on that jay?"

I gave Make Love the joint, and he took it but kept talking.

"Steinson says his father will get him out of trouble if he's drafted. Says he'll get a cushy posting down South or out West. Says he'll never have to go to Nam. But dig this—if I lose *my* deferment, they'll send me to some godforsaken place like *Da Nang* or *Nha Trang*. It has to end in *ang*, or they won't send me there. I'll end up dying or losing my legs. Eating food through a straw. I've got no connections like Steinson, the *general's* son."

"My father's a naval officer," I said.

"No shit."

"Yeah. He says it's important to serve the nation. My mother says I should go to Vietnam if America calls. She says it would be an honor to die for my country."

"What the fuck could women possibly know about it?"

"What I'm saying—I've got no connections either. I'd rather have a beer and forget it."

"Me neither," said another voice. "No connections. But I'll *never* go."

I turned to see a tall, thin kid with curly hair down to his shoulders.

"Far out, Melberg," said Make Love. "But how can you be so sure?"

"Like I said—I'll never go. I'm not going to die facedown in some rice paddy. Or impaled on punji sticks in some jungle."

I had seen the documentaries on the CBS news. Booby traps snapping open, impaling men on sliced bamboo stalks, puncturing chests and bellies and protruding out their backs as they wriggled and flailed, hanging in air until they bought it.

"What'll you do—run away?" I asked.

"Who's this guy you're with, Bornes?" asked Melberg, looking at Make Love and hooking his thumb at me as if I'd just crawled from a hole in the ground.

"I don't know," said Bornes in his Make Love tee. "Let's ask him."

"Name's J-Bee," I said.

Melberg then turned to me, "If it comes to running, I'll run. If you're smart, and you don't want to rot in the jungles or drown in the paddies, you've got to plan an exit. I haven't decided how yet, but we've got options. Run to Canada, be a CO, go underground, disappear into some cave out west."

"It's a big country. Lots of space to get lost in," said Bornes, smiling big with teeth.

A tall guy, about six three with a thin black tie that reached only halfway down his shirt, came stepping through the bodies. He had straight white hair and gold rings on his fingers; one was a prep school ring with a gemstone and "NESSEX" carved in it.

"Peace, brothers," he said, holding his fingers up in a vee. "Who's the new kid, Bobby?"

"Let me introduce you. Milo, this is J-Bee. J-Bee, Milo."

"Sorry it's such a mess here," said Milo to me, apologizing but not apologetic. "We've got girls from Barnard, FIT, NYU, Finch.

There's even a couple of women I met at the West End Bar and another girl from Vassar."

"Gracie Slick went to Finch," said Bobby Bornes.

"Very cool," said Milo. "Come in and make yourself at home. We've got black hash from Turkey and weed from six different countries—go see Damien Archer MacNeish, the Fourth, and have a toke. Over there."

He pointed to the serious group, passing the hash pipe around. A stack of black squares, like sheets of darkest chocolate, lay on the mattress next to them. A girl picked a sheet and cracked off a piece, placed it in the pipe, and lit up.

"Thanks," I said. "Mind if I have a beer first?"

"In the cooler," Milo pointed.

I snaked my way through bodies, plucked out a Bud and side-stepped to the mattress, fascinated by things I had never seen. There was a vague familiarity in the ritual—incense, haze, sharing and groupishness. I almost expected the Sisters to pop out of a closet and begin a Latin chant, proclaiming a higher power.

"Dig this—he's got marijuana drying in the closets," said Bornes, following right behind me. "Once they're dry, he's going to bag 'em and sell."

"How do you know?" I asked, noticing the closet rods draped with hanging plants.

Bornes smiled proudly. "I went to school with Milo, and that's his *modus operandi*. He supplies every prep school in New England. He motors his father's yacht to Mexico, picks up bales of the shit, and brings it to a secret location on the East Coast. Piece of cake—if you're *him*."

"Why bother with college if you're such a successful dealer?" I was baiting him, but he wasn't the type to see it.

"Milo? A simple dope dealer? No-no-no. This is a sidelight. A hobby. Recreation. Milo's going to medical school. He's going to be a cardiologist like his father. His father has a lot of clout, and he's holding a place for Milo at the University of Pennsylvania School of Medicine. Milo told me he could get Cs and Ds, and he'll still go to one of the best medical schools in the world. No, Milo's going to be a cardiologist. Rich, like Daddy. Probably buy his own fuckin' yacht too."

"And you believe that?"

"Why not? Everyone's got to grow up and do *something*. Even Milo."

I looked at Bornes, and he looked back, smug as a philosopher who was the first in history to discover the meaning of life.

I popped my beer with the community church key and took a long, quenching guzzle. The bitter cold liquid cleansed my mouth and gullet, making me feel all the fresher. Then I found a spot on the mattress, next to Milo's friends.

"You MacNeish?" I asked the average-looking guy, sitting to my left. He had middling hair, a paisley button-down collared shirt, khakis and penny loafers.

"Who wants to know?"

"Milo said you were a nice guy who would give me a warm welcome. My name's J-Bee."

He looked me up and down like a pasha appraising property. He had too much interest; it put me on guard.

"Yeah, I'm Archer MacNeish. Care to try some of the Turkish black hash that Mandy is modeling today? It's on the house this time." He pointed a finger at Mandy who was holding the brass bowled pipe and pulling in smoke.

I took another swig of cold beer and thought it over.

"His father's a naval officer. He's not a smoker, this one." It was Bobby Bornes, who took a seat on the floor between Mandy and me.

"A naval officer?" asked MacNeish, his interest heightened. "Your father's a naval officer?"

"Right."

"What rank?"

"Rear admiral."

"Rear admiral?"

"That's right."

"I'm impressed. And your name is?"

"Like I said, J-Bee."

"From where?"

"Norfolk. In Virginia."

MacNeish raised his eyebrows. "Yeah, I heard that's where Norfolk is. What a pleasant surprise. Welcome, J-Bee. Will you break hash with us?"

"Love to."

MacNeish nodded, "Julie, give him the pipe."

The girl next to Mandy motioned for me to sit next to her. I went over, and she handed me the pipe, looking at me with a dreamy dope-shine in her eyes. She was pretty, her sweat-soaked hair in a tangled ponytail. Her nipples stood out straight through her shirt, so I couldn't help but notice. As I inhaled through the pipe, she slung her arm around my shoulders sloppily and pressed her breasts against my chest, first the one, then the other, making sure I could feel each in turn. She got close to my ear and whispered something and giggled. Although I couldn't understand a thing she said, the hair on my arms and the nape of my neck stood straight up, and, in spite of the inhibitions the Sisters had sown in me, I was suddenly hard as a rock.

"I'll have to bring you to our lion's den on Riverside Drive," MacNeish was saying. "You'll have to meet the proto-Sachems."

I nodded, not knowing what the hell he was talking about.

"Sounds like you *do* have connections," said Bornes.

"You have something to say about it?"

"Nothing, MacNeish. Nothing. J-Bee, pass the pipe?"

Later Bornes told me that the Sachems were a secret society, but what they did, nobody knew except, we supposed, the Sachems themselves.

Julie was nuzzling my neck and caressing my thigh. I had had more than a few tokes, and everything seemed heavy. The air felt as dense as a block of cheese, and I was in a fishbowl, looking out. I heard voices singing, "*Fly Jefferson Airplane—gets you there on time,*" and nothing seemed to matter except primal urges and

fulfillment, an intense hankering for pizza and a roast beef sandwich or burger.

I tried to rise from the mattress, but Julie was draped on my
shoulders, so I ended up tumbling to the floor. Then, suddenly,
Julie was on top of me, kissing me, and nothing else existed. I
laughed for nothing, or maybe because nothing felt real: I might be
thrown in steaming jungles with punji sticks and snakes; I might
die facedown in a rice paddy or get knifed on an uptown train.
None of it seemed to matter; everything was too absurd.

5

Come as You Are

It was a great party.

As Julie and I rolled on the floor, kissing and groping, Bobby Bornes crawled over on his knees to crouch next to me.

"I have this unbelievable case of the munchies," he said. "Why don't you join me at The Gold Rail for some corned beef and cabbage?"

I pried Julie's arm from around my neck, a jolt of suction reverberating through my head as our mouths popped apart. I gulped air.

"Where?"

"Broadway and 111th."

"Sounds damned good!"

"Yeah. It's far fuckin' out. But it's a dump. A real dump. Sawdust on the floor and grease on the tables that the waitresses swish around with those damp rags they carry when they act like they're wiping them clean. But fuck me if they don't have the best corned beef on the planet. And beer for thirty cents."

"Beer for thirty cents?"

"On tap."

"Do they have burgers?"

"Do what? Burgers? Shit yeah—they've got unbelievable burgers. Juicy with big, thick steak fries, all fluffy inside. And ketchup! Christ, I can taste the ketchup on those fries now. And I could dig a burger myself. No. No—corned beef. I'll put ketchup on the corned beef."

"Christ. I want those fries. I want salt too."

Nothing else existed.

"Salt? Why fucking salt?"

"I'm craving salt. They've got to have salt!"

"Of course they have salt. We're in the middle of friggin' Manhattan, for Christ's sake. Why wouldn't they have salt?"

"I don't know."

"They'll have salt. Don't get paranoid."

"Paranoid?"

"Yeah, paranoid. Let's go."

Julie was licking my neck and rubbing my crotch; I couldn't ignore her. Even more—this was a strong chance to get laid for the first time.

"I'm sort of in the middle of something. Maybe you noticed?"

"Yeah," he said. "Guess I did."

"So how 'bout I join you in a few? You going down there now?"

"Yeah."

"See you in a few then."

Tetrahydrocannabinol has interesting effects, and at that moment, there were only two things in the universe of any consequence— roaring appetite and bottomless lust. It was a pity, or so my brain told me, that I could only scratch one itch at a time, and sex was the bird in hand. Julie's thick muscular thighs and rounded, marble-firm buttocks hardened me to excruciating heights. And the promise of dangling fruits and dark forbidden triangles put me at risk for losing all sense of reason.

Next thing I knew, she was towing me by the hand, down the hall to my room toward the promise of oblivion. At the door, I fumbled for the key as Julie slipped her hand down my pants and whispered, "Oooo" in my ear. The door caved in, and we tripped into the room, collapsing on the bed.

I would like to tell you that Julie and I hit heights never before imagined in the history of mankind. I would like to tell you that nirvana and the astral plane merged, and I became one with the universe—but it was not to be.

Half our clothes were off; her chest rubbed against mine. Her skin was smooth, and her breasts tumbled out, leading the way to paradise. But then, unexpectedly, she whimpered something about her stomach, and before I could understand, aching for penetration that seemed inevitably close, she turned, jolted her head to the side and ralphed all over the floor.

I was stunned as a cold mixture of horror and disbelief poured over me, all anticipation and pounding blood gone in a nanosecond, an astral plane missed like I'd arrived an instant too late for the crosstown bus. Then, with timing that couldn't have been more perfect, Nebraska staggered through the door, flipped on the lights and stood gaping like an idiot at the mess on the floor, the now unconscious Julie snoring bare breasted on the bed, and me, a tangle of hair and bewilderment with my pants half off.

"Jeez, J-Bee. What's going on?"

I was thinking: *I was going to get laid and then get a burger, and now this.* But instead I said, "Julie barfed on the floor. Can you tell?"

"Well, yeah. You going to clean it up?"

"No—you go right ahead."

As the lights were now on, I saw the lumpy puddle on the floor with splatter all around.

"What? You kidding?"

"No," I said, now as sober as Sister Mary Margaret at Saint Eustace. "Not kidding. Enjoy."

"God, it reeks."

It did. I looked at Julie sleeping hard, a natural beauty gone bad, now pasty pale, hair glued together in bunches with cold sweat. But in spite of it all, she still had the innocent expression of a little girl. I felt sad for her and remorse at having been on the verge of contributing to her dissoluteness, a pang to my Catholic conscience. So I pulled the sheets over her half-naked torso, covering her up to the neck and tucking the sheets under her shoulders.

"Hey, Nebraska—make yourself useful. Get me a mop."

"A mop?"

"Yeah. I'm going to clean this up, and then I'm going down to The Gold Rail."

"Where's that? You're not just going to leave her here, are you?"

"She won't hurt you."

I looked him up and down. He was nice enough, but I realized that Julie would be in no condition to fend for herself in a male dorm. I looked down at her face, dead to the world. In fact, she could have been dead until I saw her chest rise and fall, under the sheets.

But then I wasn't totally sure. *What if she's dead? OD'd?*

I reached over and felt for a pulse. I tried several times, but there was nothing.

Panic rose inside me, and I shook her with both hands.

She took a deep breath, sucking air and then smacking her lips.

Alive! Christ, I am paranoid!

"What is it," she croaked, fluttering eyelids. She shook her head and looked at me, some of the glassiness gone. I went for a mop and washed the floor. Then I sat Julie up and got her dressed. We walked to Barnard, just across Broadway. After a conversation in which she asked me fifteen times to call her, saying she loved me over and over, I got her into her building and stole away, jogging all five blocks to 111th. She was going to be embarrassed in the morning, but there was nothing to do except salvage the rest of the evening with a burger, fries and a crisp thirty-cent beer.

The Gold Rail was just the right place for salvation.

6

The Gold Rail Tavern

The Gold Rail was dark, highlighted by grimy yellowed bulbs, so I stood just inside the doorway and scanned the place. The walls were bare, a graying ochre, the original paint with a patina of grime laid down after long exposures to smoke from the kitchens, perhaps never washed. There was an ornate, wooden crown molding and an original tin ceiling, all beautifully made though now neglected. The floors were old linoleum tiles, many of which had torn off, exposing the bare subfloor underneath. To my left was a long row of booths of darkly stained wood. To the right was a long wooden bar which matched the booths.

Behind the bar, the bartender chatted with a waitress. He was a middle-aged man with a week-old beard, frosted gray at the edges, and he sported a baggy gray tee shirt with "Columbia Athletics" across the front. Behind him was a long mirror with shelves of bottles. A series of vertical, wooden handles at the middle of the bar counter had the usual sudsers on tap—Miller, Bud, Michelob, Rheingold and Pabst Blue Ribbon Beer. There was also a tap for a Colorado beer new to the East Coast, called Coors.

I walked in slowly and stood behind Bobby Bornes who sat at the bar in front of a plate smeared with ketchup, mustard and the remains of corned beef. Next to him sat MacNeish, lifting a beer and chewing on fries. And next to MacNeish sat an older man, looking about sixty, with whitish-yellow hair and one of those red-and-black-checkered woolen hunting shirts, the tails hanging out behind. The shirt was unbuttoned to the waist, revealing a white tee shirt, stained in front with spots of coffee and worn thin from years of use.

The two younger men were talking to the older one who sat stone-faced, staring over the bar counter into the mirror in front of him, not saying a word. Then suddenly, the old man turned on his barstool to face MacNeish and poke him hard in the chest.

"You don't have a clue what you're talking about! Why don't you buzz off and leave me the hell alone!"

"Face it, old man, I know what I'm saying. War has always boosted the economy—it's the perfect remedy for unemployment. That's why the lower classes have always benefitted from war. Like you, for example."

"You don't know a damn thing about me."

"FDR knew what I'm talking about—your favorite president."

"Right on, brother," said Bornes, slurping beer from a stein.

"The Depression had America in a hole, but World War II brought prosperity," said MacNeish. "FDR understood the value of war. He knew that war would force us to build more factories and produce more goods, and he was right. War got us out of the Depression and made my daddy rich. FDR spouted patriotic rhetoric like 'Nothing to fear but fear itself,' but the war was his plan to bring us out of isolation, and now we dominate the world economy. In the end, it's all about money."

"War destroys men," said the old man, turning toward MacNeish, his worn teeth clenched. "But you're a cold-hearted little twit, and you don't have the ability to understand. It's too human a problem for the little robotic gears in your head." He brought his hand to the side of his head and spun his fingers.

"Gears!" clucked Bornes.

"Mick," said the old man, now turning to the bartender. "I'm done here. I love your place, but if you keep letting these ignorant *pip-squeaks* in, I'm not sure I can stand it much longer. How much?"

"One twenty-five."

The old man put money on the bar.

"Keep the change."

As he walked out, he had a limp that made me feel his pain as I watched. He was thinner than he looked on the barstool, and his jeans were baggier than they should have been.

"Can you dig that?" said Bornes. "I could have blown him over with a puff of weed."

"I wouldn't count on that," said Mick from behind the bar, frowning but averting his eyes to avoid confrontation. "He's a tough man. A year ago, I saw him lay a man out twice his size. He may look frail, and he's lost some weight, but his appearance is misleading."

"It's all about money," said MacNeish. "He puts his money on the bar and threatens never to come back if we continue to be served here. He's flexing his muscle—his dollar and a quarter worth of muscle."

"He's a patriot," said Mick. "He fought in World War II. He's got a Purple Heart, and some say he received the Congressional Medal, but he won't admit it either way. No one knows where he's from originally, but he's been a loyal patron here for as long as I've been around. No," he said, shaking his head, "they don't make them much better than him."

"He's a war hero!" blurted Bornes, laughing.

"Don't be a simpleton," said MacNeish. "He may be a gullible proletarian, but he's a war hero, and you have to respect that. He risked death so my family could line its pockets. He stands for something we *must* love."

"Even if he's wrong?" I asked, keeping my sarcasm hidden.

"Even if he's totally ass-backwards wrong," said MacNeish. "Which he is."

"When did you get here?" asked Bornes, eyeing me over his shoulder. He turned, slipped off his barstool and stuck out his hand.

We shook.

"Care to join me in a booth?" I asked. "I'm here for a beer and burger, and there's too much tension at the bar. I'd rather relax."

"Sure, J-Bee. MacNeish, you coming?"

"No thanks. I'm out of here. You boys enjoy yourselves. J-Bee, you're going to visit the proto-Sachems on Riverside Drive. I'll catch you up and tell you when."

"Cool," said Bornes. "Just name the day."

"Not you, Bornes. I'm talking to J-Bee."

Bornes was insulted. "Don't worry about it, Damien Archer the Fourth or whatever the fuck number you are. I'm not interested. You're not cool enough, and your little Wall Street friends are way too blazers-and-turtlenecks conservative for my taste. Makes me want to puke."

"Like I said," said MacNeish, ignoring Bornes and looking my way, "later," and he was out the door.

Bornes and I took a booth.

"What was that all about?" I asked.

"Fuckin' MacNeish. Thinks he's so hot. You'd think he was my friend."

"Isn't he?"

"Yeah, I suppose. He was at school with me and Milo."

"It's a little club. You've all been to school together so there's this bond, right?"

"Sounds pretty weak, doesn't it," said Bornes.

"Pathetic," I said, but I felt sorry for him. "If it's any consolation, my father believes in that kind of stuff."

"Really?" He looked up with a ray of hope in his eyes, but I had to be honest.

"It's still pathetic, no matter what my old man thinks."

Suddenly, out of nowhere, the waitress was standing in front of us, the tall willowy type with cascading, curly brown hair, braless under a tee shirt that said, "Free the Chicago Seven."

"What'll it be, boys?"

"I'm leaving," said Bornes. "I'm bummed."

"Hey, man—stick around."

"No. I'm bummed. Besides, I ate already. I'll see you." And he left.

"Okay," said the woman. "It's down to you."

"I guess."

"Know what you're having?"

"Cheeseburger with those fat steak fries."

She looked me up and down, then slid into the booth across from me and sighed.

"And ketchup," I added with my mouth watering as the munchies returned.

"Ketchup's on the table. Care for a drink?"

"Yeah," I said, busy looking at her.

"Well, what'll it be?"

"Miller."

"Hey Mick!" she shouted over her shoulder. "A Miller for the man here."

"Got you covered, Margo."

She looked at me again, and I buzzed happily.

"You look like a man of sophisticated taste."

"You think?"

"How would you like to try the swiss and mushroom burger? The latest avant-garde gourmand hit?"

"Mushrooms? You mean like fungus?"

"You really know how to ruin the mood, don't you. I guess it's a type of fungus, but I like to think of it more like French truffles rather than athlete's foot."

"Right."

"Be adventurous. Taste the liberal life. Give it a try."

I thought about it. She had a point. After all, that's why I was in Fun City—to see the world and taste the mushrooms.

"Sure," I said. "Why not."

I didn't know what to expect, but I was hungry enough to eat shoe leather so that when it came, it was the best meal I'd ever had. When I told Margo, she nodded and laughed and said that whatever you were eating at any given moment would always be the best, and it was only the human condition that constantly needed improvement.

I threw back the last half inch of my beer and lay back against the bench, relaxed in every muscle, letting my eyelids close and my limb bones dangle.

When I looked up, Margo was standing in front of my table, and I gazed at her through slitted lids.

"God, that was good."

Willowy Margo with the beautiful face, bushy-haired curls and thick eyebrows, the contour of her breasts straining against her "Free the Chicago Seven" tee shirt—she stood with her arms akimbo, giving me a beady eye. She had caught my attention, and I had caught hers. I was in a stoned reverie, and I knew exactly what I wanted to do to her, right then and there. She was tough, and I thought she seemed brainy, but her tresses were thick like a jungle, and it whispered promises of a thick fur down below in the darkest of grottoes, and it made me purr like an animal, lurking in the steamy mists of the lush undergrowth, waiting.

There was a sudden movement as Margo, taking me by surprise, leaned forward and slapped the check on the table. Just as abruptly, she turned on her heels with a swish of her hips and said, "Pay me when you're back on the planet."

7

The Specter of War

As fall in the city descended and the Vietnam conflict escalated, the freshmen of the Carman 12 dorm began a ritual of congregating to watch the six o'clock news and witness, firsthand, the horrors of war. I remember one night distinctly: there were eight of us in the TV room on chairs, on the couch and on cushions on the floor. Joints were going around as some smoked, but others merely sat, elbows on knees, faces in hands, leaning forward to hear and see.

"Hey! J-Bee!"

The voice of Bobby Bornes echoed from down the hall, but he was invisible, a shadow behind a gauzy curtain of Panama Red.

"J-Bee!"

"Shut up!" shouted Kemp, a preppie in chinos and a button-down shirt. "We're watching the news!"

The voice of Dan Rather droned about jungle rot, firefights, and the bodies of the dead, zipped in black bags, lying in rows on airstrips, awaiting helicopters and jets to carry them off to unknown places of burial. They were young men our age, fighting in the mud for abstract concepts, like "Americanism," "Democracy," and "The Domino Theory."

I was a warrior's son, and as I watched these young men on television in Nam without me, I felt I belonged there, lying in the mud alongside them. It felt strange that I, after spending an entire childhood incubating for the combat life and death of a warrior, could watch them dressed in camo, firing their guns without me.

"We're losing the war," said a guy named Harris. "We've *never* lost a war."

"We've got two options," said Melberg. "Get drafted or let the authorities come in the night, bundle us in straitjackets and wrap us in chains. Dump us in secret prisons, like Chateau D'If, where no one can find us. We can either be soldiers or COs—enemies of the state—there's nothing in between."

Dan Rather was speaking again, this time about us stateside boys, twelve thousand miles from the action. "Today, President Richard Nixon has declared he is eliminating student deferments from the draft."

We had expected this, but the news hit hard. Nixon was finally, officially, withdrawing our deferments, that one formidable thing which protected us from the draft, the only thing which had stood between us as living, sentient beings and us as bodies, facedown in the paddies, food for indigenous rats. The draft lottery would be universal, and everyone's birthday would be assigned a number. Student or not, if our lottery numbers were low, we would be drafted and shipped off to Nam. The lottery was coming in February, so for now no one knew how low was *too* low, and the delay and uncertainty fed a lingering tension. When the time came, if we pulled the short straw or got the black spot, we would barely have time to adjust.

"I'm fuckin' leavin' the country before they can get me," said Fishkin, sucking a joint.

"Guys! Pipe down! We're watching the news!"

"Leave the country? You mean dodge the draft, right?"

"I can dig that," said Bornes.

"At least wait until you get a number—maybe it'll be high, and you won't get drafted. Then you won't have to leave."

"Fuckin' numbers," said Fishkin, his hair like a halo, twice the size of his head. "The number thing is a lie so Nixon can lull us hippie-freaks into thinking we're safe."

"He wants to kill us so we don't vote Democrat."

"That's bullshit," said Kemp. "I'm in the same boat as everyone else, and I vote Republican."

"It's nonpartisan," said Melberg. "The screw is nonpartisan. LBJ was a lying, son-of-a-bitch Democrat, and Nixon's a two-faced Republican. Doesn't make a damn bit of difference."

"They're all liars."

"Fuckin' LBJ started bombing the North as soon as he won the election after promising never to do it."

"I remember that."

"I'm not going to Vietnam so they can build some kind of memorial for me in Washington with my name on it after I get killed," said Fishkin. "You think I'm kidding? Kids are getting murdered there every day. Politicians always need expendable young bodies with a pulse to fight, and I'm not doing it! Even if they bring me there, I'm going to strip myself naked, leave the uniform right on the beach and swim to freedom in Borneo, so help me God!"

"That's righteous."

"You might as well be a CO and go to prison. At least you'll live," said Melberg. "We can be COs together."

"CO?"

"Conscientious Objector."

"Your geography's all wrong. You can't just swim to Indonesia—it's hundreds of miles away!"

"A thousand," said Kemp. "Get a grip."

"You think I care? I don't. I'll drop my pants and swim."

"You'll drown."

"He'll get eaten by sharks is what," said Nebraska, smiling as he said it.

"Man, that's so stupid, it's funny," said Bornes, laughing and coughing smoke.

"Shut up!" shouted Fishkin, standing and agitated. "Don't ruin my fantasy—it's all I've got!"

Maybe it was the marijuana or maybe it was the absurdity, but all of us laughed except Fishkin.

"You guys think it's funny," he said, "but I'm afraid. I don't want to get my hair shaved off, spend months in a barracks and get shipped to Nam. I don't want to die. Punji sticks sticking out of me all over the place. Scares the shit out of me."

It scared us all. In fact, I was surprised at how anxious *I* was to hear the fears of my compatriots, given that the option of fighting had been my destiny.

Bornes got up off the floor, brushing ashes from his jeans, sidling over to where I leaned against the wall. "Can you dig this?" he said. "Panic has struck. I'm blowing this pop stand. Care to go to The Village with me; do some serious partying?"

"I can't," I said, wondering how I would sit still in my current state of angst. "I have to go to the library."

"Come on, J-Bee. Give it a rest. In the words of the prophet, *turn on, tune in, and drop out.* At least for one evening."

"That wasn't a prophet. That was Timothy Leary, the Harvard professor who fried his brains on acid."

"Fuck Harvard," said Bornes. "They rejected me."

"*You* brought it up."

"Okay. Cool. But I'm splitting. Why not come along? Turn on and drop out just for one night. The prophet had an idea right there."

"I'll go," said a new voice.

"Hey, can you dig this?" said Bornes. "If it isn't the great man himself!"

It was Milo with Buck Steinson a half step behind him. Bornes put out his hand, and Milo shook warmly and gave him a smile. Steinson looked at his watch while Milo turned to me and smiled.

"How do, J-Bee?"

"Likewise," I said.

"I've had about as much of this place as I can take," said Milo. "I need a night off to clear my head, and Buck suggested we go out and have a couple beers. You game?"

I thought about it, and the lure of Fun City tempted. The Village was especially known for its thumping music, and visions of jiggling nubile young women dancing with abandon in the beer halls of Pleasure Island beckoned. The thrills that only Gotham could inject into such a boring life as mine were so close I could feel them coursing through my veins and taste them on my tongue.

But then I thought of discipline and stood strong. "Can't do it—too much on my plate."

"We all do," said Milo. "This is Columbia, and if you're not careful, they'll work you 'til you're nothing but an oily puddle in the dirt. Your whole life can be consumed by the toil that leads to an early death, but there's a time for everything, and now is the time to press your fingertips to the throbbing pulse of Manhattan. Come out for a night; we'll hit the town running. It'll be fun with four. We'll have an experience to remember, an adventure that will always bind us together, even after we graduate and go our separate ways."

"You *can't* say no after *that,*" said Bornes. "That's poetry. That's *life equals art.*"

They both looked at me, awaiting my response while Steinson stood straight-faced and expressionless, gazing into space.

"This is a persuasive brother," said Bornes, looking up at Milo with admiration. Then he turned to me, "Come on, J-Bee—don't be a drag!"

I felt the charm; I felt the tension. I felt three sets of eyes, but something within me reared itself up, perhaps perversely or perhaps on principle, refusing to buckle under pressure. I told myself, as I had done before, that I was resolute and would never succumb to the will of others against my own dictates; I would follow the path I would choose for myself.

"Another time," I said.

"All right, but if we're not going to The Village with *you,*" said Milo with an honest smile, "then we're off on our own expedition. Off to secret places, to parts unknown. Good luck with the studies."

He winked at me.

Steinson raised his eyebrows.

"Yeah," said Bornes smugly, "and good luck with the motherfuckin' books."

8

The Sisters of Saint Eustace

The reality of the draft and the resultant paranoia which had descended upon my collegiate brothers precipitated a sense of indecision in me. Forgetting about the library, I grabbed my coat and fled the dorms like a shell from a cannon, my trajectory at random. Questions squirmed in my head, challenging me as to why I, son of a warrior, would be so panicked by talk of the draft or possible rendezvous with war.

"Hey, J-Bee!"

A man of medium height, medium build and straight brown hair to the waist stood before me. His flannel shirtsleeves were rolled up, and his Popeye-type forearms, thick below the elbows, dangled from his shoulders and bounced like drumsticks. He had on bell-bottom blue jeans and a large circular peace symbol, made of copper, strung around his neck.

"Good to see you, man. Peace." Billy Wing held up his two fingers, palm side toward me in greeting. "Where're you going?"

"No idea," I said, my breath misting.

"You're movin' pretty fast for a guy who's going nowhere. Like a bat out of hell."

"True."

"Well then," said Billy with a gentle smile. "Why don't you come with me to The Apocalypse Café? We can get a cup of tea. Or coffee. Maybe there'll be a recital—poets hang there all the time."

"Where's that?"

"Basement of Saint Paul's Chapel."

I liked Billy, but I wasn't sure I was supposed to like him. He was a nice sweet-tempered guy, and he had once done me a good turn. I had overslept one day and missed my freshman bio lecture. The notes from that day were important, and even when I went around with a tin cup, begging to borrow notes from my class-mates, they gave me nothing. Some were even smirking because I was absent the much-needed notes.

But not Billy Wing. He was in the same class, and he waved me over, giving me his notes to copy.

I had looked at him hard. Here was this hippie-dippy kid, smil-ing, out of step, offering me what I needed most at the moment. And me—I wasn't sure that it would be worth borrowing notes which did not come from a starched-collared boy with his anus sewed shut. I didn't think anyone who would be willing to lend me notes, without any regret, would be someone worth borrowing from.

Of course, I was prejudiced and a hypocrite, and Billy Wing's notes were golden, better than any I could have hoped to borrow. After all, he was a Columbia boy. Going further, he was genuinely happy to share whatever I needed that he might possess, and he asked for nothing in return.

"We're all brothers, man. People have to love each other. The world needs peace."

I didn't know then about peace, but I liked Billy, and I knew I could trust him.

"So," said Billy, "*Bat Outta Hell*, you coming?"

"Sure—but I've only got eighty-three cents."

"You're in luck—coffee's thirty-five. And as a bonus, there's a guy there who's reciting diatribes tonight. Strange guy, but you might like him."

"I could use a change of scenery. Coffee's good."

He led me across campus to Saint Paul's Chapel and The Apoc-alypse Café. As we descended circular stairs, dim sconces holding live torches lit the way to a clammy stone crypt under the nave of the church. The walls themselves were quarried stone blocks, stained with the sterile breaths of holy men, the soot of the city and the sweat of generations of students. A sniff of that dank air brought me visions of nuns in billowing habits dragging boys to secret corners where, imbued with the Holy Spirit of the Inquisition, they would rack them until they broke their wills. Now from the dim café ahead, I heard the clank of teacups, reminiscent of rusted chains anchored to dungeon walls. The sounds evoked visions in my head of heavy, iron rings that Gilly had once sworn were in the bowels of Saint Eustace where, he said in a moment of hyperbole, the Sisters had taken him years before to pay for his sins and for those of mankind. I heard their murmuring voices, too muffled to comprehend.

"You can hear the dead whispering in the catacombs," I said.

"I knew you'd like it! They say that when Ginsberg and Kerouac were students here, they used to recite in this very place."

Clusters of droopy longhairs, men and women, were sitting around several candled tables, talking in huddled tones. Some of them recognized Billy as we sat down, and he nodded and twinkled with happiness. He was a regular, comfortable in surroundings where he was understood.

"You come in here a lot, don't you?"

"It's a special place," he said. "They have a selection of teas like nowhere else. For me, tea has a mysterious history. I think of Marco Polo and the Silk Road. Samarkand, Kashgar and Ancient China. I think of the initial, civilized entanglements of East and West."

He looked at me with inner peace, but his face changed as he saw my expression.

"You all right?" he asked.

"What?"

"You look like you saw a ghost."

"Just a flashback."

"Bad trip? You on something?"

"No. Nothing like that. Just some not-so-fond memories of me and Gilly getting beaten by nuns in elementary school. You know, when we were kids."

"Beaten? For real?"

In my first few years at Saint Eustace, I obeyed and listened, always with half an eye on the switches on the wall. I lived in terror of the power of the Sisters as they swished through the corridors in their black, billowing habits, pouncing on unsuspecting boys. Initially I showed them respect, and because of my deference and because I was smart, I became a favorite with the nuns who otherwise hated the boys. But Saint Eustace didn't choose nuns for their ability to teach: the Sisters were married to God, and that was all that ultimately mattered. At times the lessons bored me, and I often read a book in class, nodded off, or talked too much to the kids sitting next to me.

So they hit me.

It was in fifth grade. Sister Moira caught me napping and whacked me on the back of the head with a ruler. I jumped in my chair, still half in twilight, and she darted in quickly like a prizefighter and slapped me hard across the face. "You think you can sleep in *my* class?" The eyes of every child were upon me as she pulled me by the ear to stand in the front where she made me turn around.

I was still getting my bearings when she hit me on the rump with a switch. It stung physically, but it shamed me badly, and I hated her. Some of the children bent their heads down to hide their faces but looked up to sneak peeks; others turned their gazes away, afraid to watch, while a few brazen kids sniggered into their shirtsleeves. I stood there feeling naked, maybe like Christ himself, in front of this classroom rabble, my masculinity ripped to shreds by nuns who were nothing less than Romans. From that moment, I decided that if I were going to be hit, I would get my money's worth. If they hit me for breaking the rules, I would make sure that I broke enough rules to justify whatever they did to me. It was war; the gauntlet had been thrown, and I had no idea how I'd ever win. But it didn't matter; I had to fight, and backing down wasn't an option.

It got worse. I had been a favorite, but now I found myself getting whipped once a week, and hatred boiled my blood. The Sisters demanded I apologize to them and to God, and I flatly refused. They got under my skin, and I lost it. I acted out, rebelled, railed against all authority. My rebellion made me think of something I had seen on television around that time: as a Buddhist monk sat cross-legged in the middle of the street with a shaven head and loose black robes, a man came and doused him with gasoline and lit the monk on fire. The flames exploded in an aura of orange haze, engulfing the monk as he slowly burned to death, his skin turning black with black smoke rising off his surfaces. He did not move from his position until, in a final gesture, he lifted his arms upward before tumbling over, onto the ground, in a burning, smoldering mass.

"What's that?" I had asked.

"Immolation of monks in Saigon," said my father, looking up from his evening paper, "protesting Diem's regime."

The scene was otherworldly. Such a demonstration of determination in the face of unimaginable agony both chilled and awed me. The incredible conviction, the will of this monk, the selflessness in dying for his cause in such a way was an impetus to motivate me beyond any other example the universe could possibly provide, and its power was far greater than that of the Sisters. I became the Breaker of Laws, the Iconoclast, and Shiva, the Destroyer. I would be a burning monk; I would defy the Sisters, but I vowed I would never lift a hand to hit them back even when the temptation was almost unbearable as they sneered and beat me. At the time, I told myself that such self-restraint must count for something when God would finally come to weigh my soul and judge whether I might enter the Gates of Heaven.

The summer after fifth grade was a breather, but my career at Saint Eustace entered a new phase in sixth grade, the year that Gilly was left back and was placed in the same class as me. It started when Sister Mary Margaret locked me in a closet in the basement, next to a bucket of ammonia. I sat in the dark against the wall, my feet drawn up to my chest for lack of space, the caustic fumes burning my lungs, making me cough and leaving me in a blaze of indignation.

I was let out of the closet at the last school bell and led to the priest for the first of many "chats."

"You're a top student, Joseph," he said with a trace of brogue, his tiny eyes watering.

"J-Bee," I corrected him.

"Joseph is a great name—the father of our Lord Jesus."

He had a mound of cheese cubes on his desk and was popping them into his mouth between sentences, his jowls aquiver with delight.

He took a grunting breath and went on. "You've been doing well, J-Bee. Why the change? Why so defiant?"

I said nothing.

"You should answer when I speak to you."

"I'm afraid you'll beat me, Father. Or lock me in a closet."

"I won't beat you," he said, leaning across the desk to touch my arm, chuckling as he attempted to become my confidant.

"Well—then you'll get your nuns to beat me. They'd beat me for far less than what I might tell you."

By now I had been struck so many times, I wasn't afraid. They could do what they wanted to me, but my hate had gelled, and my resolve had hardened to the abuse.

"Maybe I *will* have you beaten—for insolence!"

"*Do it!*" I said. "If there's one thing I've learned, it's how to take hard corporal punishment. *Father.*"

He eyed me narrowly. Then suddenly, craftily, he leaned back in his chair and beamed me a big, bald-faced Irish smile, transforming himself into a fat-faced cherub.

"J-Bee," he intoned, pausing for drama.

"Father Croghan," I said, echoing his lilting voice.

"We know you're a smart one. And I see you're an angry boy, rather tough and stubborn."

"Never stubborn, sir. My father is a military man, and I am resolute." I didn't deny my anger. He was right about that though I would never confess it—certainly not to him.

"Yes," he said. "That's right. And obviously, you love him and look up to him."

This idea struck me in a funny new way. It was true I revered my father, but then where did he go when the Sisters beat me?

"Yes, *Holy Father*," I said, my tone dripping with contempt.

"Holy Father is a title reserved for the Pope as you well know. You may call me Father."

"Yes, *Father*."

"Well, you should know that even your own father wouldn't want you to place him ahead of God."

"Is that what I'm doing?"

He sat smiling, dough-faced with crinkles around blue eyes, waiting for me to speak further, but I didn't.

Oddly, I behaved better after that, taking solace in the idea that, for the moment, I was merely a passenger, biding my time until I could escape from Saint Eustace and Norfolk. I surmised that as my father's world had shaped *him*, my world would eventually shape *me*. Where I might escape *to*, and what that world might be was the subject of fantasy, a dream that relieved the pressure of my trapped existence, giving me hope where there was otherwise no light.

So life went on. I got the occasional beating, but in those days, in my neighborhood and at my school, getting hit was not considered abuse. As my mother would say, sitting at her vanity in front of her mirror, powdering, "It's merely an occasional straightening-out like all boys need." For me and the other boys, she explained, it was at the hand of the Sisters that our normal growth was assured as we moved toward high school where the physical punishment mysteriously stopped.

In the meantime, however, I had no choice but to suffer the Sisters. Yet every once in a while it would get the better of me, and, against all that my father stood for, I would return to the school at night to soothe my defiant nature, throw a rock through a window, and run like hell.

9

The Serpent of The Apocalypse

"You've got to be kidding! You were beaten?"

As I sat across from Billy, the change in his face from joy to pain—pain for me and for what I had been through—smothered me. It was too intimate; he was too close. Sure they had beaten me, but the actual events had been distorted over time, and it was this distortion, viewed through the lens of a child's fearful mind, that had placed me in the dreaded dungeons of that school forever.

I leaned backward and mumbled, "Yeah, for real. Me and Gilly. When we were in grade school, they used to kick the crap out of us. They made me into the man I am today. I've got them to thank for everything."

"Far out. That's some very dark humor. They had no right to do that."

"They had the power to do it, so they did it. *Right* had nothing to do with it."

Something clicked in me. A gate had opened, and an intangible undercurrent of emotional stew boiled. Here was this guy I didn't really know, who actually cared about what I had been through, and I was bristling at him, churning like molten lead. Suddenly I saw that he had innocence and belief; the truth was with him.

My father's view was different. "It's a matter of perspective, son," he had said. "Respect for authority is crucial, or society breaks down. There will always be those in power and those who aren't, and you should align yourself with those in power, especially if you have ambition. With your intelligence, you'll climb the rungs of power as I have. Cling to the established order—that's the ticket. It puts bread on the table, puts the car in our garage, and provides a safe neighborhood for children."

"But what about the other kids? What about Gilly? Shouldn't we stand up and say how unfair it is?"

"It's survival of the fittest, Darwin straight and simple. You can't improve the lot of everyone else on the planet. You can't expect to succeed if you run with losers, like Gilly. You have to look after yourself and fight to get ahead. Or perish. Ultimately, there's no other way."

I wanted to ask him: *where are you hiding when your son is being whipped*, but I was afraid. Funny that I was more afraid to question *him* than I ever was to face the whips of the Sisters. As much as I had loved him, I now resented him, and the idea of confronting him filled me with dread. His feedback helped from time to time, philosophy through which lens I might see the world more clearly. Such scraps of thoughts, when I was younger, were far better than the later aloofness that accompanied his rapid military promotions and escalating responsibilities.

I obsessed over my feelings. I stewed on what he had said, but I could neither rid my mind of his insouciance to my corporal punishment nor escape my fears of confronting him. One day, coming home after a beating that left me unable to sit down, I went to his office door and knocked. I knew he must be inside, so when he didn't answer, I placed my ear to the wood and heard him on the phone.

I was afraid to bother him so I stood in the hallway, feeling the soreness from my whipping, angry at having to submit to so much pain and humiliation and then to tiptoe around at home as if nothing had happened. Indignation grew as my anger and impatience ratcheted. I felt the beating of my heart and its echo in my head, waiting for the door to open.

After some minutes, I pressed my ear to the door again, and, hearing nothing, knocked louder. Still there was no answer.

I turned to walk away, but the pain over my bottom conjoined with a mounting sense of injustice made me turn back without thinking, lift both fists and bang hard on the door. He would hear me now, and I sensed I would awaken the slumbering bear who lurked in its cave. My heart raced with stimuli of fight or flight for the danger I had created and for how he might retaliate, but I stood my ground: running was impossible.

The door opened a crack, and he showed his face, sinews tensing in his neck, his anger glaring at mine.

"What do *you* want!"

My fear made me mute, but I forced myself to stand and face him.

"Look," he said, changing his tone, "I'd like to talk, but I'm under a lot of pressure. So tell me what it is, and let's be done with it. Right?"

Trying to keep my voice from wavering, I said, "The nuns are beating me!"

He clamped his stare upon me; his face remained placid as the brain behind the face worked overdrive, organizing thoughts to articulate.

"Oh *that*," he sighed. "Buck up. You were always a tough kid. That's how the world works."

"You want to see my rear end? It's purple! I can't sit down!"

"Of course you don't like it, but I have faith that the priest and the nuns are giving you the education I expect: they're vaccinating their lessons right into your skin. It's not a public school; I pay tuition. I made a conscious decision because there's more to education than academics."

"You think what they're doing in that damned school is *right*?"

"I know you derive perverse pleasure in arguing, but I admonish you to watch your tongue. Now please, if you don't mind, I have work."

"You're going to *let* them beat me?"

"Buck up, J-Bee—I've got boys dying in Southeast Asia, and you've got bruises on your butt. Get it?"

—ℳ—

"That's a world I don't understand," said Billy, hair hanging down, slowly shaking his head.

"It's a dungeon full of ghosts where they keep Satan chained to the wall," I said, "in case he's needed."

"I want to hear more," said Billy, "but first, let's have tea."

A light came on behind a translucent, white curtain. A man was sitting behind it, in silhouette. Voices hushed; the room became still.

"What's this?" I asked.

"You're about to meet The Serpent—patron saint of The Apocalypse."

The voice behind the curtain spoke, whispering through the microphone which both disguised and amplified the speech and accentuated all sounds of "s."

"I have a confession to make. It's been on my mind for some time. It disturbs me; it gnaws at me like the creature that gnaws at the root of the tree. It was a crime I committed. It had to be done—it was a blow I struck for freedom, for America, for the Land of My Fathers and for all the things that we protect when we go to war.

"But it came at a cost, My Brothers, and this time it was *I* who paid.

"It was a rat's nest of firepower, a hole in the dirt on a hillside in the South Pacific. A machine gun volley killed a squad of my comrades, pinning down the others. I was there, and I stormed the rat's nest alone. I put my bayonet through the chest of one of them, feeling bones crunch in my fingers, ramming the blade through rib and lung. The blade was stuck so fast, I couldn't pull it out. So, turning to the only other rat in the hole, I pulled my service revolver and blew off the front of his head.

"It was a worthy cause. I was celebrated for bravery and deco-rated by important men at a solemn occasion. A regiment came to attention, and marksmen in dress uniform serenaded me with a rifle salute. But as I say, there was a cost, and I paid it. Years of twisted, sweat-drenching dreams of horror. All at once, I grew from youth to man, but at the same instant, it broke that man and made me an emotional cripple.

"War is never a 'good cause,' but sometimes it's a moral imper-ative. Without moral imperative, it's nothing to ruin your soul for. Beware of wars of questionable merit, born of dubious motives from the minds of scheming men of power. In the current conflict, it will put you in the path of a people's revolution, a fight to the death over their self-determination where they have too much at stake to fail. Powerful men may have a Domino Theory, but such a mighty collapsing wall of dominoes will not be stopped.

"I warn you—I beseech you! Beware."

10

Grunt

I wondered who The Serpent was. He said that war with a moral imperative was worth fighting while other war was not. I pondered whether a soldier ever had a choice, and the more I thought about it, the more absurd the question became. Soldiers weren't able to vote themselves in or out of a war; they weren't allowed to stand up and leave on the eve of battle because, as they might think, "There is no moral imperative here." My father would laugh at the notion; then he would say what he always said concerning the only choices a young man had, "Don't be a grunt, be an officer" and "A boat is cleaner than a ditch."

As college life ground into routine, I became a grunt of a different stripe. I spent many hours on the rock pile studying Mill and Locke, Dostoevsky and Freud, Euripides and Aristophanes. I studied physics to learn how the world worked, and calculus because I had to. It was eat, sleep, go to class, and study. After a while, I knew I needed to add some color to my drab life. I called Julie to go for a coffee, but she pulled some dope from her pocket, and we smoked in a stairwell along the way. The thread of our purpose was lost, and we ended up pigging out on ice cream and Twinkies.

She took me back to her room after that, and just as things were heating up, her roommate burst in with two more giggling girls, all with high-pitched, excited voices, shrieking with laughter to be so fortunate as to discover us together. They called me "the trophy," straight to Julie's face, and she liked it. I got too much attention, too many questions from female minds that I had to think hard to answer through a weedy haze. I wanted to be left alone, the inscrutable *id*, a silent, hairy gargoyle unawakened from his anti-cultural torpor, left in his benumbed existence on the underside of his favorite rock, fulfilling only basic needs and feeding his mind without the ultra-violence of intrusive female chatter.

I fled Julie, back to my limited existence. It was during this period of man-beast incubation, sometime in October, that I sought The Gold Rail as a thirsting beggar seeks paradise, late in the evenings for dinner and beer. The dull yellow light of the place made everything and everyone appear in the faded sepia of old saloons, a colorless world that soothed all stress. Mick would station himself at the end of the bar, drying off mugs with a towel when he wasn't taking orders or serving pints, a sentinel on the battlements of a fortress of male reclusion that never seemed to change.

It was there, purely by chance, that I ran into the old war hero on three successive nights, sitting at the bar, three stools away from my usual perch. At first he eyed me suspiciously, keeping his distance, no doubt associating me with MacNeish and Bornes. But by the third night he was sitting only two seats away, and as we each chomped our food, a bond was created by mere happenstance. Perhaps he began to accept me as one accepts the furniture in a familiar room. Or perhaps, I felt, I was to be his anointed successor, he who would inherit the old man's lonely place at the bar when he was departed.

I discovered from his conversation with bartender Mick that his name was Bloom and that he was not only kindhearted, but also a serious poet although there was no way I could know whether he was good or not. Initially he only addressed me a few times, in each instance with only a few sentences to see if the gap between us might be bridged. It was interesting to view him up close and observe our interactions objectively. We were two damaged men, haphazardly seeking points of commonality in a lonely world ruled by entropy.

"I see you come in here to eat," he finally said to me. "You're always alone. What happened to your friends?"

I knew he didn't like my "friends," and he could have sneered, but he didn't. He said it straight, and I liked him for it.

"You mean," I said, "'*the pip-squeaks*'?"

Bloom smiled with a full set of teeth. "Yeah—the pip-squeaks. Or maybe it was the pissants. Whatever. Did they ditch you?"

"He's not bothering you, is he?"

It was a woman's voice jangling from across the room, and it seemed she had been monitoring the situation. I hadn't known she was there, but I turned and saw her, and immediately I had a point of reference, a beacon in my storm: the willowy waitress with the brown bushy hair, braless under her tee. Suddenly, I had lost that rudderless feeling of being unanchored on a sea of *what for*.

"Hi Margo."

"Is he bothering you?" She pointed her chin at Bloom, and he raised his hands in the air, looking downward in submission. She stood in the middle of the room, narrowing her eyes, waiting to be the judge.

"We're just two guys getting along," I said.

"Ditto," he said. "Despite age difference, we share a sense of humor."

Bloom turned and gave me a wink from the eye that was hidden from Margo's view.

"You two, a sense of humor? That's the funniest thing I've heard all day," she said, walking off. "Don't let that old fart give you any problems."

"She doesn't talk to me," said Bloom. "She's an angry woman."

"It's half a facade," said Mick, who had been listening in. "She's a very good egg. Works hard. Smart as hell."

Mick turned to me. "She really likes you. She treats you differently. Play your cards right, and you may be going places. Looks like you're special."

Bloom eyed me with suspicion, but he spoke to Mick. "So you're saying that she thinks he's special?"

"That's right," said Mick, walking away. "So what's it to you, anyway? You don't have a secret crush on her, do you?"

11

Monk's Paradise

Gilbert O'Daly was a soldier, but he didn't volunteer to have a choice about his fate in Nam. He put his trust in the gray-haired oligarchy that ran the country; he left his fate in their wizened hands.

He hadn't written, and I didn't have his address. With all the news pumped to the American public, I was alarmed, worried for his safety. No prior war had TV crews crouched in the bushes, only feet behind soldiers who were firing on the enemy and taking fire in return. These live firefights on the nightly news shocked us all as we witnessed teenage men, dressed in bloodstained drab, dragged away by their comrades, their bodies limp in death.

After I heard The Serpent's philippic, Gilly was on my mind. He could have been slain in any of the ways I had seen others murdered on camera. There were firefights on beaches, in jungles, on the Mekong River, in ancient cities amidst sacred Buddhist shrines. So, I wondered, what had happened to my friend, the six-year-old who used to knock me down only to come over the next day, smiling with heartfelt apology? The young man who bequeathed his coveted minibike to my little brother, Jerry? The boy who, the day before I entered school, forced me to peek through the windows of Saint Eustace at a rack of whips on the wall?

"They don't hit you with those!" I said.

"They hit me all the time. If they catch me looking in the wrong direction, they click their tongues, grab me by the hair, and yank me to the front. Then they whip me with the whole class watching."

"They won't whip *me*!"

"Why not? Think you're special or something?"

"They won't do it!"

"If you go to school here, they'll whip you. They don't care who you are. I heard Sister Margaret say, 'All boys need to be whipped sooner or later.' Can't you see the blood on the whips?"

"Yeah," I said, but I wasn't so sure.

—∞—

As dormitory hysteria continued to mount after Nixon's promise to remove student deferments, and as my anxiety for Gilly precipitated in my dreams, awakening me in hectic sweats and palpitations, I received his first letter.

Dear J-Bee,

I'm sorry for taking so long to write, but life here is complex. It was great to get to Vietnam after being on ship so long. I didn't sign up to be on some boat, bobbing around, polishing metal from dawn to dusk. There were times I just wanted to barf all day with the boat lurching around in the waves. But now that I've arrived, it's exciting. I've never been so far from home. The trees and land look so much different here (in Nam) than Norfolk. No crepe myrtles, but lots of other blooming plants, beautiful things I've never seen.

And the people are so different. Exotic even. It was hard to imagine just how bizarre it would be. To think they're people the same as us; I don't know. To a Southern boy, I'm staggered by how racist I really am. It's scary, but the differences are wondrous beautiful. The women, such beautiful faces, but so alien, like they dropped from UFOs. I mean—I've seen Asians before, but so many together, such tiny people. Skinny.

Scrawny even. No disrespect intended. Different. And they just squat down all the time. No chairs! Not like back in Virginia where people sit in restaurants and eat at tables with spoons and forks. They squat down (like they're going to shit) right in the street or wherever they happen to be, and they eat from bowls, scooping rice with their fingers. I swear it's like another planet. If I weren't fighting here, I might just love to live among them and learn the deep Eastern secrets of their ways.

Right now I'm on base, but I'll be going into the jungle tomorrow to face the enemy. I mean the VC, the Viet Cong. They told me to write letters, as many as I can because it will be hard to send letters while I'm out there. I'm excited to serve my country, but I'm not sure what to expect. Some of the guys say it's going to be horrible and that we'll be fighting for our lives. Many of us are going to be killed they say. But if it's noble to die for America, I'll do it. I'm not afraid to die. Well, not always. Anyways, the Sisters sure did prepare me for facing fear or even death, like it was always somewhere nearby.

Wish me luck, J-Bee. Pray for me. It's like being on a roller coaster because once you're on it, you can't get off. And I'm on it now.

Your friend,
Gilly

I read Gilly's letter in the cloister of my room. It was no place to study, but it was my refuge from the outside world. Even so, I still had to share it with Nebraska.

I slumped back in my chair, gazing out the window at the night. The glow from the interspersed lamps on campus made rainbows in the mist and reflected off the freshly fallen sheen of rain, covering the grassy quads and brick walkways.

My mind wandered. I saw sunny rice paddies with tiny Asian women and children, bending over at the waist, their lampshade hats tilting to keep their faces in shadow. They moved inch by inch, planting clumps of straight, green shoots which poked up over the ankle-deep waters in which they would germinate and from which their grain would later be plucked. It was a marvel of the natural world; it took my breath away to imagine. And though America was there to protect the daily, agrarian life of the South Vietnamese, I saw on TV that we were despoiling their land, even destroying it, while waging war against their unification with their cousins in the North.

I wrote back to Gilly with as much stateside news as I could muster. I wrote about academia and books I was reading. I wrote about campus and The Apocalypse Café. I wrote about The Serpent, the café's "patron saint." I wrote about hippies and pot and The Gold Rail Tavern where beer was thirty cents a mug. I told him how we saw the war on TV and about Nixon's decision to end student deferments, ensuring that I would enter the draft lottery for a one-way ticket to Nam.

Then I told him that, in many ways, I felt I should be there. There was a part of me that wanted to be in a ditch by his side, giving him cover and taking shots at the enemy. I told him how I was conflicted and how I saw the benefit of college. I wrote to him that after the sins of my own violence, I could probably live with killing an enemy, but what I didn't write was that somewhere in my heart I doubted the very words I was putting to paper—daily I was becoming less and less certain. In the end, I told Gilly that no matter how I felt, I might end up getting drafted and sent to Vietnam anyway. Although there might be panic in the dorms as student dreams were threatened, I was able to see the justice inherent in a draft that was based on a lottery, blind to my socioeconomic status and unaware of the color of my skin.

As I finished, Nebraska burst through the door and bounced around the room with an animation surpassing anything I'd ever seen in him. His hair was pointing in all directions like sticks of hay, and the stubble on his face was an irregular chop.

"I'm so glad you're here, J-Bee! You can't guess what I've got! I just bought a truckload of comics!"

"Comics?" I asked, seeing the stack under his arm.

"Comics! But no ordinary comics—these are from the San Francisco Rip Off Press! Robert Crumb's Fritz the Cat, Mr. Natural, the Snoids, Bo Bo Bolinski, Shuman the Human . . ."

"What?"

"That's right! Can you dig it?"

He dumped the whole pile on my bed.

"You're stoned," I said.

"Far fucking out stoned; you betcha. Perfect for reading these. Here, take a look."

I had never seen the like before. It was an impressive collection, and I told him so, which made his eyes bulge with glee.

I sifted through and read the titles out loud. *Motor City Comics. Zap Comix*, some starring Mr. Natural, others highlighting Mr. Peanut. *The Hog Ridin' Fools* by S. Clay Wilson and *The Fabulous Furry Freak Brothers* by a guy named Shelton.

"Go on and try one."

I picked up *The New Adventures of Jesus Christ*, a comic so outrageous that it took me away from the war in an instant, transporting me to another headspace and a better state of mind. I thumbed the pages as characters in the modern world swindled and abused Jesus during a visit to the twentieth century. He got so fed up that he lost patience and blew civilization to oblivion, proving that in dealing with humanity, it helps to have supernatural powers.

Underground comics were an effective escape: the good guys won but life's hollow randomness was as obvious as the Snoids, little folk who disappeared by scampering down sewers. But when Nebraska asked me to stick around and get high, he unwittingly roused me from my comic-induced trance. I felt the irresistible pull of academics which demanded justification for my living and breathing the elixir of Gotham.

I packed my books and humped out the door in search of what monks call paradise. After climbing the wide marble steps in Butler Library to the dizzying heights of the second floor, I sought a seat at an open table where I could spread my books and wallow in thought. The room I preferred was high ceilinged like a cathedral, its great skylight filtering afternoon sun. I liked it there, in the company of civilized thought as it hovered above me and above the heads of the ruminating minds seated near me. There I was connected to heaven, history and the ethers, and on that fateful night, the library was packed, every chair at every table taken. But then a single round table appeared amidst the others, a table layered with papers but with only one chair occupied, a woman alone, and with just enough space for one more.

As I approached from behind with the intention of asking if I could share her space, she abruptly turned and caught me in both eyes, her gaze unyielding, her lush brown hair cascading onto her shoulders. She was braless, and her "Free the Chicago Seven" tee shirt was as provocative as ever.

"Oh," she said. "You."

"Yeah. Me. Name's J-Bee, by the way."

"Well, I'm not at work right now, J-Bee, but can I get you something?"

She was smirking, mocking, and I felt it like a pinch.

"I thought only guys wore the same tee shirt twice in the same week."

I had nailed her, and she knew it. She flushed deep over her face and neck and pursed her lips tight, turning away.

"Hey, Margo—I'm sorry. I didn't know it was you. I had no idea you were here. I didn't even know you were a student. I mean—are you? A student, I mean?"

"So what do you want?"

I was standing stupidly, talking to the back of her head.

"I was going to ask if I could share your table; that's all. You took me by surprise."

"I took *you?*"

She turned and looked at me, gauging my honesty by my face.

"Sure," she said. "Sit down. Lots of space."

I sat at the opposite side of the table, and because Margo seemed too engrossed for conversation, I was forced to study. It was nice just to be with her, with her thoughtful silence, knowing all the while she was a woman with a role in my life, serving me food and beer in moments of intense male need at my favorite oasis. And now she was here, keeping the man-beast company so his mind could wander the intellectual world without the hindrance of feeling alone.

Somewhere along the way, I lost the thread of Kant and fell asleep on my books. When I awoke, it was dead quiet. The clock had advanced, and many of the tables had emptied. I lifted my head and saw Margo still there.

I put my head back down, just for a moment. With my eyes closed, my hearing was acutely sensitive. I heard a book snap open and pages flip. I heard someone in a far corner of the room clear his throat. A girl, far off in a different part of the building, laughed and yelled, "No way!" It was faint but reverberated through the tubular hallways, and it was followed by two people running in the same direction, maybe one after the other, feet slapping the floor, until a door slammed shut with a heavy, echoing *bam*.

"You were snoring." Margo's voice. "I know you can hear me so no point faking some alteration of consciousness."

"Does this mean I have to get up?"

No answer. I heard no sound, not even pen scratching paper though I still felt her presence.

12

Margo

I lifted my head. She had her nose to a newspaper on the table, a finger on the page.

"So—what's up?" I asked.

"Have you heard of Attica? And I don't mean Ancient Greece."

I had heard of it. Attica was an upstate maximum-security prison for violent felons, murderers, and drug dealers. Only a month before, the inmates had rioted and taken over part of the prison, forcibly kidnapping innocent people as hostages. They made demands of prison officials and threatened to murder the hostages with homemade weapons.

"Yeah, I heard of it. Prison riot outside Buffalo; a thousand state troopers storming the prison. Forty dead bodies—prisoners killing prisoners; prisoners killing hostages; prisoners gunned down by state troopers. Total absence of law and order."

"That's the one," said Margo, searching my face to gauge my position on it, her mouth pruney and tense. "That's, '*What's up.*' Rockefeller sends in troops, and Nixon and Rockefeller are shaking hands on the eleven o'clock news. Then *I* read about it next day in the papers with a hundred million other Americans. But if Rockefeller had just gone to the prison as the inmates requested, the whole mess could have been defused and needless loss of life prevented. Instead, authorities send in the militia to kill Americans, without due process, just because *these* Americans aren't in lockstep with the prevailing views of mainstream, conservative American society, aka Nixon's 'The Silent Majority.' It's Kent State all over again—same principles."

I wasn't so sure, "It's hard to sympathize with murderers taking hostages and telling us what we have to do for *them* while they threaten to kill more people."

"Shhh . . . !" said a girl, finger to lips, frowning at a nearby table.

"Appearances can be deceiving," whispered Margo, reaching to grasp my forearm, making her point. "They're stuck in prison, many for life, and they want basic improvements to make life bearable. Surely the Constitution would agree. Society could have listened." She looked at me to see how I was reacting. I was sponging it up, storing it to make sense of her view over time; I said nothing.

"Deaths may have been prevented—those ten innocent hostages," she continued. "Your governor pulled the trigger too fast. So you better not find yourself on the wrong side of The Establishment's point of view, or you may be facing the very same state troopers, gunned down by the might of the state, right or wrong, and before your time."

I wanted to say, "Not *my* governor—I'm a Virginian." Instead, I thought about her linking Attica to Kent State University in 1970. Students there were protesting the Vietnam War widening into Cambodia, and the university called in the National Guard, who were the same ages as the collegians they were ordered to oppose. The Guard lined up in front of the students, all of whom were unarmed and nonviolent, and fired sixty-seven shots at the crowd. Four students were killed, innocent youths who would never fulfill the promise of their lives. Nine others were wounded. It was a waste of life, to no purpose, and it brought the war home to America making stateside a battlefield with more force than any other single contemporary event. It fed a media frenzy and sparked protests across the nation, impacting the academic lives of four million undergrads.

I began to realize that as Vietnam intensified, I was witnessing the polarization of an entire generation—my generation—into two irreconcilable halves. It was a conflict pitting Americans against one another, but it also planted the seed of conflict within *me* as I brooded over two polar dogmas. I had one foot in the world of my fathers, the bastion of the military and the Catholic Church, and the other foot out of the box in a land I had yet to recognize fully, the rarified realm of ivory towers where professors smoked pipes and conjectured, everything lost in a smoggy haze of thought, a citadel of turbulent intellect and ideology.

My father had come down clearly on one side and had told me to retake the university. "Plant a flag on the high ground at Columbia, son, like Iwo Jima. Be a patriot and support the country against this bearded rabble." The military was strong in him. However, Margo didn't yet know from which father's loins I sprang, and I wasn't ready to tell her. I was too ashamed, too fascinated by her mind, too afraid to lose her before she taught me what she knew. I was floating in limbo, attempting to put my lips to the apple of knowledge that Margo was brandishing, ready to spill my soul into Tartarus if that was the cost.

"Hey!" said a guy at the next table. "You wanna take it outside?"

"Right," said Margo, packing her books. "Sorry."

"Where're you going?"

"I'm done here. So are you. Come and buy me a beer, and I'll teach you about what's wrong with the world."

I followed her out, realizing, surprisingly, that I was enjoying this woman's guidance.

"Where?"

"The Rail—where else can you get beer for thirty cents."

"You allowed to drink where you work?"

"Of course. They need all the business they can get."

I glanced on and off at Margo as we marched from 114th to 111th. She was a woman with direction and opinions. Julie held an attraction for me that made me want her, but it was all physical. Margo turned my brain. She made me want to trot along beside her and listen. This was all new for me, totally different from my mother. Different from the Sisters.

We sat down in a booth, and Mick the bartender came over.

"This is a first," he said.

Margo blushed. "Yeah—never saw you come out from behind the bar before. Never knew you had legs."

Mick ignored her and turned to me, "You're a lucky laddie. She hasn't had a boyfriend since that guy in Sha-Na-Na in '69."

"How do you know I haven't had a boyfriend?"

"Sha-Na-Na?" I asked. "Like at Woodstock, Sha-Na-Na?"

"I know things about people," said Mick to Margo. Then to me, "Yeah. When Margo was a little freshman girl—or maybe a sophomore—one of the guys in Sha-Na-Na snapped her up. They were all Columbia students, or didn't you know?"

I hadn't known.

"And she's devoted her free time to politics, planning with the most famous Columbian activists of the day while reading Marx and Kerouac at night. This is a brilliant woman—so beware."

"Mick," said Margo, "bring him a beer, and I'll have a glass of Chardonnay. That is, *if* you wouldn't mind."

"Comin' right up!"

Emotions raged within me as I sat with a woman I barely knew. I was suddenly an idiot, a wide-eyed, love-struck mooncalf. She had had a life, a vibrant, intellectual and sexual life before I was even sentient. I had been a virgin while she was being plowed by a rock star.

"Were you at Woodstock?"

"Yes, I went as Sha-Na-Na's guest. I hung out backstage, and before you ask, yes, I met a lot of stars. I met Jimi Hendrix—he was the one who promoted Sha-Na-Na to the Woodstock producers. He played on the program after Sha-Na-Na, so he was there when we were there. I met Gracie Slick and Paul Kantner—they were an item. I met Stephen Stills, Neil Young, Janis Joplin—she was surprisingly shy until she got drunk, then all hell broke loose. Sad to think she and Hendrix are dead."

"Impressive. Did you do a lot of drugs? Was there free love everywhere?"

"There will always be promiscuous people. Yes there was free love, but to answer your question more directly, there was no free love for me. I wasn't a paid roadie, but I did try to help. We did a lot of work: moving the set, carrying things from vans and trucks to the stage and back, taping down wires which were running all over the place. They were a real hazard. Anyone on stage could get killed jumping and dancing if the wires weren't taped down securely." She smiled. "Then someone appointed me 'coffee girl.' Now I was getting coffee for everyone, running back and forth to the truck, taking orders for milk and sugar—or no milk and sugar. Good practice for my later life as a waitress though I didn't see it at the time."

She laughed and shrugged, "Thing is, when you're in a situation like that, suddenly the world changes, and you're at the hub of everything! Things swirl around you—you're in it, but you don't have time to think about it. It was a rare event for me; probably never happen again. It was Sha-Na-Na's moment in the sun, and I was there. If you're the Jefferson Airplane, you're in the eye of the hurricane, and your whole life revolves around being at the hub of the rock world. For someone like me who had no constant connection to that world, my momentary presence was an irrelevant coincidence. Still, I want to do more important things than be a rock star or a groupie. Gracie Slick dropped out of school, but I want to delve into the world in a deeper way. Education is the key to my future. I have no ambition to be another 'Acid Queen' like her or to be dead like Janis Joplin."

I was in awe. "Just to be there allowed you to see into a window that no one gets to see through," I said. "I'd bet that not even the stars themselves get to be such objective observers—they're too embedded in the scene to see past it."

Her face changed. She wasn't just looking at me; she was scrutinizing me, judging me. "That's right," she said. "Good insight. I was taking it all in, storing it in my head like news footage so I could review it again later. I've examined that footage over and over to extract every drop of meaning I could. The whole experience was jam-packed with life lessons. It was also full of great music, but it was so loud I had ringing in my head and lost my hearing for weeks."

I should have smiled back at her. I should have been magnanimous and complimented her for having been at the epicenter of an iconic event, a watershed in the history of our generation. Instead, I sat staring vapidly, scowling inwardly at my inexperience, disappointed in myself. I was jealous and simultaneously appalled at being so petty as to feel jealousy. I had nothing in comparison except an austere existence, like a monk, studying amongst nuns and living at home in a barracks. Even with Julie, nothing had been consummated. I wanted the romance and beauty that Margo had already tasted, and I sensed I was way behind. She had lived life, and I was a starving homunculus, living under a goddamned rock.

"Staring isn't polite," said Margo.

"Sorry."

"J-Bee, you look awful. Are you angry?"

I wasn't angry. No, I was sullen, an id-beast repressed, holding back tides of molten emotion.

She reached over and touched my hand across the table, and—just like that—the lava cooled and flattened into glass.

"No," I said, feeling the change. "I'm starting to feel pretty good."

13

Stoned in The Village

I sat deep in thought, proofreading a paper, sun in the windows and the American flag painted around me.

The door bammed open, and Nebraska shouted, "That's not true!"

I jumped.

"Damn right it's true!" said Bornes.

"Guys—I'm studying."

"Not anymore!" Bornes tried to snatch the paper from my hands, but I pulled it away.

"You're stoned."

"You got that right. Hey Nellie—where's that bag of chips?"

Nebraska smiled.

"Don't just stand there—find the damn chips!"

"How do you two know each other?" I asked. "*I* sure as hell didn't introduce you."

Nebraska began rifling his half of the room. "I had *Motor City Comics* with me in freshman English—*Bornes* borrowed them."

"Ah," I said. "Robert Crumb."

"He never gave them back."

"You'll get them back," said Bornes. "When I'm done."

Nebraska found the chips in an open bag on the closet floor, and Bornes grabbed them, stuffing his hand in the bag.

"You'll crumble them!"

"So?"

"I like chips with the bubbles intact!"

Bornes was taking chips from the bag by the handful, stuffing them in his mouth. Nebraska lunged; Bornes swung the bag up and away. Straining and grunting, they wrestled for the bag until it spilled on the floor.

Nebraska was miffed. "Look what you made me do!"

"There's got to be a university regulation against you two knowing each other," I said.

"Relax," said Bornes. Then to me: "Get your coat—you're coming with us."

"The hell I am."

Nebraska was downcast. "That was my private stash."

"God you guys are *stupid*!" I laughed.

"We're going to The Village," said Bornes. "There's a shop there, Feds 'n' Heads. On Bleecker. You're coming."

"I'm studying."

"C'mon!" said Nebraska. "You've been studying since five A.M.!"

"Nine."

"It's one o'clock!"

"Can't do it."

"Okay," said Bornes. "Dig this. First we'll smoke some pot, then you'll be expected to come. That's the deal."

"You call that a deal?"

My resistance was low after hours of work; I gave in quickly. Bornes lit a joint, and we smoked as we walked to the downtown subway. We stepped off at Times Square and followed an underground maze in search of the A train. The corridors were lined with shops, alive with activity. Aromas of sweetened tomatoes on pizza blended with the biting smells of axle grease as hot stale air from the subway tunnels blew against our faces. Nebraska wanted pizza, but Bornes was impatient and physically restrained him.

"Maybe I wouldn't be so hungry if you hadn't spilled my chips!" They looked at each other and broke out laughing.

We moved on, passing souvenir shops packed with hundreds of tiny Statues of Liberty and newsstands piled with tabloids and porn mags. At every store counter sat a grubby cashier watching the browsers, eager for coveted nickels and dimes. Without warning, Bornes walked into a shop and began flipping the pages of a *Playboy* magazine. Instantly a hunched-over woman rounded the counter, sidling up to Bornes.

"If you wanna look, you hafta buy."

"I'm examining the merchandise," said Bornes.

"You can't touch—give it!"

The old woman suddenly grabbed for the magazine, but Bornes lifted it in the air out of her reach.

"You want I call the cops?" she yelled. "Help! Help!"

A squat, paunchy man with no neck and a stogie in his mouth scurried out of a door at the back, his short legs moving fast. Bornes took one look, dropped the magazine and bolted. We followed, running full speed to the platform where we caught the A.

We got off at 4th Street and walked. At a small secluded park, Bornes found a bench and sat down. "Nellie—roll another joint."

Nebraska sat next to him, rolled, and passed him the joint.

"Give me a light."

Nebraska lit a match, and Bornes toked heavily, not realizing that the stray ends of his hair, hanging near his face, had caught fire.

Nebraska screamed, and Bornes shouted, "What!"

"You're on fire!"

"What?" Bornes dropped the joint and jumped up, slapping himself on the head and face. Nebraska took off his coat and threw it over Bornes's head, yelling, "Hold on!"

Bornes flailed his arms as Nebraska beat on the coat with the flats of his hands until Bornes fell over and yanked the coat off.

"My hair!" was all he could say. "My hair!"

Nebraska stood over him with open palms in a gesture of calm. "You're okay. Nothing's burning."

Bornes patted his head and realized he was out of danger.

"You lit me on fire for Christ's sake! You trying to kill me?"

"I saw the whole thing," I said. "It was an accident," but I wasn't sure. I was oddly suspicious, imagining that perhaps Nebraska had meant to do it all along. I touched my own hair to make sure it wasn't on fire, caught myself, and realized how crazy I was. I quickly withdrew my hand so the others wouldn't notice.

"I'm not trying to kill you," said Nebraska. "Get a grip. You're paranoid. You weren't paying attention, and your hair lit up."

"I'm not paranoid," he said. "I just freaked out."

It was a sunny day, and the world was madly funny. I laughed and couldn't stop. Nebraska picked the joint off the ground and handed it to me. We smoked it down to the roach, put it in a clip and then smoked until nothing remained.

Bornes led the way to Bleecker Street. On the way, he stopped on the steps leading down to the entrance of a private residence, unzipped his fly and peed on the wall.

"What the hell are you doing?"

"I'm commemorating—can't you tell?"

Nebraska was laughing, "Commemorating?"

"Yeah—today marks the three hundredth anniversary of Peter Stuyvesant's defiant protestations against the British, who subsequently expelled him from Manhattan for urinating in this very doorway."

"That's such bullshit."

"To honor this event, the City of New York has erected his statue a few blocks away."

"You'll get arrested is what!"

Bornes shrugged. "I'm stoned. There's no one else around. I had to go."

At Feds 'n' Heads, the air was heavy with incense and tobacco. Inside the glass counter were carburetors, bongs and brass hash pipes. The man behind the counter had a huge frizz of reddish-brown hair contiguous with a huge frizz of reddish-brown beard. He wore round wire-rimmed spectacles with pink lenses, reminiscent of John Lennon. Because his face and eyes were invisible and because he didn't move, it was impossible to tell if he were asleep or taxidermically stuffed.

Bornes haggled with this man while Nebraska and I looked around. The shop was packed with objects for sale: giant hookahs, black lights, strobes, drying racks for weed, flowerpots, potting soil, shelves with vials of plant vitamins, headbands, tie-dyed pants and tee shirts, carousels exhibiting beads and peace-sign jewelry.

"I'm about to come into a lot of hash," said Nebraska. "Maybe I'll buy a brass pipe." Instead he gravitated toward a corner with a rack of comics, and I followed. I flipped through *Fritz the Cat*; he thumbed through *Zap Comix*. "Look at this," he said, pointing to a page which featured a mob of tiny men scampering out of a sewer. "Sewer Snoids. They remind me of that woman in the shop with the fat guy who chased us."

"When did you get so interested in comics?"

"My mom's an English teacher. She used to buy me comics when I was a kid to get me to read. I was a misfit; all the other kids picked on me. I would never have survived childhood without her. Comics were a fantasy land where I was safe."

I thought of my brother sitting on the floor and reading *Casper the Friendly Ghost* at Bolduc's stationery store, and I immediately felt for Nebraska. "What about your dad?"

"What about him?"

"What does he do?"

"He's a professional alcoholic. Before that, he was a hardware salesman."

"Drug of choice for that generation."

Bornes was arguing with the bearded man and suddenly turned and slammed out the door. We caught up to him muttering to himself. "I'm going back to that son of a bitch later, and you two can't be there."

We headed off to Washington Square Park, a few blocks away. "This is NYU territory," said Bornes. "You know what they say about the women here."

"No," said Nebraska. "What?"

"They fuck like rabbits."

"Really?"

"Of course," said Bornes. "Are you stupid?"

Because it was sunny, students were out in numbers, walking, tossing Frisbees and basking. Nebraska and I edged over to a line of chess tables where clusters of older men watched and played. I glanced over my shoulder to keep track of Bornes who had stopped to talk to a female student. She was nodding as he spoke, and, at one point, I saw him reach up and touch her hair. When I looked over again, they had vanished.

—ᴧᴧᴧ—

Nebraska was sure that Bornes and Milo had a deal going with the bearded man at the head shop. I asked him what it was about, but he didn't know. I asked him if the deal was drugs.

"Drugs? Are you paranoid?"

I *was* feeling paranoid. Then he said, "Come to think of it, maybe you're right."

We then wondered where Bornes had gone and decided he went with the girl.

"Drugs, the girl," he said. "I'm bummed. Let's get out of here."

We headed back to campus. Nebraska could be sensitive, and I thought his mood had changed because Bornes had ditched us. We descended the steps to the underground and caught the first train, the Uptown A. With each successive stop, the A got more crowded, and the passengers got darker, until we were the only remaining specks of white. It was a strange feeling for a boy who grew up in the South where, until recently, "coloreds" drank from separate fountains, urinated in different lavatories and sat in different sections on public transportation. In certain Southern backwaters, segregation lingered like the slow-moving Chicahominy River, not too far from my home. But now I was on a different planet, out of my depth, feeling that I could be torn apart in an instant, lynched, hung, beaten or knifed. I felt like the spawn of a posse of White

Knights, a sign around my neck proclaiming, "This descendent of bigots dares to come amongst us." But at the same time, I knew I was suffering from reefer paranoia.

They completely ignored me. I was an invisible man, and the irony was palpable. Their indifference to me amplified my personal sense of guilt, and I reflected on the violent beating I had inflicted back home on Jerry's tormentors. I had done something evil—I had exacted revenge, and I had found out as the Sisters would say, "The Devil was within me." And yet at Catholic High I had been praying during the day even while unworthy to kiss the boots of my classmates who went through the Catholic motions in as meaningless a fashion as I had done before. I had tasted sin, and I saw myself as corrupt as the nuns. They had taught me to cross myself, but I stopped doing it. My parents had given me a cross to wear, but I stopped wearing it. My best friend Gilly had said, "Where's your cross?" and I had replied, "Oh—I forgot to put it on." But he knew why I had stopped, and I knew that he knew. And so I despaired, trapped on the wrong side of Paradise.

Nebraska and I stepped through the subway doors at 116th Street and ran up the steps, ready to cross the threshold into the academic cloister of fortress Columbia. Freed from the grease that clung to my skin in the tubes below, we burst into late afternoon sunshine, gulping the air, gophers fresh out of a hole. As my eyes adjusted to the dusk, I saw there was no university, no Broadway. The street signs said Lenox and 116th, and the sidewalks were teeming with people, all of them black.

"This is Harlem!"

We jolted. Behind us, a man stood bent at the waist, hands on his knees, clucking at us.

"You must be lost," said another voice. It was a gray-haired man in a white suit, a white short-brimmed hat and black shined shoes. He looked at us in earnest, awaiting an answer.

"Yes," I said.

"Where are you trying to go?"

"Columbia."

"It's up there." He pointed west. "You took the A train, but you should have taken the Number 1."

"Yes," I said, trying to cover any trace of Southern accent in my speech, feeling the guilt of the South hanging over my shoulders like clanking chains.

"Would you like directions?"

Nebraska stood dumbstruck like a statue.

"Thank you," I said. If I had had a hat, I would have tipped it. Strict protocol was in use, and we were lucky it was *he* who had found us. Later Nebraska said it was as if we were diplomats from different planets, calmly discussing directions.

"You have two choices. You can cross the street, take the A train back downtown and then switch to the Number 1 uptown. Or you can walk through Morningside Park. Columbia is about a half a mile from here, but you'll need to walk fast and not talk to anyone."

The man shifted his feet, thinking. It began to look complicated.

"The park is on a steep hill. Columbia is at the top of that hill, on the other side of the park. You'll have to walk through the park to the staircase, which climbs a granite wall. If anyone approaches you, just keep walking. Fast. There's a lot of crime in that park, and people avoid it now."

I looked at the man's face from across the great American divide—it betrayed no emotion, but he was helping us escape his home turf to flee to safety. I was grateful, but my heart pounded with fear, and at the root of this fear was a choice we had to make.

"What crime?"

"Robbery. Rape. Last year, a decomposing body was found hanging from a tree. But it's safer now. Even the police go in, from time to time."

He examined us with expressionless eyes. Would we go through Morningside Park or return to the trains to be packed in a car with throngs of the faceless, banging through tubes to Times Square?

Nebraska looked at me for a decision.

"We'll go through the park."

"The park," echoed Nebraska.

The man nodded, and he shook our hands. "Good luck," he said. "Walk fast."

We walked four blocks on 116th, past a screaming toddler on a fire escape and kids scampering down sidewalks. An aged woman with a dowager hump inched along, pushing groceries in a two-wheeled wire-mesh cart. She nodded, and we nodded back.

The park was green and high with overgrowth, and the path diverged into opaque walls of vegetation. I trotted forward, Nebraska behind, arriving at a sheer granite cliff, an old fault line which was the site of a previous earthquake where the ground had lifted on one side and had subsided on the other. It was the height of an eight-story building, and we took to the stairs running. About halfway up, a path joined the stairs from the side, and three teenage boys emerged. They put their hands out and said, "How 'bout some change." For an instant I imagined being knifed for my money, and I ran for my life. We blew by so fast; those boys had to lean back to make way. At the top, gushing with sweat, we turned to see Harlem, now merely dots of light in the dusk, spread out behind us.

14

The Art of Lying

"You impressed me with your family's military background," said MacNeish as we walked to the den of the proto-Sachems. "Our ideology dovetails with the outlook of the military brass. Like them, we're always looking for a few good men."

"I know a sachem is an Indian chief, so what's a proto-Sachem?" Although I didn't like MacNeish ever since I saw him taunt the old man, Bloom, I was curious to see his elitist club of the privileged.

"The Sachems is a secret society of campus conservatives," he said. "Establishment. Moneyed people. *Silent Majority* types. They're snapped up by Wall Street magnates who want new blood. My father was a Sachem, and I'll be a Sachem. I'm already rich, and you can become rich if you follow me on the Sachem trail to Wall Street. You can find the Golden Trough of Happiness at the end of that trail with the rest of us."

I smiled to myself as I imagined MacNeish's face on the body of a pig, his mouth wide open as he grunted and slopped from the Golden Trough.

"So why me?" I asked.

"I've taken a shine to you. I see something in you—I believe you're one of us."

"Okay," I said. "So that's the Sachems."

"The proto-Sachems are guys ripe to be tapped by the Sachems."

"Tapped?"

"Yeah. A secret invitation. You get 'tapped.'"

The secret well of power, connections and influence where the blue bloods drink to the exclusion of common, everyday folk. As I thought about it, I realized that *I* was common, everyday folk. But then I heard my father's voice: "Drink from the well of privilege, son. Take refuge in the oasis of money and power, away from the meaningless desert of failure of the weak and disenfranchised. Away from the empty bellies of the poor and the miserable." As he spoke, I could envision this oasis: the corpulent rich seated at table inside, ladling nectar from the well while hungry skeletal figures peered in from without.

"And when we get there," said MacNeish, "for God's sake don't tell them you saw me smoke dope. You never saw me do it."

"But I *did* see you," I said. "I won't bring it up, but I'm not going to lie if they ask."

"By all means, *lie*. Don't tell them. Dodge the subject. You don't have to answer their questions with words. Make a face as if to say, 'No way,' but just don't tell them. They'll never understand. They might forget it after a while, but it would disrupt the *status quo* for a time. If you have to tell the truth, tell them a truth they're able to understand—that their friends don't do that kind of thing. That *I* don't do that kind of thing. Otherwise, they'll never recognize me."

"But if I don't tell them, they'll find out from someone else."

"Who? Who would tell them? Milo won't tell them. Bornes won't."

"You don't think Bornes would say anything?"

"Absolutely not. Bornes may not like me, but he knows the code. He would never rat. Not a chance. We were at Nessex Academy together, and he'll want to preserve his name and reputation, whatever little he's got left, without getting embroiled in a mini scandal about who's smoking pot."

My mouth dangled in disbelief.

"What's the matter?" said MacNeish.

"But you *do* smoke pot. Doesn't it bother you, living a lie?"

"Listen, righteous virgin—the illusion of my friends imagining that they know me is a more important truth than me paying homage to the petty truth that I indulge in an occasional high from marijuana."

"Sounds like you've thought about lying a good bit."

He looked me in the face. "That's right. Everyone lies. Generally people resort to a kind of disorganized lying, on the spur of the moment, without planning. So pointless. Lying is an art—I like to think that one has to cultivate one's lying. One should lie for a reason; for example, to uphold a higher, more important truth. Like telling your dying friend that he looks good, helping him in his efforts to maintain his self-esteem and sense of well-being in the face of his demise. Another good reason for lying would be to protect one's ideals, even at the expense of virtue."

The proto-Sachem den overlooked the Hudson River from the sixth floor of a grand, old building on Riverside Drive. It was a rambling flat with a kitchen, billiard room, several studies lined with books, and two sitting rooms, one with a TV and ticker tape, the other with a wet bar and big, poofy couches around a coffee table. The decor was simple, but the furniture was *Roche Bobois*.

MacNeish marched me to the wet bar and fixed me a scotch on the rocks. His arrogance was repulsive, but his idea that I needed refinement was close to the mark, making me laugh because I knew I was as yet a crude stone block for the sculptor.

Three other guys in blazers sat on the couches, and we sank into cushions alongside them. A maid in uniform popped in and set a tray of canapés on the table.

"J-Bee's father is an admiral in the US Navy," MacNeish was saying to Nelson Butterfield, who sported a Columbia sapphire ring and was thumbing through a copy of Buckley's *National Review*.

"We support the military," said a guy named Prince, sipping a gin. "Southeast Asia is real estate we must protect."

"The French walked out on it," said MacNeish.

"I know you, Archer," said Butterfield with a smile. "You love to provoke. You'd take any side in an argument just to hear your own voice. You relish the fight."

"MacNeish is *such* a troublemaker," said Prince, rolling his eyes. "He loves the attention."

"We should nuke them," said a big guy next to me with a stern, catatonic face. "Nuke Hanoi and be done with it."

"That's Doncaster," said MacNeish to me, sneering across the back of his hand. "If you haven't noticed, he lacks finesse."

"You're killing a lot of people with that," I said.

"That's how we saved American lives and ended World War II. Couple of bombs, and presto."

I was five or six when the sirens went off in school. One minute, all the kids were chattering happily; the next, they were hushed, shaken, reminded that at any time the Russians might unleash an atomic arsenal to annihilate the East Coast. We listened to the sirens, hiding under our desks. A year later, we had a bomb shelter in the school, maybe a hundred steps deep underground with a door to seal us off from toxic gases. As we sat in that sealed chamber during bomb drills, there was nothing to do except wonder if we would ever get out alive or remain entombed until they found us, perhaps a thousand years later, like King Tut. We heard rumors that we had a separate generator for electricity and air filters to protect us from radioactive fallout. But as we sat on the floor in that shelter during those drills, cramped for space, I knew that if it came to a bomb, we would die.

"I'm sure the Chinese would have something to say about an atomic bomb in their backyard," said MacNeish. "You're forgetting the ten-million-man army they're amassing just north of the North Vietnamese border."

"We've got to preserve our interests," said Prince. "My father's got tin mines in Malaya. You can't just let the Viet Cong waltz in and take whatever they want. We *own* those resources; America has to protect American property."

There was silence. As we all sipped drinks, my gears were turning. I could go to Nam and fight to preserve American business interests so that these proto-Sachems could, perhaps with a meaty donation to a campaign fund or with the flourish of a pen on gold gilt stationery, protect their tin mines with the bodies of young, disenfranchised American men. I might even go as an officer leading those men and become a hero, dead or alive. It would make my father proud, but I was discovering that I didn't like this scenario. As I imagined heroism, I was reminded of Bloom, which naturally led me to recall, again, how MacNeish had taunted him that fortuitous night I had run into them both at The Rail.

"I hear Milo is running for University Senate," said Butterfield.

"I hear he deals drugs," Prince snickered. "I've also heard he'd knock his grandmother over for a plug nickel."

"Milo's a charmer," said Doncaster with a derisive curl of the lip. "He wouldn't do that."

"Don't be hypocrites," said MacNeish. "You'd do exactly the same."

"*I* wouldn't," said Butterfield.

"Okay, maybe *you* wouldn't, Butterfield," said MacNeish turning to Prince and Doncaster, "but if *you* two guys want to be hypocrites, go ahead and lie to yourselves about it—although I hope you don't actually believe you're any different than Milo. He's a friend of mine, and I know the meaning of friendship, and I'm not going to sit here and listen to your tripe about a man you don't know from a hole in the wall."

This talk soured Prince; he frowned.

"I heard that Schuyler's working for Rockefeller next summer."

"I like how Rockefeller handled Attica," said Prince, eager at the change of subject. "Stood his ground. I was shocked that there are people who would support convicted felons over lawful society."

"That was outrageous," said Doncaster. "Criminals making demands."

"But can you believe the student protests against the governor? I mean—what's happening here?" Prince shrugged and lifted his eyebrows in disbelief. "Sometimes I think we should remove the vote from the rabble."

Doncaster chuckled.

I knew they were only half serious, but every joke is rooted in true feeling, and I didn't like the serious half of their joke. In truth, I felt indignant. I resented that they might consider depriving young men of the power to vote while simultaneously wanting those same young men to fight and die on the other side of the planet.

I probably would have ignored them except that Margo had shown me another point of view. Now that I was hearing the inversion of her argument, I was conscious of a dislike for its proponents. Butterfield seemed okay, but Prince and Doncaster were not. There was an uncomfortable shift within me: as I looked over my shoulder, backward in time, eyeing what might have been my own sentiment only months before, I was mortified, concluding that MacNeish was not far off the mark in recognizing me as someone like himself. An unknown force arose in me, and I wanted to make a statement to set the record straight, to take a stand against the selfish attitudes that had been inculcated within me from birth. I was a pupa in a chrysalis, and as I metamorphosed, I looked back at my former self, disgusted.

I looked at Prince and Doncaster. "You want boys to die, but you don't want them to vote?" I said it in pugnacious tones, abandoning my polite-Southern-boy persona.

Butterfield looked up from his reading, "Honestly, J-Bee, I don't think Prince's remarks were entirely serious."

MacNeish stared; this wasn't in his script. From his perspective, if I were to be a Sachem, my questions were anathema. As for myself, I was conscious that somewhere within me was a dream to be the embodiment of the heroic persona that my father represented; yet despite this, I felt a vibration, a deep rumbling in my viscera which threatened to shatter this dream in the way a persistent hum, at just the right pitch, shatters glass.

MacNeish laughed and turned to his cronies, "You want a monarchy here? Bring moldy old George Washington back so he can be king? Listen, you don't need to abolish democracy and restrict the vote from the average Joe. We can control elections by pumping money to candidates and by buying TV ads that spoon-feed our message to the masses like pabulum. Such is the magic of the media."

"Whether they vote or not," said Prince, "the rabble will never back our candidates."

"Yeah, they will."

"Why would they?" said Prince. "I can see their point of view; they don't want what we want. What could you tell them in a TV commercial that would resonate enough to make them vote our way?"

"We tell them we'll cut taxes."

"But we won't cut *their* taxes. We'll cut *our* taxes."

"Right, but we can't tell them that."

"That's lying."

"Oh, I dunno. Maybe we can cut their taxes a little. Listen, we tell them what they want to hear. Just like we tell them they should serve their country and die in Vietnam for the glory of our nation. They're doing *that*, and the consequences of *that* particular lie are much greater."

"Well," said Prince, "aren't soldiers *supposed* to die for their country? But *you* want to sell a candidate with lies, and that bothers me."

"Ladies and gentlemen," said MacNeish with a dramatic sweep of his arm, "another righteous man who believes we should fight in Vietnam but who would never go himself. Another hypocrite with principles."

"You're being a little hard on me, don't you think?" said Prince.

"You think eighteen-year-olds should die for their country while you sit on your asses and watch them on TV in the safety of your penthouse?" I said, my gut churning.

"Why not?" said Doncaster, smirking. "Someone has to do it."

"Hey," said MacNeish. "You want the convenience of living your life of luxury and spending your family's fortune, all of which is built on the backs of other men and is based on lies like the American dream, yet you don't want *me* to say the lie out loud because it makes *you* feel guilty? Make a decision—do you want your tin mines protected, or don't you?"

There was an uncomfortable, lingering silence. I looked from one to the other, and I couldn't tell them apart. I observed them eyeing me askance, trying not to be noticed, but the looks on their faces revealed their horror as they awakened to the revelation that they had been discussing their innermost private thoughts in the presence of an outsider. Initially they had mistaken me for an ally, but now they saw me otherwise—I was an enemy and the focus of bitterest enmity while for me, they had transformed into objects of repugnance.

"MacNeish has told you what he thinks," I said slowly, deliberately. "Now I'll tell you what I think."

"You judge us?" said Prince, narrowing his eyes in contempt.

"It's impossible *not* to judge you." I stared at Prince; I wanted to gouge his eyes out. "You make my skin crawl."

"Whoa!" said MacNeish. "Wait just a second, J-Bee. This is merely banter. This is play fighting. Word sparring. Don't be so serious."

"No one's playing," said Doncaster, face hardened. His remark was in response to MacNeish, but he was staring at me, and I had an irrepressible urge to flatten the nose on his face.

"Guys," MacNeish pleaded, "don't!"

There was pressure in my chest; I thought I would explode. My brain seized, and I moved involuntarily in one rapid motion, putting my hands under the edge of the table and standing abruptly, upending the table so that it fell over with a great "BAM!" canapés and drinks flying into the air, glass shards everywhere.

"Christ!" said Prince, jumping up.

Doncaster stood. He wasn't only big, he was inches taller than me, and his scarlet face was nose to nose with mine, his arms stiff and fisted at his sides.

"If you want me to kick your ass," I yelled in his face, feeling the veins in my neck pop, my whole body shaking as I jabbed him in the chest, "make your fucking move! It better be goddamn good!"

He didn't respond, so I said, "Because you're only getting *one* chance before I take you down!"

MacNeish put his hand on Doncaster's arm. "Chill, Brian. Carmelita will clean it."

There was a pause. No one moved. We all stood frozen, the pressure in me rising until I thought the top of my head would blow off.

"Hah!" I vented steam. "Fucking cowards!"

I walked to the door. Carmelita ran into the room, her eyes bugging out at the mess.

"Pigs!" I blurted, turning again. "I'm out of here!"

I walked out the door and stood at the elevator, waiting as my spirit cooled. Stepping into the elevator with its door closing behind me, I felt the floor cave in, and, for a moment, I was light as air. Surprised at the emotional outburst that had seized me and at the relief that washed over me, I laughed in silence, my smile fixed like plaster upon my face and my chest rocking in and out like a convulsion until tears of mirth filled my eyes and ran down my cheeks, quenching the firestorm inside me.

15

Tug of The Heart

November. Fall tightened its grip on Manhattan, draining the heat from the city, forcing me to button my coat and put on a scarf. One such night found me sipping beer at The Gold Rail, across the table from Bloom in one of those worn booths with hard-backed benches, while he peppered me with questions not only about my study habits, but also about my life before New York. Having met through random circumstances and being several generations apart, we were now discovering a kinship and becoming unlikely friends. I hadn't known him much more than a month, but he could read my face and the tone of my voice, his mind digging and questioning, excavating emotional ground that my parents had never recognized. I wasn't used to being interrogated, especially without feeling resentment, but his manner was both benign and candid which relaxed my guard. It was the first time any person had ever wanted to know so much of my life's detail.

"Something's eating you, J-Bee. Something's boiling under your skin. Spill it—I won't tell anyone—I never tell anyone anything. I'm alone in the world; I've got no one to tell."

I looked at his lined, clean-shaven face. His white hair, grand-fatherly smile and crescentic twinkling eyes reminded me of a patriarchal bust.

"So if you're so old, tell me *how* old."

Bloom smiled again. "Clever boy, trying to change the subject. But let's just say I'm old and leave it. The mysteries of my life have been solved, and the fateful decisions have been made. It's been a journey, and soon the train's stopping at the end of the line. When I get there, I return to the dust I was made from. You, on the other hand, have just begun. First time living away from home, freshman in college. You have issues to address, conflicts to face."

"What do you mean, *issues*?"

"All young men have issues as they go into the world. There are forces in your life that must be understood and dealt with. I don't mean you have issues beyond those of your peers—not unless you say so. Hell, how would *I* know, given that you haven't told me *anything*! What all young men *don't* have—and that you *do* have—is a mentor, a male compatriot who has experience and wishes to pass the baton. So why not tell me what's on your mind?"

It was impossible not to confide my life's story, babbling answers to everything he asked, so different than with my father who was absorbed in his world of naval affairs. Here again I was a child, sitting in front of a large, hovering, comforting face in whose eyes I saw both my own reflection and an umbrella of protection that mandated trust. Yet somehow these positive feelings conflicted with deeper instincts which reminded me of what I had learned from my father and all other men around me: it is unmanly to discuss one's feelings. I felt a resistance to telling Bloom the secrets of my personal life while, at the same time, I felt the tug of my heart as it whispered to me that I might have a hope of being understood—*of understanding myself*—if I merely took the chance of confiding in another human being, another beating heart behind a kind and understanding face.

In the end, I went with my heart and spoke out. "I've done something bad. It shocked me that I did it, and I haven't been able to put it behind me. A mortal sin. I don't know if you're a Catholic so I don't know if you'd understand, but I know that God won't forgive me."

"You mean *you* can't forgive you."

I expected to be angry in the way direct eye contact accompanied by disagreement always made me feel, like with my father or the Sisters. Unexpectedly, I found I wasn't angry, and strangely, I recognized companionship. Bathing in the odd sense of security that I felt with this older man, my mind relaxed and drifted into daydream, flooding me with visions of my eight-year-old brother, Jerry, whose existence had become an enigma that gnawed at me.

I missed him. I envisaged his physical resemblance to me, but I also recognized what made us different: there was a vulnerability etched into his facial expression which was wholly unlike mine, yet this expression was the impetus that drove me to protect him. Ultimately no matter how much I floundered while trying to define myself in a changing and dangerous world, my ferocious instinct to protect the defenseless had solidified into something immutable as stone.

—⁓—

"Are you having an *absence* attack?"

It was Bloom's voice, filtering through the fog of my reverie.

"No, of course not."

"Do I have to get you drunk to hear the story? Let me get you another sudser."

"What's an *absence* attack?" I asked.

"Forget about that. Tell me about those sins you just mentioned. Tell me *some*thing, for the love of Pete."

"Okay," I said, raising my hand in acquiescence. "I'll tell you about my brother." It was a history that eventuated in the act that changed my life. Although I was unsure that I would be capable of revealing the brutalities that *I* had committed, I was able to begin the story by recounting to Bloom the birth, the early unresponsiveness and then the deafness of my brother.

"I'm so sorry," said Bloom, his eyes saddened. "How did your father take it?"

I described my father's agitation, walking back and forth next to Jerry's crib in his military uniform, staring at the floor with his hands clasped behind his back as he and my mother talked heatedly in muffled tones. He was incapable of fitting Jerry neatly into the mosaic of his life. It was complicated, and my father was stunned with uncertainty and pain. He couldn't figure out whether his son had a chance at some kind of normalcy or whether he should abandon him emotionally, write him off as some kind of cripple or lost cause, someone who would need nursing support in order to be fed, wiped, and clothed for a lifetime.

"He didn't take it well," I said to Bloom. "It was messy—not shipshape like on a boat. He sort of disappeared for a while. He was distant."

"And your mother?"

I told him about my mother. When Jerry was about one and a half, I heard her yelling from her room. It scared me, and I ran there to find her lifting Jerry in the air, holding him under the arms, shaking him with force.

"Mom! What are you doing!"

I grabbed the baby, prising him from her grip. When she let go, I held him in my arms, pressing him against me.

I stared at her. I hated her. I boiled. "What the hell's the matter with you!"

Her face dropped in shame. I knew she wasn't ashamed of her behavior; rather, she was humiliated because she had been caught. She regained her composure in an instant, reddening and grimacing in anger. Looking me square in the eye, she snapped, "How dare you talk to me like that! I'm your mother, in case you've forgotten! I won't stand—your father's not going to stand for this!"

At the time, I didn't care a whit about what my father might do.

"It was a stressful time," said Bloom. "People aren't themselves when they're under stress."

"Are you for *real*?" I was disappointed in his giving my parents *any* benefit of the doubt, and I wondered if I should have ever trusted him in the first place. "I thought you were on the level.

You might just as easily say that people are *more* themselves when they're under stress."

"Okay," said Bloom, "Please, no hostility. I'm on your side. You're right, of course."

We eyed each other. He seemed sincere, and I was remorseful for my doubts.

"Sorry," I said. "Don't know what got into me. I've never really discussed this with anyone, and my parents make me berserk. I don't want to make excuses for them—they sure as hell don't deserve any."

"Please, I understand. I don't like the portrait of your folks, and I see why you're angry. But if it's okay with you, I'd rather not judge them just yet."

The story drained me. It wasn't going to end well, and thinking about it made me feel lousy. I looked through the frosty sheen on the glass in front of me, its tiny bubbles floating up through the amber fluid, up to the foamy crown. How easy it was to get lost in beer.

"I'm listening," he said.

"Right." I took a breath. "When we found out he was deaf and not brain damaged, I was ecstatic. My mother wept as if a torrent had been unleashed from a dam of tension. My father sighed and inched back toward rejoining the family. He still didn't seem to know whether to reject Jerry or embrace him, whether to regard him as weak and undeserving or to see him as a normal boy worthy of his fatherly time and affection. He perceived that my brother's perfection had been blighted, and I even heard him say, from time to time, that in the vicious world in which we live, my brother's chances of survival were reduced."

"Why? What did he mean?"

"He said that a hundred years ago, Jerry would've had to beg for a living. Three hundred years ago, he would never have made it to adulthood. Three thousand years ago, his tribe would have abandoned him as an infant in the forest to die at the hunger of wild animals."

Bloom stared at me bug-eyed.

"He said *that?*"

My father had indeed said this. I could only hope that even he, in his compulsive verbalization of homegrown Darwinism, did not truly believe that Jerry was unfit to live. However, whenever I considered that his thoughts might be genuine, I wanted to smash him.

"His own son?" said Bloom. "What can one possibly make of it?"

"I don't know what to make of it, but whenever I think about it, I want him in front of me so I can punch him!"

Bloom slowly shook his head. "That's over the top."

His comment struck me as argumentative, critical.

"Well, you haven't heard the rest of the story, *have you?*"

"No, of course not," he said, his expression showing sympathy and patience.

I hung my head; my impulse was unjust. I was picking a fight out of sheer belligerence, aiming my anger in the wrong direction. "Sorry," I said. "It's not your fault."

"I understand. It's difficult."

"Anyway, my father wasn't always like that. There were times when he was able to forget his hard-core warrior ideals and love my brother, and after Jerry got the hearing aids, there were times when I even saw him smiling, like when they played together." What I didn't tell him, out of shame for my father's behavior, was that mostly he looked the other way when Jerry was there and that I took up the slack.

"I spent a lot of time with him—reading to him, playing with him. But as he got a little older, I became worried that he might be sent to Saint Eustace and get beaten by the nuns, like I was."

"Come again?"

I had forced my own hand, so I had to tell Bloom about Saint Eustace, the Sisters, and my old friend Gilly.

"You were beaten by these nuns?"

"In elementary school."

"That's outrageous! Did your father know about it?"

"Absolutely. It must be a cultural thing, a rite of passage. The beatings made us Irish-Catholic boys into strong men."

"*Now* who's making excuses for your parents?"

I realized that my intellect forgave the very thing that my anger had condemned. Maybe he had a point, but I flapped my hand at him, and when he was finished admonishing me, I continued.

"I begged my parents not to let Jerry set foot in that damned school. I actually got down on my knees and clasped my hands together like an altar boy until they agreed to send him to the local public school—though not for the reasons I cited. They said they would send him so he could be in the disabilities program, which Saint Eustace didn't have. Still, public school wasn't any better as he was bullied relentlessly by other kids."

I told Bloom about how Jerry was tormented, and when I had finished, he said, "I'm not sure who had it worse."

"What d'you mean?"

"I mean I still can't get over those damn nuns. I can't fathom what kind of people they must have been to treat you like that, and I can't decide whose childhood was worse—yours or Jerry's."

"Jerry's. There's no comparison."

"I'm not so sure. You were both neglected. You were both abused, but *you* were abused by those in power. The authorities."

"You can't compare us!"

"Yes, I can. Don't forget—*he* had *you*. Who did *you* have?"

I didn't want to hear it. Maybe he was right, but I couldn't see past the horrors that my brother suffered.

"I'm sorry I interrupted," he said. "I'm outraged both for you *and* your brother." The lines on his face had changed from strong and chiseled to tired and stressed. He put his hand through his hair. "Tell me more."

I told him more. I narrated, step-by-step, Jerry's last day on earth, ending with his violent, meaningless death. After that, I choked and couldn't continue. I couldn't tell him about the revenge I took and the effect it had on my life—I was truly afraid I might weep in my beer and not be able to stop.

16

Punji Sticks

Bloom asked how my parents had coped after Jerry's death, but I found myself unable to talk about it. Later I would tell him the rest of the story, but at the time I could only slump forward with my head on the table, drained of energy, and recall my own violence and Gilly's kindness. "I'm sorry, J-Bee," he had said. "I loved your brother; he was a sweet kid."

I left Bloom; he said he understood. I headed back to my room, stopping at the student mailroom where I discovered, coincidentally, a letter from Gilly. I tore it open, but at that very moment Milo burst in with Buck Steinson and another two preppy-looking kids, all of them hooting over their own jokes.

"J-Bee!" said Milo with a smile, slapping me on the shoulder. "We missed you the other night. Had a great time downtown. Wished you'd been there. Didn't we, Steiny?"

"Right," said Steinson, his lips a thin line.

"Sorry I couldn't come. Maybe another time."

"*If* you're lucky," said Milo, pointing at me with his fingers in the configuration of a pistol. Then he noticed my letter and leaned over to examine the envelope. I disliked his nosing where he didn't belong so I folded the letter and stuffed it in my pocket.

"You've got interesting mail. That looks like a bona fide letter—very few of us get any of those." He turned to Steinson. "You don't get letters, do you?"

"Nope."

"I sure as hell don't. Where's it from?"

"I'd guess Vietnam, from the stamp," said one of the preppy-looking guys.

"Far out, J-Bee—who d'you know in Nam? Your father there?"

"Just a friend."

"You have a friend in Vietnam?"

"Yeah. Where I come from, kids volunteer to serve their country. I'm sure Buck understands, coming from a military family as he does."

Milo looked at Steinson who shrugged. "Yeah, I know some kids who went."

"No you don't," said Milo, and he chuckled. "You went to school with us, and you know damned well no one volunteered."

"No," said Steinson, "I knew a few kids."

"Liar!" said Milo, laughing. The two others laughed as well.

"Anyway," I said, "maybe I'll see you guys around."

"Sure," said Milo. "Stay cool."

—⁓—

Once in my room, I wanted to read Gilly's letter, but since my parents hadn't called and it was almost Thanksgiving, I decided to ring them first. When my mother answered, she tweeted happily that she and my father were going to visit her sister.

"There's just no point in you coming home," she chirped. "We'll all be in Richmond."

When my father took the phone, he told me not to be afraid to serve the country if my number was picked in the lottery. From his voice, I knew that he meant what he said, but I also heard a subtle reluctance, an unexpected unhappiness that I might leave Columbia and go to Nam. Maybe it was because he preferred the navy and a sparkly clean ship to the army and jungle mud, or maybe it was because he realized that if I died, his seed would die with me, ending the Darwinian succession of his progeny.

"Gilly went off to Vietnam," he said, a fact I had known for months. "The poor devil's volunteered to clean latrines and wade through paddies during the monsoons. He didn't have the marks to go to college, but the army will make him a man. It'll teach him a trade that he'll use when he gets back home. They'll build him a career—if he lives. He built that car in his basement, so maybe they'll teach him to be a mechanic."

"Yes, sir."

"How's school? How're your grades?"

"I'm doing okay."

"When I think about you, I always wonder if you're the only kid there with a haircut." He chuckled. "Are you fitting in? Making friends?"

I told him I had a few friends, but the one thing that struck me was that since I'd arrived in New York, I hadn't yet cut my hair. It had been close to three months, and now it was well over my ears. What would my father have said if he saw me? I knew men back home, guys who were hanging around the barber shop or chewing the fat with the grease monkeys in the local garage who used to say they would shoot a longhair—meaning anyone with hair as long as mine—if they could ever get their hands on one. I had heard them lament that part of the problem was that no sane person in Norfolk would dare grow hair long enough to be shot, and this meant they couldn't find anyone worth shooting. In the old days, those kinds of comments seemed to be worth a laugh. The good old boys loved to share their enmity of the Yanks. Sharing hate brought them together; it made them a brotherhood, I supposed, like the White Knights. Back then, those Northern boys with their long hair struck us as the opposite of manliness; they were soft and weak, so-called pussies, who'd get fucked up the ass in prison. However, now that I had the advantage of a more complete view of the world from New York, and now that I knew good people like Billy Wing, I realized that in spite of how angry I was as a youth and how much I would hoot at those jokes in the barber shop, those sentiments no longer had a place in my life.

I opened Gilly's letter:

Dear J-Bee,

How are you? How's your folks?

Being on base is much more like being back home, but at the same time, it's not. You can't imagine what it's like fighting over here—it's totally out of control. It's a free-for-all. It's the Wild West. Drugs all over the place. Everything. Marijuana, heroin, smoking, shooting, pills, LSD. Unbelievable.

We go out on patrol, and some grunts I came in with were killed three feet next to me. Gunned down. Bits of flesh got on my skin. I had to pay attention, all the while feeling them stuck on me. Nasty. I couldn't wash it off for days during patrol. I try to get used to it, but the idea of someone else's innards on me is disgusting. Back at base I scrub myself, but I never feel like I get it all off. Maybe I'll never get used to it.

There are booby traps in the jungle. The VC bends back saplings to snap up and hit you if you step on the trap-release, and the saplings are rigged with slices of bamboo cut at angles to make sharp, rigid points, like knives. They're called punji sticks, and believe me, they're terrifying. I saw a grunt get hit by one, and it was no joke. The bamboo stakes punched him full of holes, the blood just poured out like a fountain. He was screaming the whole time we pulled those damned sticks out, one by one. Some of the guys vomited just watching. He was whacked in the groin, the thigh, the belly and the chest, all from a single trap. The medic said he punctured his lung and cut an artery. He bled into his chest and all over the stretcher. We dragged him back to base, but he was dead. He was a young guy, about our age. We might've played pick-up basketball with him in better times.

It's murder. They murder us, we murder them. Horrible. God and Christianity are nowhere. We are the cutting edge of a military tool, we are blades looking to slice other people. We're a gang, we tramp through jungles looking for a firefight.

There's something else. I go to the whorehouses in Saigon. I know it's wrong, I know it's a sin, and I hate to admit that the Sisters were right about me. But I need it, and when I'm with a woman, it releases the stress. It may not be love but it feels like it. I need to be touched sometimes, in a good way, even though they don't love me. But it upsets me how we use them. These whores. They're having our babies. I see the babies crying in the same room where I'm lying with their mother. That part feels awful. They're trapped and have no choice. They're like children, and they're trying to survive like me.

Some of the guys have raped women. I know because I've seen it. There were others hanging around acting like nothing was happening. That's the way people act, because it's all like this bad dream, and if you don't interact with it, you feel like it might go away or that it's not really happening.

I'm ashamed. I've seen such bad stuff, and I've done nothing about it. I feel like I should do something, some kind of cleansing, but I don't know what. I have no power to do anything, anyway. Everything we touch here goes bad. I pray sometimes, but I don't hear anything. Some of the guys say everything's fine, but they just tell themselves that. They paint over the horror with some notion of patriotism, but it feels like a lie.

When I first arrived, I was a newbie, and they stuck me in front of the patrol so I'd get killed first. I was a human shield protecting them. But I'm not a newbie anymore. I have friends, other guys like me from all over the US, and we watch each other's back. New guys keep coming, and their survival isn't good. I feel bad about it, but I'm not sure what can be done. I feel like I'm back on the football team with the same old numbskulls, except this time we're carrying M-16s and the other team is the gooks. They want to kill us, and we want to kill them. You and I were taught that God is everywhere, but here, God is nowhere.

You're my only friend. These guys aren't my friends. They're comrades sure. But we're close by mere coincidence.

I'm not sure who they are, really. We're all Americans, whatever that means. Out here we're killing others who are fighting to protect their homes. If I get killed tomorrow, they'd forget me in a day. I'd be another faceless grunt in a black zip-up bag they'd want to forget because I'd remind them of the possibility that they're going to die. We have very little in common with one another, but we're bonded by a hatred for another group of people. Do you see how evil this is? Which is why I think we're going to lose this war. And I'm so glad you're not here to see this awful mess. Stay in school so that I can know that even though I'm here fighting, sitting in mud up to my waist or with skin rotting between my toes, you're safe getting an education for both of us. And if I live for a while longer, I'll come visit you in New York. I always wanted to see The Big Apple.

Talk to you later. Your friend,
Gilly

17

The Confession of Billy Wing

I left my room, disturbed by Gilly's descriptions of jungle fights and Saigon whores. I could palpate his need for humanity and kindness, but I was too far away to give it—divorced from hardship and reality as I was, tucked away in a rarefied academic atmosphere. It was outrageous what MacNeish and his cronies had said about young men like my friend, considering them mere fodder for the protection of assets.

As I worried about things which I couldn't control, I envisaged fault lines within my generation, lethal cracks which delineated different classes of men, struggling one against the other. Why couldn't the world be as Billy Wing saw it? Why couldn't we all be brothers?

The sun had gone down so I hunkered in the library for five solid hours. When my eyes had finally melted from their sockets, I blew out of there, bursting through the doors onto the quads, my breath a chilled mist hanging in the air. I walked, cold and directionless, in a patternless dissipation of entropy while the walkway lamps shone on puddles and wet sidewalks.

I made a snap decision to head over to Furnald Hall where MacNeish had told me, a while back, about a coffee shop. It had a separate entrance, a set of steps going down under the dorm and into a basement rathskeller. I heard his political thrumming in my head. "There are three classes of people: me, other rich people, everyone else. In that order. I believe in a pyramidal society just like the English: King at the top, Peers of the Realm, then all other Englishmen. After them come the hordes of non-English rabble: colonials and heathens. We were colonials once, but in view of the ascendency of America and its having supplanted England as *the* world power, I've made a revision to the English paradigm when structuring my own egocentric world: me, other rich people, everyone else. Very American, right?"

I would have laughed, but he was serious, and I told him I'd think it over. I had never met anyone like him before, and now, of course, I disliked him. I also decided that he disliked *me*, but there was a difference in the quality of our dislikes—I was repelled by his elitist views, but as he mostly disliked or hated *everyone*, I was not as distinctly repulsive to him as he was to me. For him, I was just "everyone else," which apparently had not been enough to disqualify me from being one of his cronies. Interestingly, even though MacNeish was so seamlessly integrated into his rich society, I suspected that he was universally disliked by his "friends." I wondered how moneyed elitists could tolerate his abrasive personality within their ranks. But then I thought, "Me, other rich people, everyone else," and I got it. For the world in which MacNeish belonged, his character would mean little compared to his money, as long as his repugnance remained hidden beneath a veneer of propriety and didn't intrude or distract anyone from the main purpose of their class. Money must stick together against the tides of the masses.

So I walked over to the basement of Furnald Hall to see what kind of coffeehouse it was. The moment I opened the door, I knew it was dodgy. A beaded curtain hung in front of me with a darkness behind it which was a shade of gray just this side of black. I pushed past the beads which clinked to announce my arrival, and I staggered two steps in, inhaling a mixture of stale sweat, sulfurous incense, and a tinge of moldy humidity. Unable to focus in the dark, I glimpsed a dim figure which came and took my hand, leading me to a couch where I sank until my coccyx bounced on the floor.

"A drink?" she asked.

I looked up—long blonde hair, peasant blouse, rounded breasts, muscular arms. I'm a young man, and it aroused me, but the air of the place and the forwardness of my new companion put me on guard.

She sat next to me on the inescapable couch and rubbed my thigh, leaning close with a guttural noise in her throat. The raw sexuality of this woman, mixed with disequilibrium in a place with the scantest of light, made me feel on the edge of something terrible. My adrenaline surged, my eyes dilated, and the hair on my neck and arms piloerected. Vision adjusting, I began to see that the blonde purring next to me, all smooth curves, had cheeks a shade too dark and a jaw too angular. Then I realized everything, all at once: *a man*. I stood up, surprising myself with the strength I mustered to escape both the couch and the nails which clutched my arm.

She-he laughed, not maliciously, and said, "Sit down, sweetheart, and I'll give you a massage you'll never forget."

"No, thanks," I said over my shoulder, stumbling through the beads into the cold, still night.

Fuckin' MacNeish.

Waves of blood flushed my face; I sweated from heat and mixed emotion. I pounded the brick walkways between the quads, my boots crunching snow. I thought and rethought of the sinking couch and the exotic creature, beautiful and repulsive, who had rubbed my leg.

It freaked me out. I couldn't unravel my feelings. Part of my bewilderment was due to limited experience—I was as yet an unfledged male; I had never gone all the way. I wondered: is sexual attraction based on what is real, or is it illusion? I had been attracted to a man, and though I thought him to be a woman, his facade had fooled me. Must I therefore reject the physicality of attraction and seek only the soulful? On the one hand was the doctrine of the Catholic Church; on the other was physical biological coupling. Sacrament or coitus; mindfulness or mindlessness. I wondered whether there were moral underpinnings to the sexual act, but then I thought of something else—perhaps I might find love.

Cold night air brought me back to my senses; I was in motion, making heat as I walked. It was then, by chance, that I collided with another body moving through the empty stretches of campus. "Peace, brother," he said in a generic monotone, raising two fingers in the shape of a V, a peace symbol dangling around his neck.

It was Billy Wing, and when he saw it was me, he grabbed my arm with both his hands.

"J-Bee—thank God it's you! I'm in so much trouble. When I think about what I've done! God, why did I do it!"

"Do what?"

He was licking his lips, twisting from side to side in order to look behind him.

"I made a mistake, and now I'm going to pay for it!"

"For what?"

"You can't tell anyone—they might kill me!"

"Who?" I looked in his face, a mist rising between us. His cheeks and lips were drawn taut over the bones of his face like colorless skin on the frame of a drum. He was shaking with cold. Or was it fear?

"You've got to swear! If you don't swear, I won't have the nerve to tell you. Please swear because I need someone to tell so I don't go completely insane!"

"Okay—I swear."

I felt his fear; it made me afraid even though there was nothing for me to be afraid of. Still, I had the irrational sense that if he told me what he feared, that if I became privy to his nightmares, they would become *my* nightmares—pounding themselves into my head—and then I would be forced to shoulder some part of his burden. It reminded me of Gilly's stories about the Sisters and how *his* stories eventually became *mine*, like the fulfillment of some bizarre prophecy. Intellectually I rejected this notion as ridiculous, but emotionally I believed it anyway. This premonition was so oddly terrifying that I felt it might change my life, and the animal forces within me bellowed against involvement in Billy's entanglements.

Motionless as if my feet were frozen to the paving stones, I watched Billy Wing as he gathered the courage to divulge a tale that I didn't want to hear. I waited in dread, trapped, knowing that soon I would be forever incapable of escaping the net that his story would cast.

He swayed back and forth, hugging himself with his arms. His breath came out with a low-pitched shudder as steam rose from his mouth and clouded the air. "I know it's uncool," he said, "but I did it for the money. I needed money, so I sold some drugs. I sold them for a distributor, a dealer, and now his minions have got their hooks in me."

He stopped to wet his lips and tongue.

"They want me to sell more, but I won't! It's wrong, and I want it behind me, but now they want me to give them more money. They're calling it *severance pay*; they're saying I'm breaking a contract. For Christ's sake, J-Bee—*there is no contract*! I didn't sign anything! I paid them everything I owed—everything! I swear to ever-living God! And now, what do I do? I don't have any more money. Even if I wanted to fork it over, they've cleaned me out— I've got nothing left!"

I looked him in the face, but I could find nothing to say to ease his fear. I felt powerless, a feeling that had been hammered into me by the Sisters.

"I believe you, Billy."

"Why should I worry about dying facedown in a rice paddy when I might be murdered right here before winter is out?"

"What happened?"

"These two guys—I saw them with Milo, so I thought they were all right. They gave me four hundred grams of hash to sell, saying I could make some money. Hell, they were preppies! They looked like kids hanging out at their parents' yacht club. Loafers and button-down shirts. They looked so safe you'd let them babysit your sister!

"Everything was okay for a while. I sold what they gave me. Just hash and marijuana, nothing heavy. I thought everything was all right until they came over one day, looking for more money. They brought along another guy I never saw before. Some big guy with a thick, pink scar across his throat. The preppies said something in Spanish to him, and while I stood there gawping, this guy grabs me in a headlock! I mean, what the hell? The preppies just stood there, talking to each other—you know, discussing something on the quiet as if nothing was going on. Meanwhile I couldn't move, bent over at the waist, that big guy stinking like armpit sweat with my head in a vice. It hurt! It was humiliating, and I was afraid I would pass out or maybe choke to death.

"They scared the living shit out of me—now I'm looking over my shoulder every five seconds! They said they would make it worse if I didn't give them *the money*. Then they said that I had to stay in their employ. They said if I tried to leave, they wouldn't be able to trust me to keep my mouth shut. They said if I tried to quit, they'd have to shut it for me! They told me that Miguel—the big guy—couldn't talk normally because someone slit his throat last year, but that he loves to kick the shit out of people and that he would gladly kick the shit out of me. They knew I was scared, and they had a good laugh. Then they said something in Spanish, and Miguel let go of the headlock, grabbed my shirt collar and punched me in the mouth. My lip swelled up and bled on my coat. Then one of the preppies said something like, 'Friends?' and stuck out his hand. I just looked at him, and he broke out laughing."

I hadn't seen it in the dark, but now that Billy mentioned it, there was a smudgy discoloration around his mouth, and his lip was swollen. I looked into his eyes, and it was like looking through a window into his soul. My Catholic antennae sensed that he might already be at one with the damned and that his soul was not to be tampered with. I thought I saw the mark upon him, and I was no exorcist. My heart wondered if he were past saving, possibly under the protection of an evil force that would never let him go until it knew how to dispose of him. In my gut I was uncertain about what *I* could possibly do—I had fear, and I felt myself shrinking away as I witnessed the demons circling, sniffing, telescoping in.

18

Bloom's Web

Billy Wing was in fear for his life. He was right next to me, yet there was a gulf between us I couldn't bridge. Here within the confines of the great university, unassailable fortress of knowledge, on a lighted path between the snow-sprinkled greens of the quads, I felt the powerful grip of the universe, and it was far too strong for a mortal like me.

Or was it? I wanted somehow to ignore my fears and stand up for my friend. I felt the urgent turbulence of his demons as they beat their wings. But could I really believe that Milo was at the root of Billy's problems? On the surface Milo seemed affable, but who were these others who followed him around? I realized that before I could attempt any kind of intervention to protect my friend, I had to have further information to clarify what exactly was happening.

I took him to The Rail and bought him a Coors to lift his spirits, but it had no effect. He looked pasty, nervous, and his hair was plastered to sweat on his forehead. When Bloom came over and sat with us, Billy surprised me by recognizing something about him.

"Have we met?"

"I don't think so," said Bloom.

"Maybe it's your voice. Are you on radio?"

"No. Never on the radio."

"I can't put my finger on it," said Billy. "Maybe I'm just spooked, but there's something familiar about you."

Billy was fidgeting with the saltcellar and avoiding eye contact. He couldn't sit still. He took two swigs of beer, said he had the heebie-jeebies, and unexpectedly skipped out the door.

"He looks awful," said Bloom. "*You* look awful. What's going on?"

Blooom had lost weight so I said, "You don't look so hot yourself."

"I know I look like a scarecrow, and I know why. But that kid— I've got a bad feeling."

I didn't want to betray Billy's confidence, but I trusted the old man and felt so bad for Billy that the words just rolled right out.

"I've got the same bad feeling, but I don't think there's anything I can do short of committing a crime."

"Sometimes there's nothing a sane man can do. Bad things happen, and the world keeps turning. That's what we inherit—the world God gave us."

"Exactly what I'm thinking."

He looked at me, surprised that a young man might possess the same philosophic lens, the same curtain of irony through which he himself saw the world. He looked me in the eye and saw that we shared an understanding of the human condition, a similar resignation to powers greater than ourselves. I could be reincarnated many lifetimes in far-flung coordinates throughout the space-time of the cosmos, but it would be rare for me to share such a moment again with another. A wave of empathy passed between us, a whole universe of mutual comprehension linking two men across generations. We had been drawn together initially by chance, and then sluggish gravitation kept us there.

Bloom turned his head to the bar and raised his voice: "Hey Mickey—give me another beer so I can mumble in it like a crotchety old man. How the hell can I mumble if I don't have a sudser?"

"I thought your limit was two."

"Special night. I've got this young fella here wants to talk. It's an experience I don't want to miss."

Mick looked over at me. "You don't actually want to talk to that broken-down warhorse?"

"Did you say cart-horse?" said Bloom. "I think you meant sawhorse."

"Actually," I addressed Mick, "I was hoping to talk to *you* so's I could order that corned beef and cabbage special you've got going for three fifty. That's if you're not busy."

"I think you better talk to the kid, Mick," said Bloom. "He's an Irish Catholic just like you. You can spot 'em a mile away. And he wants to reaffirm his identity in this melting pot by eating some corned beef and cabbage. And mind you boil those potatoes, laddie."

"I swear by Saint Patrick and the snakes that left Ireland," said Mick, "it's coming right up."

My friendship with Bloom continued to grow. He looked like an Irish Catholic, and maybe he talked like one, but there was something else. From the first time I met him, I knew he wasn't one of us; I saw no leprechaun there. He was a proverbial onion, a man with a layered and complex soul. He was an enigma, a puzzle, with relationships to Mick and maybe Margo and a past that had something to do with war. He was someone who wouldn't surprise me if I ran into him at the Metropolitan Opera, suddenly clean-shaven and wearing a tux. I smelled a world of culture behind all his gruff talk, like a pond of clear water behind a screen of vegetation, planted purposely to appear scruffy and wild to fool all those who wouldn't take the time to look past the ruse.

Was this man secretive or just very private? I knew virtually nothing about him, and it felt odd to trust him the way I did. We had a saying back then, "Never trust anyone over thirty," yet here I was, a fresh-faced teen from the brackish waters of the South, moving slow as molasses, ignoring the wisdom of the age. However, when he wanted to hear more about what happened after Jerry's death, I still wasn't ready to tell him. I had taken revenge, but I would never get my brother back. Perhaps when I premeditatively beat those kids, *their* guilt transferred to *me*, and then when no one came after me, it further compounded that guilt. If I had been properly punished, perhaps I would have been absolved—I felt certain that if anyone had seriously looked for me, they certainly would have found me. Maybe no one came after me because I had been so effective in scaring those kids. Maybe their parents saw the injuries from the beatings and asked what had happened, or maybe not: maybe their parents just told them they got what they deserved. Some parents are like that, knowing justice when they see it. Or maybe they told the two kids to shut up or the cops might find out what they had done and lock them in a juvie prison and lose the key.

The students at Catholic High heard about Laureen and Stankewicz through the typical gossip mill, but no one knew who had beaten them. No one guessed it was me because no one connected Jerry's death to those two kids except Gilly, who accosted me in the hall between classes.

"You didn't bring me!" he said.

"Lower your voice!" I said in hushed tones.

"Why didn't you bring me?"

"I didn't want to get you in trouble if I got caught."

"No one's getting in trouble."

A bolt of fear ran through me. I hadn't reflected thoroughly on what I had done, and now I realized that I had no idea how seriously injured they might be. I wondered if they were still alive or if I had killed them.

"Are they okay?"

"Someone said they went to the hospital. Broken bones, broken ribs—the girl was coughing up blood. But I heard they're back in school."

"Did they say anything?" I was nervous. I didn't want the cops after me, and I was horrified by the possibility of jail.

"No one knows about *you* if that's what you mean. That big-mouth, Sue Campbell, was going around telling everyone that she knew the girl. She said the two kids were hit by a truck."

"*Hit by a truck?*"

"Those kids aren't going to tell anyone anything—you must've scared them half to death! I heard another version—some cocka-mamie story about them falling in a ditch on their bicycles. No one knows what to believe, but those two kids just won't say."

—◦◦◦—

"Okay," said Bloom. "I know there was more that happened after your brother died, but since you're still not ready to tell me, let's talk about the draft and the importance of staying in school."

He advised me that all people of intelligence should integrate into society, which was, according to him, the umbrella of safety for a sane and civilized world. Graduating from college was the start of that process. "Without society's rules, there'd be chaos that would end in a bloodbath. People are savages, tending to war, and it's only the umbrella of government that forces us to tolerate each other and work together." His words were a counterweight to what my father spouted about survival of the fittest and every man for himself.

While Bloom was opening my indoctrinated mind with a crowbar, Margo was waiting tables. She came over, crossed her arms and glared at him. "Don't you have anything better to do than come in here night after night and drink beer?"

"What's it to you?" he said.

"Hanging out with a young man less than half your age, filling his head with whatever you're peddling at the moment."

"He's a smart fella. He can judge things for himself."

It sounded hostile, bitter. There was something between them, but I was in no position to pry or to judge.

Margo's mouth puckered and eyes narrowed, but then she looked at me and took a half step back from the table. Her face changed to a tight-lipped smile. "Sorry," she said. "I'm having a bad day."

She turned on her heels and disappeared into the kitchen. I asked Bloom what this altercation was about.

"I'm not entirely sure," he said. "She's a bright girl, but she's got strong opinions. Maybe I said something she didn't like."

He became subdued after that, and when he left, I stayed to sip beer and review the Lorentz-Fitzgerald Transformations for my physics class. I was deep in thought when Margo came up behind me, catching me off guard and whispering with her lips nearly brushing my ear, "Don't let the old man fool you. He's got tricks up his sleeve." Her breath on my ear made the base of my spine tingle. As I craned my neck, turning my face to see her, she was leaning over, and I glimpsed the tops of her breasts through the crewneck opening of her shirt. She caught me looking, and her face turned red. She straightened up to obstruct my view and then sat down across from me, squinting a mistrustful eye. I had an urge to put my hand through her hair or stroke whatever part of her was nearest, but I realized this was far from the right moment.

"He'll charm the paint off the wall, that old man," she said, lifting a finger both to emphasize her point and to warn me against any advance. "Be careful you separate the substance of what's really him from the web of words he spins."

19

Libation

Throughout Christmas break I was alone in the dorms except for a few kids, mostly from out West or the deep South. I had called my mother, but she said, "Your father and I are busy—you know the holidays, so much to do. The Edwards are having a party; the club is having its Christmas party; the admirals will have a holiday get-together . . ."

I wasn't interested in going home amidst a whirlwind of social activity, so I elected to stay in the city. Without school or family obligations, I could explore the landscapes of Gotham, a student on furlough, looking for random adventures flowing with women and rivers of beer. Nebraska was gone—God knows where—and I had the room to myself, sleeping at any hour. I could have women without any concern for Nebraska's rights to his space.

But what women?

Julie had gone home to New Jersey. And Margo was a woman who would call the shots as she saw fit; she wouldn't be coming to my room on a whim.

Or would she? She was a senior; I was a freshman, and the gap between us was even bigger than that because she had taken a year off from school. She was experienced, smart and sophisticated, and I was energetic but disorganized, clearly at a disadvantage. I could imagine all I wanted, but the chasm between male-beast fantasy and student reality was far too great for me to straddle. I was no match for her in the eternal conflict of gender chess, but if I could land her, perhaps the equation could change; perhaps I might even make up ground or possibly gain an advantage.

But then reality slapped me. I was jealous. I was a puppy, and she was a woman who had hung with a rock star. I couldn't compete; I was angered, even grieved. Wallowing in my pathetic proto-anthropoid shell, I decided that I wasn't even sure that I wanted her. So maybe I'd hop a subway and find some pub or dance palace, somewhere women might be looking for a raw, unpolished thing like me. The idea got me juiced. Thrust into the battle of life forces in which every man enlists, I had to find out where I stood in the hierarchy of desirability—I would take my place in the struggle to spawn or be damned.

One evening near the end of break, I was leaving my room to hop the Number 1 train to The Village. But going out my door, The Grateful Dead grabbed my ears—"*I lit out from Reno*"—and I followed the notes to Milo, sitting alone in his room, on a mattress, in his underwear with the black shortie tie around his neck.

"Greetings, J-Bee. Come in. Pull up—something. A chair, a mattress. How are you?"

"I'm not going to stay. I'm headed downtown."

"I dig. But first, get your ass in here and sit down. Tell me the news of the world. Have a cup of tea and keep me company for a few. It'll warm you up before you're on your way. It's cold out there. December, in case you forgot."

Milo intrigued me. His name came up unexpectedly and more frequently than anyone else's. He was a prep school bigwig with connections to everyone and everything. There were whisperings that he controlled Columbia's drug trade and that he put the finger on people, who later disappeared. Often he was seen with his shortie neckties next to the dean of students or playing touch football on South Field with the university president. He also had a steady stream of women dropping by his room. Bobby Bornes worshipped him; MacNeish spoke of him with respect as if the walls would report him if he dared say anything negative, but Billy turned white at his name.

As he glided around the room, his naked muscular torso was impressively formidable. I didn't feel afraid of Milo, but I was wary. I had to be cautious, looking in his eyes, searching his depths for whatever and wherever his soul might be, wondering if what I would see would be luminous and sparkling or hideously deformed and rotten. So it was with special people: there was no middle ground; there were only the extremes, which sometimes blurred together.

"I have some black Turkish hash if you want."

"What would the dean think if he knew his favorite protégé smoked hash?"

Milo laughed. It was good-natured, but I couldn't tell if it was phony or genuine.

"Your father's an admiral. MacNeish told me. He wants you in the Sachems."

Milo was up and tiptoeing around in his skivvies, heating water and rummaging through some tins for just the right mixture of teas.

"We'll see about the Sachems," I said.

"You and me both, brother. I'm thinking that we're cut from the same cloth."

"You think?"

Suddenly I was uncomfortably too close to Milo who was calling me kinsman and brewing tea like we had some kind of bond. This took me by surprise, and I discovered that I didn't like us having anything in common. Vulnerability mixed with horror slithered up the back of my neck.

"I have an idea, J-Bee. Why don't you come and work for me? Just so happens I have an opening at the moment."

"What kind of work?"

"MacNeish says you're a good guy. It'll be good money."

"I don't really need money. What kind of work?"

"Selling marijuana or hash from time to time. Nothing major. What d'you think? Everybody needs money."

"Not interested. But thanks."

"You sure?"

"No interest," I said.

"That's cool, but too bad. Too bad for me. You'd be perfect—everyone likes you. Must be the Southern charm."

"Listen, Milo. I don't like tea, and I'm hitting the road. What's with the tea, anyway?"

He looked up at me, and I could tell he read my face in a nanosecond.

"After I went to all this trouble to brew you something special?"

I was a fly in a web. My heart fluttered in apprehension as my limbs and voice went numb.

"Just stay where you are," he said, pointing at me as I braced to hoist myself out of my chair. He moved close and put his hand on my shoulder, pressing me back down. "Sit yourself. You don't owe me anything. I'm giving you a gift. A libation. One straight man to another. Just unstress for a minute."

He took the few steps back to where he was making the tea.

"Chill out," he said over his shoulder. "Stay and have a sip. You take sugar?"

Intently focused on his task, he got out the sugar and stirred the tea with a spoon pinched between two fingers, the wrist of his other hand resting on his hip with the fingers fanned out. As I gazed on, mesmerized by the comedy he enacted, it struck me how un-self-conscious and disarmingly innocuous he appeared. He then walked back to me and passed me the mug. It was a funny thing, but suddenly, as if I were being pulled by magic invisible strings, the tea beckoned, and I was drawn to it.

Milo sat down, cross-legged on his mattress, and smiled. Norman Greenbaum was on the stereo, singing—*Spirit in the sky-that's where I'm gonna go when I die*—and I lifted the mug to my lips and drank. Orange spiced tea warmed my gullet; it was very good.

I drained it and bounced to my feet, ready to bolt out the door. Milo was gazing into space with an occasional brief glance in my direction.

Such a weird fucker.

Then I felt a strangeness, a disorientation, a sensation I had never felt before. The hands of the clock on the wall began to spin, zipping around the dial and suddenly stopping at what I supposed was the real time. It was weird but fascinating. I glanced around to confirm that I was still in Milo's room with Milo still in it, sitting on his mattress, sipping his drink as Norman Greenbaum warbled.

I looked back at the clock, and now the hands were spinning propellers, so fast they blurred, and a rainbow of color was part of that blur. Then the hands stopped and swelled into thick, drooping cucumbers, which broke from their attachments at the center of the clock face, snapping off and clattering to the floor from their own weight.

I stared at them as they transformed into the heads of Laureen and Stankewicz. They rolled across the floor, staring at me, saying, "You did this! You did this!" Then they sprouted bodies, and I was hitting them with a bat, and Stankewicz was holding his head and shrieking, "He was just a little kid! He was just a little kid!" And Laureen was laughing and sputtering, "He was this little deaf kid! We never did anything wrong!" Now I was hitting them with a machete, and the machete was flashing silver in the moonlight. It was very beautiful; the glinting of the blade effervesced in a magnificent arc. The silver blurred into a shiny red-maroon as the machete ripped their heads off, and the heads were rolling away, blinking and babbling, "He was just this little kid!" while another voice was shouting, "No! No! No!" And it was my voice; I was shouting, and it was a horror. Then Bornes was standing there with a joint in his hand, smiling in a tee shirt with the lettering, "Make Love Not War." He was giggling, "He was just this little kid! We went to school together, you know." His face was one big laugh, his mouth wide open when suddenly punji sticks sliced through his body from behind, all their points sticking out the front of his neck, his torso, his arms and legs. Like Jesus on the cross with all his flesh quivering, his wings spread like a wriggling butterfly, pinioned to a board. He winked. "We went to school together, Milo and me. He was a very big shot."

I was staggered. There was a bright fog in the room, and Milo emerged from the fog as Norman Greenbaum was singing, *And when I die and am able to rest*, and Milo said, "Sit down, J-Bee. It's cold outside."

I brought my hands up to either side of my face, and a voice shrieked, "Fucking Milo—what the hell have you done!"

There was laughter everywhere, and I saw cracked plaster faces, hundreds of them, pure white and stuck to the wall, laughing and shaking with laughter. A million outstretched fingers were pointing at me, and I knew I was going to die. But I wasn't going to die with Milo. He did this to me. He had handed me the poisoned chalice, and I had drunk, so now I was going to die.

I tottered from the room. The halls were dark, and tiny arms were reaching out to touch me, begging for everything I had in the world, every bit of me, so that they could live for only a few minutes more, sucking away my energy, my soul and my life force. They were children, lining the walls, crying with their hands outstretched, tugging at me, fingering my shirt and clothes, reaching their hands into every crevice of my body and being. I moved forward to escape, but they hung on me, heavy like chains, dragging behind me, wailing little toddlers without their mothers, terror on their smeared faces, bloated bellies, spindly legs, bony knees, hanging onto me for dear life, dragging me down as I trudged.

I made it to the elevators and pressed every button I saw. I wouldn't jump off a building; I wouldn't lurch in front of a moving truck; I wouldn't tumble onto the tracks in front of an onrushing train. I was tripping, and I would force myself to be a voyeur and see and feel the universe. I would surf the astral plane and attempt to live 'til morning.

The elevator doors burst open. If it were an empty shaft, I knew I wouldn't know the difference, and I could free-fall twelve stories down and die on a cement slab in the basement, a shivering pile of pulp. But the odds were against this, and I took my step forward into potential oblivion.

Someone grabbed me by the shoulder from behind and said, "J-Bee, wait!"

I turned in panic and shoved him as hard as I could, sending him backpedaling. He slipped on the floor, falling on his rump in his skivvies and shortie black tie.

The elevator clanged shut. I was inside, lights fizzing and flickering, shadows shifting as the bottom fell out and I went into freefall. I was a monkey in a space capsule, plummeting to Earth after a voyage to the stars. Spiraling down, down, down, a BB in an inverted, hyperbolic singularity, I was sucked into the great vortex at the event horizon, the atoms of my bones and organs to be pulverized into a particulate plasma so that the history of the existence of what I was and where I had been, the body in which I had walked the planet would be vaporized into the gaseous soup of nothing randomness at the center of the great maelstrom, the hole at the bottom of the universe. I braced for my demise. The stars, suns, planetessimals, positrons, pions and quarks all circled above me, inaccessible, as I reached up to claw my way out of the abyss. But then a great weight pressed upon my legs, and the elevator braked, and the door bounced open, ejecting me. I hit a wall full front, and a great wave broke on me in undulating pain. Sweat poured off me and ran through the cuffs of my pants onto the floor, gushing red as my life's blood drained, flowing like water from an unplugged pipe. I was drenched over every inch of my body, pain throbbing my head, pulse pounding my veins, and I knew what it meant—I was alive! A beacon shone down from heaven, and voices sang, telling me to go and see Billy Wing. If I could find him, he could be my guide through the chaos.

I trudged to his dorm, Hartley Hall, dragging a flood of stains in my wake until I came to a very dark hallway where I faced growling dogs and smelled a stagnant, deep-rotted smell of death. Chirping, swirling bats led me through a tunnel of darkness, the fluid of dead water lapping at my ankles. Shrieking faces pierced the shadows with fluorescent bulbs buzzing and sputtering dangerously from loose wires hanging from overhead. A black portal loomed in front of me, black from both an absence of being and an absence of light, and I pounded on it with fists. With crying bats behind me, I faced a scrabbling of rat claws from inside the portal which was Billy Wing's door. The door hissed, exhaling a long shushing rattle accompanied by a fetid white vapor that wafted from the door, sticking to me like ashfall, but stinking with such intensity that I could smell it in my skin. Such was the power of this intense aroma that I flickered in and out of consciousness, a strobe light gone mad.

On the fringe of suffocation, every nerve in my body screeching in agony, I felt a massive presence as Death stepped forward and announced itself at Billy Wing's door. I fell backward from the full force of the hallucination, knowing that acid was tearing my reality to shreds. This great presence used all of my senses at its disposal to possess me so that my only escape was to find my legs and reach the crisp air outside. Without Billy Wing, I was lost in the oblivion.

A shimmering half-crushed face with one eye hovered above me in the white sticky cloud that had formed under the sputtering lights, and I saw it was my brother. "Go, J-Bee!" he said. "Run! Escape this awful place!" I croaked, "But I can't leave you!" He said, "I am not real. I am not here. Go J-Bee! Go my brother! Will yourself onto your feet and flee the Lord of the Flies before he clutches for you—because *he is here!*"

20

Lady Luck

There was no sound above the hush of the snowfall when I found myself facedown on hard ground, rimed with crystalline crust. My right eye was iced shut between the lashes; the right side of my face was numb. I touched it with fingertips, but no sensation.

I was lying on Columbia's South Field. I had no idea what time it was, but it was dark, and my clothes were damp. I sat up, and snow sprinkled off in a powder. The sky was charcoal and purple with occasional orange flashes, reflecting off the clouds. New York was on fire; Columbia's buildings surrounded me on fire, and I was on fire. I was a burning monk; orange flames burst from my skin which seared in pain. The snow kept falling, but it was cold, not hot, and now I was no longer on fire.

I took the Number 1 train, but I don't know how. It was a roaring metal tube, a catacomb with an infernal kettledrum sound, a dancing rhythm clicking and clacking, bound to Greenwich Village or maybe to Omaha. The lights got dimmer the faster it moved. Bulbs on the catacomb walls, shooting past the train, crossed shadows with bars of light on the grimy faces of anonymous riders, sitting inert on plastic train benches. I watched them, their faces mutating into random shapes and colors with expressions as still as hewn Mayan gargoyles.

I debarked at 4th Street, Sheridan Square, where a lone man in rags played harmonica. He sat on the station platform on the opposite side of the tracks, propped against the wall, both his legs lopped off at the knees. He wore a khaki shirt with "US Army" across it, his two crutches beside him and a red bandana around his head. He shook a tin cup as people passed by. "Pencils!" he shouted. "I was a soldier! Look at me now! Buy some goddamned pencils to help a fuckin' vet!"

Then he laughed a loose phlegmy sound and lit a cigarette.

When I climbed the subway stairs to the street, I felt him behind me. I turned, and he was there, standing with no legs on crutches, stumps dangling in air. He said, "Brother, will you buy some pencils? Help a fuckin' veteran? I have no place to live. I have no life. Help me, for the love of God. Have you got no humanity?" My voice croaked something inaudible, but I knew what it said: "Of course, I'll help. I'll give you money." He coughed and inched closer. His breath was on my face. I could smell his rotting teeth, but it was stronger than rotting teeth. Then I saw it was Bloom, and he had medals on his chest. He said, "The medals don't mean anything. They ripped my heart out and gave me a bunch of tin."

He tore the medals off and threw them onto the ground. They morphed into seeds which suddenly sprang to life as little crouching Asian men. These men stood up all at once, surrounding us with punji sticks in their hands. I heard a scream and felt the blood rush to my head. I was screaming, and the men were laughing. They sliced Bloom's chest open and ripped out his heart, leaving a large dark bloody hole in its place. One of them held his beating heart; another pinned a cross to his chest. Then they all laughed— even Bloom was laughing. "These gooks are my brothers; whatever I have is theirs. We owe the bastards—they can have my heart in a bowl of rice. I don't want your money, but I need another heart. Give me yours—help a dying veteran!"

I turned and ran. I ran into people on the sidewalks. I ran into parked cars. I ran until I couldn't run, and when I turned, Bloom and his gooks were gone.

I slowed to a jog, but I didn't stop. Bloom had to die for the Japanese, Koreans, Vietnamese—somebody. He had thrown in his lot with them years ago. But not me; I wasn't going to die for them. Maybe I had to die; maybe I was going to die, but please God! Not for this! Let them unite their country, choose whatever government they want. I wasn't going to stop them. I wasn't going to die in a rice paddy to be eaten by rats—I wasn't going to do it!

I was walking. Although the hallucinations were less intense, faces in the street still terrified me, and the buildings moaned and twisted in the snow-dusted wind. Doorways bellowed like mouths, giant and obscene, beckoning me to enter and despair.

At the corner of 4th Street and Seventh Avenue, I sat on the sidewalk to reflect. At first, I was visited by horrors; voices interrupted my thoughts as did visions of throngs of souls akin to my own, maimed and disemboweled, inching through mud, dying bewildered and never knowing why. Never knowing or seeing the beauty of things as I did as I lived in my small gifted life. The disparity skewered my heart—such a weird lottery, imposed by the universe and executed by mathematical emptiness.

I sat for an hour or maybe just minutes. I fused with the landscape: I was brickwork, asphalt, a chunk of the pavement. Ice cold faces came out of the dark, smeared with reds and pinks, contorted with pain and ferocity. Bodies radiated colored halos like infrared maps—they may have been star-children, or maybe just aliens, or maybe just auras of those walking past.

Abruptly something deep inside me—a ragged hairy beast locked away, chained for a lifetime to dungeon walls—was roaring, his sound percolating from the depths of my subconscious into my waking state. I felt him shake off his chains, stretch his arms and legs, and burst forth from his shadowy cell. Stupefied, I felt life renewed. As cars and people danced down the street, I sat spellbound at the spectacular parade, consumed by love. I had magic within me, and though the people I saw were grotesque—striped, angular, dog-faced—they were magnificent, and I was the gifted witness. Enraptured, I feasted on beauty, grateful to be alive in such a vibrant, colorful painting. So abject yet so privileged amongst all living things, I sobbed to be gifted such sensual wonder.

I was now tired, sitting on the frozen sidewalk, watching my breath billow to steam, chilling to crystals, refracting the neons and headlights into millions of rainbow shards like shimmering plasma. I was still tripping, and though I knew I had to find refuge from the cold, somehow I didn't care. With the back of my head against cold brick, I closed my eyes, knowing I might freeze or die in the gutter. Unless the clouds parted for Lady Luck to shine down upon me, there was nothing between me and oblivion.

"J-Bee?"

It was a soft voice, a gentle voice, and it sounded like wind chimes on a sunny veranda.

"J-Bee?"

I knew it was cold, but my body told me I was warm with Southern heat. It made no sense except that I was tired, and it was hot, and I would give in to the overwhelmingly heavy need to slumber, leaning against the brick wall.

"J-Bee! Get up! Wake up! Are you okay?"

I was being shaken, and I opened my eyes. The image was bleary; I saw shapes and then a face with a halo of shaggy hair, cascading down to a pair of shoulders.

I heard a croaking voice, my voice, "Margo—what're *you* doing here?"

21

Echoes of Sunshine

Sun streamed through the lacy window curtains, and I was alone in a warm, soft bed, the covers over my head.

Fucking Milo! Thank God I'm alive!

I had vague feelings about where I might be; it wasn't my bed, but I didn't care. I had thought I was dead and buried, and I was thankful to be among the living. With such beautiful sunlight, whatever did anything matter?

I remembered Death outside Billy Wing's door, its rotten smell in my nostrils. Had it been real? Or some bizarre reverie, invented by my brain, without meaning? Even if illusory, it had to mean *some*thing.

"Oh—you up?"

It was that jangling voice. It was music in my head.

"Margo?"

"That's right. Or don't you remember?"

It was a big bed, king-size. I rolled over, and there she was, standing in the doorway, draped in a striped djellaba, feet in flip-flops, a cup of coffee in her hand. I smelled a hint of cloves and cinnamon, kitcheny smells, mixed with the java.

"How the hell did I get here?"

She giggled, "Do you remember *anything*?"

Murky visions. Hallucinations. Psychosis. Things had happened, and I remembered. But in spite of remembering, I wasn't sure which parts were real and which were not.

"I hope you do because I want to hear it. You seemed to be on some kind of drug. Do you take drugs, J-Bee?"

She looked at me, wide-eyed. She asked the question, and, what was different, she really wanted to know the answer.

"No, I don't do drugs."

But this wasn't right.

"I've smoked marijuana."

"That wasn't marijuana last night."

"No, it wasn't."

"So, what was it? Something's happened to you. Do you feel like you can tell me? Maybe it's none of my business, but it feels like I'm allowed to ask."

Where would I begin? I had discovered something. I could tell Margo because she might help me uncover its meaning, and sifting through last night's wreckage to uncover its meaning suddenly became a priority.

"It must've been LSD."

"LSD?"

"Something's happened; not sure I can explain. Don't know if I can put my finger on it, but it's as if my eyes are suddenly open, as if they were shut before. Somehow, everything looks—*feels*—different."

I had seen the beginning and the end of everything, all at once. I had seen incomparable beauty; I had seen unparalleled misery. I had witnessed Evil—an unbearable smell—and it knocked me down as it came.

"I saw Death last night. I know you'll think I'm ridiculous, but it's the God's honest truth. I thought I was going to die—no, I *knew* I was going to die. But here I am, and now everything's different."

Everything was wonderful: the sun was shining, and I was in a room with Margo. I was in *her* bedroom, in *her* bed. Everything now had to be reevaluated; I needed new perspective. I wasn't quite sure *how* things had changed; I didn't quite know what it all meant, but I felt an unreasonable optimism and happiness. It felt like a good start. I glanced at her, but she didn't move or speak. She looked me in the eyes but said nothing.

"God, Margo—say something."

"Well, yes, you may have changed. You don't sound like the J-Bee I recall. Not that I've known you very well, but you sound serious. You sound more—"

She hesitated.

"More what?"

"Focused. Clearheaded."

"Focused? Lost, more like."

"I could be wrong, but you seem to be more purposeful. Driven by questions. Lost maybe, but there's a spark there. I think you're wrong about not knowing where to begin; I think you've already begun."

I sat up, and I had a good look at her with her arms folded, leaning against the door frame. My head felt scrambled, fogged, yet I was evolving in some enigmatic way. And now here comes this woman with a voice, and she was making sense. She was watching out for me, like she cared, and it made me feel grounded. She told me I had direction and purpose, and although I didn't know where or what, it gave me a tang of self-belief, which made me itch to move forward. And then, almost not to be believed, through all this ran the fact that I was in this woman's bed.

I suddenly had new questions.

"Did I sleep here last night?"

"Evidently."

"And did you sleep here with me?"

"I slept in the bed, yes."

I couldn't remember a thing about it, and she was giving me the beady eye. How could I not remember sleeping with Margo? How could having sex with a goddess have made no impact? *I must be cursed.*

She read my mind.

"But no, we didn't have sex, in case you're wondering. You were whimpering, having a bad time until the effects of the drug wore off, and you finally settled down. I just kept you company. Besides, I have nowhere else to go—this happens to be my flat."

She was smiling, and I felt heat for her unlike for any other woman.

"You were like the little brother I never had."

I groaned out loud. "You sure know how to kill a guy."

"I've had plenty of practice," she giggled. "I'm kidding. You're not like a little brother, but there's something else about you, and I'll have to think about it before I can explain."

"*You're* not like anyone *I've* ever known."

She looked down at the floor, suppressing a smile, but when she looked up she couldn't contain it, and she beamed. "You're a lot younger than I am, much less experienced than the men I'm used to. But I'd be lying if I said that I've seen your charms before in other men."

She stopped there, but I was hungry for more. "Go on," I said.

"Well—since you *ask*. After you settled down and slept, feeling you next to me in bed was oddly comforting. It seems that you're a man who comes across as steady enough to make a woman feel a certain humming. A warmth. Maybe I felt secure. I don't know—as I said, I'll have to think about it."

Margo's romantic experience in the past, with other men, made me nauseated. Whether she knew it or not, she was playing me like a musical instrument—perhaps a simple thing like a single hollow pipe—and she was calling the tune.

—∿—

Margo lived on 107th Street, so I hiked back to campus on 114th. Christmas break was ending, and I expected an increase in campus activity with students returning from holiday. As I entered the campus gates, I saw a throng on the Van Am Quad in front of Hartley Hall. Students were milling around in the cold, and a dozen New York City cops stood guard at the doors, talking on radios and chatting with campus security. On 116th Street, in the middle of campus, an ambulance sat silently, its red lights circling.

I walked over to Hartley to watch the drama. Having cops on campus was a rare event, and I was drawn to witness the shadowy traces of possible crime. A cop and a campus security guard, both toting guns, were conversing. I sat on the steps with my back to the pair, perking my ears like a cat.

"It was me," said the guard. "I was the one who responded to the complaint. The smell in the hallway, outside the room, was enough to KO an elephant."

"Took a while to report. How come no one else smelt it?"

"It's Christmas break. The place was empty; the students had all gone home."

"The kid must've been dead a week or two."

"You think?"

"That's what forensics said. Body's pretty decomposed. A hundred seventy pounds of aromatic rot."

"That's why I almost passed out when I opened the door; the smell was horrible. He was at his desk, slumped in a chair. The syringe was hanging out his arm."

"Reclusive hippie kid. Dabbling in drugs, overdid it and killed himself. That's one explanation. But they'll have to rule out foul play. It's an ME case."

A plainclothesman walked up.

"Officer, there's kids walking around. Keep a lid on it."

"Sorry, Lieutenant."

"Lieutenant," I blurted, standing up and turning to face him. "Who died?"

The lieutenant looked me up and down, narrowing his eyes. "We have an ID, but I'm not giving any other details. We've been here four hours, and we're packing it in. Body's coming out; then we're out of here. There'll be an official statement later."

The next day, the details were printed in the *Columbia Daily News*.

BODY FOUND IN HARTLEY HALL

"A dead body was found in Hartley Hall after going undiscovered for weeks during Christmas break . . . 'An unbearable odor' from the victim's dormitory door prompted a complaint that was called to campus security by a returning student . . . Columbia security guards responded, entering the room with handkerchiefs over their faces . . . Guards and police, New York's finest, were seen retching while examining the room with the body present . . . One guard was quoted as saying, 'Some hippie kid shot up and killed himself. Accidental OD. The Office of the Medical Examiner is on the case.' The victim has been identified as William Humboldt Wing."

The smell I had encountered must have been my friend's corpse, rotting behind the door as I knocked. Upon reading the newspaper account, I felt pulled by invisible strings, lumbering forward like a sleepwalker until I found myself again in that same hallway outside Billy's door, trembling as I relived the moment. My nostrils filled with the same powerful decay that I had smelled the night before, and then, out of nowhere, came a tweeting in my brain, an echo of LSD. I heard a rumbling voice addressing me, shaking the walls around me, speaking a language of the damned, ushering in a swarm of flies which hissed and buzzed through my ears and into my head. The low-pitched, vibrating voice became so loud it shook the walls until I lost my footing and fell. The redolence of rotting flesh seared my throat, making it swell to the point of closure and asphyxiation. Lying on my belly I was a mere lump of clay, a foe of the evil forces arrayed against me, and I was powerless to protect myself, paralyzed by inescapable horror. I found myself on all fours, and a sound was erupting from the fear within me, a long unintelligible rasping howl.

A door down the hall flung open, and a young man stepped out.

"You okay?"

It was so simple, so mundane, and yet these two words broke the spell which had taken hold of me. The rumbling and odors were suddenly gone.

"Yeah," I said. "Yeah. I'll be okay."

"You sure? What are you doing on the floor? You look terrible."

"It's an echo of a bad trip. And Billy Wing was my friend."

"Yeah, it's too bad what happened to Billy."

He stretched out a hand, and I took it. He pulled me to my feet.

"We were all shocked that he would use heroin. We knew him, but we couldn't believe he was shooting drugs. I mean, he studied all the time! We saw him walking around in a towel to go to the showers—he had no tracks on his arms or anything. He was very serious about his schoolwork and wanted to go to grad school. He talked about it a lot. A couple of guys down the hall are saying he was murdered. But how could they know? No one was here over break except Billy. Some guys are saying he kept talking about someone threatening him, but no one wants to tell the police. Everyone's spooked. One guy mentioned a name he heard Billy mention—Manuel or Miguel. Ever heard of him?"

"Thanks," I said, "for helping me up."

"It's cool. Why don't you go down to the bathroom and freshen up. You look like you saw a ghost."

I thanked him again, stumbled down the hall to the bathroom and stood facing the mirrors over a line of sinks. I ran cold water and rubbed my face; the stimulation roused me.

I saw myself, truly saw myself, for the first time in over a month. I had been living a life of the mind and neglecting my physical self. My hair was longer, stringy. I hadn't shaved for three or four days, which left a heavy stubble. I was metamorphosing from a raw, undeveloped grub into something new. I could see the tangible alteration, as if the change in my mind was triggering a change in my outward appearance, an accretion of some new persona.

In the mirror my face contorted, the colors smeared, and my image shimmered and changed. I saw the face of Milo where my own face should have been, and I knew right away what this meant: it meant Billy's death was murder, and it meant Milo did it. The rotten smell was Milo's signature and nothing else. I could discern no single thread of morality or empathy anywhere stitched into the fabric of his decaying soul. It was Milo who dosed me, and it was Milo who killed Billy Wing. He may have been there when Billy went down, or he may not. He may have sent his cronies, who stuck a needle in Billy Wing's arm, or he may have done it himself. But ultimately it was Milo who OD'd poor Billy and then left him there to rot and stink so that days later, I could smell him outside his door while, thanks to Milo again, I was tripping my shredded brain to oblivion.

22

The Acts of Saint Paul

Classes started after holiday break, but I couldn't focus; my mind was stuck on Billy, dead in his room. We had sipped tea together, and now I'd never see him again. The world would forget him; unstoppable time would move on. I wondered: had his death been woven into the fabric of time by a dark and unforgiving God, even before the innocent thread of his life had begun? Or had it occurred on the spur of the moment, a mere confluence of events, the random collision of his lively spirit with an onrushing freight train of evil?

I went through motions but was numb to humanity's traffic. I wasn't hungry; I didn't sleep. As I lay on my back at night staring at the ceiling while Nebraska sawed wood eight feet away, I had visions. Faces of the dead and things I had imagined but had never seen came out of the dark: phantoms murdering my innocent friend, schoolboys chained to dungeon walls, nuns in black habits in candlelight chanting monotonically. I saw Jerry's face and remembered as car tires thumped over him, crushing his life.

One cold night I couldn't fight it anymore; it must have been four in the morning. I leapt out of bed, slipped on my coat and walked out to Broadway. Normally a place of bustle and bodies, the sidewalks stood deserted, pressed by a thick sky hanging above the rooftops. Icy scum in the gutters reflected the reds, greens and blues of twinkling neons, and wind blew empty pop cans clattering down the street.

I tramped forward along a lifeless row of storefronts while the voice of reason and a blind instinct for vengeance battled in my head. Reaching The Gold Rail, I stopped at the dimmed set of windows and peered through the glass; it was too black to see the upturned barstools on the tables.

I moved on. As I walked downtown, a dog with gray clotted fur jogged past on spindly legs, crossing the street in silence. Behind him skipped a larger black bitch, heavily muscled but equally indifferent. They evaporated into darkness, throating low-pitched dissonant growls.

I crossed myself instinctively. Buffeted by numbing wind, I reached 96th Street where I stopped at the stairs to the subway underground. There was light down there, and a warm stale blast hit my face, saturated with soot and ozone from the subways. The heat relaxed my muscles, casting a pall of lassitude upon me, and I heard, somewhere deep below in the bowels of the slumbering city, the rumbling of great metal behemoths, the contrivances of mechanically oriented minds, rattling and banging their ways through the black corridors of another world. For an instant that world beckoned, tempting me below, curling its lip at me to come and feel its comfortable warmth and escape the cold of real, waking life.

Gazing foggily, I noticed the name "Taki 188" in black Magic Marker, scrawled in a modest hand on the white tile wall of the stairwell. I recognized this name as a pioneer in the contemporary world of graffiti, the despoilment of walls and trains throughout the city, a movement spawned for a host of nameless individuals, living in squalid apartments in anonymous realms of New York, to achieve a spot of dubious recognition, distinguishing themselves from the oceans of humanity which churned in the great urban tidal bore. The scrawl was one boy's proclamation of, "I am Ozymandias," a muted voice in asphalt wilderness. I stood on that brink between two worlds, not so much thinking as waiting for some spark in my soul to make a fateful decision between the cold, living world above ground and the warm, polluted world of artifice and conveyance beneath.

A tall shadowy figure with long white hair now stood at the bottom of the steps, the gray and black dogs at his feet, mouthing words I was unable to hear above the screeching of the trains. I discerned a sulfuric smell mixed with necrotic decay, not in my nose but in my brain, and I felt the impulse to climb down the steps to smash the insolent face and kill the wraith as he stood. He must have known my thoughts as he lifted his arms in an invitation to hug me, waving me forward without words. I stood inert, again on the cusp of indecision, when the figure and dogs disintegrated into shadow.

I snapped from my reverie, wondering if I could ever overcome the ingrained propensity for violence that had been pounded into me by the hands of the Sisters. In front of me was the great Thalia Theater, product of a grandiose bygone era, its ornate facade decorated with the visage of the muse herself and numerous colored bulbs, now unplugged and darkened, bereft of audience. As I turned to walk away, I heard two voices and the scuffling of sneakers about fifty feet away. Then I heard a yell and saw two men, one punching and the other backpedaling, falling on his back to the ground.

I shouted, "Hey!"

The aggressor stopped. He turned, and our eyes met, an act of intimate engagement. At that instant, I felt no ill will, no call to violence, no personal stake to intervene, but I stood there rigid, fixed in readiness, awaiting the unfolding of events. Such an interlinking of eyes by two male strangers on a deserted street in the context of violence is a significant confrontation, an invitation to combat. We were trapped together, locked in each other's vision, caught in a moment of indecision as the cosmos whirled around us, awaiting our response.

In the next instant, the man on his back on the ground coughed, breaking the spell and rupturing my connection with his assailant. It was then that the aggressor turned and escaped, jogging away, assuring we would never meet again. The victim slowly rose to his feet and faded into the inscrutable night.

I walked farther. At 72nd Street, at a place they called Needle Park, there were several inert bodies sleeping on benches, wrapped in blankets and sleeping bags, smeared with the ambient filth of the city. A bearded man in a green hooded jacket, marked US ARMY, came forward as I walked by. Hands in his pockets, he was hopping from foot to foot in Converse All Star sneakers.

"Lids, acid, speed, smack, *bombita*. You want it; I got it."

"No thanks," I said.

I felt his hand on my shoulder.

"I got great deals. I got anything you need, brother."

I kept walking, lifting my hand to knock his arm away.

"Well, fuck you then," he said. "Fuck your mother!"

I turned and saw Milo; it was his face. "Fuck your mother!" he said again and laughed. Somehow his visage triggered impulses in my sensorium—the same sounds of scraping trains filled my ears and the same smell of necrotic decay suffused my brain. A strangeness rippled through my consciousness which laced me with an involuntary blast of anger. Milo had been following me all along, and now I moved to kill him, to crack that face, to end his overwhelming malice. I swung as hard as I could, striking his jaw obliquely instead of flush on the face as I had intended. He crumpled to the ground with a howl, allowing me to scrutinize his features and see, with horror, that it wasn't Milo at all—it was simply the bearded man I had seen in the green army jacket.

"Oh God! He hit me! He hit me!" the man shrieked, rolling on the ground, waking the bodies on the benches. "Oh my God—he's hurt me! Please somebody help! He's trying to kill me! *Help!*"

The others sat up, and one sprang to his feet with an incoherent squawk. I bolted several blocks toward the river, my knuckles throbbing. No one followed so I slowed to a lope.

Something inside me was simmering, an emotional froth bubbling. How could I have mistaken that man for Milo? And who was the figure at the stairs to the underground? It must have been more echoes from the acid trip, confounding me again and again, tricking me. Yes, I wanted Milo dead, but how could I be certain that he killed Billy? I was in a fog, but I had to be perfectly sure before committing so final an act as murder.

It was then that the gravity of my intentions became apparent for what they were. I had reached the deepest layer of sin, that profound recess of Hades in which was hidden ultimate depravity and self-degradation. There could be no redemption from such a place if I chose to act. I would be lost for the entire infinity of time, unable to be saved, at the very bottom of the inverted pyramid of Hell.

Hadn't I already glimpsed this Hell after battering Stankewicz and Laureen? Would I again react to evil and conform to what Milo had done by responding to him in a way that echoed exactly what *he* had done? Suddenly I was afraid. I knew that violent action could result in sin, but was the mere contemplation of violence *equally* sinful?

No, I thought, it couldn't be. At least not according to The Acts of Saint Paul. This rationalization made me feel better, but then I saw the hypocrisy. I laughed at myself for such crude thinking. There I was, squirming out of all responsibility for contemplating murder without recognizing my self-deception. I was too close to the problem; I needed another lucid mind to confirm or reject my reasoning. I would seek that woman with the "Free the Chicago Seven" tee who lived along the route back to campus. The sun wasn't up, but its pink and orange lights were brightening the sky, a beacon guiding me to her door just several blocks ahead on 107th where West End Avenue emptied into Broadway.

A small truck stood curbside in front of a narrow store; a florist was taking delivery as I approached. The shop's metal cellar doors, normally flat and flush with the sidewalk, were open and upright revealing steps to the cellar below the shop. As the florist moved bundles from truck to cellar, the scent of fresh flowers was sweet on the crisp cold air.

What better way could there be to thank Margo for bringing me home from The Village and giving me refuge from the cold?

I approached the florist. "Can I buy flowers?"

"We're not open."

I put my hand in my pocket and pulled out three dollars. I handed it to the man. "It's all I've got."

"Okay," he said. "Whaddya want?"

"I don't know. It's for a girl—a woman."

He eyed me. "It's like that, huh?" He took my money and went into the cellar, returning with some pompons and baby's breath, wrapped in delicate green paper.

"She'll like these," he said. "Lots of color."

"Do you have a little card so I could write a note?"

"A card? Get lost—I'm not even open! What you *ought* to do is thank me."

"Right," I said. "Thanks."

—m—

Down another block, I turned to cross the street and saw a gray car moving from downtown toward me with such speed that it went airborne as it hit humps in the asphalt. A beat-up white van was overtaking this gray car on its right as both ran red lights, one after the other.

Stuffing the bundle of flowers in my coat, I fled from the street, flattening my back against a building, glancing about for a door-way to hide in, afraid of being apprehended by cops pursuing me for assault. I heard backfires, and the van swerved in front of the car, forcing it onto the sidewalk, across the street from me. The vehicles skidded, hitting trashcans and lampposts; then six long-haired men in tuques and overcoats burst from the van, like clowns from a phone booth, toting guns. They swarmed the car, flinging its doors open, yelling, "Get the fuck outta there!" and throwing the men from the car at the wall, their faces and arms up against it.

The cops—if they *were* cops—frisked the criminals and cuffed their arms behind them. One of the men from the car was hurt, and the cops dragged him bleeding and laid him on the ground. Other cops unloaded weapons and duffels from the car, placing the materiel in a line on the sidewalk, taking inventory with pencil and pad. Then they loaded the men who were against the wall, along with the bloody one, into the rear of the van before shutting its doors. The weapons were bundled into the trunk of the car before both car and van drove into the darkness, uptown.

In awe of the display of their power, I had stayed out of sight in the shadows.

23

Tea with Flower Children

I opened the building's glass front door. Stepping into the foyer and out of the cold, I found "Margo Rankin" on the list of tenants, written on a paper strip next to her buzzer.

I pushed the button and waited. I pushed the button again.

"Who is it?"

Her voice was grumpy, and I felt my stupidity. *Could she be with another man? Had she been dead asleep?*

"Uh, it's me."

"Who's me?"

"J-Bee."

"J-Bee? What time is it?"

"I don't know. Six maybe?"

She buzzed me in, and I ran up the stairs. She leaned in her doorway in a housecoat and slippers. "It's okay if you don't mind I'm a mess."

She was a goddess. I would be her lump of clay.

"Come in, now you're here."

I smelled the flaking plaster and the dust of old-time hot-water radiators.

"I've been walking," I said.

"Walking? Okay, young men need to walk sometimes. Sometimes they think better on the move. Where'd you go?"

"Down Broadway to 72nd."

"72nd? I know what that place is. Not drugs again, is it?"

"No, it's not drugs. I just couldn't sleep, and I ended up there. It was Billy. He was my friend, and now he's dead."

"Billy?"

"Billy Wing."

"Oh—you knew him? The kid in Hartley Hall?"

"Yeah. Him."

Out of the chaos of my emotions, I suddenly thought of something one of my professors had said about the purity of "The Word" according to Saint John, how enlightenment was the ability to transmit thought with total clarity through words. But I couldn't formulate words; I stood dumb as stone.

"I'm so sorry, J-Bee. Come and sit in the kitchen. Can I make you coffee?"

Could I let this woman past the barriers of my armor? Those heavy plates of defense that I had installed against the Sisters? Could I trust her with the underbelly of my soul?

"Let me take your coat," she said.

I opened my coat and took out the flowers. They were a bit squashed but the thin green paper seemed intact.

"These are for you," I said, thrusting them forward.

"For me?" she squeaked happily, which surprised me.

"For you."

Her eyes went wide as she took them.

"I wanted to thank you for looking after me the other night. You were very good to me."

Her eyes never left the flowers as she brought them to the counter and unwrapped them. "You shouldn't have," she said. "So thoughtful of you. They're beautiful." She examined them closely. "They're a bit rumpled—you had them under your coat!" She turned to me and giggled. "You silly! I'll put them in water. They'll be fine."

They did look a bit rumpled now that she mentioned it, and I felt rather pathetic, but Margo seemed happy, bustling industriously about her kitchen, finding a vase.

"I thought of getting you chocolate—"

"Did you? No, I love these. See?" she said standing back to admire her setting of the pompons in the vase. "They look great. Now sit down—I'll make that coffee."

I did as she told me. She prepared coffee, first attempting to straighten her hair and then curl it behind her ears. She rummaged through drawers, coming up with an elastic and tying her hair in a ponytail.

She served me a cup and sat facing me.

"You have such a nice place," I said.

"Are you all right, J-Bee?" She gazed into my face.

"I'm not sleeping well," I said, "but I'm happy just to sit here."

I asked her what she was doing lately.

"I'm doing a research project on the inequality of sentencing amongst different socioeconomic groups inherent in our criminal justice system. I'm working with a very hip professor at the law school."

"Nice," I said, but it didn't feel nice. I was jealous to hear about how wonderful she found some hotshot professor. "So what's your idea of 'hip'?"

"What kind of question is that?"

"If you make a statement with that much matter-of-fact conviction, I should be able to ask a simple question about it without you getting your knickers in a twist."

She pinched her face into a prunish wrinkle and glared. "What's this about knickers? I don't have knickers! You're a bit impertinent for six A.M., and I'm serving the coffee, not the other way 'round!"

"C'mon Margo, I'm kidding."

Her face was red, but she took a deep breath and burst out laughing.

"You should see the look on your face! God, you're funny."

After we had both laughed enough to clear the air, I took my chance to press for an answer to my original question.

"So what's this 'hip' thing about?"

"Hip? It means someone who 'gets' the counterculture. It means someone who understands and subscribes to the revolution we're living in. My law professor friend, he's not as stuffy as most lawyers. He's not shackled to the suit and tie uniform they all wear, and he sympathizes with liberal politics. He does high-profile criminal defense work."

"Probably gets paid pretty well."

"In some cases. But I know for a fact that he also does pro bono for political rebels who can't afford anything. Look, what you're saying sounds jaded, but let's be honest—you may be right. But why shouldn't he take credit for high-profile work? It helps his standing amongst the law faculty, and it helps with potential promotion. He earns money from wealthier clients while, at the same time, he helps indigent criminal defendants with the Legal Aid Society. He's part of the establishment, but he also reaches out. I respect that. When I'm admitted to the bar, I hope to bridge the gap between the elitist attitudes of the greediest attorneys and the idealism involved in helping those who cannot help themselves."

I admired her. Her analysis was evenhanded; her insight was clever and precise, and her values had to be applauded. Given her determination, I couldn't imagine that anything would stop her from fulfilling her dreams.

—⁓—

I asked her to breakfast, but she groaned and said no: "I've got toothpicks holding my eyelids open. Besides, I look terrible."

I headed out for eggs and potatoes and returned to my room for my books. Nebraska was gone, and the winter sunbathed the room in lemony yellows. Sleep-deprived and emotionally drained, I lay on my bed, locked safely in the dorm, unsure if I had enough energy to make it to class.

I slept. I awoke in dusk, my room awash in lavender gray. Out the window, the walkway lamps popped on, and waves of students poured through the plaza, exiting classes for the day. I was hung over from exhaustion, muscles flaccid from the deepness of sleep. I righted myself on the edge of my bed and raked fingers through my hair.

Again, I thought of Billy. I wasn't going back to his room, but I wanted to feel his presence. I left the dorm and walked across campus, descending the stone steps to the crypt of The Apocalypse Café. I would sit with his long-haired gentle-minded brothers, peaceniks and flower children, whom I might never understand because of our divergent states of mind: their inner peace and my instinctual, lingering, subsurface tension. I eagerly hoped that the simple act of sitting near his friends would allow me to absorb their serenity and rid myself of my preoccupation for vengeance. Irrationally I hoped even further that they might exorcise my recurring hallucinogenic echoes. In honor of Billy Wing, as if at a wake, I sat quietly and had a cup of tea, an uneasy labor in view of my recent experience.

Without introduction, a silhouette appeared behind a diaphanous screen, and the figure of The Serpent spoke to us in faded tones, his voice damped by the stones which were hewn into blocks and built into walls all around us.

"I am talking to you, O My Brothers, about the death of a fellow collegian, one of your own found ripening, rotting, decomposing at his desk. The smell was so strong that the blood hounds of the police were howling as soon as they entered the building.

"He had a needle in his arm. He had succumbed to the devils of heroin, a scourge in this city, but also a scourge to our boys in Nam. You and those boys are churning through separate and distinct societal mills—you in an Ivy League university, poring over books at desks and libraries; they in the United States Army, toting guns, sweating bullets, trudging through jungles and paddies. You and they are destiny's twins, two faces of Janus, door to the world. You and they are heads and tails of the same coin, currency of The Military Industrial Complex. You and they have come into this world the same, naked and exposed without defense to the elements, screaming bloody murder, society's imprint stamped on your rumps forever. And you and they will leave it the same, dying the same, fodder for the lilies in Flanders Fields, by knife, gun and overdose.

"I see that your generation is beset with a terrible conundrum at its core, a conundrum which creates a polemic at the very heart of this age. It is everywhere in the media, pitting two groups of men against each other by creating a false and baffling argument. It is tearing you apart—you and they who should stand in solidarity against the forces of injustice in this world but who instead stand on either side of the rift we call enmity. One group of you is calling the other 'cowards' and 'un-American,' while the other is calling the first the stupid lackeys of imperialism. I tell you it's all rhetoric, generated from a smoke screen being used to make two sides out of the same, exploited generation of men. It is divide and conquer, a strategy of the powerful elite. I am telling you that you and these boys, fighting in the sweltering heat of Indochina, are brothers and should see each other as such. There is no time for animosity and distrust between you. Flip a coin, and you could be them. Pick a lottery number, and you *are* them. Whatever differences you may have between you are as thin and evanescent as gossamer thread in the endless fabric of cosmic time.

"So, you may ask, who is killing you boys, poisoning your souls with hate, death and war? Turning you one against the other as each of you strive to serve what values are best in this painful, throbbing world?

"Should we believe *CBS News* who says you are fighting for different causes? Should we believe the *New York Times* who says you are champions of different factions? I tell you to look deep within yourselves for the answers. I tell you that you should not drink from the well of the media for truth for they will only sell you the cheap lies they purvey.

"So should we believe Nixon and his cronies, who sit in plush chairs around long tables, gathering wind to assail our ears with polished, duplicitous rhetoric? God knows what any of them are saying, My Brothers, but whatever they may say, they do it to retain control.

"I advise you this: say *no* to it all because if you hearken to what they say, you will kill one another which is tantamount to killing yourselves."

24

Jump

What was he telling me, this Serpent? His words and voice were suffused with import and seemed familiar. It felt like he was speaking to me personally, telling me that what happened to Billy paralleled what was happening to the boys in Vietnam. More specifically, it was a parable about Gilly and me—we were exploitable, interchangeable, and seemingly expendable.

Margo had told me to meet her at the West End Bar, away from her cronies at The Rail. So I went a bit early and took a booth in the back room where old men played jazz in the evenings. I had no idea what she wanted, but it made no difference. I grimaced at the certainty that whatever she bade me do, I would do it. I was her obedient servant or slave, more like, if she wanted one. I was powerless to do otherwise.

I scanned the place for familiar faces, but saw none. A gaggle of waitresses stood at a corner of the bar; I raised my hand for attention.

One came over.

"Waiting for someone, hon?"

I thought she winked.

"Uh, yeah."

"She cute?"

She pulled out her pad and pencil, staring at me, her arms pressed inward against her breasts making them swell under that black leotard top that waitresses often wore.

"Got a Rolling Rock?"

"A-course."

I pulled out Machiavelli's *The Prince*, required reading for philosophy class. I tried to read, waiting for beer, the jazz wafting gently in air. The music relaxed me, and in a minute, I was lost, pondering the Italian's dog-eat-dog world and the vengeance I took in the vacant lot near Bolduc's. Then I thought of a man whose shortie black tie and prep school patina cultivated a nonthreatening facade to hide the lizard underneath.

I closed my eyes. I recalled my friend Billy, his long hair and bell-bottoms, the peace symbol around his neck. He had lost everything. I put my face down on the table, my nose in the crease of the open book, letting my arms dangle. I dreamed until I heard a voice, tinkling like wind chimes on grandma's veranda back home. It lifted my heart.

"You all right?"

I felt her sit across from me, but I didn't lift my head. Her voice was enough. If I looked at her, I would be lost in the vision of her, and it would distract me from the pleasure I had from her voice alone.

"J-Bee, please look at me."

I sat up.

"Coming here was a bad idea," she said, glancing at the waitresses who stared back.

"It was?"

"But we're here, so what the hey."

"Right," I said. "What the hey."

The waitress came over, and Margo ordered a gin and tonic.

"You don't like this place?" I asked.

"I prefer The Gold Rail, of course."

"So let's go to The Rail."

"It's not that," she said. "I don't want them to see me with you too many times. I like to keep my private life private, you know?"

I had no idea what was going on, but I nodded my head as if I did. "So why is it a bad idea to be *here*?"

"It's not really a bad idea. I mean, I *feel* like it's a bad idea meeting *you* like this."

I was crushed. "You do?"

"Well, no. Not really."

I'm sure she knew, from the look on my face, that I was baffled. I stared at the walls, and neither of us spoke until the waitress returned with her gin.

"This is not going according to plan," she said and drank it half down. "I need to buck up my nerve."

"What do you mean, *buck up your nerve*?"

"I need more alcohol."

She called for the waitress and ordered another. I was still nursing the same Rolling Rock.

"Alcohol's good," I said. "Why're you nervous?"

"Why do I feel like this?" she asked herself.

"Feel like what?"

"I'm a grown, experienced woman. I'm not sure I want this."

"What don't you want?"

"I can't feel this way about you. But it's an emotional fact—*I just do*. No point in hiding it. No point in playing with you."

I was shocked. This was not expected. I could feel my body and mind move from disappointed lethargy to an acute hyper-awareness as hope reentered my system.

"But I'm angry at you."

"Angry? Why? What did I do?"

She looked at me like an adult looks at a child who was lost but now is found.

"Nothing. You didn't do anything. Except that you made me feel this way."

"It's my fault? Christ, I didn't have a clue. I'm really sorry."

"You silly; don't say you're sorry. Come over and sit next to me."

I got up and moved to her side of the table. She edged closer and put her arm around my shoulders.

"What I have for you, it's the kind of feeling—okay, love—that can screw up your life. You give the other person power over you, and he can crush you."

I was stunned. I wanted to get up and do cartwheels even though I had never been able to do them. Then a horrible thought occurred to me—perhaps Margo was kidding. I was an easy and inexperienced target, and she could be toying with me. She could lead me anywhere and then laugh at my gullibility, an idea that struck me with fear. I felt my emotional self shrink away, putting up walls for protection.

"That's how you feel about me?" I asked.

"Why the surprise?"

"I don't know. You never show it. How do you know that's how you feel?"

"Oh, gosh. Do I tell you? Where's my gin."

I'd never seen her drink anything but an occasional Chardonnay, but there she was, having another slug of gin. She was more than nervous—she was panicked, and I suddenly reverted to a rational man and left my emotions behind. No, Margo was not playing—how could I ever have imagined that she might play with another's feelings? She was as genuine a person as I'd ever known, and I realized she was saying she loved me.

I sat like a paralyzed lump. I waited for her to continue, scared to death. This was all new to me, to be loved by a woman. And not just any woman—a woman whom I thought to be both brilliant and desirable. She was so far ahead of me; I didn't stand a chance. I was vulnerable in front of her, and I knew this had to change fast if I were to meet the challenge.

"When you're in the room," she said, "I get some kind of hormonal storm. My brain short-circuits, and I don't think straight. I'm all humid like the tropics."

"How?" was all I could mouth. Sex with this goddess just seemed much too advanced, but she had planted an image in my head, an image of misty heat, a flooded sinkhole veiled in lush jungle undergrowth, sticky and moist like rain forests after a downpour. I glanced at her, the hair eddying in rivulets to her shoulders, and I trembled with the thought of all she had hidden. I was dumbfounded by fantasy, and all I could mumble was, "Oh, right. A physical thing?"

"Well, there's that. But it's more than that. You may be raw, but you're honest, and that's rare. And you're intelligent. Analytic. Then you've got this Southern accent when you explain things to me." She arched her eyebrows. "That accent really came at me from nowhere. It's not heavy or redneck; it's genteel. Wasn't expecting it. And then you're willful. You have ambition. You have a moral compass too. No question—there's a lot going on in there."

She caressed the side of my head with her palm and fingers; it took me totally by surprise. It was a spectacular feeling of such well-being that I involuntarily shut my eyes and emitted a low-pitched glottic hum with every stroke of her hand.

"You like that!" she said in a high-pitched giggle.

"I do," I said. "So how do you see all this in me?"

"I've been watching you. I'm not stupid. You have a hold on me, which I like but don't like. I'm not used to it. I've got my own ambition. Gosh, why am I saying this? This is hard. It's like confessional."

There it was, finally—I was her confessor! She was confessing as I sat, eunuchoid, with a miter on my head. I was sitting in the finery of silk embroidered costumes, my hands folded neatly in my lap, listening to the sins of a young woman, saying, "Yes, my child."

"You're Catholic?" I asked. "I'm Catholic."

"No, I'm not Catholic." She thought about it. "The use of the word 'confessional' was a metaphor. Actually I'm Jewish."

It was all new. I wasn't at Columbia to meet bomb-throwing Jew-boys after all. I was there to meet bomb-throwing Jew-*girls*.

"Okay," I said. "Okay. What now?"

"Do you like me?"

"Yes. Of course. Maybe I even love you, but I'm not sure what that means."

"Well," she said, "then I guess you should come up to my place."

—m—

I lay on my back, bathed in the grays of urban night. Slats of light filtered in from the lamps on the avenue, projecting across the ceiling in diagonal beams. Blushes of red and white were moving in other directions across the ceiling, coming and going, accompanying noises of tires on wet asphalt.

Margo's face nuzzled the side of my chest, under my arm. Her breath brushed against me in feathery waves; her arm was draped over my chest.

I purred, not daring to move.

She murmured inaudibly.

"Hmmm?" I responded.

"I said your hair's getting longer. I like it."

"Uh-huh."

"And why aren't you wearing a cross? I thought Catholics wore crosses."

"I used to wear a cross," I said.

"Not anymore? Does that mean you've lost your innocence? An exile from The Garden?"

"Yeah, I suppose. The Sisters would say I've fallen from Grace."

Would I tell this woman how I fell? Of my torment at the hands of the Sisters? Of my tainted soul and evil deeds?

"The Sisters?" She touched her tongue to the side of my chest. "What flavor am I today?"

"Tell me," she said, "about the Sisters."

"The nuns."

"They were nuns?"

"I still can't figure out whether they gave me hell because they knew—in that holy, preordained way—that I was destined to be damned and so deserved to be punished. Or maybe they were intrinsically evil themselves and had wandered from the path of righteousness of their own accord, just people using God as a pretext to exact abuse against us boisterous boys.

"Or maybe there is no God. Maybe none of it really matters. Maybe the Church and the Sisters, the priests, and even the bishops, the cardinals and the almighty Pope himself make the rules on earth merely to empower themselves while appearing righteous as they hide behind cloaks and finery. I don't know about *all* of them, but some of them are greedy, piggy-faced toads, beating children and feeding off the nickels and dimes of the poor."

"Were you beaten, J-Bee?"

I nodded. I remembered their hard faces, their mouths taut in the grimace of attack. I remembered getting hit, but it was the faces which told me I was an object of hatred.

"What did it do to you?" she asked, worried. "Did it twist you inside? Did it deform your soul?"

"Probably."

She sat up, propped herself on her arm and looked at me. She passed her hand over my chest, over the soft hair, and it felt good.

I reached for her and kissed her. I stroked the curves of her buttocks and thighs, coming to rest on the fur of her deepest recesses. I wanted her. I wanted her, and I didn't want to share her with any other man. She had transported me to underground secret passages, to grottoes secretly shrouding limpid, tropical waters, surrounded by the lush vegetation of the paradise that was her. I was lost in her, and love flowed from me like a river. It was powerful, and whether it lasted ten minutes or for all of eternity, there was no mistaking what I had discovered.

"Tell me a story, J-Bee. Tell me the story of your life before you got here."

"There's a lot to tell."

"There's always a lot to tell, and if you don't start, you'll never tell it."

She had me cornered. I would be baring the tender underbelly of my soul at the risk of being sliced to ribbons. If I confessed and revealed my story, it would rip from me like a torrent, and there would be no way of stopping it.

I wanted to protest. I bleated like a sheep, "You haven't told me a thing about *you*."

She said nothing. I got a pair of cow's eyes.

"You want me to trust you?" I managed to say.

"It's hard, I know. It's harder the more you have to hide."

I looked at her, the imp, now smiling with her face on my chest, licking me again.

"It's like mushrooms on your burger," she said. "It's a new adventure in the terrifying labyrinth of life. Will you find a monster lurking in the maze? A tantalizing siren who will drown you? Or will you find the woman of your dreams, a woman who may protect you from the storms of life and more? Yes, J-Bee—trust a woman, and you may be injured, damaged, maimed beyond recognition. Trust a woman, and you have everything to lose. But think what you might gain: understanding, sympathy, and an end to the solitude, loneliness and emptiness that is the hallmark of a hermetic male life."

I looked at her again, my mind squirming like a worm on a hook.

"Christ, that is well put." It came out like a groan from a man who knew his destiny and had no power to alter its course.

"The cliff is there," she said. "Jump."

I looked at her in horror.

"Oh what the hell, J-Bee. Go and jump! What do you have to lose besides everything?"

I was in the grip of an intangible thing, pushing me ever forward like a lemming to the cliffs, promising elation while subjecting me to extreme risk, taking away all rational thought and laughing at my powerlessness. I stumbled forward and leapt from the precipice, and my life plunged into free fall. I told her that I was the son of a naval officer from Norfolk. I told her about my best friend, Gilly O'Daly, who went to Vietnam. I told her how I was beaten by the nuns and how their rigid behavioral rules got under my skin like bugs in my pajamas and how I lost it, acted out, rebelled and railed against authority. I told her how it made me do all kinds of "bad" things, and when I acted out, I paid for it with my skin. I didn't want to tell her more because I was afraid that I might lose her, that she might reject me; yet I couldn't stop. Something within me wanted to be heard, forcing me to continue so that I finally told her what only Gilly knew: I had committed what society calls a felony and what the Church calls mortal sin; I had taken revenge against my brother's killers with full premeditation, ambushing them in a violent and savage act. Within the entire span of my young life, it may have been isolated as an act of depravity, but it was the one exception to my behavior that made me a sinner; it was the moment with the single most powerful impact on my soul.

I told Margo everything about the planning and beating of Stankewicz and Laureen and how it changed my world. It was this event, I explained, that had been the catalyst for my choosing Columbia, a place where I imagined the forces of Good and Evil would come face to face and battle for my soul.

When I had finished, Margo lifted herself from my chest and, kissing my forehead, said, "I had no idea that being a Catholic was so difficult." Then she hugged me and didn't let go.

It had a strong effect. There was a trumpeting within me that shook the fortress walls of my soul until they tumbled down in submission, allowing light to penetrate where it had been absent a very long time. Then the tumbling of the walls became the quaking of the earth, and the quaking of the earth became the convulsing of my torso. I was horrified—how could the telling of my story, the trusting of another soul, have such an effect? How could I be sobbing so uncontrollably without the power to stop?

25

Nebraska's Dilemma

Margo and I got along. She made me talk, and she was a good listener. I was blind to whatever it was that I gave her in return, that made her so interested in me, but there must have been something. Perhaps it was because she was curious and had a free, unfiltered look into the mind of a male who was too dumb to put up defenses. Perhaps it was simply because she was creative, and I was such a wet lump of clay that she could mold me however she liked. Or perhaps, dare I say it? Perhaps it was because I was young and full blooded, a testosterone-ridden Southern boy replete with the occasional hormone-induced acne, and she wanted her sex with rockets and firecrackers.

No matter. But when I asked her, "Why me?" she giggled about how my accent turned her to jelly. I really didn't believe her because the Norfolk accent isn't too strong, and I supposed it was all a tease on her part, yet my adoration for her left me no choice but to trust her as she led me around by the nose. It was stress and excitement to know that I was her man while *not* knowing if, at any minute, she would cut me loose to float away into emptiness, adrift on a deep green desolate sea of unknown consequences, as lonely as a sailless dinghy in a storm amidst whitecaps and sharks.

One afternoon, humming with satisfaction, I arrived from class at the threshold of my room and heard voices inside. I ducked back into the hallway and listened.

"What're you talking about?" said Nebraska's muffled voice. "You owe me."

I knew the second voice; the hair stood up on my neck.

"You sold me some grass," said Nebraska, "and I paid."

"You didn't."

"I paid MacNeish."

"What's MacNeish got to do with it?"

"He said he went to school with you. He said he collected money for you. Why should I pay twice?"

"You borrowed from *me*. You pay *me*. It's not complicated."

"I shouldn't have to pay twice—it's un-American."

"Can you dig this? You owe me, so pay. Or you'll find yourself lying in Morningside Park with a couple of broken legs. And don't even think to rat me out—nobody can help you. It's your word against mine, and I'm well connected. I've done nothing you haven't done: smoked a little marijuana, got a little rowdy. If you say anything, I'll sue you for smearing me, and my father has lawyers."

I glanced around the doorjamb and saw a tall man with straight, white hair to his shoulders and a shortie black tie. There were love beads around his neck. He held my roomie by the throat of his shirt, thrusting him against the wall so that only his toes touched the floor.

"I don't have any more money! It took a lot to get the money that I paid MacNeish. Ask him. How can you get money from me if I don't have any?"

"Just watch me. You really think some prairie dog can stop me? I'll fuck you up the ass for fun, and *then* you'll damn well pay me."

"Put me down. This is way uncool."

"I want to hear you agree."

Nebraska licked his lips. "All right," he said, "I'll pay."

"That's more like it," said Milo, and he let Nebraska down.

Nebraska straightened his collar and said, "Can you give me a receipt?"

"What planet are you from? No receipt. But if you want, you can work to pay it off."

The faces of my brother, Jerry, and Billy Wing rushed my head; I felt a force from within compel me to thwart any threat to Nebraska.

"Fucking Milo!" I said, stepping through the door, the words erupting.

He didn't turn, but he knew it was me.

"Lay off!" I said.

Milo turned from Nebraska and faced me. "You're a nice guy, J-Bee. You and I understand each other. Things got a little out of hand, right? No harm done."

"Get out," I said.

"This isn't your business," he said, narrowing his eyes and pointing at me. "*You* need to keep out of this."

I wanted to kill him; I wanted to rip him to pieces. With the sudden power of steam expanding in a boiler, I jumped, howling uncontrollably, and attacked him, swinging and landing both fists with force, one after the other. He wasn't ready and fell backward with a shout, whacking his head on the floor. I landed half on top of him, putting my elbow in the center of his face. Somehow he got to his knees and was behind me, and I felt a blow to the side of my head. The room grayed; I saw bright flashes of light. I heard the universe shudder, a vibration rippling the ethers of the cosmos like a pebble warping the glassy surface of a pond. Planets orbiting through space for billions of years skipped over the micro-perturbations of my violence.

My vision returned, but I was kicked between the shoulder blades, snapping my neck back and knocking the wind out of me. I gasped once and then coughed, but I didn't taste blood. I heard him make a guttural rasp, and then I heard him spit. A warm gel hit my face, lumpy and sticky on my fingers when I instinctively reached to swipe it.

He stepped over me on his way to the door and said, "Maybe we're even; maybe we're not. You better keep looking over your shoulder."

I heard Nebraska shouting as I lay in a fetal position on the floor, painful bells clanging my brain. I kept my eyes shut, unsure how long. As my senses reclaimed me, I opened my eyes, face throbbing, and I saw Nebraska sitting on his bed, his head slumped forward, hands in his hair, whimpering.

"Where's Milo?" I asked.

"My God—you hurt him! Why did you *do* that? You're a fucking madman!"

"Where did he go?"

"God, I'm in trouble! But you—you're out of control!"

"Nebraska, where's Milo?"

"He ran out. He was clutching his head. His nose was bleeding."

I rolled on my back and closed my eyes again, horrified at the inner mechanisms that could allow me to undertake actions both unpredictable and immoral. As my head pulsed with hammering in the nerve endings of my skull, I realized that Milo was now the enemy and that I would always have to be looking over my shoulder, ready for aggression. I laughed out loud at the paradox, though it hurt my head—I was living in a male hierarchy in which reticence to fight went against evolutionary instinct while, at the same time, that very same reticence was the key to preserving societal peace.

"Why are you laughing?" asked Nebraska with concern. "Are you all right?"

"Christ, my head hurts. What the hell was that about?"

"He said I owe him money. He wants me to work for him, to pay him back."

"I thought you said you paid MacNeish?"

"Yeah, I did, and now I'll have to pay Milo."

I had a flashback: MacNeish and Bornes were having a conversation in the hall as I was passing by. It was only a fragment, but it stuck in my head.

"We all work for Milo," MacNeish was saying.

"I don't," said Bornes.

"Milo thinks you do. I tell you, Bobby, it's a risky business. It's your choice of course. He may be your friend, but you know the risks."

Fuckin' MacNeish.

—ᗰ—

Nebraska didn't look good. He was beginning to realize he was tangled in something he shouldn't be, and I was in it too.

"How much do you owe?" I was nauseated now, and my head still pounded. I reached up, and it was tender.

"Not much."

"Christ, Nebraska, what the hell for?"

"I bought some pot, and he loaned me the money. I didn't know he would charge me twice with loan shark interest. I mean, out on the plains, we have fields of the shit, growing wild. It's all free to anyone who gets off his ass, drives out to the country, snags a few shoots and dries them out. No one charges interest for pot. No one makes a fuss. It's like living off the fat of the land. Everybody's part owner. Sort of."

"Just don't work for him. I'll give you the money. No interest."

"I couldn't do that."

"Yeah, you could. And I think you'd better."

"Why? Maybe I *should* work for him. He's not a bad guy."

"Are you stoned?"

"Usually."

"Didn't you just hear what he said? Don't you see what he is? He'd step on his grandmother's face for a nickel."

"He would?"

"You're a space cadet! Are you tripping? Do you have any judgment at all?"

I wanted to tell him what I knew about Milo. I wanted to tell him that I thought Milo and his thugs had killed Billy Wing. I wanted to tell him that he was being recruited to take Billy's place, but I knew that I couldn't. No one could know that I pegged Milo for Billy's death, not until I knew exactly what I was going to do about it, and that would mean that I had to be absolutely certain that Milo was a killer. It would not be enough that it was logical and that I had a conviction of his guilt.

"I like to see the good in people," he said. "I'm a hippie through and through."

"Yeah, but you won't survive long like that."

"Maybe not. That's what my mother says. She always says I'm too soft-hearted."

"Listen, I know things about this guy."

"Like what?"

"You wouldn't want to know after I told you, and I don't want to tell you. It's bad information."

"Maybe you're right," said Nebraska. "He scares me. He threatened me! He warned me not to tell anyone, so please, J-Bee, don't repeat it."

"You don't have to worry about *me*—I took a punch for you, in case you hadn't noticed. Damn good punch too. My head's killing me."

"I noticed. You're gonna have a shiner."

"I stuck my neck out for you, so listen to me. It'll be worse if you work for him because you'll be in his power; he'll have his hooks in you."

"Fine. I won't. I just don't get what you've got on him. I'd like to know what I'm up against. But at the same time, I'm tempted to work for him because I could use the money."

"The money? What's with that? The kind of money he'd give you wouldn't solve any problems unless you make a *career* selling dope. And that's if he pays what he says he'll pay. Which he won't. You can't trust him. Do something else for money. Go to the bank. Get a loan. Get an honest job. Anything!"

"I don't know."

"*I* know. Think what he could do if you worked for him. You couldn't tell anyone anything because it's illegal. You couldn't tell the cops if he got violent. You wouldn't be able to tell the dean's office either. Stay away while he's got nothing on you because once you've done something illegal, you'll be all alone. And he'll know that. You'll be in his grip. He'll own you."

"Okay," he said. "Okay."

But I wasn't sure what he'd do. His willpower was no stiffer than the stem of a daisy. He was an optimist who lived on the path of least resistance, a flower child who reminded me of Jerry in some ways and Billy in others, bringing out my protective instincts so that in the end, I scraped the money together and shoved it in his pocket.

26

Lottery

The alarm rang to get up for class. My head ached, my belly was empty, and my bladder was full. I slapped the alarm and cracked my eyes: Nebraska was across the room, comatose. I sat upright, head in a fog, scratching and yawning, fighting the urge to flop back on the bed. It was ritual, ending in the miracle of waking on my feet, walking toward coffee or sitting at a desk, amazed at how I'd put on my pants and pulled on my shirt prior to consciousness.

I left my room to encounter young men swarming the hallway, roving back and forth, laughing and shouting, overflowing with joy or buzzing with panic. Guys whom I hadn't seen since freshman orientation were milling around, hooting with upraised voices and gesticulating hands. It was a scene that reeled me in to where the bodies were densest, near the TV at the end of the hall which blared the morning news.

It was too much activity at too early an hour. Groaning at the barrage of invasive sound and light, I slammed into Kemp who was running at speed.

"It's February third!"

"Okay," I said, my head still spinning. "Yesterday was Groundhog Day."

He flapped his hand in derision and resumed his run.

I heard Dan Rather on the tube, "The draft is the only thing left in society, other than taxes, that forces Americans to do something against their will. This year has something new—young men previously exempt from the draft because of student deferments no longer have that exemption. This year, for the first time, they are eligible to be drafted."

Harris, Melberg and Bornes were poring over the *New York Times*.

"Fucking thank God," said Harris. "I'm 299!"

He jumped and whooped, punching the air.

"Christ," said Melberg. "The nightmare is happening. It's a lottery for who gets the black spot. Cancer. It's me."

"What'd you get?"

"Forty-six."

"Man, that's bad."

"Cheer up," said Bornes. "You'll be all right." His back was to me, and he was in a sweatshirt with the hoodie over his head, but I knew the voice.

"I'm doomed," said Melberg. "I'll run to Canada. Toronto."

"They call it Pigtown," said Bornes. "The pigs come in on trains from Saskatchewan, and they run them through the streets from the stockyards to the slaughterhouses. Sad little piggies never see what's ahead, never see what's going to kill them."

"They call it *Hogtown*—not Pigtown!" said Harris.

Bornes smiled. "I like Pigtown better. It has a ring."

"Pigtown sounds about right—I'll go to Pigtown."

"What're you complaining about?" said Potts over his shoulder. "Have you heard about Steinson? Bobby, tell 'em about Steinson."

Everyone looked at Bornes.

"Steinson? Big Buck Steinson?"

"That's right."

"It's true," said Bornes. "Everything you heard is true."

"What's true?"

"Spill it."

"All right," said Bornes. "Calm down." He lit a cigarette and took a deep inhalation, holding it in and blowing it out. "Steinson's left school. He's not coming back."

"Why the hell not?"

"His draft number is three."

"Three? Like one, two, three?"

"Yeah," said Bornes, nodding. "That's the one. Three. He left last night after the numbers were announced."

"He's fried."

"He's as good as drafted."

"But his father's a general!"

"At the Pentagon," said Bornes. "So Buck's joining the National Guard. Or the Coast Guard. He told me his father's going to get him stationed in El Paso or the Chesapeake Bay. Someplace safe to sit out the war."

"Nice to have a father who's a four-star general."

"He's not a four-star general," said Potts. "He's three stars."

"Who the fuck cares?" said Melberg. "I'd take a father with two stars."

"I'm up for adoption," said Fishkin, who wandered over. "My number's not so hot."

"I'm going to Toronto. We can go together."

The TV droned, and I heard tidbits from the talking heads. "Middle-class boys are being drafted, and they don't want to fight . . . Casualties are mounting . . . Kids from down the street are being killed and maimed . . . Officers being murdered by their own troops . . . Dead bodies in coffins going home."

"It's half-assed, the whole thing," said Melberg. "No one's ever declared war."

"Not officially," said Bornes. "Congress has never declared war in Vietnam. In Korea, at least we were complying with a UN Resolution."

"That's not entirely true," said Potts, now out of his seat and standing with the rest of us. "The 1964 Gulf of Tonkin Resolution was a formal approval of action in Vietnam by the executive branch. Though as you said, it's no declaration of war."

"You know everything, don't you, Potts."

"Who cares?" said Fishkin. "It's chicanery. Political sophistry. There seems to be logic, then poof! There's no logic at all. It's all quicksand."

"How the hell can we go from Woodstock to Nam, just like that?" asked Melberg. "I was at Woodstock three years ago. Sweet sixteen, smoking dope, dropping sunshine. Whatever happened to my misspent youth?"

"It's over—whatever's left of your youth will be spent in rice paddies with foot rot."

"Or worse."

"That's right, little piggy," said Bornes, talking to Melberg but winking at me. "Now there's a good boy. You run to Canada like you promised." He flapped the back of his hand at Melberg to shoo him away. "No one wants to be the last to die in Nam, just before we lose the war and leave Southeast Asia in disgrace. You can join the National Guard—that's what they're doing at Yale."

"I heard you can't just join the National Guard to avoid being drafted."

"You can if your father's a four-star general."

"Three stars."

Dan Rather was speaking again, "Morale is low . . . Drug problems on base . . . Marijuana on the increase . . . GIs addicted to heroin . . ."

"So what's your number, J-Bee?" asked Melberg.

It was a bucket of ice water. I was finally awake, facing the reality that I was in it, like them. I was a cog—we all were—caught in the gears of history. The irony was that I had grown up with the mindset of a warrior; it was my self-image. Yet something wasn't right. A warrior had to have the power of choice; it was part of being a warrior. One could choose to join the fight, and that commitment enhanced one's prowess in battle. Now, however, I had no control, no choice. The government had the power to use my body, break me down and rebuild me, put me in jungles and drench me with toxic defoliants raining from jets overhead. I'd be government property, ripped out of school, shipped overseas, a body with a pulse and a dog tag, thrust in front of the enemy for slaughter.

Fear rose within me. My heart palpitated. How was it that I, son of an admiral, brought up to uphold the might of my country, could feel such fear? I wasn't alone. Not only the boys in the TV room but also big Buck Steinson, son of a three-star general, was afraid and had bolted.

Politicians, as Fishkin had said, clearly were not to be trusted. Energetic men, speaking from both sides of their mouths, always for personal gain. JFK himself, charismatic as he was, spent World War II on *PT-109*, a Coast Guard boat, seemingly to avoid the horrific fighting in the Pacific. Someone had written a book about him, a biography before his election. Inside it, I had seen photos of him, shirtless with big white teeth, sunglasses and a fabulous tan, lolling on the deck of his boat. Later, it was he, this same JFK, who sent the very first combat advisors to Vietnam, just as the occupying French were leaving, opening the floodgates so that American boys like Melberg, Steinson and me could get drafted and go there to die.

"I don't know my number," I said.

"God, J-Bee, what happened to the side of your face?"

It was Milo's mark.

"You look like you walked into a lamppost!" Bornes laughed. "You must have been pretty stoned."

"Forget it," I said, my head clanging for coffee. "I'm okay."

"You don't look okay."

"Tell me your birthday," said Melberg. "I'll look it up. Or take a look in the paper. The numbers are listed by birth date."

I looked up and saw their eyes upon me. I glowered, but I was caught, not knowing in advance how I might feel but suddenly unwilling to tell them my birthday. I felt my fate was a private thing, and it surprised me to feel this way. It made no sense, but it wasn't their business.

But then again, why not? Why wasn't it their business? Weren't we all in it together?

No, we weren't. This was a circus, and each of us played a sideshow for the others, a perverted, impertinent sideshow in which each drama unfolded, and the character of each man was unmasked. How we received the news, how we reacted, what our resolve was—all of our personal inner workings were paraded in front of the others. Who were the clowns, who were the winners, who were the losers, the cowards, the patriots, the philosophers. It was all on show for a laugh, and the stakes were never higher.

I didn't want to play. I was outraged that they expected me to reveal myself, show them who I was; it was none of their business. No, they weren't my brothers. The diversity of our fates broke the bonds of our mutual allegiance. Some of us would be free to pursue our educations while others would be hauled off to the front. Others would run for the hills. If we were brothers, as The Serpent had said, then we would empathize and console one another, but we had not learned the lesson. Some of us rejoiced at the demise of our peers; others of us were solely self-focused, unable to sympathize with our comrades.

I didn't like what I was witnessing, and I reconsidered. Perhaps my initial reaction of pride and resentment wasn't right. Even if we fulfilled the stereotype of insensitive louts, even if we were a generation professing one thing but behaving another, all our souls were still in the same cauldron together. Whether we realized our commonality or not, our ability or inability to see that we were in chains together could not change the fact that we were all one generation of men, exploited by the times, helpless to take our lives in our hands in the face of a greater power. I saw we were linked after all, and I would have to join them.

I eyed Bornes, who was entirely devoid of empathy, and asked, "What's the cutoff?"

"About 90 or 100. Maybe 110."

"No one really knows," said Harris. "It can change from year to year. It depends on the number of boys they need."

"August 19th, 1953," I said, standing with the others, facing what I had to face, grim and serious like every other bewildered young man, all of us beautiful miracles of God, all of us bound one way or another to extinction.

"Your number's 105, J-Bee, right on the cusp."

"You're in limbo. No telling if you're headed to paradise or hell in a handbasket."

I knew what it meant, this limbo. My number wasn't high enough to guarantee I wouldn't be drafted, and it wasn't low enough to force me to choose between running to Canada or waiting for the government to ship me overseas. It could go either way—it was a lottery, a game devoid of reason while paradoxically infusing meaning into randomness. My destiny hung upon its outcome, my lack of choice was vexatious, but my inability to know my future was alarming. I wanted my uncertainty resolved so I could decompress and make concrete plans for the future; instead, my life remained chained to the game.

I went back to my room after the day's classes to write Gilly. He would understand. I wrote about the death of Billy Wing and how it made me feel both sad and vulnerable. I confessed that Billy had foreseen his own demise and that I had done nothing to help him. I recounted how Milo had dosed me with LSD and how I suspected him of killing my friend. I wrote about Miguel and the preppies and how Milo went after Nebraska. I described how I knocked Milo down and how I saw stars when he punched me. I wrote how he had threatened me, and that it was possible that one of us might kill the other.

Unloading my woes made me feel better, so I wrote how the lottery made my future an unknown prospect: I might continue at school or be shipped to Nam. I wrote about Melberg and Pigtown, Steinson and the National Guard, and Fishkin vacillating between cutting off his fingers or undergoing a sex change operation in Sweden. I also mentioned a guy named Bellis who was talking about declaring himself a conscientious objector, like Muhammed Ali. "Maybe I'll go to jail, or maybe I won't, but anything's better than Nam."

"You're not Muhammad Ali," said Bornes. "You're too frail. You'll get tied to a bedpost and gang raped in prison, and then you'll wish you'd served your country."

"No, I won't."

"I'd rather die with honor in Nam," said Bornes, "than get fucked up the ass by felons."

Worse than the torment at the hands of the Sisters, the idea of being sodomized was harrowing. It was the total capitulation of masculinity; it was disempowerment, humiliation and castration. There was also physical pain to remind one of the helplessness involved in rape, the total loss of honor and identity. I had to stop and wonder about the innate male hierarchy of force. The truth seemed to be that the world was the way Bornes drew it—and my father too—relentless, unyielding and brutal.

I mailed the letter, which eased my stress. I had resolved nothing, but facts don't matter when one feels relief. I was blind to the idea that reason might have little impact on my emotional state and that, conversely, emotional well-being might be impervious to reason. All that was important was to grab my coat and head to The Rail where I might find Bloom and celebrate limbo with a beer.

When I arrived, Bloom was alone in a booth. He beckoned.

"What happened to your face?"

"I walked into a lamppost."

"Looks more like you walked into a left hook."

"A guy was picking on my roommate," I shrugged. "I had a small fight."

"Did you hurt *him*?"

"I hit him; he hit me. We both walked away, but I'll be looking over my shoulder. He won't like that I hit him."

"Anything I can do?"

I shook my head no.

"Hungry?" he asked. "Dinner's on me."

He waved to the waitress, and I ordered a Rolling Rock, brewed in flag-waving Latrobe, Pennsylvania. I ordered a burger with swiss cheese and mushrooms.

"What's with the mushrooms?"

"One of the ladies who works here told me to walk on the wild side and taste the mushrooms. I tried it; I liked it."

"Really," he said. "Impressionable, tender youth. Bet I know which one said that."

"Where's Margo?" I asked. "I don't see her around."

"Why so interested?"

"I like her."

"You like her? She's a bit old for you." He narrowed his eyes. "And seeing as you just sat down, you should do the polite thing and ask how *I've* been."

I said I was sorry and asked how he was. He surprised me by saying he had prostate cancer "riddling my bones." He said he refused the therapy that "the goddamn white-coated doctors wanted to give me."

"Refused?" I asked. "Why'd you do that?"

"I don't like to tell you because it's embarrassing. But I'm going to tell you because you're a man, and you need to know the decisions we're forced to make. Also I've got no one else to tell."

I was shocked by the news but touched by the sudden intimacy of our relationship. I liked him, and now I felt bad for him.

"You can trust me," I said.

"I bought you off with that mushroom burger. I know how it is." He looked at me deadpan. "I'm kidding. I *do* trust you, but we need to lighten up because the truth is grim. I've refused their therapy, and my bones are filling with cancer. It's only a matter of time. Soon they'll be so full of tumor they'll fracture from my own weight, just from standing up. I'll have to lie in bed, unable to move. And the pain I have now will be nothing compared to what it's going to be."

"There must be something you can do. Have you told your family? I mean, of course you did."

"No. I've got no family anymore. They're all dead. Well, there's one still left, but she's disowned me." He looked away for a moment. "Let's not talk about that. Back to the doctors. They gave me narcotics for the pain, but I don't want to cloud my mind. After they wore me down, I did finally agree to radiation therapy although I'm not sure how much good it'll do. What they really want is to cut off my balls to slow the growth of the tumor, which I will *not* do."

"You're joking!"

"Wish I were. Testosterone fuels the tumor. The therapy is castration. Plenty of men do it so they can live longer—brittle old men, shuffling around. But I won't! I'm going to die, so I'll die like a man with my balls intact."

I walked him home. He was in pain. I asked if I could help further, but he shooed me out the door. I vowed I would go back and see him again, and I did, doing whatever small errands he needed. I could only think of the irony: a war hero, dying many years after the battle, alone and in pain, away from the eye of a cold, forgetful world. It made me feel guilty that I had someone to talk to when I was upset, but that didn't stop me from going to Margo's and ringing the bell. She was my confidante, and she might be the one to unlock the medicine cabinet to soothe my sadness for Bloom. She would also know how to remove the stress that the lottery had injected, and then, of course, she would give me sympathy for getting hit in the face. No matter what, I could count on Margo.

"What happened to your face!" she asked, insisting on every detail. I told her about Milo, which led to more questions. She wanted to understand my "reckless behavior." She made me feel shame, so I changed the subject and addressed the reason for my visit.

"It's Bloom," I said. "He's got cancer."

"*What*?"

"It sounds bad. It's in his bones. He's in pain."

"Oh my gosh!"

"I feel really bad; he's such a nice guy."

"I *thought* he was losing weight! I was worried last time I saw him, but he never said."

"He's not a big talker. You know that. Just don't tell him I
told you. I mean, if you see him at The Rail. And please don't tell
Mick—he told me in confidence, but I just had to tell you."

She had shown concern when I told her about my fight with
Milo, but now, hearing about Bloom, her eyes misted. She kissed
my bruised cheek tenderly and put her hand on my shoulder with
her face close.

"You're such a good fella. Such a good heart. I feel bad. I wasn't
paying any attention to the old man. Maybe I'm too wrapped up in
myself. Do you think I've been too tough on him?"

She looked me in the eyes, searching for an answer to her
question, open to being hurt. I saw that she was expecting the
truth and that she knew this truth could hurt her. I didn't know
why her behavior toward Bloom would make so much difference
to such a tough-skinned lady, but she was much more sensitive
than I expected.

My instinct was to tell a small lie because I loved her. I had
seen her be prickly to him, but I didn't want to hurt her more than
she already was. Still, there would have to be some truth mixed
with the lie so she wouldn't reject what I said.

"How could you have known? He's just a regular at The Rail.
There's no deep relationship with you. He's a tough man; I don't
think you're too tough for *him*. He takes things in stride. He knew
you two were playing a game, and he seemed to enjoy the attention. He knows he keeps secrets from people, and he doesn't hold
it against them if they come to the wrong conclusions. I think he
likes the game in a perverse sort of way; I'm sure he loves the
whole thing."

She had tears in her eyes, but she broke a little smile. "There's
something I have to tell you."

I waited for her to continue, but she sat biting her lip and said
nothing.

"I'm listening."

"Since I've been at Columbia, I haven't told a living soul. Please
don't tell anyone—not Mick, not anyone."

"Okay, I won't even tell Bloom."

"No—don't tell *him*, even though he already knows."

"Bloom already knows?" I was puzzled at how such a great secret would be already known by Bloom. "I thought you didn't tell anyone."

"I didn't."

"So how does he know?"

"Because—he's my father."

She sat expressionless like a sphinx.

"Bloom?"

"Yes."

"Wow!" I felt like I had stuck my hand in a socket. "You never said! So why's your name something else?"

"Why do you think? C'mon, J-Bee—you're a sharp guy."

Electric jolts were coming one after the other. "You were married?"

She nodded. "It was a stupid decision. I felt like I was smothering, and I just wanted to escape. My father never stopped telling me what a big mistake it was."

"You're divorced?"

"Yes."

"So why is everything so secret?"

She looked uncomfortable. "It's complicated. I've been upset with my father for a long time, and lately I found out something that I never knew, something he never told me. Something that redeems him. So now I'm ashamed of how I've been treating him, which makes it even harder for me to talk about. I'm also angry he never told me about it himself—the man's so damnably secretive! Though in retrospect I can understand why he didn't. The whole thing leaves me with conflicting feelings, but I have to admit: it's a great relief to confide in *you*."

I had questions, but I was on a cloud—she valued my confidence! Then I realized that her confiding in me was a turning point that I had to acknowledge and solidify immediately. "Whatever you tell me is no one else's business," I said. "I won't repeat anything."

"I know you won't—there's something about you I trust."

I was leaning on my forearms which were flat on the table in front of me, and she reached forward and rested her hands on them. She looked into my eyes to confirm our understanding.

"In my senior year of high school, my mother got breast cancer. After her surgery, life seemed to normalize, but then my parents began arguing. At the time I figured they were stressed and that things would get better, but they didn't. They got worse.

"My father usually began the fights—he was angry about *something*. I could see he was frustrated though I didn't know why. Honestly I wasn't too interested, and when he raised his voice, I became more and more disconnected. I conveniently shrank away into my teenage world.

"My mother's response was to disappear. There were nights she didn't come home. She would say, 'I'm going to my sister's,' and off she went, slamming the door. At other times she defended herself with violent outbursts, accusing my father of being unromantic, a brute, an oaf, a moron. I remember," she said, starting to chuckle, "my mother throwing a dinner plate at him—he was standing there with an expression of shock, holding an empty dish with a lamb chop on his head and vegetables stuck to his shirt. It wasn't pretty, but I felt sorry for her, and I tended to believe that he was the brute that my mother said he was and that she was the injured party. Ironically I ended up discovering that things are not always as they seem.

"The cancer returned, and she got sick from chemotherapy and radiation. She got weaker and lost weight until she finally died. My father took it hard, and I added to his misery by blaming *him* for making her unhappy during her final days. Since then I asked him to justify his behavior, but he never defended himself. He usually said nothing at all, but one time he said his silence was a 'matter of honor.' He refused to mention anything that might be critical of my mother, and I remember him saying, 'She's lost everything, and I'm still here.' He said he would not allow me to see her in a negative light, but I couldn't help thinking that he was being secretive, possibly covering up something unforgivable.

"The whole episode didn't feel right, and I didn't want him near me. When I went off to college, I told him to stay away. He went along with that for a while, and during that time my attitude softened, but I just couldn't speak to him. When I was getting married, he and I had a few conversations, but he thoroughly disliked Mitch Rankin, my ex. In retrospect, he had cause not to like him, but at the time it only alienated me further.

"After my divorce, I began working at The Rail. Bloom—my father—sold his house and moved here to be near me. He began coming to The Rail, which I didn't want, but we struck a deal: he wouldn't talk to me, and I wouldn't object to his coming in."

"I'm thinking that you didn't want anyone to know he was your father?"

"I know. Sounds terrible, doesn't it?"

"What about him?"

"He said it wasn't important to him either way, but I know him—he prefers secrecy because he doesn't like to deal with questions from other people."

"Are you his only child?"

"Yes."

"He obviously wanted to be near you. He was starving for a way to reconnect."

"When you put it like that, I feel awful." Her eyes moistened again. "But you're right."

"So what happened? What did you discover that 'redeemed him'?"

"I've been in touch with my aunt all along, my mother's sister. I hadn't seen her in ages so I went last weekend. I wasn't expecting any news, but she said she had something important to tell me. She said it was time I knew because it might end the estrangement I had with Bloom. It turns out that for a few years leading up to my mother's death, she was having an affair with another man, and when she was in the hospital for her cancer, this man visited her.

Things blew up when my father ran into him there and found out, for the first time, what was going on. As I listened to the story, I became so alarmed that I expected to hear that Bloom decked the guy. But according to my aunt, he never touched him. He never reacted physically. In fact, I've reflected on my father's behavior a lot recently, and I've been guilty of imagining him to be something much worse than he is. He's never been physically abusive to anyone that I've ever seen or heard of. Even though he's a tough man, I shouldn't have had the wrong impression.

"Meanwhile, lying in her hospital bed, my mother told Bloom flatly that if she were going to die, there was no point in her waiting for happiness. Apparently she said she had no reason to hide anything from anyone, and that if she lived, she was going to leave him for this other man."

"Who was this other man?"

"Nobody important, really. Someone she met by chance. In fact, I met him once, and he was so unimpressive that I never gave him another thought. The whole thing sounds so much like my mother, I knew it had to be true the moment I heard it."

"You're sure it's true? Your aunt did wait years before she decided to tell you, and Bloom never said a word."

She sighed. "I wish it weren't true, but it is. My aunt produced a diary that my mother had written; it was a popular thing for women of my mother's generation. I never knew that my mother kept one, but it was in her handwriting. The two women were very close, and when my mother died, my aunt managed to obtain possession of it. She gave it to me, and I read it on the spot. Every detail of the story was confirmed."

It was a story which went far beyond the confines of my jejune imagination. Just the idea of imagining one's parents having sex— let alone with someone outside of their marriage—was something I had never thought of. It must have been a humbling experience for Bloom, and I felt for him.

"I'm sorry," I said. "It's a difficult story. But the upside is that now you can get closer to your father again."

"How do I tell him I found out what my mother did? After all the suffering he endured just to prevent me from finding out?"

"It's simple. Secrets run in your family. Don't tell him anything—just get close to him again. I'm sure there's nothing he would want more than to have you in his life."

"Gosh," she said. "The brilliance of your solution is its simplicity!"

—⁂—

We made love. I never felt so close to another human being. After, we lay in bed in the dark, deprived of all visual input and with a trust for one another that allows for uninhibited free association of thought. Words were spoken into the blackness by one, and answers mysteriously returned from the other. I was marooned on my island so that later, after having thrown a bottle with a message into the sea, I plucked her answer, as the tide returned, from the sands of my beach.

"They're planning demonstrations," she said. "Students called a meeting, and I went because I was curious. I sat in the back and made a few comments, trying to guide them a bit. When I was with Mitch, I used to go to SDS meetings. I was this wide-eyed little girl tagging along because he was friends with Gonzalez and Rudd, and I wanted to hear them speak. It was all new and exciting, and *those* boys were radical. Some of that group ran off to join the Weathermen, and I never saw them again."

Just the idea of "Mitch" made me jealous, but the darkness helped me let it go. A line from Dylan's "Subterranean Homesick Blues" sang in my head: *You don't need a weatherman to know which way the wind blows.*

"Anyway," she said, "they used to plan all kinds of stuff: marches, boycotts, strikes. We took over Hamilton Hall one time and locked the dean in the basement. The guy was a bastard, probably deserved it. We went into Hamilton through the tunnel system—you know, the one we use in winter to walk between classes to avoid the snow? The university will never allow that to happen again. They'll call the mayor to send the cops to campus before they'll ever let students take over buildings again. Cops would be a disaster, by the way—the media would have a field day; the coverage would be horrific for the school. Anyway, I'm dreaming of going to law school, and the idea of protesting and getting arrested scares me."

"Law school!" I hooted.

"That's what I said. And why are you laughing?" She whacked me with the flat of her hand, but I couldn't help it.

"I can picture you shredding the opposition into paper streamers!"

"Really?"

"Absolutely."

"But what about the protesting?"

"Protest now; go to law school later."

"It's not that simple. If I get arrested, no law school will ever take me."

"You're right," I said, remembering how Gilly had warned me about *my* future.

"Follow your principles," I said, "but restrain your activity. Carefully plan your involvement to minimize your risk."

She thought in silence. "Maybe."

"*I'm* also stuck on a fence," I said, "and I don't like it."

"What fence?"

"The draft lottery."

"What happened? Were you drafted?"

"No, I'm in limbo. My number is too high to be drafted right away, but too low to know I won't be drafted later."

"That's awful."

"I hate waiting. Worse, if I have to make a decision, I have no clue what I'll decide."

"Maybe you won't have to decide. Maybe you won't be drafted, which would still be better than a lot of boys. But if your number ends up making you draftable, hopefully you'll have sense enough to see there's only one real choice."

"Oh?"

"I can't see you in Nam or prison. You'll run."

I had no answer to this, but the uncertainty gnawed.

"You're not answering," she said

"I've got no answer. I'm absorbing."

"You must see it," she said. "The ideological font from which every 1950s American male used to drink—in order to grow into manhood—is polluted. America's run of never having lost a war has come to an end. Slogans like *fight for your country* and *my country right or wrong* have become hollow mantras. The warrior ethos has run out of time."

"The warrior ethos," I intoned, but I couldn't quite let it go.

"Anyway," she said, "I can *go* to the meetings. Maybe I can go to the demonstrations, but maybe not. Whatever I do, I can't be taken for a ringleader. I have to be careful because the government is probably monitoring me. J. Edgar Hoover keeps files on dissidents and student radicals, and there's probably a file on me already. I don't want to get arrested, but I also don't want to end up in some secret FBI prison where they detain me without *habeas corpus*. I run that risk if they discover I'm involved again. God knows—they could even kill me and dump my body in some culvert."

"That sounds paranoid."

"It does, doesn't it? But the government *is* covertly infiltrating campuses. And let's not forget Kent State. They pointed their guns and shot innocent, peaceable, demonstrating students. Four killed. Did we think we'd be gunned down on our own leafy quads like an enemy? Are we the enemy? Would you have called me paranoid if I said this was going to happen before it actually happened? This nation is feeling its way along a dark corridor, and there's no telling where we'll end up in five or ten years. Or fifty. Meanwhile the government might send you to Vietnam, and you might die. Is that paranoia? No, what I'm telling you about our government is true. They have secret files—even the *New York Times* reported it, and it's rare for the media to get anything right. It's an FBI routine, spying on citizens. They're opening our mail, taking photos of us at demonstrations, spying on campus groups. It's a fact. And I don't want to be sent to the gulag. Going to law school is too important; I want to help change the world."

"I think you should. God knows you've got the brains."

There was silence, so I told her about Steinson leaving school and Melberg going to Pigtown. I could feel her thinking. I wanted to hear her voice; I wanted her support like warmth from the sun.

"I want you to live, J-Bee. If you want to subjugate yourself to the will of the government, do it for a good cause—*not* for Vietnam. The world is big—go to Canada if they draft you. You should know by the summer whether your number is low enough to get you drafted. Of course, if your number is higher than the cutoff, no worries."

We fell asleep, entwined limbs and torsos, naked in paradise.

A green snake appeared. He was the serpent of knowledge, intact with arms and legs from the time before he was cursed to slither on his belly. He didn't look like a serpent, but I knew he was. He walked on all fours and stopped in front of me. He lifted a finger in the air, warning me in a silky voice that he planted in my head: "I see that the soldiers returning from Vietnam are appreciated by many—though not by all. America may yet lose this war, and if so, there will be shame. I see that our boys in fatigues are angry at you, their brothers, because your protests fill the streets. They feel you don't appreciate the sacrifices they make, offering themselves on the altar of freedom. Do you appreciate what they do in your name?"

"Yes," I replied. "I feel guilty about them fighting without me. But I don't want to fight this war."

"You know," said the serpent, "Of course, you're right. But so are they. They're making the ultimate sacrifice, throwing their bodies in the line of fire although their cause is flawed. But what is *your* cause? Do you live for something better? And is there no place for détente between these two camps? Is there no mutual respect to be shared within your generation's terrible paradox?

"Listen to me," he said, "I am talking to you."

Now he was hissing, this serpent, his talk no longer silky. "I'm telling you something. I'm whispering a secret in your ear because I see the future. You're all victims; it's not about *them* or *you*. Two-faced politicians, The Military Industrial Complex—these *giants* suck your blood. They make this nation great, but they do it at a cost; nothing is free. The pendulum of power has swung too far, and the swing is at the expense of the masses: your generation. The giants paint their plastic faces with smiles to lull you into complacency, but as they sit together, whispering across the backs of their hands, they dictate legislation that molds your futures.

"Woe to you, powerless and dying, dazed and without a compass in the wilderness. Woe to you who foot the bill for the American dream, the construct of those in power, a drug they dispense to keep you all believing what they'd have you believe."

I saw the image of the four-legged serpent emblazoned in my brain. And then I was in front of a mirror, and the serpent was there, and he was me.

I awoke with a start and a shout and peeped about in the dark. I was covered in a sheen of sweat. The serpent who walked on all fours was gone, and I was sitting erect in bed in blackness.

A hand reached up and gently stroked the back of my neck.

"You all right?"

"It's a dream," I said, though I knew it could be truth.

27

Quarks

I devoured information nonstop, reading books at a fevered pace, buying them secondhand at Salter's Books. Aeschylus, Homer, Nietzsche, Descartes—they quenched the thirst of my ever-feasting brain, molding my cortex like plastic. The minds who came before me and the language used to express their ideas imbued me with waves of revelation and pleasure. For me, it broke new ground, like being on the prow of the *Pinta* as it spied the beaches of San Salvador or like lifting a burning ember with Homo erectus as it first harnessed fire.

None of this could compare with the ultimate mysteries of Relativity, the Principle of Uncertainty, the Lorentz-Fitzgerald Contractions, the unattainable speed of the photon, or the forces which hold together the enigmatic structure of the atom, that ultimate box encasing a box, encasing yet another box, each ever more bizarre, ever more primordial, ever more guardedly invisible than its overarching predecessors. It was in that direction, toward the evanescent and bottomless world of physics that my curiosity drew me, a simpleton, a rounded bead on a string, rolling linearly in an infinite and multidimensional universe. My mind was ready to be set alight by a new theory that would forever change humanity's view of the world. I was going to a lecture by Murray Gell-Mann on the vision he had of a tiny new particle, a revelation beamed into his mind by an omnipotent God, shining through the murky haze of quantum mechanics and differential equations to burst into his consciousness. He would reveal it to us, and I could only *hope* to understand such abstruse dark matter.

In Pupin Hall, the physics building, I came across a grubby, unbathed, bearded man, slumped in a doorway on the fourth floor, with blackened grime in the creases of his pale white face and under his uncut fingernails. He reminded me of a man I had seen some months before in front of Barnard College at 117th and Broadway. A grizzled old man had been squatting over the sidewalk in full daylight with all those pretty college girls walking to classes. No one seemed to notice but me, the stark dichotomy in human experience, two colliding realities in the planet's richest city. The man himself was as oblivious to the others as they were to him as he hitched up his pants and walked on, leaving his spoor behind.

A security guard appeared with a graduate student in tow and approached the bearded man in the doorway.

"Sir," said the guard, politely but firmly. "You can't stay here. These are the professors' offices."

The man in the doorway had a very soft voice, and I barely heard when he said, "I'm waiting for T. D. Lee."

"I'm sorry; I don't know how you got in, but you can't stay."

"I'm waiting for Professor Lee. I got tired, so I sat in the doorway. I've had a long trip. I'm here to listen to Gell-Mann speak. He's my friend."

I couldn't believe what I was hearing; the man knew Murray Gell-Mann!

"Wait a minute," said the graduate student. "This may be a mistake."

"No mistake," said the guard. "He broke in the building without ID."

"Could you ask his name?" I said. "At least ask him who he is."

"I'm Richard Feynman," the man piped up. "Ask anyone. I'm waiting for Dr. Lee. I'm here to listen to Gell-Mann speak on

Friday about his new theoretical discovery. He's going to talk about quarks."

At that moment, T. D. Lee, the youngest winner in the history of the Nobel Prize in physics, appeared in the corridor, smiling. He identified Dr. Feynman to the guard, welcoming his colleague to come to his co-op "for a place to eat and shave." As we gawked, they walked off arm in arm. It was Feynman's book that I was using in my first-year course in physics, but how could anyone have known it was he? The bizarreness of the players in the field of physics was a match for the strangeness of things erupting from the atom. Now nothing would keep me from Gell-Mann's lecture.

Margo had assumed that I would protest against Gell-Mann coming to Columbia. She saw me at times as an outgrowth of herself, and she couldn't imagine that I, the dark unkempt id whom she had liberated from under its rock, would ever make a free choice to go in a different direction. She was shocked when she found out.

"We're having a protest against Gell-Mann. A demonstration. He's a dark agent of The Military Industrial Complex. He works for JASON, which means he actually works for Nixon! He's the engineer behind the placement of land mines—bombs, J-Bee—to kill Viet Cong. He builds war toys for money! He's the genius planning the mining of the Ho Chi Minh Trail. *He* is the enemy."

"He's a professor at Caltech."

"But his preferred extracurricular activity is getting paid to blow up Vietnamese. He's escalating the war, and he's ruining the democratic self-determination of an entire, sovereign people. We're talking about an ethnic population in Indochina that's been overrun and dominated for over a thousand years, mostly by China. He's mercenary! And the time has come for Vietnamese home rule."

I knew what she was saying. I had misgivings. But as we are made of carbon, calcium and iron, and since the only place these elements are created is inside the furnaces of stars, then we are made of the dust of such stars, stars which lived and died long before the earth ever existed. I was determined to know more about these things and to leave the political churning of earth-bound humanity behind in order to hear Gell-Mann's solitary voice, speaking for the cosmos, as it filtered down though the primordial interstellar dusts.

"He's a brilliant scientist," I said, "and he's found something no one else on the planet has ever been able to find, and he did it with mathematics and imagination. It'll probably take another thirty years before they ever physically discover what he's found theoretically."

"He's a criminal."

"He's a luminary. His mind is a mind to behold. I want to see the corporeal body of the man that houses that mind, and I want to hear that mind speak out. Is that so terrible?"

"J-Bee, please. You can't go!"

"Watch me."

"You don't appreciate anything! Don't you see the evil there? He's prolonging the war, and you might die as a result! And for what?"

"For the chance of a lifetime."

She stared at me.

"You don't get something either," I said.

"Like what? What don't I get?"

I couldn't explain. Either that, or she was unable to open her mind to allow my thoughts to seep in. I knew she was not so different from me: young, headstrong, stubborn and unable to see the other side of the coin before rejecting it wholesale. The dark side of the moon, the inscrutable mystery of the atom—one had to look hard and want it in order to see it.

"Are these brilliant minds," I said, "are these beautiful, luminous beings with thoughts so crystal clear really so corrupt that they're plotting the killing of the Vietnamese people? Mining the Ho Chi Minh Trail?"

"Yes," she said. "Of course they can be evil. Edward Teller was brilliant, but he was also evil. Nuke-level evil."

Friday arrived. The protest began early, demonstrators confronting everyone who entered Pupin Hall with a prearranged
scripted talk, telling them, "Gell-Mann is mining the Ho Chi Minh
Trail . . . Working for Richard Nixon . . . Working for Satan . . .
A murderer, killing innocent Vietnamese people with the remote
push of a button . . . impersonally . . . with the flip of an electronic
switch."

Some used tact and persuasion to convey the message, some
railed and accosted those walking by. Others waved Viet Cong
flags and carried angry banners. All of them handed out pam-
phlets against the war. As the day wore on and the lecture began,
the crowd swelled to several hundred. I heard loud chants from
outside the building, among them, "*1-2-3-4, we don't want your
fucking war!*" and the repeated mantra, "*Ho-Ho-Ho Chi Minh!*"

But I was inside in the amphitheater now, one of fifty attend-
ees, safely settled in a hard wooden chair bolted to the floor, in
front of a tall wall of black chalkboards and a single, stark, wooden
lectern. Pupin Hall was the same as the day it was built in 1901,
without a single upgrade in comfort or decor for the now seventy-
one years it had stood. Below us, in the basement in 1939, Enrico
Fermi and Leo Szilard had worked on developing a self-sustained
neutron chain reaction on the way to creating an atomic bomb.
Now, thirty-three years on, there was a cyclotron there, a racetrack
for nuclear particles accelerating in circles to smash atoms, creating rainbows of subatomic particles both wondrous and fleeting.

Professor Lee introduced Professor Gell-Mann. With faded
chants of protest in the background, the audience hushed, awaiting a revelation in academic history. As new as the idea of their
existence was, quarks themselves had to be as old or older than
the universe. They were antecedents to the concept of time, and
Gell-Mann posited these tiniest of particles were the most basic
components of the building blocks of the atom; they were the basic
interlocking pieces forming the substratum of mass in the maelstrom of the space-time continuum.

I looked at Feynman in a clean white shirt, sitting between the seats of Lee and Gell-Mann, rapture on his clean-shaven face, angelic with the purity of an altar boy. Feynman's brilliance was different from that of Gell-Mann, and his appearance seemed strangely irrelevant to himself, his body a mere encumbrance to the world of the mind in which he lived.

Meanwhile Gell-Mann was preppy in blazer and loafers and stood up to polite applause, answering his introduction with a poem in Swahili, a language which he said was an interest of his ever since he had picked up playing the African kora.

The lecture was casual, and the odd listener may have been confused into thinking it was a survey course on the foundations and comparisons of Eastern and Western civilized thought. When the mathematics came, there were lines of calculus that I recognized but could not follow, and there were references to theorems I had never heard of. The Columbia faculty posed the occasional question, and so brilliant were their words and the daisy chains of their ideas that it made me believe I understood everything they were saying. Afterward, however, I remembered little detail, but I realized that I had listened to the words of the gods. Unfortunately the concepts and mathematics were beyond my abilities to retain them; I had drunk from the River of Forgetfulness immediately after Gell-Mann sat down, rendering it impossible for me to unlock any secrets after the fact. It seemed a fantasy; I had been tricked by the brilliance of these men and their words, tricked by their excruciating luminosity. I had witnessed a revelation that only *they* had achieved, thinking falsely that I had understood when, in fact, I had only been bathed in the golden light of their knowledge, like the proverbial swine wallowing in pearls.

I did understand the irony. Should this particle, small beyond the bounds of comprehension—a blur, a smudge, laughingly insignificant in its visibility—truly exist, then it would be a "small" of mighty significance despite its trivial name. I imagined Gell-Mann was secretly laughing at the world, twinkling with delight as he drew symbols on the chalkboard.

The Columbia faculty were polite and good-natured, but there were skeptics. The club of physicists of this high order was small, and they all knew each other and their foibles. They knew they had to keep the peace and maintain their dialogue. It was a union of super-intellectual oddballs, and without each other, there was no one else with whom they could share their visions.

"You'll never be able to prove this. We'll never be able to find them. We'll never have the energy to be able to dislodge one."

A discussion ensued. It was well known that Gell-Mann had tried to find evidence of a quark in the physical world, but the physics community did not really accept his evidence. Not yet. I thought I heard whispers of "angels on pinheads." It seemed that the amount of energy required by a cyclotron to manifest a quark was too great to be achieved in the current state of the world.

"We'll find it," said Gell-Mann. "And, God willing, I'll be alive to see the day."

"Why does the world need another layer of subatomic particles? Are they really necessary?"

"They are necessary if they are real," said Gell-Mann. "And if they are real, we will then have to ask why they were necessary in God's paradigm. We seek the truth; there is no invocation of need, purpose or anything else. The world exists; we are there to plumb it. Why should there be a reason? There's no need to plead for one. If the thing exists, and I've said it does, then do with it what you will. We are voyeurs in the cosmos, here only to witness. The grand scheme is not accountable to us. Any demand by us for reason be damned!"

The applause was polite for Gell-Mann, and the faculty rose to shake his hand and pat his shoulder. My mind buzzed with swirling particles, pinwheels of milky white specks, all churning in a thick black soup. I tried to retain these visions, Gell-Mann's new universal construct, before it might evaporate from my recall. It was hard, and his paradigm receded from me faster than water sucked down a drainpipe.

As I stepped out of Pupin Hall, I stepped into another kind of maelstrom. Angry voices, chanting loudly, were moving from Columbia's quads and spilling onto Broadway. I moved with the rear of the crowd, finding myself at the top of a staircase which cascaded down to the gully of the boulevard below. I perched myself there, a vantage point above a sea of hundreds of students, pumping their fists in the air and moving in a current downtown.

"Hell no, we won't go!"

The meaning was clear. Here was my generation, powerless against The Military Industrial Complex, against Nixon and his cronies, forced to follow his bidding but showing a unity with steely defiance, railing against the forces of the established power, forces they could never overcome. The protest was planned to be small, but it had risen spontaneously as a wave rears up before breaking on shore. Here was youth washing into Broadway, the surge of a storm-driven river, a sea of heads, a sea of uplifted arms, all moving together, bodies flowing in one direction, bearing downstream like a tide.

I stood on the steps, a safe haven of solid cement over which my comrades had just swept, and I watched. I don't know why I hesitated. I knew they were right. But within me there was an immutable presence hunkering at the root of my bowels, a great stone anchor, fixing me to the ideology with which I was inoculated at birth and which had been spooned into me for years like pabulum. This ideology had forced me to suffer, and I knew it like the figurative chains in the dungeons of Saint Eustace. So why could I not release it?

I watched my brothers flowing in the same direction, a blood in the veins of the great society in which we lived. For myself, I lacked the power to break from my roots.

I could not yet flow with the others.

28

Hatred

After the demonstration, I went looking for Margo. She wasn't at the library, so I headed for The Rail. I examined the many passing faces for Milo, looking over my shoulder, peering into doorways. Faces were bundled against the cold in high collars, some with smeared red lipstick, others with shadowy beards, all emerging from clouds of misted breath. I felt Milo's presence when a man suddenly spat in the gutter in front of me; I felt him again as four raucous men burst from the doors of a bar, though he wasn't among them.

When I reached The Rail, I found Bloom and sat across from him.

"How's your friend, what's-his-name?"

"Billy Wing."

I missed his hippie spirit. "He was murdered," I said.

"Murdered? I heard about a student who OD'd in his room, but I haven't heard about murder."

"That's him," I said. "He *was* murdered. He told me he was dealing drugs just before he died. He said he'd been threatened, and then he was dead."

Bloom squinted at me without blinking.

"That doesn't prove he was murdered. But if you know something, tell the police."

I was used to fending for myself, yet here was a man speaking to me in fatherly tones. It was uncharted waters, this mentoring, and previously my instincts had struggled to subsume it. Yet now, because he was Margo's father, I felt something new: a bond of kinship, like blood, which made me more docile and more receptive to what he might suggest.

"My father always told me to avoid the police. It's not that I care what he says, but the police are like military—they have power; they use it, and people get hurt. *I* could get hurt."

"Okay, you don't want to get involved. But if you've got information, it might clarify events surrounding his death."

In the nicest possible way, Bloom allowed me to see my intentional avoidance and exposed my guilt. I imagined myself walking down Broadway, a sandwich sign slung over my torso, "Behold the Catholic, fallen from grace—he turned away from his friend."

"But there's another reason you won't go to the police, isn't there?"

He was right; there was another reason, and I recoiled from the idea that he might uncover my motives even further.

"Does it have anything to do with getting into that fight and getting your face smacked?"

My chest tightened. My sandwich sign was now two metal plates, a device with screws, squeezing. Bloom was forcing me to confront an unspoken ugliness inside me, a monster that was safe only when chained to dungeon walls behind a bolted iron door.

"No matter why you're so reluctant, you should tell the police what you know."

"I can't."

"Why not?"

The pressure was unbearable. Bloom was on the verge of unchaining the beast and unlocking the door.

"Just tell me why not—" he said. "Give me a *reason*."

I shouted so loudly that the few other patrons turned and stared as the lid blew off the pot: "*Because I want to kill the son of a bitch!*"

—m—

After the shout, I was drained. I slumped back in my seat. The waitress came flying out of the kitchen like a goose with Mick in tow, thinking they had a customer in distress. Bloom apologized for the noise and told Mick to go away, ordering beer and burgers from the waitress. After they'd gone, he told me he understood how I felt, and when the food arrived, I had a few bites and felt better.

"Have you mapped out how you're going to do it?"

I didn't have a plan, but I reflected on what I already knew. I had ambushed Laureen and Stankewicz, and I could do something similar. I could trail Milo, unseen, to a suitable location where I could attack. However, the problems he posed were different than what I had faced with the two bullies. He was big, and at any given moment, he might be with his lackeys. I would have to confront him when he was alone in a desolate place where I could corner and immobilize him. A baseball bat might work, but I would have to get close and move fast. Killing with such a blunt tool would take vigor; it would be messy. Another alternative, a gun for example, might kill him impersonally without a single bead of sweat; but while a bat could be easily bought in a sporting goods store, buying a gun would be complicated and traceable.

"I've thought about it," I answered, "but I have no definite plan."

He nodded.

"Except maybe," I said, "to shove him out of an airplane at forty thousand feet."

"You know," he said, "You can't just go around killing people."

"You're right," I said, "but I loathe him."

"Killing another person will damage you. And it's risky. The police, whom you don't trust, could find you. You could get a prison term with dangerous felons who might sodomize or kill you. The friends of your victim might retaliate—they might hunt you down. It's a bad idea."

"I know. But I can't help thinking about it."

Bloom was the catalyst for my introspection, and now I was mortified by what it revealed. Did this hatred have such control over me that I was incapable of breaking its spell? Had I learned nothing from my prior violence? Was I prepared for a murderer's utter darkness of soul?

Bloom looked through my eyes like he was examining my brain.

"I'm trapped," I said. "If I don't kill him, he'll probably kill me."

"And you're 100 percent sure he's the one who killed your friend?"

I said nothing.

"I see," he said. "Well, you'd better get sure in a hurry. Otherwise, what if you kill the wrong guy?"

"It's *got* to be him," I said, but I wasn't wholly certain. My feelings made no sense: I hated Milo; I wanted to be the instrument of his death, but I definitely didn't want to be a killer.

Bloom swigged beer. "Okay, so tell me about this guy and how he murdered your friend. And what you plan to do about it."

"Are you sure you want to know?"

He didn't answer, and I realized that I couldn't tell him anything further. If I told him any specifics about my intentions, and if Milo ended up dead, Bloom could be a witness against me.

We ate in silence, each in his own bubble. Finally he said, "So what else is bothering you? This death is old news, and you're edgy. I'm guessing there's something else."

I didn't look up.

"Schoolwork? Grades? Family?"

He squinted at me, looking for a hint. Then he smiled.

"Women!" He chuckled. "It must be a woman. They bring joy; they cause pain. So what's happened?"

"I didn't follow instructions."

"Be specific."

"She was part of a protest against a lecture being given by a visiting professor, and she wanted me to be part of the protest."

"And you didn't go."

"I didn't go. I went to the lecture instead."

"The lecture she was protesting against?"

I nodded.

"Hah!" He clapped his hands. "You're a pistol, all right."

"Glad to be so amusing. Even at my own expense."

"It's nothing—I'm laughing because you're an underdog who bites back."

"I can take a ribbing."

"If she's strong-minded, you may have a problem. Is she strong-minded?"

"Definitely."

"She wants you in lockstep, but she should let you be yourself. Otherwise she's not getting anything out of the relationship, only what she's already got. But at least you stood your ground. I like your assertiveness. You can't let women lead you around *all* the time—sometimes you need to stand on your own."

29

Neanderthal in a Fog

By the time I left The Rail, it was dark and cold. I walked downtown, newspapers eddying in barren streets. Bums slumped in doorways or lay on grates in the sidewalks where blasts of heat rose up from the pressure of subway cars, rocketing through catacombs below. With my face huddled in the upturned collar of my coat, I pressed south to 107th Street, occasionally glancing behind for Milo and his thugs. Once at Margo's I ran up the stairs to her door. She had left it cracked open, affording me smells of simmering pepper steak and sweetened marinade.

"Not sure why you're here." She was standing in her kitchenette, never turning to face me, her ponytail bobbing as she took long strokes with a carving knife.

"I wanted to see you," I said. "I miss you."

She ignored me, slicing and mashing, tasting her gravy. Then she said, "We're very different people. We don't see eye to eye on important things. I don't know why I'm explaining it to you—I shouldn't have to explain myself."

"How are we different?"

"You're a hypocrite."

After my disobedience, I had expected a reprimand, but my male mind could not wrap itself around the specifics of this new charge. It made no sense; somewhere there had to be a misunderstanding. I was being sucked into the wrong argument, and I was muddled about how she had gone off on a tangent. I wanted to get back on track and clarify what we were really arguing about, but all I could say was, "Why am I a hypocrite?"

"I don't know *why*," she said. "Search your own soul for *why* you do things. It's got nothing to do with me."

"I mean, why do you *say* I'm a hypocrite?"

"You let me run at the mouth about my politics, and all the time you've got absolutely no respect for them. You nod and smile, acting the sycophant, but in reality you've got no interest in what I'm saying. Ergo, you're a hypocrite."

"I respect your views. I really do! But you know my roots are conservative. It's not easy—I have to digest your views slowly and think them through. You're teaching me new things, and I'm devouring everything, every drop! I'm trying to make sense of this new world view, but it takes time."

She threw me an eye over her shoulder. "I'm not sure I'm interested in your roots or your perspective. They're evil, and you're supporting them. By going to their lectures, you're consorting with the enemy, giving them heart. There's no middle ground. I've run out of patience, and I'm not going to deal with it!"

"Deal with what?"

She put her knife down with a clatter. "With a person making a stupid political statement because of his lack of political awareness."

"I'm not making a political statement."

"Right. Fine. Let's just say I don't want a conservative in my life. Or a warmonger."

"Margo, why are you giving me such a hard time?"

She turned to face me and wiped her hands on a dish towel. "What could be more important than the very politics that may send you overseas to fight and die in a war against innocent people who want nothing more than to be left alone to govern themselves? They don't need a self-appointed world policeman!"

"I'm rethinking *everything*. I'm trying to understand how the world works—"

"That's something you damn well need to learn in a hurry."

"I'm starting with the most fundamental truths, like how mass warps space, how atoms are constructed, and how quarks glue everything together."

I may have thought my logic was unassailable and that Margo was finally about to see the merit in what I was saying. I may have felt that the relevance of what I wanted to learn was so self-evident that she would take a step backward and look at me with epiphany written all over her face and say, "Wow, J-Bee, honey, of course the secrets of the universe are manifestly important," but I must have been delusional because I was never more wrong.

"*Quarks!*" she said, throwing her hands in the air and looking to heaven. "A footnote in James Joyce! And you think *that's* important?"

I felt like the wind was kicked out of me. I wanted to explain myself further in case I hadn't expressed my message correctly, so I said, "It's the name chosen by Gell-Mann himself to reflect the irony of the small yet mighty."

"You're not only politically irresponsible," she said, narrowing her eyes and grabbing her carving knife, "you're a hopeless ass without any sociopolitical perspective! You have no clue what it means to be a citizen of the civilized world. You're a stupid lout without any justification for existence like all the other establishment toadies!"

"And you're a goddamned control freak!" I shouted, surprising myself at the anger that had suddenly burst forth. "You're a bully just like the Sisters at Saint Eustace—rigid, unwavering obeisance to dogma, unremitting self-righteousness and judgment of others, unforgiving intolerance and punishment! What you really need is a parrot so you can train him to do tricks and say all the correct witty liberal things! You're a narcissist in search of a mirror! You don't want a companion or a relationship; you want a robot so you can dial in what he should be thinking and how he'll recite exactly what you program him to say, methodically plugging the latest avant-garde language into his brain!"

"And *you're* a spineless, unprincipled moron! Why did you bother to come over? Get the hell out! We're done! And don't come back—I won't see you again!"

I was crushed, swept aside by the great wake of Margo's battle-ship presence, by the cyclonic winds of her rage, dashed against the sharpest rocks in the tiny dinghy of my intellect, my emotions shred to tatters, a useless sail against the forces unleashed by a Circe. I felt weak in the legs, wobbly, so I sat down and put my head on her table.

"I won't be bullied," I said so quietly that she couldn't have heard it.

"I said get out!"

She took a step forward, brandishing her knife like a machete before swinging her blade to point at the door.

"Get the hell out! Get out of my life!"

—⁂—

You can love a woman, but that's no gateway to understanding women.

I loved Margo. I loved talking to her, and I loved her talking to me. I loved looking at her; I loved holding her, and now she would remain a mystery forever. She was a willowy figure, a shimmering mirage, a silhouette veiled in mists. But whatever love I had didn't add up to any ability on my part to understand what made her act or behave. My lot had been to be thankful that I had been with her and then to be devastated whenever she might leave.

I thought about what she had said, and I could only conclude that I had to be the master of my own thoughts. Now that she had said it was over, there was an emptiness inside me, a loneliness. Her rejection left me in an emotional fog. There was no way out; I would have to live with the pain.

—⁂—

Gilly wrote me a letter to say he had been given a temporary leave of absence and would be allowed to go stateside. He was making his way to New York, tired of war and keen to visit, hoping a spell of "normal life" would be good for his mental health. The letter was posted overseas and had taken so long to be delivered that when I finally got it, his arrival was imminent.

I was eager to see him, and when the time came, I took the subway to Times Square. The rattling tubes were warm, making me sweat in my coat. At 42nd Street I got off, shoulder to shoulder with a phalanx of city dwellers who ascended the stairs en masse. Outside, a wall of cold air spanked my face, chilling the sweat on my neck. I wound myself in a scarf and pushed to the street where iridescent neons refracted through icy particulates of breath.

It was dusk and rush hour all at once, and I entered a sea of people. Tides of bodies pushed me along. I bobbed like flotsam past glass-sheeted storefronts with clusters of face-painted whores who hissed, "Wanna party," and "Suck your dick for a twenty!" They leered, hiding their sagging breasts and needle-pocked skin in order to advertise bursting cleavage and flounce as something worth poking for a little bit of cash. In other doors stood pimps and hawkers, calling at male passersby, occasionally yanking a man by the arm, brazenly culling him from the human surge.

I moved west on 42nd to the Port Authority bus station, past any and all the tempting distractions. At the station, I sat on a bench amidst several slumped figures with another three bodies asleep on the floor. Now sheltered inside from the cold, they smelled of urine and feces, their faces and coats smeared with grime from a life of lying on floors and sidewalks. Once, Margo had put this in context over a beer. "These poor people carry their possessions on their backs like refugees. They're lambs, too innocent to protect themselves from the brutal world, too uneducated or insane to read the papers or vote. America needs to reach out and help them."

Gilly's bus arrived. I smelled diesel fumes as the bus bay doors flew open, a smell of tanks and jeeps and battleship engines. A stream of passengers came through these doors, many looking for futures and fortunes, others prowling for fun or prey on Gotham's streets. Gilly appeared, and I saw the shaven stony face of a soldier, a pink scalp shining through a crew cut, a duffel slung over his shoulder. We embraced, long lost brothers, whispering each other's name.

"Great to see you!"

"Same!" I said.

We eyed each other, scanning up and down as men do, absorbing the data that visuals bring, turning them into judgments.

"You look a little hippie there, J-Bee." He flicked my hair with his fingers. "Hair's just at your shoulders. Your daddy catch you, and he'll go to the barn for the shears."

"You'll meet a hippie or two, but I'm no hippie. More like I'm too lazy to get it cut, and nobody here really cares."

We laughed.

"You *should* be a hippie—hell, why not? Better than being a soldier; I'm telling you. We hear about you boys smoking dope, but the fact is, we do it too. Some guys even shoot H."

"You're *not* shooting up!"

"Not me. I avoid that shit. It's a killer. But I tried marijuana, and it's not half bad. Some of the guys smoke up before heading out on missions, but I think that's just stupid. Makes it dangerous for all of us."

We walked off, arms around shoulders.

"I want to ride a subway," he said. "I want to walk where there's lots of normal, human activity. I need normal. And how about a beer?"

We made our way back through Times Square. Gilly's neck craned up at the sights, his head swiveling back and forth. "There's nothing normal about *this* place," he laughed. I felt safe with him; the threats of thugs and pimps ebbed away, leaving me to enjoy the color and weirdness on the New York stage.

The week before Gilly came, I had spoken to Jake McCann, a guy down the hall, whose roommate had dropped out of school.

"Hey, Jake."

"Peace, brother."

"My buddy needs a place to crash for a week, can you—"

"Sure, man. I dig. Roommate's gone; bed's empty. Just let me know when—key, shake hands. The gig."

Once at campus, we found Jake's room and left Gilly's duffel. It was Gilly's first time at a college, and as we exited the gates, he said, "It's a citadel. It'll open doors for you that no one else can unlock. Make good, brother, because we're dying over there."

The Gold Rail never changed. The dirt on the floor and the grime on the ceiling got older all the time, accreting layers of sediment. We sat in a booth and had beer.

"I hear they're taking away student deferments."

"Yeah. That's all the guys in the dorm want to talk about, besides grades and women. And Milo."

"Milo? You wrote me something about him and your friend who was dead in his room. Remind me again."

I told him how Milo had dosed me with LSD from a cup of tea, and how it had sent me to Billy Wing's door. I told him how I had smelled Billy's rotting corpse during my trip and how he was found later in his room with a needle in his arm. As I told the story, the smells came back, and the visions of swirling bats and sputtering bulbs echoed fresh in my head. It was almost as if Milo, when he dosed me, had sent me on a mission to reveal his own guilt, as if it were a message from the realm of the supernatural, beckoning me to come forward in pursuit.

"I'm sorry, J-Bee. I knew guys who didn't deserve to die—I also knew guys who did. I've seen people incinerated from napalm dropped from jets. If you've seen jets dropping this stuff, it's not a pinpoint procedure. The jets boom in at speed, spraying the stuff all over the place and roasting absolutely everything. Jungles scorched to the ground. GIs, Vietnamese, roasted alive. Not to mention animals. And burning alive is a painful, horrible death.

"I've seen guys gunned down too. I saw others booby-trapped in the jungle. I wrote you about one, and then there was another one, a new kid. We were in the jungle, and he stepped on something. The next thing you know, a wooden door swung out of nowhere, hinged around a tree trunk and whacked him full in the face and chest. It would have knocked him twenty feet except that the door was studded with bamboo stakes sliced into points. Punji sticks. Anyway the door hit him so hard that about ten stakes stuck right through him. He screamed and then hung there, on the door, trembling, with all these pointy stakes poking out. We just stood there and gaped. He was a nice kid, but there was no time for a postmortem. We went into hunt mode to track down the killers and blow them away. Gooks."

"That word 'gook' sounds bad."

"It *is* bad. I'm ashamed of it. But they're killing us—heck, they may end up killing *me!* Or, if you end up there—*you.* No point being polite about it. They hate us for being there, and we *have to* hate them if we're going to have the will to kill them. And we've got to kill them, J-Bee, or *they'll* kill *us.* It's a mean fact. It's hard enough to kill a man you're pretending to hate. Try to like him, and you'll never be able to do it. You won't have the heart."

We sat sipping beer.

"I think you said you suspected that this Milo killed your friend. I thought this was college. This doesn't fit with gentlemanly behavior and college."

I recounted what Billy had told me: his panic, the preppy boys, and the big thug Miguel with the scar on his neck. Then I told him how it all connected back to Milo and that I thought Milo had ordered Billy's hit, possibly by his thugs. I repeated how Milo and I had fought and how he had kicked me and then threatened me, which had made me constantly paranoid.

"*Now* I remember the story. If this guy wasn't your enemy before, he is now. Well, so now you want to attack this Milo, like those two kids back in Norfolk."

"I want to fucking kill him."

Gilly looked surprised. "You need to calm down."

I took a slug of beer. I was amazed at the power of my temptation: one moment I was plotting how I would kill Milo; the next moment I was mortified, imagining clanking chains awaiting me in Hell.

"You have any proof he killed Billy? I mean, before you even think of revenge or killing someone—which you shouldn't because you're supposed to be getting an education—you better be damn sure you know the facts."

"I feel like I've got to do something, and I'm sure as hell not going to the police."

"Just sit on it. Don't do anything while I'm here. Heck, I just got here! I need a rest. We can talk about it, but don't do a goddamn thing. Nothing should distract you from your education."

"And what if I'm drafted after I lose my deferment? That's a distraction I won't be able to ignore."

"Cross one bridge at a time. Anyway, ever hear of Canada?"

"Canada?"

"I hear the women are gorgeous, and they dress in the latest from Paris and Rome."

"You think I should run to Canada? Be a coward?"

"Why not? It's a civilized country."

"Cold as hell and me, a Virginia boy."

"That's right. A Southern boy running to Canada isn't what I'd call cowardice."

We laughed, but what I didn't tell Gilly was that, at that very moment, I was in the midst of another flickering echo of my acid trip, disturbing visions of deformed faces and abandoned, hopeless toddlers. Perhaps I *was* an id under a rock. Maybe I was a Neanderthal caught in a fog, but I began to see that the way to my own redemption might not be through violence but down a different path. If nothing else, acid had etched a window into my world that hadn't been there before, and I was looking through that window now—soon I might have to go one step further and jump right through it.

30

Kinship of Warriors

The next day, Gilly and I were sitting in The Rail when the front door swung open, admitting the figure of a slender man blown in like a leaf by a bolt of cold air. He stepped into the dimness of the tavern limping in pain, clothes hanging on his bones like a coat rack. His hair was longer, the shafts standing out with the effect of a halo as sunlight flooded through the storefront's plate glass and caught him from behind.

"Bloom!" Mick shouted from behind the bar, turning heads.

"Mick," said the man.

"What'll it be?"

I waved to Bloom who came to our booth and sat next to Gilly, across from me.

"Gilly," I said, "this is Mr. Bloom."

Bloom winced. "Bloom," he corrected. "Save the Mister for important men."

He turned to Gilly. "So damned polite. Not sure I can trust a man with such silky manners."

"We Southern boys, Mr. Bloom," said Gilly, smiling. "Polite is what our mommas teach us."

Bloom grunted. "Looks like you've been overseas. Indochina?"

"That's right," said Gilly. "How'd you know?"

"Crew cut. Military boots. The look in your eye. I can spot it; I've a gift for seeing things about people."

"Right," I said. "When we first met, your 'gift' couldn't tell me apart from the back of Aunt Viola's barn."

"You mean when you wandered in here during my altercation with the pip-squeaks?"

"There's that," I said, "but it took a while for you to warm. You were slow. I had to creep up to you in tiny increments to get some conversation."

"Tiny increments? Very fine talk."

"Oh," said Gilly, "J-Bee is known for fine talk. Silky tongue. But watch out when he's riled; he can strike you with that tongue. He bites. With words, that is—though he *can* get physical."

"No," said Bloom, turning back to me. "It wasn't like that. I pegged you real fast. I'm a frosty man. I'm gruff. At my age, it's impossible for me *not* to know what I am. So I didn't want to scare you off. I gave you small *incremental* doses of my personality to reel you in without spooking you. Inch by inch. I knew you were a sensitive man—I had to bide my time, right?"

"A sensitive man!" snorted Gilly with delight, slapping the table. "Oh my, that's rich! That's what he is, all right! But he'll rip your guts out if he's cornered. He'll come at you, that one."

He tipped his pointy-topped beer bottle at me.

"I saw that too," said Bloom.

They were snickering in their beers.

"Like sport fishing," said Bloom, "I had to reel him in like a bone-headed tarpon off the Keys. *In-cre-mental.* Wear him down. Landed him good and proper. Now, many burgers and a bunch of beers later, we're friends."

"What a pain in the ass," I said, but my smile betrayed me.

Bloom and Gilly got on well. They had something between them I didn't share; they were warriors with a mutual bond, and they knew it. I could see them together in some dim beer hall in the future with horned hats on their heads, sitting on benches with a host of their dead comrades, singing and drinking themselves to oblivion. Coming from a military family, I had the sad revelation that I was never to have such a bond even though I had been born and conditioned all my life to inherit that very thing.

"So," said Bloom turning to Gilly. "Tell us how they're treating you over there."

"Brutal." Gilly lost his smile. "Have you been to war?"

"I have," said Bloom.

"Then you know *how* brutal."

"I do."

"You killed people?" asked Gilly.

"Yeah."

"I'm not talking about shooting someone thirty yards away. I mean up close. I saw their teeth; I saw the pores on their faces."

"I know what you mean. The killing gets personal. Intimate."

Gilly looked at Bloom carefully. "Sounds like you've thought about it."

"I have."

"That's exactly how it is. I'm possessed when I kill people. They've trained me to be a killer, and then I wake up at night in a cold sweat. I can't stop seeing the faces."

"I feel for you," said Bloom. "After you come home, you'll find yourself again. I promise."

"You can't say that."

"Yes, I can. I'm not saying you won't change—you'll change. But you *will* find yourself, and then you'll decide what to do with it, and that decision will reflect the kind of man you've become."

We ate. Bloom lamented the lack of parades for the heroes coming home from Nam, news which surprised Gilly who said he expected appreciation from an America who had sent her sons to put their bodies in harm's way. By six o'clock, dusk seeped in grain by grain through The Rail's front windows. Bloom left for an appointment, and then we split. The Serpent was going to speak at seven, and I needed a coffee, so we trudged off to The Apocalypse Café.

The basement of Saint Paul's chapel spoke to Gilly like it had spoken to me. The damp stone steps leading down to the café and the sconces shimmering with orangey light re-created a dungeon with quivering shadows along the walls that ignited the imagination. Gilly said he saw the dark hooded figures of the Sisters lurking in every corner. He said he smelled the dank and moldy corpses of boys, those who had been lost in the labyrinthine cellars of Saint Eustace, left there chained and naked to die and then decompose, so many years before.

"The distance in time and space between here and the dungeons of Saint Eustace is closer than the thickness of a batwing," he said. "Wherever or whatever those boys are now, they're always with me because Hell is everywhere—it has no respect for time or space. Just the idea that those boys were there, dead in the cellars of Saint Eustace, was terrifying. Once you've been there, it's always with you—or just a step behind you."

I knew what he meant; I couldn't have said it better. I felt those boys somewhere near, perhaps only feet away behind some dodge in the crypts, seemingly on the other side of the walls which enclosed the café itself. It was as if there were some eerie connection, like a wormhole between this place and the subterranean world under the little school where boys had been tortured and then perished, long ago, beyond the protective gaze of society.

We sat down amongst the longhairs who nodded at us, restraining themselves from staring too hard at Gilly's pink shaven skull. Then, amidst the hushed voices, which were themselves damped by the surrounding stones, the profile and whispering utterance of The Serpent emerged as if from a soupy fog, a primeval being rising from a primordial ooze, hidden behind the veil of his diaphanous screen.

"I have a message for you, O My Brothers. I hear a voice, and it's the Voice of the Revolution, whispering in my ear, burning in front of me like a shrub at the top of a mountain. It is a voice which must be heard, and you, Sons and Daughters of the Revolution, must hearken.

"A conflict is upon us. I see students betrayed and enraged by the hypocrisy of government. I see their anger flowing. I see them taking buildings, marching and protesting against the mining of the Ho Chi Minh Trail in the widening war, now spilling into Cambodia and onto television, into living rooms across our land. Helicopters are flying, dropping men, while planes are dropping bombs to destroy the VC infestation that's proliferating along the Trail. It's an aerial ballet, filled with the music of diesel engines and jet turbines, played out in a dance of flying war machines and a smell of gasoline, the drama supplied by the lives and deaths of the troops and villagers on the ground as thousands of tons of bombs explode. And there above, God pulls strings in a lottery, choosing which boys will live and which die.

"I've been in Nam, but it had a different name. In 1942, it was Guadalcanal, the Battle of the Solomon Islands. I know the terrain, and it's all the same. I know the smell. I know the price that has to be paid, and I know the outcome. We young and fresh-faced boys must always foot the bill.

"But I also know the difference between Nam and the Solomons. World War II was a moral fight, the lines of Good and Evil clearly drawn. We were fighting monsters, and they had to be defeated. These evil agents were fighting to take over the world, committing genocide as if they were slaughtering cattle. They espoused racial superiority and gave themselves the right to destroy and rule others. It was our enemies who justified that war and gave us the moral impetus. It propelled us, the Americans, to the status of world saviors.

"But what of this current war in Vietnam? We're told it's a fight to stop 'Communism,' a mantra spooned us like dog food from a can. The Voice on the mountain has spoken to me and has bid me to implore you, My Brothers—do not die for someone else's mantra. Do not die facedown in the rice paddies or up to your thighs in jungle mud and rain in order to protect the tin mines owned by the capitalist elite. Do not die for any of them, the dog tag numbers dangling from your necks. Die on your own, and die for your own sakes, and let the Vietnamese rule their own lives and die in their beds of old age."

31

Nietzsche, Supermen & the Death of God

"You know," said Gilly, "that's where I'm headed. Dying for someone else's morality. 'Cause it just ain't mine no more. The only thing I can't tell you is *when* I'm gonna die. Or where—jungles, paddies or digging a latrine."

We left Saint Paul's Chapel and headed back to the dorms where another of Milo's parties was cranking up. As the elevator doors banged open, we were hit with billowing smoke and the din of a boozy, dope-happy crowd. When we got to my door it was open, and Gilly and I ducked in.

Nebraska lay sprawled on his bed, alone in the room, reading his favorite comics from the Rip Off Press. "Hey, J-Bee! This Mr. Natural is an icon. A guidepost for our generation."

I liked Nebraska's comics. It was hard not to get stoned, lie down on the floor and have a good laugh. But there was a time for everything, and this wasn't it.

"South, meet the Midwest," I said. "GI Joe, meet Huck Finn goes to college."

Gilly and Nebraska shook hands.

"Any friend of J-Bee's is a friend of mine," said Gilly.

"Nice to meet you."

"So why you holed up in your room? Why not at the party?"

"I can't go. I don't want *him* to know I exist. I'm flying under the radar."

We said goodbye to Nebraska and wandered down the hall through the haze of reefer. Gilly remembered from my letter why Nebraska was spooked and how I had confronted Milo.

"You should have kept your cool," said Gilly. "You don't show feelings to the enemy."

"I was angry."

"Right," he said. "Go figure."

As we got to Milo's door, I leaned in and pointed out Milo.

"The tall one?" he asked.

"Yeah."

"Long straight white hair, skinny black tie?"

"That's him," I said.

Gilly stood squinting, taking it in. But before he could enter the room, Julie sidled up, having noticed my good-looking friend, and hooked her arm lazily over his shoulder.

"Gilly," I said, "this is Julie."

"Hi," she gurgled.

Julie was already stoned, but even with her glassy eyes, her high beams went up and down Gilly in a flash.

"You call this partying being a student?" he said. "Nice life!"

"Well," squeaked Julie, "I study hard to play hard. Know what I mean?" She winked at Gilly and, leaning forward with a soft-ish belch, lurched a bit, her breasts juggling against her tee. She grabbed his bicep to steady herself and then looked up at him, a rock of masculinity, sipping his beer calmly.

"Thanks," she said, smiling at Gilly.

"Don't mention it," he said.

"Uh," I said, "later."

Gilly tipped his hand at me, and Julie giggled. She turned to Gilly and put her fingers through the stubble of his hair, her female mind and motivation undraped.

I had no worries for Julie; she would get what she wanted, and Gilly would get the exercise and catharsis which have been the balm of soldiers throughout human history. For me, however, it was back to the crucible of learning, the library where I hoped to see Margo but ended up amidst words of dead philosophers. I threw down an armload of books and waded into the pool of deepest thought: Kant droned ethics while small, anemic, near-blind Nietzsche sat in an attic with a candle, dreaming of supermen and the death of God. After a while, their words blended together, numbing my overworked brain which escaped by envisioning something else: The Serpent lounging in a poofy armchair, feet up on a table in front of him, his big green head thrust through the collar of his white shirt and smoking jacket. His elbow rested on the arm of his chair while his fingers held a cigar to his green, puckered lips. He inhaled smoke and blew out one ring after another.

"I have something to tell you," he said. "You must choose, or I choose for you."

I stared at the creature, and he stared back. I realized I was looking at an image of myself, and it was me who was holding the cigar and blowing smoke through a leathery, toothless mouth. Membranous reptilian lids closed over my eyes. I succumbed to the power of sleep and did not try to understand.

—⚹—

"You're sleeping again!"

It was a giggling voice, and I felt her buzz of energy next to me, rousing me from my twilight state. I felt her touch my head. Gently.

I cracked an eyelid without raising my head.

"Margo."

She was smiling. I felt sun where there was no sun, beaming down upon me.

"I was hoping to catch you here," she said.

She sat down. There were a few others studying, sprinkled lightly among the tables under the cathedral ceilings in the rarefied air of Butler Library.

"It was Kant. He's a dead man who puts me to sleep. I don't know how he wrote it—*I* would fall asleep writing that stuff."

"Uh-huh."

In the short time we had been apart, I missed her. Now that she was next to me, I felt a sudden jolt of energy. I wanted us to talk and never stop, but then I restrained myself, deciding to be calm and measured in order to avoid seeming rash or foolish.

"I took Gilly to The Apocalypse Café," I said.

"Your soldier friend. Did he like it?"

"He felt the same way I did. It's a spooky place, like the dungeons of Saint Eustace."

"That Catholic school you went to—they had dungeons?"

"Probably not."

"Probably not? What does that mean?"

"When I think of that place, I remember it through the lens of the mind of a little kid, like I was then. We were always hearing about dungeons under the school. There *was* a basement. It scared the hell out of me, and kids seemed to disappear down there. The Sisters would take them down, and they'd never come back. Everyone said the Sisters chained them to the walls, but who knew? Maybe their parents just took them out of school. Maybe they just moved away. But they were gone, and everyone whispered about it. Some kids said they heard them screaming down there. Or they heard chains."

"And you believed it?"

"We were *kids*. It was Catholic school, and we all knew that strange things happened in Catholic schools. They beat us, and everything was about 'The Devil' and 'Satan' and how we had to be punished in order to dislodge the evil spirits from our bodies. We *believed* that stuff. It was plausible, considering the state of the world at the time."

Margo leaned toward me, examining my face for distress. Her forehead was furrowed and her brows arched. She kissed my cheek. Maybe it was love, but it felt like pity.

"I don't want pity, not from anyone." I was bleating like a sheep. "I guess I can't escape my emotional attachment to the Church; its ideas are so deeply baked into me. It's like an addiction—I just can't imagine a world without the framework of Catholicism. I'm afraid that if I lose this anchor, I'll be adrift in a life devoid of any meaning. It frightens me."

Margo leaned back in her chair. Her face hardened, and her eyes narrowed, indications that thoughts were crystallizing. She was my guru, and I awaited her pronouncement.

"So what's the answer?"

"Catholicism," she said, "is successful because for Catholics, morality in this world can get you to heaven in the next. They might have nothing in this world, not even the shirts on their backs as they scratch out their lives, but they get something later that the rich who exploit them can never have. Therein lies a powerful inducement—you can get the better of your oppressors in the next world if only you do what the Church tells you. To throw away heaven, even if the chance that heaven exists is very slim, is risky. It's a system that's hard to reject. There is an analogy to this in the Vietnam War. We have a moral responsibility to fight in order to avert the takeover of the world by Communism which threatens to take over America. It's a terrifying thought. It's also a convenient moral imperative for those who want us to fight."

She was my oracle; she had answers. Then, just for a moment, she reminded me of The Serpent. I asked her, "Do you know who The Serpent is? The one who speaks in the basement of Saint Paul's Chapel?"

"No."

"Well, you remind me of him."

"Who is he?"

"I don't really know, but I thought maybe *you* did. Your ability to unravel things in order to analyze them is like his, and your views feel similar." I was jealous, and I was afraid she might discover it. I was jealous to think that another man had shared his thoughts with her and had formed her mind on the subject. *Who was this man who pretended to be The Serpent?*

"What do you mean?" she asked.

"I was wondering how it is that you're so fluent with The Serpent's ideas. At times you almost seem to parrot his views. Is he someone you know?"

"I don't parrot *anyone's* views. What's this about?"

She was angry that I was accusing her of being an intellectual acolyte. I felt a sinking at the bottom of my belly as if she had pulled the plug, such was the power of her disapproval. Where the ship of my soul had been skipping along on a placid sea, she would now unleash a storm, and I was to be sucked into the loveless void where all uncompassed ships are destroyed.

Then her expression changed as she read the emotions on my guileless face.

"Oh, don't tell me!" she squeaked with innocent delight. "You're jealous! Come on, J-Bee, tell me! Are you jealous?"

I felt as green as the hills of Erin, land of my forefathers, but also red hot with the anger of one whose secrets were betrayed. In short, I was confused over emotions that only Margo could incite. To make it worse, I reminded myself that *she* had broken off with *me*—I was jealous and had no right to be.

"Why should I be jealous? Do you know him, or don't you?"

"Of course not. I didn't know about him until you told me about him."

"Do I believe you? Or did you sit down with me just to taunt me."

"Should I swear to God and hope to die? Would you believe me then?"

She leaned over and gave me a hug, which had the effect it always had. The steam blowing out my ears turned off like a valve, and the lion that was me was suddenly bleating again, like a lamb.

32

Atrocities

Margo said there was something she wanted to tell me, so we packed up our books and stood outside at the entrance to the library in the cold.

"When it finally sank in that I might never see you again," she said, "it was absolutely unbearable. 'Why?' I kept asking myself, 'why does this boy have such a hold on me?' When you're not there, I miss you terribly."

She looked up at me with her brown eyes in the way she always did, rendering me paralyzed with an intensity of affection that could only be love. Why should she be so amazed at her feelings? Why would she fight how she felt? I respected love. I paid homage to the great god Love, and I couldn't understand why she would mount even the slightest resistance.

"Will you take me back?" she asked, her eyes closed and her lips slightly parted. "I can't resist any longer. I submit to this power, this spell you've cast over me. Please tell me you'll have me back."

To think that I had the guile or manipulation to cast a spell on anyone made me chuckle. I was too unrefined for any of that, yet there she stood, her eyes closed, waiting for my response.

"You really want me back?"

"I can't study anymore. I sit there; I read, but I can't retain anything. I can't sleep—I lie on my back and look at the ceiling. I'm losing weight; I have no appetite. When I think about how I've lost you, I'm sick to my stomach. Yes, I want you back, but do you want me?"

"Of course I want you back!" I said, smiling like an idiot. "It was *you* who wanted out."

We hugged tightly, and I knew happiness again. As we relaxed our embrace, she said, "I was wrong—you need to discover who you are without me pressuring you. It's *your* life, and you have to find your own way. I know that now, but wow—I've missed you!"

—∿—

Dreaming of Margo, I sat on the Sundial, the very heart of the campus, and waited for Gilly. Yellow-green shoots of spring were poking from the hibernating browns of twigs on either side of the campus walkways while the sun dripped warmth on my shoulders. March was turning the corner to April, and the campus was teeming with people. Some were marching with purpose while others strolled aimlessly, happy to be there, sharing the grounds with the pigeons that strutted about.

I saw Gilly as he approached from Amsterdam Avenue. He came over, sat down and put his arm around my shoulders.

"My oldest friend in the world," he said.

"Where've you been? I've hardly seen you the last few days."

"I've been with Bloom. Nice fella. I went to see where he lives. He's struggling with pain. Not walking much. Says it used to be his old war wound, but now it's prostate cancer, and it's gotten worse. He says it's in his bones."

"Yeah, he told me about it."

"I brought him some groceries. Says his daughter started shopping for him, but it sounds like they don't get along. Sounds like it's hit and miss. He makes excuses for her; says she's studying and works a job so she can't always come by."

"He told you about his daughter?"

"He did. We got to talking about a lot of different things. He's a war hero, you know."

"I heard something about that. From the bartender at The Rail."

"He was in World War II, in the Pacific, under MacArthur. He understands Southeast Asia. He's fought in the jungles on those outpost islands. He calls them 'rocks.' We talked about fighting hand to hand—he really knows what I'm going through. He's a piece of history, an interesting man. Interesting opinions too! Who knows? I could grow up to be *him* someday."

"Good," I said. "I'm glad you got to know him."

"We've got another thing in common: he's taken a shine to you. He thinks about you like I do. We want you to grow to be somebody special, to *do* something special. We agree you belong here in this 'Ivory Tower.'"

We sat at the epicenter of fortress Columbia, bastion of academe and cloister of all human knowledge. Students, professors, long-haired freaks and blazered preppies swirled everywhere around us, all with ambition, all going somewhere important. Gilly swept his arm slowly in front of him as if unveiling the campus from behind the curtain of its history, descendant of medieval enclaves of learning, its perimeter replete with spiked gates and fences.

"It's a special place," he said. "No question, it's where you belong."

We sat side by side, two connected solitudes.

"You should go visit him, J-Bee."

"Bloom? To his apartment? I've gone a few times."

"You should go again. He'd like to see you."

"Yeah, I haven't gone lately."

"You should. He's an old 'war horse'—his words—and he's probably going to die in there alone. I thought I'd tell you since you and I don't have much time left together."

"You leaving? I've hardly seen you!"

"I'm going back to Nam."

He was my oldest living friend, the kid who, in his innocence, would knock me down and beat me up when we were five and six. We shared something I didn't have with others. Two Southern boys reunited on the streets of New York.

"I can't believe you're leaving. I'll miss you. And back to that hell-hole too."

"I joined up by choice—it's my own fault. I just hope I survive to finish my tour."

"You'll survive," I said. "How long 'til you're out?"

"I don't know. Months. It doesn't matter. I'm not the same boy anymore, and I don't see any way back."

"C'mon—you'll be out soon enough, and a stretch of normal civilian life will change you back to your old self."

I knew I was lying. I still felt guilty that I wasn't in Nam with my friend, and I *was* guilty for lying to his face, but I didn't regret what I said.

"No," he said. "I don't think so. It's not like you knocking those kids around with a stickball bat in Norfolk. It's mortal sins. I'm damned to Hell. I've got nightmares. I can't sleep. If I hear a car backfire, I hit the sidewalk, chest down. I can't watch westerns on TV—too nerve-racking with all those guns going off. I'll never be able to go near the Fourth of July. Normal folks think I'm wired, and I am. I *see* how they look at me. And there's a reason for all this—I've killed men with my bayonet in their ribs, up to the hilt, their face in my face, their breath so close I could smell their breakfast. I've seen men rape women with babies looking on. What the hell was I doing there? I've seen so much death it's sticking to my skin—I can't wash off the odor. I went to the Saigon whorehouses, and I paid those women more than what they asked, but it didn't wipe away my sin. God showed me there was nothing I could do to cleanse myself. And no matter what I gave them, the women hated me anyway. I can't say I blame them. I see what we're doing, and they've done nothing to deserve it."

"Have you gone to Church? Did you go to confession? Take communion?"

"You're asking if I performed the sacraments to purge my sins? You know I can't take communion. My sins are mortal; I'm eternally damned. My soul isn't clean enough to receive the host."

"It's not your fault, Gilly. You're a soldier. You have no choice."

"I've told myself that a thousand times, but it doesn't work. Of course I had a choice—I volunteered, didn't I?"

"But we're young and stupid," I said. "We believed what everyone told us. My own father even told us! That the war is for a good cause, that we're protecting democracy. Christ, I still half believe it myself. Even now it's hard for me to let it go. And when you volunteered, it made me feel good, like part of me was absolved for not being there. So it's not your fault. The truth is you didn't volunteer for what you got. For the lies."

"You're right. They lied. But it doesn't matter because I still have no way back. I'm a soldier, and I'm a murderer. It's my trade. Even if our country has stamped its approval on my butt, and even if they lied to me, it's still a mortal sin. A filthy, unforgivable sin. And I'm soaked in it so deep it's running in my veins."

I looked at my friend's shaved head. I looked in his eyes, and the light there was dull like the eyes of fish on ice in the market. He was not the rope-skipping kid I knew in school; he was way older than me now. He carried more on his shoulders than I ever did, and I was helpless to free him from the trap in which I found him. It was sad—he was missing the joy that *my* youth had found, the freedom to live in a wondrous, enchanted world and the exciting expectation of a future which could yield great things.

"I did something for you, J-Bee. Call it a gift from a friend. I also thought it might cleanse me; do me some good. But it didn't. I'm deeper in the dungeons of Saint Eustace than I ever was. I'm chained to the wall. I'm never getting out. I feel the evil spirits closing in. They're marking me so Satan can find me. They're pissing on my soul so The Devil can smell me. But I'm glad I did it. I'm a soldier. I'm trained to do this kind of thing. I *could* do it, so I *did* do it. I did it for you. I may be a goner, but you're still okay. Your sins are nothing compared to mine, and I couldn't bear to see you do anything to dig your small hole deeper."

"For Christ's sake, what're you talking about?"

"Now that I'm about to tell you, I'm not sure I should. I don't think you should share any part of this."

"Part of what?"

Gilly's dull stare was upon me, and I stared back.

"What?"

Then it hit me—it all fit. "Oh for the love of God! I *know* what you did!"

He just sat, unblinking.

I swallowed. My throat was dry. I crossed myself without thinking.

"Why, for the immortal love of Jesus, did you do it!"

He stared at me deadpan, a very tough man. I watched and could do nothing as he sank in quicksand in front of me, up to his waist and then to his neck, his face as stoic as ever, his mouth a tough-tight line of determination until, gasping his last breath, he went under the liquidy surface.

"I remember," he said, "when you stopped wearing that cross in high school. I stopped when I was in Nam. I confess—I'll tell you even though I don't like saying it: God is gone from my life."

He stood up for a moment and stretched; then he sat back down next to me. "I shadowed Milo. He covered a lot of ground, going in and out of that Morningside Park, going back and forth to Harlem. Running drugs or whatever the hell he was doing. He had that big guy with him—that guy Miguel with the scar on his throat, the guy you told me about.

"Anyway, I bought a six-foot length of bamboo and sliced off the end at an angle to make it razor sharp. An old gook trick. I went looking for Milo, but I ended up spotting Miguel instead. It turned out lucky that I found him first as he was the more danger-ous of the two. He wasn't expecting me, so I tailed him into the park down a narrow path. I followed him to a small clearing sur-rounded by thick brush where he sat down on a big rock. The rock was in front of a tall bank of weeds, and behind that was a thick wall of brambles and scrubby trees that encircled the clearing on three sides. I hid and watched for a while to see what he was up to until I realized he might be waiting for someone—possibly Milo. I decided to act fast. I went over, step by step, what I was going to do in my mind; then I jumped him, running out of the brush and screaming like a banshee.

"I took him by surprise. He stood and put his hands up, but I ran the bamboo right through him. I aimed the pole at his chest, but he hit it with his arm, deflecting it up. I had so much force behind it; it deflected only a little and went through his neck and out the other side. He staggered backward into the high weeds and pitched on the ground. He was rolling around, grabbing his neck and pulling at the spear, but there was nothing he could do. It played out in seconds, blood pumping out his neck and running out his mouth. God, how he gurgled, choking on blood. Must've hit an artery."

"Christ! You killed him?" I was horrified. My mind saw Miguel on the ground, rolling in agony, blood gushing out of him. Thoughts streamed through my head—I was trying to escape from violence while Gilly was in its embrace. "I can't believe it!"

"Believe it! This is what I do in Nam—that's why they sent me there! So let me finish. I need to tell you the whole story." He took a breath and wiped his face with his hand. "When big boy stopped moving, I grabbed the bamboo shaft, put my boot against his head and yanked it out. I dragged his body to a dense area of vegetation and scrubby trees so he was hidden—I didn't want Milo to see him and freak out. Then I went back to my hiding place and waited. Sure enough, I heard someone coming along the path, and it was Milo. He sat down on that same rock. I heard him say something like, 'Where the fuck is he?'

"I let him sit and stew for a while, then I came out of the brush and stood a few yards in front of him, blocking the path out. The wall of trees and vegetation trapped him; I knew he couldn't escape. I took care to put the end of the spear on the ground with the point straight up, in a sort of a neutral position, so as not to scare him. I stood stock still at attention while Milo just stared at me, probably wondering what the hell I was doing there with a bamboo pole. He tried to be cool, but he looked pretty rattled. Me,

I was in battle mode, ready to do anything, and he was the target. I saw him like Viet Cong. I hated him like the enemy.

" 'I'm waiting for someone,' he said. 'What are you doing here?'

"I didn't answer. He asked my name, but I said there was no need for that. 'We have business,' I said. 'I'll tell you my name when it's time. But let's be frank—you killed Billy Wing, am I right?'

"He said, 'Not really.'

" 'Okay, so you had someone else do it, probably Miguel.'

"He didn't answer. He just sat on his rock staring at me. I said, 'Try to be a man. I'm asking you again—you killed Billy Wing, am I right?'

" 'What's it to you?'

" 'You're not leaving until you answer the question.' I noticed he was about to get to his feet, so I added, 'And don't stand up or you'll make me nervous—no telling what I might do.'

" 'I'm waiting for someone,' he said, looking past me down the path. 'He'll be here any second.'

" 'If you're waiting for Miguel, he's not coming.'

" 'He's never late. He'll be here.'

" 'He won't.'

" 'You're very sure of yourself,' he said. Then he pulls out this switchblade and says that, if he wanted, he could 'cut my eyeballs out' or some such thing. 'Miguel's coming down that path as we speak, and then you'll have some explaining.'

" 'You have no idea what you're doing,' I said. 'Miguel's lying yonder, dead on the ground.'

" 'Bullshit,' he said, but he was afraid. I pointed to the patch of brush where I had dragged the body, and he noticed some blood.

" 'I'm saying for the last time, you're not leaving here until you tell me you killed Billy Wing.'

"He licked his lips and put away his switchblade. 'It was purely business. If he was something to you, I'll make it up to you. I'll pay you for it. You can come and work for me. I can always use a resourceful man.'

"I couldn't let it go. I was in too deep. I wasn't going to let him put *you* in danger. I had him in my sights. He knew I had killed

Miguel so there was no way I'd let him go. 'That's a nice offer,' I said. But then I was curious, so I asked him how he fooled the police into thinking it was suicide.

"'Simple,' he said. He was smirking now, acting like we was all friends. 'We put on hospital gloves,' he said. 'I have access to those kinds of things.'

"'That's all I wanted to know.'

"I stepped toward him, but he stood up and stepped back. 'Stop. I'll pay you whatever you want.'

"He was a squealer, J-Bee. A boot-licking coward. He stood there, tall and awkward with his little black tie. He looked stupid and afraid, but I knew he was bad to the bone, so I moved closer and said, 'You asked my name.'

"'Yeah,' he said.

"'My name is Billy Wing,' I said. 'But for you, I'm the end of all things.'

"I struck hard and sudden, like a copperhead. I used the same bamboo pole; I rammed it through his chest. Those punji poles are amazing sharp. I leaned on that thing 'til it came out his back. He grunted and swore 'til his legs gave out, and then he passed out on his feet and fell down. I watched 'til his eyes went cold. Then I left them both in the weeds to rot. That park is a jungle, and I know what a jungle is if I know anything. And I know how to do these things. They trained me for a killer. Between the army, the Sisters and the Viet Cong, I'm a professional killer now, God help me. I feel the evil in me. It's some kind of force, an urge, a reflex to do bad things. I have no idea what'll happen after the war when I have to live stateside with civilized people. I don't know if I've got any hope. I killed that man. Two men. I know you didn't ask, but I did it for you. I did it because I knew what kind of people they were and what they did to your friend Billy. I was sure you were going to try to kill them yourself, and I was afraid they might hurt you. Or worse. You've got to promise me you'll keep clean—you had nothing to do with this. I'm the one who's damned."

Horror, anger and guilt gripped my brain. My greatest friend had jumped off a cliff into insanity. Desperately I now searched for a droplet of hope with a divining rod in the sand dunes of the Sahara, but nothing. My mind came to rest at the helpless despair etched on the tattered banners that flap over the gates of Hell. I had wanted to be with him in Nam, but the chasm between us was now complete. Worst of all was the part I had played, wittingly or unwittingly, in luring him to the revenge he had enacted on my behalf.

I wanted to yell. I wanted to curse. I wanted to undo what couldn't be undone, yet all I could say was, "You can't do this!"

"It's done, J-Bee. There's no going back. Please accept it—I did it for you."

I was stunned. I couldn't reject my friend's request.

"Anyway," he said, "is this really any different than me killing the enemy overseas? They're people too, but it's just that they're hidden from view, unknown people in Southeast Asia. Another race. We don't know their individual stories, so it's all impersonal. People who've never been to war think it's like football. Just a game, know what I mean? 'Better luck next time,' or, 'Take one for the team.'

"But it's not like that. Killing is killing, and death is death. It's final. This time, I did the dirty work so you can go to this great university and get the education you deserve. And when I leave here, I'll still be doing the dirty work over there, in Nam. I'm so proud to be your friend. It's one of the few things I've got. I need you to stay clean, and I want you to always let me call you brother. That's all I ask. I just need to know you're there, and that you're my friend."

"Christ, Gilly! Of course you're my friend!" But all I felt was horror and an urge to vomit. Milo, a prep school boy gone wrong, would never be a cardiologist now. No matter what he had been— and God knows I hated him—I was no judge to sentence him.

Or was I? Was I a hypocrite by hiding myself behind excuses, trying to run from the part I had played in his death? Or was I merely conflicted, still lost in the Babel that was New York, weak and unable to make up my mind which side of the fence I was on?

"What the hell did I ever do for you that you would *kill* for me?" I asked.

"You were my brother in arms, back in Saint Eustace when we were babies. We fought the Sisters together—you gave me heart. You're my brother, J-Bee, more than the guys in my platoon, and there's nothing I wouldn't do for you."

"Gilly, why? Why have you done this! I wouldn't have killed anyone!"

"I know you, J-Bee. I know you'd have done it. I had to stop you, so I did it myself."

"No really—I wouldn't have."

"Yes you would. Just look at how you battered those two kids back in Norfolk. Look how you planned it. And you didn't tell a soul—not even me—until I confronted you. Oh, yes, J-Bee, you could've done it. You *would've* done it!"

His face was strong and determined, filled with the certainty in what he had done and why.

"Christ, Gilly, don't you see? If you believe that, then it's my fault you did this!"

He looked at me quizzically as if he didn't quite figure how the guilt could shift from him to me so easily, especially as he had already thought it all through. Then his face took a darker, half-terrified look as he began to imagine that what I said might be true and that his entire plan might have backfired. But then his face changed back to stony certainty and confidence once again, and he said, "You're mighty wrong, J-Bee—the guilt lies squarely with me."

If Gilly was depraved, I was at the bottom of it, and I was dizzied by my complicity in the acts of horrible violence he had committed. I heard the voices of the Sisters, shrieking, telling me that I had led my friend to the destruction of his heavenly soul and that I was to blame, that I had sent him to his ruin so that I could survive and live a good, happy life. I felt their presence swirling over me, their black billowing habits flying them through the air until they transmuted into women with beaks and wings and talons, coming down upon me to rip the skin off my back, leaving me to perish and my bones to decay from exposure to the elements.

For a moment I lost my balance, almost toppling over, my brain whirling from the vortex of imagery.

"J-Bee?" Gilly said, grabbing my arm. "You okay?"

I took a sigh and let my hands drop. I looked at Gilly, a fellow lost soul, but deeper in blackness than me. I was, at least, beginning to see light in my life while he was heading the other way. I knew that right now, there would be no point in telling him that what he had just done, what he had thought was a gift or some kind of divine intervention wherein he was the instrument, was really a meaningless act of depravity and bottomless evil. It would not help him if I were to explain this to him, and it would not change his point of view. At least not now.

"I'm fine," I said.

"Your life is ahead of you; the guilt lies squarely with me."

I nodded my head to agree, knowing full well that my agreement to his assertion was a lie but realizing that it would be cruel, even inhuman, to argue with him about what might be, or could be the truth. Maybe, like me, he would get another chance to wipe his slate clean, sometime in that distant haze ahead of us that we call the future. Meanwhile his life was in the balance, floating in the space-time continuum, subject to that great lottery, that universal randomness that governs all fates. As he was headed back to the jungles of Southeast Asia where every man had to harden his soul to be able to execute just about any unspeakable horror in order to survive, it was not the time to soften him up, to tell him that he had made a grave mistake or to cause him to doubt what he had done. No matter how horrible his life was, his immediate survival depended upon him being a warrior. Intellectual truth and understanding—and even his redemption—would have to wait until, and if, he might survive. It was not the time to remind him of his days as a choir boy, nor was it time to tell him that maybe, just maybe, in a tomorrow loaded with uncertainty, it might yet be possible for him to rediscover the simplicity of happiness and the innocence of his youth.

33

Gift

As I jogged along the river on my way to visit Bloom, I recalled a conversation from a few days earlier. MacNeish had sent Bornes to warn me, "I've got something to tell you—dig *this*."

"What?"

"Milo's on the warpath. You know he can be nasty when he's like this. He's *not* cool. But don't tell anyone I warned you. I don't want to get myself killed for something stupid like *this*. No way. I'm all peace and love at the moment. Ya dig? Are we cool?"

"We're cool."

"Good. You need to get real because when Milo's like this, I head for the hills, you know what I mean? We may be cool, but he's definitely *not* cool. He's off his fuckin' rocker. No point in talking to him about being cool. He doesn't give a flying fuck, I can tell you. No way, man. And there's no way out."

The next day, MacNeish sidled up as if by coincidence. I knew his duplicity, his style to act nonchalant while knowing exactly what he was up to. He had it all planned, every step choreographed.

I wanted to tell him that his friend was feeding the dandelions, but I had to be careful. It was ironic that I could say nothing about Milo's death, and I knew it might be a long time before someone would discover the body. Until then, Milo would molder in Morningside Park, a place no one was brave enough to penetrate because of the criminals it harbored.

"Milo's coming back soon," he said. "He may be out of town at the moment, but he won't like that you're influencing Nebraska. He won't like it if he finds out you're trying to dissuade Nebraska from working for him. He's not going to take a shine to you. Guaranteed."

"How do you know? Did he tell you?"

"He has ways of letting people know how he feels. He doesn't have to tell anyone anything."

"You didn't answer the question, MacNeish. What are you, his agent? Did he send you to tell me, or not?"

"No, he didn't tell me."

"He's got a mouth. Let him tell me himself."

"I'm just being a friend."

"Whose friend?"

"Your friend. I like you, J-Bee. I'm warning you so nothing happens to you."

"That's not a very veiled threat."

"I'm not threatening you—I'm warning you about Milo. He's dangerous, unpredictable. He gets unstuck."

"Right."

"You don't have to do anything. Just stay out of it."

"He's his own man, Nebraska. There's nothing I could say to affect him either way."

"So you don't deny meddling?"

"What's it to you? You're cross-examining me, so it's obvious he sent you. I always figured you for a pimp. You're Milo's little pimp."

"For your information, I haven't seen Milo in a couple of weeks."

"Really? Well maybe he's changed his mind. Why don't you ask him again."

I was getting worked up; I could feel it.

"And another thing," I said. "I know you pimped my roomie out of his money, money that was meant for Milo. I know you, MacNeish."

MacNeish turned on his heels and walked.

"If I were you," I said, "I'd move a little faster before I have a mind to run you down and take Nebraska's money back."

McNeish broke into a trot and was out of sight, around the corner.

—ɯ—

Bloom saw me half in and half out of his bedroom doorway. I felt hesitant to trespass in his inner sanctum where he lay on his bed.

"Don't worry about it. Come in."

It was a vintage Upper West Side apartment, built in the 1920s with hot water circulating in pipes to heat the place and flaking plaster in the corners of the ceiling. The air was warm, sullied with odors from his urine-tainted underwear and the stale sweated linens on which he slept. He lay there, limbs flaccid, bony ribs showing through an unbuttoned shirt.

"Sorry I'm such a mess," he said, laughing. "It's no fun dying, and it's worse to die falling apart, little by little. The cancer in my bones has aggravated the old war wound. The doctors said the blood vessels to the wound are impaired by the cancer, so the antibiotics can't get in to heal it, and the body's defenses can't get in to repair it. Something like that."

"Dying?"

I took a step into the room and saw dull green pus soaking through gauze bandages on his leg. I was dizzied by the sweetish, rotten smell.

"Sorry to disappoint."

My stomach clenched, and just for a second I heard flies buzzing. My vision grayed, and my legs wobbled.

"You look pasty—you all right?"

The ridges on Bloom's brow deepened with concern.

"Fine." Sweat beaded on my forehead and ran from my armpits.

"Sit down."

I found a hard, wooden chair against the wall and pulled it toward the bed.

"I know what it is," he said. "I can smell it. I smelt the same thing at Aola Bay, in Guadalcanal. War doesn't just kill men; it makes them rot before they die. The stink made me vomit. All those rows of bodies ripening in the sun, bloating as they cooked. Some were dead, and some were only half dead. But they all stank."

He looked me square in the eye. "And now it's me."

His jaw tightened. "I lived through war, but somehow it's all caught up with me, lying here, limp as a dishrag. An old soldier, finally getting what he deserves after all the hell he's caused his enemies. Other human beings."

"They would have killed you."

"Yes, that's right. But the fact remains: *I* killed *them*. I took everything they had. Some of them up close, with my own hands. It's hard for me to forgive myself, and some days I don't want to."

He put his face in his hands and rubbed. Then he dropped his hands and shook his head.

"Good of you to come," he said. The jaw line was hard, the neck ropey with tendons and muscles. Yet the eyelids were puffy, and under the eyes the flesh was pouchy.

"Good to be here," I said.

"I've got something I want to give you."

He made an effort to lift himself, then decided not to try and eased back down.

"I can still walk, but not too far. Even with my bones falling apart. But I'm tired right now so you'll have to get it yourself."

I stood up.

"Go to the chest over there in the corner. Top drawer, on the left, under the white shirts."

I opened the drawer and rummaged under the shirts.

"It's a small box. Take it out."

I found the box and brought it to the bed.

"Open it," he said.

Inside were two small metallic objects.

"I don't have much, but I'm giving these to you. It's all I've got. Take them out of the box."

I did as I was told. One was a Purple Heart medal, dangling from its ribbon, and the other was something more important: a golden star with an eagle perched over it, maybe brass, hanging from a blue ribbon of the same color as the American flag with thirteen tiny white stars on the blue. I had seen one once on one of my father's naval comrades, but without the eagle. Still, there was no mistaking it, the Congressional Medal of Honor.

"I can't have these!"

"Why the hell not?"

"These are treasures."

"They're mine, and I can do what I like with 'em. And I can't take 'em with me where I'm going."

"Don't you want to keep them in the family?"

"I only have a daughter, and she doesn't want them."

I was caught between them. I was keeping a secret from Bloom at Margo's behest: that I knew she was his daughter. Conversely *he* was telling me to keep his medals rather than give them to her, and I had the feeling that that was supposed to be secret too.

There was a knock at his front door.

We looked at each other, but abruptly I noticed that he was looking at me differently. His eyes narrowed. The mood was changing; I felt uneasy. Something was about to happen. He was looking at me not as a friend but more like someone about whom he had just realized something, and he was rolling it around in his head. The moment before we were casual, close. Now he was judging me. He was walking around me, eyeing me from new perspectives, and he hadn't yet made up his mind.

He said hurriedly, "Put the box in your pocket. Do it!"

I heard a key in the front-door lock, clunking as the dead bolt slid. The knob turned, and a light step entered and shut the door.

I put the box in my pocket.

"I can't get around too easily right now so my daughter comes over once in a while. I didn't have a daughter for a long time. Then she heard I was going to kick it, so she decided she wanted to rebuild her relationship with the old man before his demise. She's been angry. Many things it seems. Very complicated. In fact, much too complicated for me to understand. A woman thing. Inner rage. The wringing of hands. Guilt because she was forced to turn away. The only thing I understand is that she's just like me, but a woman."

"I got some milk, coffee and eggs like you wanted." It was a voice from the kitchen, muffled by the walls, but I knew the voice.

"I have a visitor," he said.

A few drawers closed, and a cabinet slammed shut.

"I'll come right in. Or should I leave? You need privacy?"

"Come in and say hello."

Steps on the tiles approached, and there she was, in the doorway, bushy brown hair and all.

"Hello, Margo."

"J-Bee?"

"You two know each other?" said Bloom, looking at Margo with some confusion. "I mean, I know you know who he is—from The Rail and all. But you *know* him?"

"You know I do," said Margo, pointing her chin at me. "I told you about him."

"This is the guy you were talking about? You never said!"

"You never asked!"

Bloom paused a moment and then turned to me. "I suppose you didn't know she was my daughter because her name is different. Well, she got married very young."

"Bloom—Dad—you don't have an opinion. Save it, *please.*"

She went over and kissed her father on the top of his head.

"Progress," said Bloom, pointing at his daughter. "I get a kiss." He was smiling now, uncharacteristically.

Margo rolled her eyes.

"She ruined her life because of me," Bloom went on. "Or so she says. She also accuses me of ruining her mother's life, which is unfair. Then she ran away with Mitch Rankin to escape the family her mother and I had tried to build for her."

"That's not quite the way it was," said Margo.

"Your mother wanted me out of her life, and you wanted me out of yours. Men have no rights when it comes to what women want." Bloom looked miserable. He waved his arm, "Well, I wouldn't go away. I wouldn't do what I was commanded to do. I never had a chance from the start." He turned back to me. "Does she treat you any better?"

I looked at Margo, and her face flushed crimson. She looked away.

"She treats me fine," I said. "Margo can make me happier than anyone I know."

Bloom glanced at his daughter.

"He's a good lad."

"Don't I know it," whispered Margo. "I don't treat him too well, but what would you expect?"

"My fault again?" said Bloom.

"I didn't say that!"

He ignored her. "J-Bee's a nice fellow. He's got a clean slate. Why make him pay for whatever's making you angry? Wake up and smell the roses. Or be angry, if you want, but keep him out of it."

"Too late," she said. "It's always too late."

34

The Weathermen

It was the middle of April. Multicolored spring burst upon campus with flowers in the beds, dew on the grass, and a warm yellow sun. Students washed like tides across the main plaza while others perched like puffins on the great stone steps of Low Library, some basking, others reading books. Classes would be ending within weeks.

At the very heart of the campus, orators with bullhorns stood on the round, flat-topped monolith of the Sundial and spewed rhetoric with an angry edge. It was an event ignored by many, but for others there was a compelling urgency, and a crowd had formed to listen.

The message was simple though the problem was not. After Nixon had promised not to ramp up the war, our B-52s were now bombing Phnom Penh and Hanoi. The Southeast Asian theater of war was widening, and our troops were invading Cambodia, signaling an escalation of the draft to facilitate the war's expansion. More boys were needed to populate the schemes of the Pentagon, and more boys, perforce, would die.

Along with speeches through bullhorns, plans were emerging for more demonstrations. Students clamored to exercise their rights to assembly, organizing anti-war protests on campus.

I sat on the steps alone in the crowd. I listened at a distance to the words from the Sundial, but mostly I attempted to read a letter from my father. One passage stood out:

They're spoiled, long-haired kids, looking to be in the spotlight. I don't understand the selfish mentality of putting oneself ahead of the needs of a nation.

I say join the navy and fight for your country. If you join the navy, you follow your forefathers. Boats are clean; you won't die in a ditch. Moreover, Vietnam is not a naval war so it should be safer on a boat. Can you join an officer training program at Columbia? It's a good career and might be a springboard into other careers, like oceangoing commerce or politics. George Washington, Teddy Roosevelt and Ike were all great warriors before they were presidents. Be amongst them.

Margo was excited I was going to an SDS meeting. She skipped alongside me, talking as we went. She thought she had convinced me to come, and though the truth was different, I didn't want to displease her because it was better to keep our peace. I was a political agnostic with a strong curiosity, and my desire to explore the issues was the reason I had come to college in the first place. Columbia was a litmus test for my soul, and I was placing myself in situations to see if I would take sides. I didn't know what I was or what I would do. I didn't know in which direction I would be blown, but I wanted to discover the properties of the sum total of the subparts that was me.

Margo had been at Columbia in the spring of 1968 as a freshman during massive campus protests against government-funded military research and CIA recruitment. She knew the leaders of SDS from her connection to Rankin, and one by one, I had heard the stories.

"They were crazy boys, and I was this little wide-eyed girl, you know, in pigtails."

I looked at Margo through both the objective lens of intellectuality and the prism of my desire. She was a serious woman, blessed with talent in every facet of her life, but now I imagined her in pigtails. It was a brief but powerful daydream, leaving me in love with her for having an innocence somewhere in her past. It aroused me to conjure this image in pigtails, and then it turned to the jealous roar of a freight train as I imagined how she had been broken in by another man, her innocence torn away to be replaced by the worldliness that adulthood must bring.

I suffered in silence.

"In '68, hundreds barricaded themselves in campus buildings, but the entire effort was much bigger: thousands protested, and close to a thousand were arrested when the cops stormed campus. It was one of the biggest, if not *the* biggest student protest in American history. Near the end, most of those occupying buildings had fled; only a few dozen of the most determined radicals remained. The finale was in Hamilton and Lewisohn Halls where the last of the students were cornered, refusing to come out. The police had them inside with no witnesses—no media, no photographers—and they beat the crap out of the kids with nightsticks. When the boys were dragged out, their heads were flattened. A bloody mess. Blood out their noses and ears, blood running from their scalps. They were beaten, but no one lost an eye. No one was paralyzed. No deaths. Most were arrested, but some got away and went underground, on the run. Unlike what happened later at Kent State, no one was shot. But there were massive, ongoing student strikes and boycotts, canceling classes for the rest of the year.

"Mitch was arrested and then, after being released from jail, hung around campus. That's when we got married. He insisted, and I was too young to know better. I was this little empty-headed girl, but that changed fast when Mitch left me. He joined the Weather Underground and eventually got a stretch in prison for building bombs in the basement of some rat hole in the East Village. I went there once, but I never went back. The paint was flaking off the walls in sheets, and ceiling plaster was falling to the floor in chunks. *My* apartment's got roaches, but *they* had roaches in the East Village the size of Yorkshire terriers. If you left the table for half a minute, the roaches would carry away your dinner. I never went back; the marriage was pointless, and my father was right all along."

"And you didn't like that."

"No, I didn't. Did I say I was perfect? Anyway, Mitch's arrest and his radical activities got in the papers. I was interrogated, but I didn't know what he was up to, so they let me go. My father was livid. He hated Mitch all along. I eventually understood, but I never openly sided with either of them. I felt caught in the middle. After that, there was another group of radical Weather-boys who were killed when their homemade bombs went off in another basement downtown. It was a dangerous business."

"Where were you when the bombs went off?"

"I missed two semesters at school, but only because I was depressed and had to work for tuition. I didn't return to Mitch. He left me flat for the radical left, worse than if he'd left me for another woman. In the end, I didn't love him. He wasn't a man of warmth, Mitch Rankin."

"What did Bloom say?"

"He said 'Good riddance' and told me never look back. He's a strange man, but he's always stood by me."

"I don't think he's all that strange."

"He's over thirty, and you know what they say—*never trust anyone over thirty.*"

She burst out laughing, and I laughed too.

"Who invented that?"

"Jack Weinberg. A guy in Berkeley's Free Speech Movement. Anyway, 'strange' is the wrong word for my old man; *enigmatic* is better. I never thought to ask him about his secrets because I never suspected he had any. He's so secretive you can't even tell he's got them. But he does. Lots."

The SDS meeting was in Dodge Hall. We took seats at the back with about fifty others. The tone was more serious than the lecture on quarks. Margo leaned over and whispered that even if it were impossible to know which ones they were, the FBI was there, somewhere in the crowd, spying on us and recording what we said. This, however, didn't bother the student standing in front.

His name was Pruitt, and he wore a hooded sweatshirt, Converse high tops and jeans. His face and neck were covered with beard, and he had a thick curly mass of hair like he'd jammed his fingers in a socket. Next to him in a chair was another man, a few years older in a crumpled blazer and a white shirt open at the neck. He was scanning the audience, and when he saw Margo, he nodded without so much as a flicker of a smile.

"Who's that?"

"Johnny Avecedo. He was a student strike leader in '68. He's very smart. He never went underground; he kept his head above water. There was never anything crazy about *him*. He had the respect of students *and* the administration. He dresses academic establishment, but he's anything but. He's got a legitimate job working for the media. He was in the class of '68 with Mitch. He graduated; Mitch didn't."

"They've taken away our student deferments," Pruitt was saying. "Many of us are going to be shipped out—unless we take a stand, here and now, and fight it!"

"Right on!" The crowd came to its feet, fists pumping air.

Pruitt motioned us to sit.

"But it's worse than that," he said. "The war isn't winding down like Nixon promised—"

"He lies!"

"—it's escalating!" cried Pruitt.

"Tricky Dick!" someone shouted.

"It's escalating because Nixon is bombing the Ho Chi Minh Trail in Cambodia and dropping helicopter troops behind the Trail, in Laos!"

"Not Laos!" shouted another.

"We're not at war with Cambodia, and we're not at war with Laos, but Nixon is dragging them in—two sovereign nations—whether they like it or not!"

"No way!"

"To add to this," said Pruitt, his voice rising, "Columbia's doing research to mine the Ho Chi Minh Trail. Columbia is at the forefront of war technology, getting money from JASON so that we, Columbia's very own, paying heavy tuition for the privilege to be here, can die alongside other boys from all walks of life. We're paying for the privilege of throwing our bodies in a line of fire from our Vietnamese brothers who fight to unite their homeland!"

"Right on!"

"I tell you now, we can't stand by and watch this happen, this meticulous and relentless laying of seeds—teeth—in the furrows of war! We must organize our plans to protest and strike—we must jam the mechanism of the university machine so that we, with the only means left to us, can take action against the powers that would otherwise send us to extinction in a land that doesn't belong to us, where we have no business dying!"

The crowd stood again at once and applauded, many with fists in the air, many shouting "Right on!" over and over.

Avecedo never moved from his seat but looked placidly at the audience.

There was talk of burning the American flag, burning draft cards, marching with the flag of North Vietnam, and carrying banners of Ho Chi Minh, but then things calmed down. Issues were addressed, and plans were made so that at the end of April and the beginning of May, just before finals, a series of sit-ins and demonstrations would take place. The culmination would be a protest on the Van Am Quad, a grassy area rimmed by a solid wall of buildings on three sides—John Jay, Hartley, Livingston and Hamilton Halls. While students on the Van Am Quad would be protesting, other students would be sitting-in, in front of the dean's office inside Hamilton.

This protest, however, was not to be the finale. It was to be the harbinger of a general student strike, the object of which would be to shut down the university completely.

"We want the university to screech to a halt! We want control! We must show them *we're* in charge—not them! We won't tolerate establishment-driven chicanery and lies!"

"Power to the people!" screamed a woman.

"There are twenty thousand students on this campus," said Pruitt. "We want a strike, and we want them all in it! We want to burrow under the skin of the administration—to irritate the dean, the provost, and the university president until their stress is unbearable! We want to goose them into reacting with force—a reaction which will create public sympathy and ignite student outrage! A reaction which will power our demonstrations and fuel the combustion of our protests! We want a battle with the administration to electrify the media and galvanize more students to join the strike!"

I was impressed with Pruitt, standing for a cause. But was he just another "crazy boy" as Margo called them? Would he be willing to sacrifice himself totally and risk his life and future for this cause? It seemed he would. This was a man with ability, a firebrand, standing in front of his peers, offering up a message like a Christ. But was he righteous? Or was he just another power broker with a talent for silky patter? Was he in it for the high that he got when he was filled with the message of his god, drunk on his own words as he mesmerized his audience to follow him into dark and risky places?

I was also impressed by the congregants. They had passion, an argument, and a cause, and they were ready for a fight.

And what of the Vietnamese people, subjugated for more than a millennium by other more powerful regional dynasties like the Chinese, the Khmers, the Chams and the Mongols? The French and now we, the Americans, were the last in a line of invading powers, conflicting with a Vietnamese people who were desperately fighting for unification. Gilly was with the Americans, and they had trained him to kill, and now he was risking his life on the other side of the planet.

And what of me personally? Could I allow myself to risk arrest in a protest that would stand as concrete evidence against my character for the rest of my life? More than likely such an arrest would taint my chances in future, not only of becoming an officer with a military career but also of getting into graduate school. But was I even capable of standing with bomb-throwing scruffy-faced Weather-boys against everything to which I had been previously connected by birth and by blood? Was it even possible that the genetic mold which spawned me might be flexible enough to withstand such violent change? I honestly did not know.

What would my great friend Gilly say about my joining an anti-war conflagration which was opposed to the stark choice he had made when he enlisted to go to the front? I never forgot my friend Gilly, in firefights for an America which we had learned about in school, an America which fought tirelessly for freedom, always winning against the evils of its enemies. As the public continued to see the televised war in Vietnam, replete with bloodied American boys, the dead were industrially zipped into bags and shipped back home in refrigerated cargo bays. Day after day, the nation watched as TV crews filmed eighteen-year-olds firing automatic weapons at unknown slanty-eyed assailants, all of it bringing back American memories of a righteous war fought only twenty-five years earlier in which the limp, dead bodies of Asian aggressors were dragged from their rat holes, burrowed into the rocky hillsides of islands in the South Pacific.

I did not know what my nature and intellect would force me to choose. If there was a God, He did not whisper the answer in my ear. Only time, which He also governed, would reveal His ultimate intentions toward me and the solution to the puzzle of my fate.

___

35

Morningside Park

Nebraska ran across campus to catch up to me. He was breathing hard.

"Have you seen this!"

He shoved the *Columbia Daily News* in my face.

"What?"

"The police found Milo dead in the park!"

"What park?"

"Morningside. You haven't heard?"

"No."

"They found him with another man. They're both dead—they've been dead for weeks. The bodies were decomposing. Dogs ate them. Parts of them."

"You're not serious."

"Yeah. It's in the paper."

He stuck it out for me, and I took it. "I guess you won't have to work for Milo after all."

"Yeah," he said, "I won't. But there's more. Apparently they'd been looking for this second dead man in connection with Billy Wing's death because a distinctive scar on his neck matched the description from a witness who saw him near Billy's room."

I opened the *News* and read. A bunch of middle-school boys, whose only crime was skipping school and hiding in the park to avoid detection, had found the two dead men. The boys had picked the park as the perfect place to hide because of its dangerous reputation and the unwillingness of people to go in. One of them told his mother about the bodies, and she immediately called the police. "He told me, so I called the police. But if he was doin' somethin' wrong, I don't care if he gets in trouble for playing hooky. He's only twelve. He ain't no murderer."

The police went on to say, "It's been a warm spring. The bodies were more decomposed than would be expected." They had identified a tall man who had a student ID on him, nineteen years old with straight white hair and a short black necktie, but they never mentioned Milo by name. They also identified the other dead man as Miguel Nunez because the body's fingerprints and scar matched those from Nunez's prior arrest record. A police spokesman said that they had been looking for him "for questioning in connection with the death of William Humboldt Wing, but they had been unable to find him."

"I'm going to miss Milo," said MacNeish.

"I'm not."

"He was my friend, J-Bee. You know what a friend is?"

"That's rich," I said, "coming from you."

"Maybe you don't have any friends, but I value mine."

"Billy Wing was my friend. Nebraska *is* my friend."

"You need to make up your mind, J-Bee. You need to take sides. You're a political mess. Your father's an admiral—I'm surprised you're still thinking about which side you're on! Your father can't be happy."

"And you, MacNeish? What the hell are you? You'd sell your kid sister for a nickel. You'd change your vote to increase your stockholdings. Come to think of it, you do that already."

"I had you all wrong. You'll never be a Sachem. You've got this girlfriend who's a subversive, who wants to tear down the country."

"Then I'm a subversive, too, I suppose."

"That's the way it looks. Especially with your hair halfway down your back."

MacNeish had exaggerated the length of my hair, but it was getting longer. It was close to my shoulders, and I was wearing a stub of a ponytail at the back. For him, the longer the hair, the more radical the owner.

"My girlfriend likes it that way," I said.

He snorted.

"I want to make it official," I went on. "I really don't care about your society of blazers and stirred drinks. I see them in my mind, sitting back in their poofy couches. They don't care about people— they've got their tin mines to worry about. You should be happy I'm not in the club."

"I don't wear blazers," said McNeish.

"It's got nothing to do with blazers. It has to do with that nose-in-the-air, greed-infested attitude y'all have."

"It's your girlfriend who's got an attitude. She's a pretty self-righteous know-it-all."

"Yup, that's her. How would you know about her, anyway? You don't truck with women."

MacNeish put on a phony grin.

"Yeah," I said. "I know about you. Not that I care, to be honest. It has nothing to do with why you're a lizard."

"She's in one of my poli-sci classes. She shoots her mouth off a hell of a lot."

"I know exactly what you're saying. You mean she shuts you down if you even attempt to speak. You're afraid to fence with her. Her mind can tear you to ribbons."

"That's a load of crap."

"You have to say that. You have to save your face. Anyway, why don't you leave her out of it? You wouldn't understand the emotions between two people anyway, so don't even try. You're this thing, MacNeish. A mechanical device with gears, someone once said. A backstabber. What do you know about friendship? With you it's all about what someone else can feed you. You require material for friendship. It's all quid pro quo. It's not about actually *liking* anybody. You're this green toad—whatever you touch turns to warts and money."

He shrugged. "Doesn't sound so bad to me. But you—what kind of subversive are you? Are you going on strike with the hippies? No. So maybe you're going to join the sit-ins outside the dean's office? No again. Or did you join the marchers on Broadway the other day?"

"No," I said, "did you?"

"I don't do that stuff; you know that. I don't believe in selling out my country. I'm a loyalist. But how about you? Which side are you on?"

"Bornes's side."

"He's not on a side. He drifts through life, stoned all the time, spewing that '*cool man, dig it, right on, get real, far out*' bullshit. He's got no backbone. No ambition. Where's your backbone, J-Bee? Are you coming out of your cave yet?"

—⚏—

Clusters of picketers appeared on campus, walking in circles in front of some of the buildings where war research was underway. They were carrying placards, "Bring Our Boys Home," "End the War," and "Stop Columbia's War Research." There were shoving matches between protesters and members of The Silent Majority, a newly formed group on the national scene, a backlash against the anti-war movement. The name was coined in a speech in which Nixon said his actions were backed by a "silent majority" of Americans. At Columbia, they were students with short hair, khakis and button-down collars, who also went by the name The Majority Coalition. The year before, I might have been mistaken for one of them, but no one would mistake me now. I was evolving, almost transformed. I had begun college under a rock, a sightless worm inching through tunnels in the mud. As my metamorphosis progressed, I came out of the darkness to emerge as a being who rejoiced in the sun, on the verge of understanding though not yet enlightened; possibility of satori was palpable.

Meanwhile confrontations on campus increased in number and intensity. As a fledgling longhair, I was occasionally an object of derision, at times shoved from behind by groups of men in khakis and oxfords, bellowing with laughter as they passed me on walkways to class.

But more serious things were happening. A sit-in at Lewisohn Hall was in progress when The Majority Coalition stormed in to drag protesters away, yanking them by arms and legs or even by the hair. *ABC Eyewitness News* arrived outside the building with star reporter Melba Tolliver, interviewing as cameras rolled and floodlights beamed. In front of the building with film footage cranking, the two groups threw punches until campus security pulled them apart and bolted the doors.

Most nights, the six o'clock *Eyewitness News* began by featuring Tolliver, and students filled the TV lounges to see themselves and their friends being interviewed while bleeding onto their shirt-fronts. In Margo's words, the media had turned serious issues into a circus and students into self-adulating voyeurs. All thoughts of war and anti-war were momentarily suspended as students sought the spotlight of celebrity cameos that only the media could provide.

"Are you fighting for peace?" Tolliver asked a student outside Hamilton Hall.

"We're fighting to save our boys from dying for nothing. We're fighting to prevent the dictatorship of The Military Industrial Complex. We're fighting to stop Columbia from making money by participating in a war machine which supports the fruitless killing of people twelve thousand miles away."

"Is that all you're fighting for?"

"No. We're fighting to avoid the draft. We're fighting to end the hypocrisy of this war. And we're fighting like hell for our lives."

36

Valhalla

Margo said her father wanted to see me, and I wanted to see Bloom to get his views on the draft. Mick, at The Rail, hadn't seen him for weeks, and Margo said he was wasting away, unable to lift himself off his bed. "He's refusing to go to the hospital," she said, alternately raising her hands to the heavens and then burrowing her fingers in the roots of her scalp. "I'm tearing my hair out! The old grouch won't listen to reason." She deepened her voice to imitate her father: "I'll die in my bed! I won't die in an institution with bustling women barking orders with their stupid white smocks and those nursing hats stapled to their steel-wire hair—they use enough hair spray to asphyxiate an army! It'd be like a barracks for sick men, and I'd be cowering under the sheets out of fear for female commandants in jackboots!" Back to her natural voice, she asked, "Get the idea?"

When I arrived at his flat and opened the door, I gagged on the smell. Lying in bed, he was smaller than I remembered, his legs as bony as a stork's. He had hollows at his temples and between the bones on the backs of his hands. Clustered around him were chairs and tables piled with all kinds of clutter: half-eaten morsels on plates, boxes of juice with bent straws, bottles of pills, and a small handheld urinal.

"I've got something to tell you," said Bloom. "Time's run out."

We eyed each other. Bloom bit his lip with the subtlest movement. When he realized I saw him, he stopped. Then he clenched his jaw.

A clock was ticking somewhere, and for a second I saw it from when I was tripping, the clock with the ponderous cucumber hands, spinning out of control. A bead of sweat formed at my sideburn; I wiped it. It felt like minutes passing, but it may have only been seconds. If there were trust and friendship, there would have to be truth, and Bloom, seemingly on his deathbed, was at a crossroads of speaking the truth or losing that moment between us.

Out of the soup of the many and jumbled thoughts in my head, I suddenly had an epiphany. I recognized something so new to my thinking that I hadn't yet sifted the words to express it.

"I know what you're going to say," I said.

The statement surprised us both.

"How can you know what I'm going to say?"

"It just came to me."

"What exactly just came to you?"

"The Serpent," I said.

Bloom and I had never discussed The Serpent before, and it caught him like a slap in the face. He sat staring at me, unable to hide, a warrior-heap of broken bones, half undraped and in bandages, his gangrenous leg shackling him to his sickbed.

"I asked Margo if she knew who The Serpent was because she talks about the same kinds of things in the same kinds of ways as he does. I couldn't make a connection, but then you popped in my head."

"How's she treating you?" he asked.

"Who?"

"Margo, my brilliant daughter."

"Good."

"Don't let her strong-arm you. She's a forceful woman, and she likes her way."

"I do know it."

"You love her, I think."

I nodded. His words were a truth I couldn't escape. I loved her. I was her acolyte, her devotee. She had taught me things and was as dear to me as Gilly, the difference being that I was forever at her feet, looking up.

"But the answer to your question," said Bloom, "is yes. I'm The Serpent. I'm sorry for not telling you before, but somehow it never came up. I'm shocked you guessed, but then why not? It only proves that I've chosen you wisely."

I felt uneasiness in my gut, a queasy feeling that something I did not want was about to fall on top of me.

"You've chosen me for something?"

"Yes. I'm a dying man. I'm wrapping things up. You don't have to take it on, of course, but I need you to. For my peace of mind. I have hope you can do this, and you're unquestionably the anointed one."

He reached over to his night table for a pill in a bottle, and he washed it down with water in a finger-smudged glass. I looked out the window and saw traffic inching slowly on the boulevard as always, the endless stream of millions of people in the tidal bore of Manhattan.

"It's for the pain," he said. "My bones hurt."

"Which ones?"

"All of them. Cancer's no picnic. Anyway I had to tell you today, which is why I sent for you. No one else knows I'm The Serpent. Or that I used to be, I should say. The Serpent persona has been a secret."

I was momentarily confused. I had come to him with the notion that I had raised the subject of The Serpent to *him*, but now I found that it had been his plan all along to settle this issue on *me*.

"What do you mean you had to tell me *today*?"

"I'm close to the end. I'm going to die. A man can feel Death at his shoulder, and I feel Him right now. He's lurking in the shadows; He'll make his move soon."

I started to object to the idea that he was dying, but he held up his hand to stop me.

"There's no time for Southern politeness. Reality can be harsh, but we have to honor the truth."

I wanted to say something else, but again he held up his hand.

"This is the wish of a dying man, and you must *hearken*."

It was The Serpent I heard, and I was compelled to hearken. Bloom was a broken warrior, yet the mind hadn't stopped as the body crumbled.

I gave in to his demand.

"There's a reason you have to know this secret," he said. "I'm not telling you for kicks. And when I die, you become the keeper of that secret. It'll be yours to safeguard until it's time to reveal it to the world in the way it should be revealed. We are linked, you and I. Not much different from how you're linked to your friend Gilly. He's a good man, but he's a lost boy because of this war. My war gave me an identity. *I'm* a hero. *His* war has destroyed his soul. There are many factors involved: the two wars are different, and we two men, Gilly and me, are different from each other as well. But we three, you included, are friends in a deep sense. And so I tell you with no malice, between friends and about our friend—he's a lost boy. I worry for him every day, and that's a fact.

"But not you. I'm not worried about you in the least. When I gave you my medals, I knew it was right. I knew you understood their value. And now they serve as a material link between us. They are the substantive evidence with which the deal is sealed. Of course, we're both linked through Margo, but that was an accident—or maybe just the divine hand of fate. So now, on to the final contract between us, and then the mantle and the aegis will have passed from one generation to the next, and I will be free of it all, relax my grip and drift off to Valhalla."

37

The TPF

I ate and slept. I studied in the library with and without Margo. When the library's silence became too oppressive, its musty air so dry that my book pages went brittle and cracked, I got up and walked the campus alone. During these gushes of freedom, I allowed my mind to wander. I replayed the conversation with Bloom in my head, over and over, asking myself if I had to be responsible for his legacy merely because he had said so. In the end, I saw that friendship demanded I take responsibility even though I felt ill-equipped to take over where he had left off.

"The medals were a gift," he had said, lying inert on his bed, his bones like so many sticks of wood. "But now I give you a burden. Or perhaps it's just another kind of gift. A disguised gift. A spiritual gift. Whatever you call it, this and the medals are a paltry legacy, but they're all I've got so I'm passing them to you. *You* will be The Serpent. *You* will carry the lineage. I can't do it—I'm finished."

"Me? I can't! I've got nothing to say."

It was an honor, but I was unworthy. It had taken me all year to crawl out from under my rock, a giant step forward in my small life. Yet now I felt hopeless and exposed by Bloom. Once again, I was oversensitive to the light. All I wanted was to slink back into the ooze and darkness from whence I had come.

"You'll find your voice. You *will* become what it is within you to be, even if it takes another forty or fifty years. Someday you'll speak out with your message. You *will* have something to say, and you'll say it when you're ready."

I felt doomed to failure. I sensed that I would feel this failure for the rest of my life, and the idea of it filled me with dread. I would carry my unfinished promise to Bloom like a stone around my neck, without relief, eternally circling my rung in Dante's pit of Hell. There seemed nothing I could do to avoid it. The decision was made, and I couldn't—and wouldn't—abandon my promise.

—⚹—

Classes were ending. Finals loomed. Spring's evolutionary carnival was crowned in pastel pinks and lavenders as tulips in the thousands erupted from muddy beds. Student throngs churned with hormonal tides in the walkways while lusty cats screeched and rutted in alleys, and birds trilled in treetops.

There had been smaller demonstrations in the prior few weeks, and Lewisohn Hall had been overrun by students who garrisoned there for seventeen days. But the demonstration planned for this day by Pruitt and the SDS was to be the culmination of all that had come before, and it would happen on the Van Am Quad in front of Hamilton Hall. Students would stage a sit-in at the dean's office inside the building, presaging a possible takeover of the building by protesters who would mass on the Quad.

"The university won't call cops on campus again," said Margo. "Not after '68. This is our chance to get involved."

I had agreed to meet her there, so I walked across campus to join the others. I was mildly uneasy, unsure about how I'd feel to stand in solidarity with "long-haired hippie-freaks," as my father would say. Yes, my hair was long, but this was a chance to resolve the paradox of my dilemma. I would test my feelings for and against the war by thrusting myself into the cauldron of the protest in order to discover which way my emotions and intellect would guide me.

The protest had begun. The Van Am Quad was a rectangular green space with crisscrossing paths and a stone gazebo at its center. One side of the rectangle's perimeter was formed by John Jay Hall; the second by Hartley and Livingston Halls. These three dorms stood next to each other with no spaces between, a solid wall of brick and cement, a full two city blocks in length. The third contiguous side rimming the Quad was formed by Hamilton Hall, home to the dean and his minions, the steps of which were almost as wide as the building itself. The last side of the Quad was open, sloping slightly upward and adjoining the rest of the campus.

Pruitt, bullhorn in hand, climbed halfway up the steps of Hamilton Hall and then turned to face the protesting students on the Van Am Quad.

"The sit-in has gone on for hours," he announced. "We've stuffed the dean's office with wall-to-wall bodies. They're the wisdom teeth that the dean never had—he'll have to yank them out or drag them out to get them out!"

I monitored the protest standing a short distance away on the Quad. I scanned the demonstrators but saw no sign of Margo. More and more students, many of whom had been watching on the sidelines, ambled in to join the protest. What had started as twenty or thirty had become a hundred, and now the hundred was doubling. Beyond these two hundred, another hundred or more were milling, both in and around the Quad, enjoying the sunshine of a glorious day. Some smoked, some lay on the grass, and some talked with excited anticipation that something important was about to happen. As I watched and time advanced, the distance between me and the protest shrank: the crowd was growing in my direction, and I edged nearer and nearer.

I knew why I was there. I knew why I was interested. I wanted to see and hear, and I was drawn, inch by inch, into the whirlpool of the times. LBJ had lied to us, and now that LBJ was gone it was Nixon, busily escalating the war by mining the Ho Chi Minh Trail, bombing Cambodia, and taking away our deferments. These politicians, old men, used us like pawns on a board in a bid to place themselves in history.

The Serpent in the bowels of Saint Paul's Chapel had told us, "If you do not do battle on the shores of the Tonkin Gulf, you will surely do battle on the campus quads where your blood will spatter the curbstones." So as the sun beat down upon me from the heavens and the flowers bled color in their beds, I found myself standing in the crowd amongst my peers in protest. Pruitt led us in chants and then preached on the bullhorn, "The second-year anniversary of the deaths of the martyrs of Kent State is nigh—we shall not forget them!"

"Right on!" roared the crowd, hoisting fists in the air.

"We stand with them today. Although they died in innocence, they died for us, never believing that armed men of our own country, in our own generation, would pull the trigger and gun them down in cold blood!"

"That's right!"

"We stand here today at a watershed in history. Our own university feeds the war machine. The stars are aligning to bring us to confront our nemesis, and I say we will not shrink away when we confront these forces of The Establishment which aim to do us harm! *Are you with me*?"

"Yes!" roared the crowd again.

"We must face this evil war as soldiers for a different cause! A righteous cause! We must stand together!"

While Pruitt's voice rose, echoed by the growing body of demonstrators, New York City cops filtered in, standing around the fringes of our host, collecting on the open edge of the Quad. They were dubbed "New York's Finest" by the media, but most of our generation on the nation's campuses referred to them as "The Pigs." Sporadic cries of "Pigs on cam-pus!" spontaneously rang out.

The cops paid no attention. At first, one cop had appeared; then there were three or four. I carefully examined them: standing near students who had come for a stroll, they may have been six foot six or seven, big and broad-shouldered with glinting guns.

They wore tinted shades, light blue battle helmets, jodhpurs and black leather jackboots. Their motorcycles looked like toys as they straddled them.

I had heard of these cops, these elite of the NYPD, identifiable by gold insignia pins worn on their collars, bearing the initials "TPF." They were the "Tactical Police Force," and I'd heard they had to be six foot three and 220 pounds to qualify, the biggest and toughest of cops, culled from this city of eight million souls.

As I watched, more TPF appeared in groups of two and three, standing next to each other and laughing with ease. They were gathering like birds on a wire. At first their presence was unobtrusive; they made little noise. Some puttered in on motorcycles, others clopped in on horseback. Then slowly, steadily, their numbers grew. The groups of two and three swelled into a battalion of fifty and then one hundred, and then two hundred big strapping beefs, their roaring road hogs rivaling the energetic chanting of the protest. They dismounted to form a wall of armed men in a tight, linear array along the open edge of the Quad, brandishing nightsticks and facing the haphazard mob of students. Behind this front line of TPF, another two lines were forming, waiting their turn. Behind all of these was a detachment of cops who stayed on their horses, accompanied by lieutenants with bullhorns and paddy wagons which had parked in a line in the middle of campus near the Sundial. Surrounding them all were ancillary cop personnel and a swarm of journalists, buzzing with cameras in tow.

From where I stood at the gazebo in the middle of the Quad, a spot where I had taken a book so many times in order to linger in peace, the situation now seemed dire. The TPF were unimaginable creatures—giant, stony, a collection of the biggest people ever seen at one time and one place on the planet. No matter how determined the students could be, believing they could change a society rife with wrongheadedness, I saw that the TPF would never be stopped.

Who had called this army of Philistines here, so obviously meant to crush us? Since the campus was private property, the call had to have come from the office of the university president.

A student leaned into me, "There's going to be some cracked heads." I saw a familiar face with hair down his back and a tee shirt which said, "Make Love Not War."

"I mean," said Bornes, "can you dig this? The fun and games are over, man. The demonstration was way cool. The kids have had their little outing, exercising their lungs, singing and chanting— *Kumbaya*, you know? But recess is over, the bell has rung, and now it's time to split. Unless of course you want to end up with a broken face wearing striped pajamas in the city jail. How useless is that? Totally *uncool*. I'm going inside the dorms to watch the panic from the other side of the glass doors. Coming with me?"

I considered my chances; the lines were drawn. I could see it all in my head, and yet there I was, heading down the garden path toward confrontation with unstoppable forces.

"It looks like Kent State all over again," Bornes said. "Very uncool. I don't want to get shot. I don't want to be one of those bodies on the evening news, lying facedown on the ground with a teary-eyed chorus leaning over me, moaning my name. No thanks. I've just gotten a lottery number that'll keep me out of the war, and I'm not about to trade going to Nam for getting my head blown off in my own backyard. Fuck that, ya dig?"

I looked at Bornes. He had a point. I knew I could die right here on home soil. More likely I might take a beating, something I knew how to take. But looking at the size of the cops, my odds seemed poor either way.

"You coming?"

"Not yet," I said surprised, still not ready to leave.

"Suit yourself." He shrugged and was off to the doors of John Jay Hall, leaving me with Pruitt and his long-haired anti-war rag-tags. The repetitive chant of three hundred jean-jacketed students reverberated in my ears and vibrated my gut. "Pigs on cam-pus! Pigs on cam-pus" rang out, making me a part of this greater whole, not unlike what I felt as a little boy listening to the organ booming in church. Our sound was loud and our arms upraised, beating the air with each syllable of the chant, a peace sign on some fingers and the fuck-off sign on others, jugular veins bulging and faces reddened.

We were trapped between the TPF, Hamilton Hall and the solid brick wall of the dorms when the doors of Hamilton burst open, and the students who had been sitting-in at the dean's office scampered out the doors and down the steps in front of the building shouting, "They're in the tunnels! They're in the tunnels!" Then the doors banged open again, and a hundred more helmeted TPF came pouring out, this time with plastic battle shields. They positioned themselves in rows on the building's steps, a spot where, only days before, students had sprawled, chattering in the shade of the blooming cherries.

We all knew about the tunnels which connected the buildings on campus, conduits built so that students could move underground between classes without walking outside. The conclusion was obvious: somewhere else on campus in a clandestine operation, a veteran TPF unit had gathered en masse before entering the tunnels and bursting unexpectedly through Hamilton's doors. They stood shoulder to shoulder on the steps, six or seven cops deep, shields edge to edge, a bulletproof, rock-proof wall. Their shields were wide and long, covering the troopers' faces, distorting and blurring their features into grotesques. It was a staged invasion, no different from the way the Viet Cong moved through their own underground tunnels on the Ho Chi Minh Trail, ready to strike the enemy.

During the seconds after the cops had settled into position, there was a moment of stillness in which no voice was heard. My heart pumped strong in my chest, and I heard its thump in my ears. The sun beat down, and no breeze blew. The wheezing of a bus on Amsterdam Avenue was heard above the continual grinding of traffic. A bird chirped briefly then stopped, self-conscious it had broken the silence. The Earth hurtled through space no different than it had for billions of years, insouciant to the human drama and struggle irrelevant to its trajectory.

I heard something faint but unmistakable from behind the lines of police. A whistle blew a single faded note, a signal. Descending the steps of Hamilton Hall, the men in blue pressed forward—one solid wall of battle shields, advancing like a single crawling organism. They marched at us in the unwavering lines of a Roman phalanx, one line after the other, forward in lockstep, leaving us no place to go. We were repelled in a crush and had to give way and move backward.

Some of the students turned and fled toward the refuge of the dorms behind us. But as they reached the threshold of the doors which were always open during the day, they found them dead-bolted. They couldn't get in, and there was no other place to run— they were trapped like the rest of us at the mercy of our foes. Some of the women in the crowd lost control and screamed, but then the anti-war chanting began again as the hardiest amongst us railed against the oncoming tide, a defiance which was our only and last remaining weapon.

I sensed a betrayal as keen as Judas's kiss—the president of Columbia, our own university, had called the mayor to send the TPF. A tremor ran through me, an anger, and I raised my right arm and pumped it, joining the chorus, "Pigs on cam-pus! Pigs on cam-pus!" My pulse was bounding in my neck, and I was alive to the impending clash for which we were raw recruits. I recalled MacNeish's words, "Join me, J-Bee." I remembered Melberg had said, "Run to Canada, J-Bee." But I had ignored their requests. There were others as well, and I had ignored them all, and now it was too late. Too late to stand up and say politely to one of the TPF facing me, "Excuse me, sir, but there's been a mistake—please let me pass and go home." I was on a battleground making history, and the only question left was whether I would make a stand or forever equivocate on the greatest issue of the times. How would I face the moment? Would my skull be crushed? Would I fall and never get up? Would I fight to kill my oppressors, or would I walk forward, head held high, a nonviolent soldier ready to fall for the cause but never to kill for it?

A second whistle blew, halting the men with shields in their tracks. The other line of TPF, along the open edge of the Quad, stood tense and unmoving, their contiguous nightsticks touching end-to-end, horizontal in front of their chests. These cops were unencumbered by the shields and gear of their counterparts, making them more mobile.

The chanting had stopped, but the protesters waved their fists and hurled obscenities at their opponents.

Within seconds a third whistle, and the TPF without shields, from the open side of the Quad, broke ranks and charged straight at us like minions of Hell. As if we were mortal enemies, they knocked us down, kicking and punching, thumping us with their sticks. The protesting crowd fell apart, but I didn't run. I knew that the time to pay the price was now, the great climax that we all live and die for. TPF were swinging their clubs with two hands like bats, others tackled students in full flight. Students ran to the doors of the dorms where the crush only worsened, and shouts went up for help as students banged in panic. Some fell to the ground and might have been trampled, but others inside the dorms who had watched the scene unfold opened some doors to let their peers in. I wasn't far from those doors, and I thought about running, but instead I turned to the oncoming blitz.

It was a slaughter. The dogs of The Establishment had nothing to hold them back. I perceived a ripple in the cosmos followed by the injection of an alien but friendly spirit into my being. It energized me, filling me with momentary passion. I felt its vibration; it wriggled inside me, urging me to burst forth from my constraints. My emergence was like a hatchling's, and my eyes opened to a newness in the world. The image of Bloom, still and motionless, lying on his bed with his eyes suddenly fixed and sightless, sprang into my head. Next I saw Stankewicz and Laureen on the ground where I had put them, amongst the weeds in a deserted lot. I saw Gilly's face as he told me, "My killings have warped my soul—I'm ruined!" Last of all, I saw a monk in black robes, sitting cross-legged in the street, exploding into flames, agonizing but unwavering in the face of gathering twilight.

I understood who I was and what I had to do.

Escalating noise and movement brought me back to my senses as I awoke to chaos all around me. The students were routed but not without a fight. Some lay bleeding and broken on the ground, but others were striking back, punching, biting and kicking their foes. Watching this infused me with rage and contempt. Though I would not be violent, I would be counted. I pumped my arm in the air and yelled at the top of my lungs in support of our cause and against the outrage of the slaughter.

I was whacked on the head by something hard, pain blinding my vision.

I wobbled. I grabbed my skull. Things blurred in front of me. I felt to vomit but retched instead. Then I was hit on my upper back, and the day became gray.

I went down. I was kicked in the chest. I coughed and sucked air. Two sets of arms rolled me on my stomach, pulling my hands behind my back. I turned my head to the side and gasped, sucking in dirt and grass. I tried to spit, but bits of grass stuck to my lips. I coughed and felt something move in my lungs. I retched again. Sticky fluid ran down my face, clotting my eyebrows and burning my eyes. There was an intense pinch on my wrists, and I couldn't adjust my arms to relieve it, nor could I wipe my burning eyes—my wrists had been cuffed. Cops yanked me up from under my armpits, and I thought my hands would rip clean off. I thought my shoulders would be torn from their sockets. They pulled me so fast that my legs couldn't keep up, leaving my feet to drag as they pulled me. Angry faces loomed through a fog, screaming profanities and throwing small objects at me. People jumped out of the crowd to hit me, one or two succeeding before being restrained by cops. These people were students of my own generation, people who had sat in classes with me, studying at night in the same libraries, living and sleeping in the same dorms as I did.

I saw Harris and Melberg watching on the sidelines, pointing to people they knew. When they saw me, they waved, but I couldn't wave back. MacNeish was there too, and I saw his face: yelling, his teeth bared, his eyes narrowed. He stood in a cluster with Doncaster and Prince and other men in chinos. They were shoulder to shoulder, safe behind TPF lines.

When we reached the paddy wagons, they unlocked the cuffs and shoved me in the back of a large van—a mobile holding tank—with comrades from the protest. They packed us in, kids pressed one against the other, sitting on the cold metal floor. All the windows were barred and closed, and the air was dense with breath, sweat and mold. From what I saw in the light of one gray bulb on the ceiling, hunched young men clutched their heads and extremities. They were compatriots in battle, prisoners of war, and we were all hauled off to the enemy stockade.

At the jail, they threw me behind bars in a room with many of the others. All the benches were taken, and there were no chairs. I was dizzy and slumped to the floor, relieved that the handcuffs were off but with my skull and brain still aching. I put my fingertips to my head and did so gingerly, feeling my way slowly over the spongy, pulpy mass that had swelled there.

38

Redemption

A young man leaned over me, his face shadowed by a thick, curly mass of hair. "You brought the fight to them today," he said. "You didn't deserve this, but as they say, no good deed goes unpunished."

"You look better than I feel," I said, the act of speaking throbbing my head.

"You were tough. I got off easy compared to you."

He handed me a paper towel and motioned for me to wipe the blood from my face.

"Pruitt?"

"Yeah. You were brave out there today. I saw you. You stood up and made a statement with that herd of gorillas from NYPD stampeding us. By the way, you all right? Do you need a doctor?"

I wasn't all right, but I said I was.

"You're one tough fucker," he said. "I'm sure the army could use someone like you, but I'm glad you're with us."

Relief washed over me. I was in physical pain, but Pruitt's words, true or untrue, bathed my soul. I repeated it to myself—I had done something good. I remembered the secret well of power and privilege from which the elite drank, and I saw the nuns with their whips encircling the well, protecting it. I saw the ragged poor as they lingered on the edge of this oasis, faces sallow and sagging, mouths empty, bellies ascitic and swollen as they dwindled, scratching the hard earth to survive, pissing in the dust to etch their boundaries and make their mark on the world. I saw them dying, flies buzzing in endless feast.

Perhaps the way of the world would never change. Nevertheless I had fought for change. I had planted my foot outside the circle with Pruitt, whose demonstration was the vehicle through which a message was delivered. His voice told me that I had done penance and earned forgiveness in an unexpected way. However, he had no idea of the demonstration's personal effect on *me*. In response, I wanted to tell him I knew how to take a beating, but my aching body didn't feel like talking. I wanted to tell him I had been hardened at the hands of the Sisters. I wanted to tell him that I may have given to the cause, but that the cause, to my surprise, had given me back incomparably more. It was baptism—my soul had been cleansed.

Pruitt and I sat with the others while surveillance cameras observed us from the corners of the ceiling. The holding cell was filled with protesters who had been with us on the Van Am Quad, and Pruitt talked to each in turn. It was plain that others were hurt: a few broken arms, bruised and swollen faces, black eyes, bloody noses. In spite of this, the room was generally quiet with only a few kids occasionally whimpering. When the cops came and saw the most severely injured kids, they immediately led them away, leaving the rest of us quiet, utterly subdued.

From outside the room, noises echoed through the cinderblock hallways and reverberated through the metal grates which covered the ceiling vents. We heard angry shouts of inmates elsewhere in the building, bursting upon our hearing out of nowhere, only to recede into the overall blanket of grayness of the place. There was the occasional "bam!" of a thick metal door, and, from time to time, there were loud but distant stentorian commands from the police, echoing from all directions, aimed at person or persons unknown. Later, for about twenty minutes, we heard a monotonous banging through the walls, a pounding as if metal on metal, irritating the senses and worsening my headache. It was as if someone had devised this as punishment, something we couldn't see or control but which amplified our miseries. Then it stopped as mysteriously as it had started.

Over and again, I watched through the bars as the same three cops approached us from down a long hall, unlocking our door and calling a name. They led us away in this manner, one by one, back down the long corridor and through the thick, heavy, metal door at its end, thereafter to some destination unseen.

Hours passed. The cell's population diminished gradually in a trickle. When they came for me, Pruitt had already been taken. They unlocked the cell door, calling my name. I got up, and they moved their arms in a gesture that ordered me to approach. One cop cuffed my hands behind my back while the other two looked on, one with stick in hand, ready for trouble or resistance. Then they stood on each side of me and one behind. They took my arms and led me onward without saying a word.

I took the walk with some trepidation, my heart pounding as I marched, escorted by adversaries, to face the unknown. It was not like being led away by the Sisters, whose powers I understood. This situation was alien to me; I could not predict what would happen.

There was blood on my face, so they led me to a sink with a mirror and told me to wash before taking me elsewhere for mug shots. They inked and rolled my fingers to document my prints, and they led me to a phone and told me I could make one call.

I stopped then to think. My first thought was to call my father, but in my mind's eye I saw him sitting at a huge table in Norfolk Naval Base with other admirals of the Atlantic Fleet, conducting meetings on wartime strategies and exercises in a room with maps and electronic screens. There would be too much brass in that room for him to understand my being thrown in jail for objecting to the Vietnam War. It was painful but clear: my parents were no longer my allies. I had crossed a Rubicon; no return was possible.

Bloom was far too sick to call, so my mind turned to Margo— I would have to call her. She had somehow been missing from the demonstration, and it might be that she wouldn't answer the phone, but she was my only realistic hope.

But what if she wasn't there? What if she didn't answer? Would I have to stay in my cell, stuck in limbo with no one knowing where I was? Isn't that what jail is, anyway? And what if she were physically unable to answer? What if something terrible had befallen her which had prevented her from coming to the demonstration—an illness, perhaps? What if she had been arrested regarding a part of her life of which I was unaware?

I thought not. I knew her for what she was, and there was no one else—Nebraska was too irresponsible, and Bornes and Mac-Neish were not my friends. I would have to call Margo and hope for the best.

"Hey boy—make your call! Don't make us wait."

I called Margo.

"J-Bee! Thank God it's you! Are you all right? Where are you?"

"I'm in the city jail."

"Oh my God—I'm so worried! I'm coming to get you!"

Margo asked if I was hurt; I said I was okay.

"The bastards!" she said. "I heard what happened—the cops beat everyone before they took you away. Did they hit you?"

"Yeah, they hit me. But I'm okay."

"Bastards! I'm coming right now."

"You know where I am? I'm not too sure myself, to be honest."

"Yeah, I've been there before. For Mitch."

Rankin.

"Where were you, Margo? I didn't see you."

"I'm so sorry I couldn't be there. I'm so, so sorry."

"Actually," I said, "had you been there, we'd both be in this godforsaken place. Who would be left to get us out?"

"You're right," she said, "but I still feel bad. I led you into this thing, and I feel like I abandoned you. But I couldn't help it. I had no choice. Something awful's happened."

"Why—what's happened?"

There was silence, but I felt her gears turning. "It's Bloom. My father. He's dead."

"Bloom's dead?"

"This morning."

It caught me blindsided. In forgetting him, even for a few hours, I had let him slip away forever. I was hurt—I sensed the sudden absence of a bedrock upon which my adult life had been building.

"How?"

"You know how. He was full of prostate cancer. His bones were crumbling. He fell apart."

"Oh God. I'm sorry!"

"I'm sorry too. I'm drained. Watching him in pain with no strength to fight and no will to live. Watching the strongest person I ever knew basically give up. It's been a tough day." She paused, and I heard her take a deep breath. "For you, too, I know—you've had a very tough day. So I'm on my way."

I was numb with loss. However, at the same time, the news of Bloom's death felt eerily familiar. I sensed that I had been cognizant of his passing at the exact moment it happened—I had felt a ripple in the cosmos accompanied by a passionate conviction to stand my ground against the TPF. Now again, as I was finishing my conversation with Margo, this same prior cognizance, this ripple, was triggering an almost identical reverberation in my sensorium, a déjà vu. It was this same awareness that I had felt on the Van Am Quad. It was a mysterious pulse of spirit from someone else, and I knew it had to be Bloom's spirit, an echo of what had been presented to me at the moment of his death.

—ɱ—

The cops took me to a large metal desk with papers all over it and a special, important-looking cop behind it. He was corpulent with a pink fat face and small watery eyes, looking like Father Croghan. The difference was that this man had sergeant stripes, carried a gun, and had arms like ham hocks, matted with thick black fur. The cops who brought me stood behind me like andirons and showed the greatest respect to this fat one.

"If you wanna get outta here," said the fat cop writing on a black-and-white form, "your bail is forty dollars." He never looked at me once.

"I don't have forty dollars."

I panicked. I didn't want to stay in this hole, but I had nothing on me.

"That's why you get your phone call. No one has any money in here. You're supposed to call someone to come and bail you out. You shoulda called your lawyer. Did you call your lawyer?"

"I don't have a lawyer."

"No? I guess not. First arrest. I get it."

I told him Margo was coming. He said, "We wouldn't keep you anyway. We don't have room for all these troublemakin' kids for more than a day. They're clogging things up. We'll send you out on your own recognizance if we have to. Until you can pay or be brought before a judge. We just can't keep all these kids here. We're not a day care center. This is the goddamn city jail."

The cops behind me laughed, and the fat one waved me away. "Get him the hell outta here and bring me the next one."

They made me go back to the cell and wait. Close to an hour passed until the same two cops came for me.

"You," the cop said pointing at me as he opened the door.

"Me?"

"Yeah," he said. "Who'd you think I was talking to? Your lady friend is here. You're leaving."

They led me to Margo without the cuffs. Margo ran to me and gave me a hug.

"Look what they did to your face, the animals," she hissed.

"How did you get me out?"

"I sprang you. They violated your First Amendment rights to speech and assembly. Such an outrage. Anyway, I paid your bail. Like I said, I've been here before. I've had lots of experience. I love visiting folks in jail; it's something I know how to do. This is what I want to do for a living some day—visit people in jail, like you. I'm going to be a sort of female version of William Kunstler."

"You mean the lawyer for the Chicago Seven? Like on your tee shirt?"

"And the Catonsville Nine, the Weather Underground, Lenny Bruce, Angela Davis, the Black Panthers. That's the one."

"You're kidding, right?"

"Well, yeah, I am. And I'm not. I *am* going to law school—I'm not kidding there. Then after I graduate, well, I can open a bail bond service so I can get you out whenever you need me."

"Margo!"

We both laughed.

"I missed you," she said, hugging me again. "I'm so sorry."

"Forget about sorry," I said. "I did it for me. It purged me."

"Bloom would have been proud—being busted for your principles. *I'm* proud."

"Now tell me about Bloom," I said.

She sucked up breath. "I knew it was coming. I called an ambulance, and they took us to Saint Luke's—I sat in the back with him and the medics. The doctors pronounced him dead when we got there. It was a very lonely experience. Sobering. I had to decide what to do with his body.

"I went through his apartment, but there was very little there. He had some books, but he was never a man who enjoyed possessing things. He had a few medals which he was awarded for bravery in World War II, but I couldn't find them."

She stopped to look at me. She gazed into my eyes in earnest, searching. I wanted to tell her, but it wasn't my secret. Or was it? Bloom had told me to stuff them in my pocket before I had time to fully think through what was happening. And now I realized it was just as Margo said—he was a man of few possessions, but he did have secrets. Perhaps now that he had passed his mantle to me, I could dispense with his secrets as I saw fit. Perhaps I would tell Margo after all, but I still wasn't sure. I decided I would hold on to his secrets for a little while longer and decide what to do after reflecting. Maybe after a modicum of meditation, I would know what to do; however, I did *not* expect to sit on these secrets for well over forty years without saying so much as a word.

She looked away from me.

"He's going to be cremated," she said. "His wishes. No funeral. No anything. It's a cold world without knowing he's here. Even if I was angry, even if I didn't see him, I always knew he was there. He was my hero, but it took me my whole life to figure it out. And now he's gone. Just like that."

39

Winds of History

The university dropped all charges against us, and Columbia's president expressed remorse for having called the cops. They left that day, and he vowed never to call them back.

Massive unplanned demonstrations broke out as thousands poured through the great gates of Columbia onto Broadway, sweeping downtown in marches against the war. They were met each time by New York's battle ready TPF on foot and on horseback. Since Broadway wasn't part of the university, the cops were in their element. Some days they escorted the marchers as they walked, but on other days they broke heads and made arrests.

Student strikes followed, crippling the university. Hundreds stood on the Van Am Quad shouting and pumping their fists, "On strike—shut it down! On strike—shut it down!" until, finally, the university's dysfunction was so onerous that it shut down. Students overran Hamilton and hung a bed-sheet banner from a second-floor window, renaming the building "Ho Chi Minh Hall." I went to take a look for myself, jogging up the front steps, yanking open the door and running straight into Bobby Bornes.

"Did you see our banner?" he asked proudly, pointing up at the bed sheet. "Get your ass in here and see what our revolution's doing."

He opened the door and beckoned me to enter.

"Come on," he said, "It's okay—you're with me."

They had trashed the dean's office, throwing every sheet of paper onto the floor from every drawer and cabinet they could find, creating a sea of papers six inches deep. In order to walk, I had to step on manila folders labeled with student names and marked "confidential." It had rained on and off for a week, and there were muddy footprints on everything. I was appalled at the destruction, aimed at the hallowed order that Columbia had safeguarded for generations.

There were no physical casualties at the hands of the students, but both the dean of students and the dean of Columbia College resigned, making way for new men. At the end of it all, Margo crowed victory, but my mind went back to Gilly. I saw no victory with him still fighting, and I worried. He was into his final stretch in Nam, and his life still hung in God's balance, awaiting a verdict in a place where the prospect of victory was fading.

I went home for a few weeks that summer to see my folks. They were shocked to see me with so much hair. My father shouted, "I'll whale that animal right out of you!" and then produced sheep shears from the garage and threatened to shave my skull on the spot.

My mother shook her head sadly, "He's got whiskers. I gave birth to an animal."

I apologized because they would never understand. I cut my hair and shaved my week-old beard which made my mother smile and my father swear that he knew me again, but he really didn't. How could he know the sedition of his son? How could he know that I had left his world behind, the military world I was born and bred to, near to where the Chickahominy River flows ever so slowly, its black waters oozing past its banks, its scum of green algae sitting atop its seemingly placid surface.

I went to my brother's grave and stood over the tombstone. I wept in silence, remembering his tiny coffin as it was lowered into its hole in the earth.

I decided to go to the weeded lot to find the abandoned trailer with the sodden walls where I had hidden prior to committing the worst sins of my life and where I would search for the ghosts of Stankewicz and Laureen. But the lot was no longer there—it had been bulldozed, leveled to make way for a shopping center with thousands of tons of poured cement. Nothing was left that I knew; it had all been buried in peaceful sterility.

Last, I went to stand outside Saint Eustace. I didn't dare go close, still wary of the watchful eyes of the Sisters. As I gazed upon that place, sitting in its treeless asphalt expanse, I saw how small it really was. I wondered that such a tiny school could cover such a vast system of dungeons and catacombs in which so many unfathomable acts of torture and degradation had taken place, in the past and presumably into the future.

I returned to New York and rented a run-down place on 123rd Street, in Harlem. Adam Clayton Powell, the congressman from that district, had been indicted for embezzlement and fled to Bimini, and the newly elected Charles Rangel had been sworn in in his place. I drove a cab out of 130th and Tenth Avenue at night, making a pittance from the nickels and dimes I was paid by the alkies, hoods and whores who waved me down, possibly fresh from nocturnal deeds of depravity.

One night, Margo and I lay in bed together with the lights out, sweated after exertions in the oppressive summer heat with only open windows to cool us. She asked why I had cut my hair, and I thought of Bobby Bornes and the hair down his back. It was a style, and she liked it, but it meant nothing to me. The next day, she drove to Miami with a bunch of left-wingers to join three thousand protesters, filling the streets outside the Republican National Convention. Front pages across the nation reported on the interruption of Nixon's acceptance speech by a Vietnam vet in a wheelchair who, rolling to the fore, suddenly shouted, "Stop the bombing! Stop the war!"

When she got back from Miami, I stopped at her apartment to say hello. We sat at her small kitchen table across from each other as she sipped tea, nervously tapping her foot.

"It's the end of an era," she said. "I'll be in law school this fall, and I can't rabble-rouse anymore if I'm going to make it in *that* world. None of the big shots are going to take some unpredictable female radical under their wings. I'll have to establish myself in the legal hierarchy as a reliable, predictable commodity, something that their eyes recognize when they see me, someone who dresses in their codified fashion with a pants suit and hair that's 'professionally' coiffed and so forth. Such a conservative group of people, *lawyers*. So it's the end of an era—my irresponsible, freewheeling, hard-rocking radical days are over. No more hidden identity for me. Every time I open my mouth my speech will be recorded, my arguments will be documented, and my reputation will hang on every word I utter, *every* inflection."

"No more bomb-throwing Jew-girl," I mumbled.

"What's that?"

I reached out to touch her arm, but she drew it away.

"I just wanted to see you," I said.

"I don't know why you bothered. Honestly, sometimes I don't think I understand men at all. Any of them. Fathers, uncles, husbands. Let's see, then there's the Wall Streeters, CEOs, presidents, rock stars, Weathermen. Oh, and *boy*friends. Who knows what *they're* thinking. Ever. I don't think that *they* even know what they're thinking."

"Are you trying to tell me something?"

She was leaning forward over her tea, sipping, but she craned her neck to look up at me with big, round wet eyes.

I felt what was coming; it hit me in the gut before she explained. I wanted to vomit—I felt my world submerging into a dark and infinite solitude. I wanted to turn away, hide under a rock, but I stayed where I was to face the oncoming storm.

"You cut your hair," she said.

"What's that got to do with anything? You already reprimanded me for that *before* you went off to Miami."

"You're no longer the innocent boy I fell in love with. You're a worldly man. Whatever the forces were that moved you to cut your hair, they must have been complex. It was a man's decision, and now you're not the same boy I loved anymore. You've changed."

It wasn't what I wanted to hear—it was "loved" in the past tense. Somewhere hidden behind the curtain of her verbs and logic was the heaviness of a rejection, a weighty jagged rock that would sit at the root of my gut and bleed me.

"Aren't you being a bit harsh?"

"Harsh? Me? I'm the tolerant one. A boyfriend who goes to a lecture by the architect of a network of mines designed to kill and maim folks twelve thousand miles away, and *I'm* harsh? If Gell-Mann were tolerant, he wouldn't have been constructing electronic networks of booby traps to kill people who didn't see the world the way he does."

"I'm *not* him."

"True. You're not him."

"Anyway, that was months ago. How about coming up with something new."

"The point is that you're still not totally committed against the damn war."

It sounded to me like she had gone off to Miami and was reinfused with a new and hefty bolus of left-wing rhetoric, but I understood what she was trying to say. I didn't like the war, but I felt a kinship with Gilly, another soul bonded to me through the trials of childhood like a brother.

As we looked at each other across the table, it may as well have been Hell's Canyon. My best friend was still in Vietnam, and it hurt that he was there, alone, but Margo wasn't ready to understand.

"What would Bloom—my father—say? He'd say we're very young and not yet fully developed into what we'll become. He'd say we're going in different directions: you're still in college, still in the incubator, and where I'm going, you can't possibly follow. Neither of us would survive if we stayed together. Law school is like high school all over again; everyone in the same class together every single day, all day long. No time for anything but thick books. After that, God knows where *you'll* end up, and *I'm* going to end up in some abstruse, arcane field of law. I'm going wherever the wind blows me. How could I be anchored to another person before I know where I'm headed? How can *you* be anchored? Don't you see how hopeless it is? Maybe if we somehow get to cross paths again in the vast and unknowable future, perhaps then we'll be free enough, wise enough, to love each other again."

I knew what she meant. We had traveled partway together, but now our paths would diverge. I didn't want to accept it, but I knew it was pointless to argue with Margo once she had staked out her intellectual territory. I didn't believe that Bloom would have felt what she claimed, and I wasn't going to let her go without a fight. Perhaps I was somewhat presumptuous, perhaps I was even wrong, but I had my own strong emotions and intuitions, and they were telling me that I was much closer to Bloom than anyone, and that I had known him better than his own daughter had known him.

"What about paying homage to love? What about putting love above all else?" I said. "What would Bloom say to that?" I felt certain that she must see that Bloom would put love first, yet I realized I should never have asked her the question.

"He'd say you've read too much Shakespeare in freshman English. Love is about feelings and emotions, and I'm telling you that this is how *I* feel. I can't change it, even if you beat me with a stick. My feelings are a fact in themselves which logic can't dislodge. You can talk 'til you're blue in the face, but feelings will always be a wall against the frailty of arguments and words."

I looked up and saw she had tears in her eyes. Her face rumpled. She ran around the table and squeezed her arms around me as I sat. Her head was on my shoulder. We were close again, but I felt terrible.

After I left her apartment, Margo's presence evaporated from my life. Whether I went to the library or The Rail, I never did see her again in those familiar places. For months, they seemed empty and forlorn as I trundled along the tracks of my life, rails that I had laid down during happier times.

—⁀⁀—

The war was winding down. Soldiers were coming home. Some had parades, others not. We were still fighting, but everyone knew we had lost. It was a first for America, and shame seared the national ethos indelibly like a branding iron. Veterans who had no parades were bewildered by their lack of recognition and had anger in their hearts. I understood, but there was nothing to be done. They had to face that their war was not loved and that they themselves were the living proof of America's fallibility.

In the fall, I was back in class. My draft number was just high enough, and I would sit out the war. Gilly had been right—I had been given another chance.

Meanwhile, at the Paris Peace Talks, Hanoi shook hands with Washington, signing an accord which presaged the end of the war. This was the "peace with honor" that Nixon had sought in order to save face for America, and it only came at the cost of a few extra lives while we waited for Nixon's terms to be accepted. Days later, Gilly sent me a letter: "Can't say where I'm going. Ho Chi Minh Trail, I think." He was assigned to drop from a helicopter over the border into Laos, even farther afield than the American incursion into Cambodia and far outside the sanctioned theatre of the war. It was months later when I learned more. Hanoi released the names of ten POWs whom they claimed they had captured in Laos. The US responded by handing a list to the North Vietnamese delegation in Paris with 317 names of "unaccounted for personnel," whom the Americans asserted were missing in Laos. Gilly was on that list, but Hanoi emphatically denied their existence.

Whatever the politics, I never heard from Gilbert O'Daly again. No one I knew from back home in Norfolk ever heard from him either, and ultimately his name joined the Missing In Action list on Washington's Vietnam Veterans Memorial. Although it's possible he's still alive, living in some remote village in Southeast Asia, I've always felt that he's dead. It's long in the past, but whenever I think about the fat kid who used to knock me down or the kid who built a car in his basement, I smile. At other times, though, now that my children are grown and if my wife of thirty years is out with her girlfriends, I might go for a beer and sit alone, brooding over the death of my friend. I've always missed him, and I pray he's in heaven or maybe in Valhalla with Bloom.

The battle for my soul had ended. I hadn't struck the stone of liberalism with the conservative hammer of my forefathers. Instead I had found my long-haired brothers in The Apocalypse Café and on the Van Am Quad, and I had, unwittingly but tacitly, sent Gilly as a proxy to fight a war overseas in my stead. Thereafter, the event of my arrest by the TPF, that act which had mended my soul, made it impossible for me to be accepted by an American medical school. Luckily Canada embraced me, and I went to medical school there where the Vietnam War had been anathema. After that, I found employment in the American veterans hospital system, giving my life to the men who had borne the burden of battle but who had nothing to show for it: so many were homeless, sleeping in door-ways, haunted by the recurrent, echoing nightmares from atrocities which they had witnessed and committed and which had taken place thousands of miles away and many years in the past. Now I care for these broken men as a personal tribute to Gilly, my lost brother, who is always with me in spirit. It assuages my guilt for not having been beside him; I give back where I can.

The events at Columbia and those like it across America were a stone plunging into the placid pond of our national conscious-ness, creating ripples and disturbing the mirror-like perfect surface in which American dreamers had seen their images within their perfect world. It was a tumultuous time, a springboard into our contemporary world. Society has wandered more than forty years since then, and perhaps it is time to reflect back on that period and recognize the secrets it holds. Soon, the generation belonging to that time, my generation, will be nothing but dust and unable to speak, leaving its drama to be blown away in the winds. The intense fervor of the times might be all but forgotten.

We are lulled to sleep, closing an eye to all that has gone before. Planets, asteroids, comets and all the dark matter of the universe, rocks without objective as old as the creation itself, move with gravity and insouciance, jostling together and then apart through darkness in the vast volumes of space as we, in stupid torpor, know nothing of where they've been or their momentous interactions. Time is the final element, pushing us ever further from the events of 1972 and toward the trifling moments of our deaths, compressing our futures into smaller and smaller intervals until we have no time remaining. But time is also on our side because time, as frozen moments in history, will always be present after it has elapsed, and the records of its events will be forever etched on the eternal cosmic map if ever we should choose to look back.

With this book, these *Serpent Papers*, I have fulfilled the destiny thrust upon me by Bloom, my friend, long dead these forty some years. There have been times that I've opened the box that he gave me to gaze at his medals and remember him. It was his force of will that, through a remote distance in space and time, over an unconnected gap in the cosmos, moved me to complete this book and fulfill some sort of meaningfulness in my life. I may be out of step with contemporary America, suffering the occasional disturbing echo from my one acid trip, but I have completed my work with dogged determination and have given forth my words to others, either for them to hear or never to hear.

This is the end. I am exhausted like the butterfly who pollinates the plants but then dies at summer's end. The plants will grow and waver in the wind, never knowing how or why but ever propagating. Still, no matter. I have completed the labor to which I was tasked, and now I must lay down my pen and rest my head and think no more upon an age and times which are all but forgotten and whose lessons are enshrouded in a world of misty gray, neatly tucked away in remote corners of library stacks, in the dusty archives of history, enwreathed within the coils of The Serpent.

Acknowledgments

I would like to thank Beth Spanier, Richard Marek, Susan Dalsimer, Kim Schefler, Aaron Kaiserman, Lizzy Hall, Miss Canfield, Jimmie Sylvester and the Columbia Fiction Foundry.

I thank the literary journal, *The Write Launch*, for publication of some chapters from *The Serpent Papers* in advance of the full book.